Hard Feelings

JENNIFER MILLIKIN

ISBN: 979-8-9909048-7-3
www.jennifermillikinwrites.com
Cover by Okay Creations
Cover art by Rosie Fables
Editing by Emerald Edits
Proofreading by Sisters Get Lit.erary

To those of you who like the car windows down, music you can tap your feet to, and the sunshine warming your face.

CHAPTER

One

Dominic: Cecily, hi. It's Dominic Bellinger. Klein's cousin.

Cecily: Hello there, Dominic. You're also Klein's literary agent, I'm told.

Dominic: Guilty. Klein gave me your number, I hope that's ok. He promised he asked you first.

Cecily: He asked. 🙂 I hear you want to take me out to celebrate his (and, by extension, your) recent professional win.

Dominic: And yours, too. It deserves at least a cocktail.

Cecily: What does it deserve at most?

Dominic: I'd tell you, but then...

Cecily: You'd have to kill me?

Dominic: ...

Dominic: ...

Dominic: ...

Dominic: I'm over here trying to think of something witty to say, but I'm coming up empty. You're the one who's good with one-liners. I saw your captions for Klein's social media posts. One might say if it weren't for your clever digital marketing campaign he wouldn't have the attention of a publisher.

Cecily: I'll never turn down a compliment, so thank you.

Dominic: You're welcome. I land in Phoenix next Tuesday at eleven. Happy hour that afternoon?

Cecily: I'll text you when and where on Tuesday morning. Looking forward to meeting you, Dominic.

Dominic: Sounds great. Looking forward to meeting you too, Cecily.

CHAPTER 2

Cecily

Meeting the cousin of a client for a drink that may or may not be considered a date is a risky proposition.

May Be A Date. That's what I'll call it.

Potential downside is that it doesn't go well, and we will face a lifetime of awkward conversations at big life events of the person we have in common. Potential upside is... Well, I don't know. Feels silly to say *happily ever after*, especially since I'm ninety percent positive I don't believe in the concept for myself. That last ten percent functions like an insurance policy. I'm not comfortable cutting myself off from something completely, so I give myself a little wiggle room. Just because something is *improbable* doesn't mean it's *impossible*.

"Not the red," I mutter, tossing the deep V-neck dress to the side. It flutters onto the heap of considered and quickly discarded items of clothing on my bed. For the record, I look fabulous in red. But my coworker, Paloma, once told me red is for hookers, and even though I know she's wrong, I worry she is slightly right. I think it's in her delivery. She speaks with confidence, and that makes me believe whatever she says. It could also be her Portuguese accent.

I'm considering my backside in the full-length mirror that hangs on my closet door when my sister calls. Tapping the speaker button, I say, "I'm nervous, Kerrigan."

No need for a greeting. We've been texting all afternoon.

"It's only a drink," she reminds me. "Don't think of it like a date, which it might not be."

"Right." Except it feels a lot more like a date than a friendly *yay us!* meeting. The tone of our texts was flirtatious. I've studied them from every angle, I'm embarrassed to say.

Looking forward to meeting you, Dominic. I hear it spoken in my voice: sultry, soft, an emphasis of the hard *c* at the end of his name.

Sounds great. Looking forward to meeting you too, Cecily. Because I've never heard him speak, I imagine how he sounds: a deep timbre that suggests worn leather boots, well-dressed but not fanciful.

Maybe I'm reading into it. Maybe it's the romantic drought in which I perpetually find myself, my imagination coloring in the man-shaped outline I've dreamed up.

"What are you wearing?" Kerrigan asks.

I glance in the mirror as I rattle off my outfit. "A denim skort that ties on my hip, and a white tank top with scalloped edges."

"Hmm," she says, and not in a reassuring way. "Add a cardigan. That way you can slide it off one shoulder when you're sitting across from him. It'll make him think of undressing you."

I make a face at my reflection, but it's meant for the ho I'm on the phone with. "I'm not sleeping with him on the first date. The first meeting. Whatever we're calling it."

"There's nothing wrong with it," my sister says, adopting the defensive but also superior tone she uses when she spouts words like *sex-positivity*. "Besides, I didn't say to sleep with him. Making him picture undressing you is a far cry from getting horizontal."

She takes a deep breath, but I cut her off before she can dive into her lecture. I've heard it all from her before, and besides, my sister has an affinity for shrooms. I'd fight a rabid coati for her, but she is not to be trusted when she's been munching on fungi.

"It's not right *for me*, Kerrigan. Now, get your head in the game. I already passed on the red dress because I don't want to look like a hooker. I'm not going to undress in front of the man."

She sighs because I'm just that hopeless. Her eye roll is almost audible through the phone. "Paloma was kidding. She's from the land of thongs and sungas."

I shudder at the memory of Paloma showing me a photo of her family on the beach in Brazil, all the males wearing sungas. I asked her why I needed to see the silhouette of everyone, including her sixty-year-old father's, babymaker. She muttered something derogatory about my being a prudish American.

"I need talking points," I tell Kerrigan, studying my shoe collection. "Should I wear flats? What if he's short?"

"We love a short king," Kerrigan trills.

"You have the worst habit of repeating phrases you see people who are cooler than you post on social media."

"I really do," she agrees readily. "Wear the tan sandals that give you a couple inches."

I examine my hot pink pedicure, toes already encased in the tan sandals that give me a couple inches. "Perfect. Thanks, Kerr."

"You'll do great. This'll be fun. Dominic will be the prize you're awarded for going on all those awful dates recently."

"Let's hope," I say flippantly. "At some point I have to break my streak of meeting the human equivalent of fruitcake."

"Dense and unappetizing," Kerrigan announces with conviction.

Over the past few months, my dates more closely resemble the punchline of a joke. Mama's boys, dude bros (pronounced *bruh*), and one ballsy kleptomaniac whose astronomical good looks did not offset the salt shaker I caught him tossing in his backpack during our first (and last) date. Further proof of my theory that even pretty people can be weird.

"Ok, I gotta go." I grab my purse off my bed, looping it around my shoulder.

"If all else fails, make a show of lowering your cardigan."

"Bye, Kerrigan."

She shoots back. "Puritan."

"You belong on a beach in Brazil."

"I wholeheartedly agree."

"I love you."

"I love you, too. Remember, your mouth can't get pregnant. Byeeee."

The connection ends, and I shake my head. Kerrigan describes herself as *unhinged*, and I'm inclined to agree.

Not in a million years would I admit this to my sister, but I nab a cardigan from my closet on my way out. Just in case.

CHAPTER 3

Cecily

I KNOW WHAT DOMINIC LOOKS LIKE BECAUSE, AS ANY SELF-respecting woman going on a date with someone she hasn't already met would do, I looked him up.

His social media is private, but I found his headshot and bio on the website of Whitaker Literary Agency.

What struck me about him first were his stern eyebrows, followed by the unusual color of his hair. Copper? No. Burnt caramel? Yes. After that, it was his eyes. Piercing deep blue, almost unbelievably so. Must've been the work of Photoshop. His lips don't make sense. Why are they *luscious*? Why is that the only word I can think of to describe them?

In short, Dominic is attractive. As long as he doesn't steal the condiments, he will automatically be my best (May Be A) date in a long time. The bar is low. The only way to lower it further would be if he set fire to the place, or pulled a red nose from his pocket and began to juggle.

This morning I texted Dominic like I said I would, telling him to meet me at Obstinate Daughter at five. They make the best blueberry mojito, and one of their bartenders is irreverent in the most entertaining way. It's also where Dominic's cousin Klein works as a bartender while he waits for Dominic to sell his manuscript. Klein isn't working tonight. If he had been, I would've suggested some place different. I don't need an audience on my May Be A Date.

The afternoon sun beats down on my car as I throw it into Park. My cheeks fill with air, the noisy breath vibrating my lips as I release it. Angling my rearview mirror down, I check my makeup, my teeth, pretty much everything about myself. My pulse flutters and my stomach flips as I make my way across the small parking lot.

Obstinate Daughter swarms with the after-work crowd laughing, drinking, and talking over each other. The vibe is hip and upscale, a place with the prettiest emerald green floor tile and ivory textured walls. The men clustered around the horseshoe-shaped bar wear slacks and button-up collared shirts, sleeves rolled twice. Professional attire is loosely interpreted in Scottsdale. The women wear all manner of clothing, their choices more expansive than the men. Give this place a few more hours and it'll turn from after-work happy hour into pre-game central, a place where the young and the sexy gather before moving on to the row of clubs nearby. Even on a Tuesday in the warmth of June, this place thrums with life.

My gaze homes in on a tall figure at the bar. From his profile, along with his unique hair color, I know it is Dominic. He's half seated on the backless teak stool, his other long leg reaching for the ground like he's ready to stand up at a moment's notice. He wears khaki shorts and a cream polo with baby blue stripes in varying widths over the chest. His forearm leans on the bar, but his posture remains upright. Halston, the aforementioned irreverent bartender, talks with him.

She catches sight of me over his shoulder and waves, eyes lighting up with familiarity. Dominic turns fully my way, his gaze coming to rest on me.

The nerves in my stomach increase tenfold, butterflies with wings of razors. Dominic is my client's cousin. My client is dating my boss. My boss has become one of my closest friends. This has the potential to be so, so messy.

Dominic rises. At his full height, he must be over six feet tall. An easy smile breaks onto his face, so different from the headshot on his company's website. He strides forward, through bodies of people who've become faceless to me, meeting me halfway.

"Cecily." His voice stretches through the growing din, rolling over me. It's rich and deep, like the pouring of a decadent sauce.

His arm extends. I place my hand in his. He fastens his grip around mine, not too tight, not too loose. Just right. It's a simple handshake, but something in me pays attention.

"It's nice to meet you, Dominic."

"Dom," he corrects. "Only my boss and my parents call me Dominic."

I nod. "Well, Dom, how about that drink?"

He steps aside, motioning toward the bar. We fall into step, and Dom pulls the stool out for me, waiting for me to get situated before he takes his own seat. He definitely gets a few points for that. I love a gentleman.

Closer now, I notice his polo is knit, and made of silk

and cotton. Not a single wrinkle blemishes the press of his flat-front khaki shorts. In fact, everything about him is orderly. Tidy. There's no way this man is walking away with a salt shaker in his pocket. Also, the blue in his eyes was not the work of Photoshop.

"Cecily, hi," Halston says after I've hung my purse on the hidden hook under the bar.

"Hey, Halston." I greet her warmly. I have a soft spot for her, mostly because she is everything but soft. I admire it. She is unapologetically herself.

"You two know each other?" Dominic asks, looking between us.

"I started coming here after I met Klein. Paisley talked about how great this place is, and I wanted to see for myself. Plus it helped me get to know Klein, and figure out his voice for his social media captions."

Dom looks impressed, and a vibrating warmth of satisfaction fills me. I not only love my job, I also love excelling at it. Gesturing toward Dom, I say to Halston, "This is Klein's cousin, Dom."

Halston executes an exaggerated once-over. "I see the resemblance." She levels her steely-eyed gaze on Dom. "You tell that jackass he owes me money."

Dom grins. "He owes me money, too. A hundred bucks. I told him he was going to fall for Paisley on that island, and I was right."

"Paisley and Klein were the only two people who didn't know they were going to fall for each other." Paisley is my boss at P Squared Marketing, and I listened to her moon over Klein before they spent a week pretending to be dating. Not to mention I'm the person Klein sent all his island photos to as part of our social media campaign for him. His camera roll was full of Paisley and he was still insisting they were just friends.

Halston laughs. "Klein doesn't really owe me money, but sometimes I tell him he does, and he believes me."

Now Dom's laughing. "I have no moral issue with telling him he needs to pay up."

"I like you already," Halston says, fluttering her fingers at him. "What do you want to drink?"

Dom does the face up palm gesture in my direction, motioning for me to give my order first.

A few more points for Dom. If he keeps it up, maybe I'll lower one shoulder of my cardigan after all.

Halston waves a dismissive hand. "I already know what Cecily wants."

My head bobs in agreement.

Dom props a foot on the bottom rung of the barstool, gaze attentive as he says, "Two of whatever is so good Cecily has made a habit of drinking it."

Halston beats back a sly smile. "He's cute," she says to me, like Dom's not there.

Dom tuts. "I'll tell my cousin you said so, since we share a resemblance."

"Ew," Halston says, tossing blueberries and mint into a shaker. "Don't do that. Klein does not need another woman telling him how gorgeous he is." She grabs the muddler and gets to work.

"Is that your assessment too?" Dom asks, eyebrows lifted. "Did Klein hit the genetic lottery?"

"Let it be known," I start, tapping the tip of one rounded fingernail on the bar top, "that while Klein is conventionally attractive, he is not my cup of tea."

But his cousin might be.

Dom presses his lips together, slowly nodding his head. "What is your cup of tea?"

"Hmm," I say, coy. My chin tips sideways an inch. "Polite men who don't live with their mothers, steal condiments, or call me *bruh*."

Dom blinks those striking blue eyes at the list I've rattled off. "That is oddly specific. And very understandable."

I shrug. "Prior experience determining future preferences."

Dom smiles again, and *wow*. The nerves had been too sharp for me to fully appreciate his smile before, but now? I can say with total confidence he has the best grin I've ever seen in-person. Easy, effortless, crooked at first like he's trying not to let it take over, then bursting onto his face as if he can't help himself.

Halston sets our drinks down. Pinkish-purple hued, mint leaves and blueberries floating amongst the ice, a lime wheel adorning the rim.

"Cheers," she says, disappearing around the other side of the bar.

We clink glasses and take a sip. Crisp. Cold. Refreshing. Halston never misses.

"Delicious, right?" The tip of my tongue pokes at the corner of my mouth, gathering a lingering drop of mojito.

"Dangerous," Dom adds, taking a second sip as his gaze firmly lands on me. Is he talking about the drink, or me? Do I want him to be talking about me? I like the way his lips work the rim, his generous lower lip pressing against the glass. Luscious was the right word to describe his mouth.

I clear my throat. Press a palm to the side of my heated neck. "Tell me about you. Where did you grow up?"

"Here, actually. The Phoenix area." His elbows rest on the bar. "What about you?"

"Not in Phoenix, but in Arizona. Olive Township. It's a small town a couple hours east of here." There it goes, that twinge in my heart. Try as I might, it happens when I think of home. I'll be honest, I miss the town a hell of a lot more than I miss my family. My sister followed me to the Phoenix area when she became an adult, and my grandma already lived here.

"I've heard of it. Klein's mom took us there when we were little. To an olive grove, I think?"

"That's what it's known for, or was anyway, until some travel magazines featured the wellness spa."

"What made you move to Scottsdale?" His gaze is open and curious. Interested. There's a lot going on around us, superb people-watching, but his eyes remain fixed on me.

"I needed to put space between me and my family. Mostly my parents. They're..." Manipulative. Exacting. Difficult. "...a lot."

"That's tough," Dom says sympathetically, but nothing else.

"What about your family? How are they?"

He shrugs lightly. "Fine. Not much to tell."

He's cagey about his upbringing. Interesting. I elbow him lightly. "Come on. I showed you mine. You show me yours."

His gaze slips from my face, landing on my neck, moving across from shoulder to shoulder. My breath hitches as I watch his lazy perusal. Then he says, "If the tale of my childhood had a flavor, it would be vanilla. Very boring. Nondescript."

"Vanilla is good," I argue. "Vanilla is a staple. A universal flavor for a reason. Me personally?" I sip my drink. "I happen to like vanilla."

His chin dips fractionally, as if to say *I accept and appreciate your defense of the flavor and my childhood.*

Something hits me square in the back, an elbow, I think, and I pitch forward, mojito sloshing dangerously close to my outfit. Before I can topple out of my seat or collide with the bar, a pair of hands catches me. Steady. Warm. One at my hip, the other brushing my upper arm.

"You ok?" Dom's voice is low, a terse murmur near my ear.

"I'm fine." His proximity is far more flustering than being bumped into. Dom's fingers dally just long enough to make my skin hum.

"Sorry about that," a voice says in a British accent. A man steps up to our seats, wearing the same post-work uniform as every other male in the vicinity, and stares at me. "You're gorgeous," he says, eyes glassy. For some reason his accent makes the interruption less annoying. "Good work, mate," the guy says to Dom. He extends a fist, waiting for Dom's tap. This move brings him closer to me, and I'm met with the skunky scent of beer.

Dom obliges. He smiles good-naturedly, eyes locked on me when he says in agreement, "She's beautiful."

"Cheers," the guy says, lifting his pint in the air, hearty and drunk and happy. He moves away. I roll my eyes. "Nice work, playing along like that."

Dom's blue-eyed gaze grips mine. "Who said I was playing?"

It's probably still part of going along with the inebriated guy, but something about the way Dom says it, the way he's looking at me, makes it feel like it could be more.

I glance away before I think too hard about it, tapping my nail against the side of my glass. I'm unsure what to do or say. Dom has exceeded every expectation. It would take a lot to make me relinquish my hold on my personal feelings of a happily ever after, but it could be a starting off point. I reserved that last ten percent for precisely this anomaly.

"So, Dom," I start, crossing my legs at the knee and leaning a little closer. He sees my shift in body language, mirroring it with his own micro-movements. The dip of his shoulder closest to me. The tightening of his hand that rests on his thigh. *Yeah, this is a date.* And a good one, too. "Tell me something you hate."

"Hmm," he rumbles. "My birthday."

The corners of my lips turn down. "Not lima beans, or people who chew with their mouths open?"

He makes a face like *fair point.* "Those are gross, too."

"What is it you don't like about your birthday?" Sympathy rushes over me, and I place my *sympathetic* hand on his forearm. I definitely do not take notice of the warmth of his skin, the light dusting of hair, the scattered freckles.

He takes a moment to ponder the answer, then says, "The attention."

I retract my hand, using it to play with the gold bangles on my wrist. "You had me worried there for a second. I was afraid you had a very sad story to tell about your birthday."

"No sad stories." He points at his chest. "Vanilla, remember?"

I run a fingertip through the condensation sweating on my glass. "I don't know, Dom, something tells me beneath this composed exterior, you might be a unique flavor."

He holds my gaze, something passing through his eyes. I don't know him well enough yet to understand what it is.

A ringing trills from his shorts, and he glances down. Frowning, he says, "I'm sorry, I don't normally keep my ringer turned on." He pulls his phone from his pocket, glancing at the screen. "I need to take this. Excuse me."

"Sure," I say, shifting on my stool to make it easier for him to get up.

He smiles apologetically. His thigh brushes mine as he steps between our seats. It's warm, strong and solid. His forearm sweeps over the curve of my shoulder, sending a zing of electricity down my arm.

He bends down, his lips near the shell of my ear. He smells so good I nearly groan. "I'll only be a moment," he says, then smoothly steps away.

Over my shoulder, I watch as he disappears down a short hallway leading to the bathrooms.

"That guy is Klein's cousin?"

I whip back around to Halston. Her disbelieving gaze flicks from the now-empty space Dom occupied to my eyes.

"Yes." I laugh. "Why?"

"Because Klein is a tremendous nerd."

"Dominic might be a tremendous nerd as well. I don't know him."

Halston smirks. "Yet."

"He's Klein's agent," I add, swirling a blueberry in my drink with the cocktail straw.

"I bet he put *Must love books* on his dating profile."

I blink twice, coquettishly. "Good thing I love to read."

A group of men sidles up to the far end of the bar. Halston glances their way, then says, "If you want another round, I need to know now. Something tells me those are the kinds of assholes who order difficult drinks. Fruity martinis, but in rocks glasses because their fragile masculinity can't handle colorful drinks in their proper stemware."

Our blueberry mojitos sweat on drink napkins, a quarter left in each. "I'm not sure." A quick look at the hallway tells me Dom is not yet on his way back. How long should a phone call take? I hope everything's alright.

Doubt slides into my thoughts, followed by little bursts of dread and panic. Dom wouldn't be getting The Phone Call, would he? The call that announces there has been an emergency and the person needs to abandon the date. Also known as the Ripcord Call.

No. He would've answered a Ripcord Call in front of me, for full dramatic effect.

Ugh, I hate this. The nerves from before have returned, and now they're sharper, laced with uncertainty.

Halston waits for my answer. She has a life to live, a job to do. She can't be delayed by my internal crisis. Quickly, I say, "Let me go ask Dom." I add a decisive nod that hides my apprehension.

Halston waves me off, telling me she'll watch our drinks. Behind me, I hear her tell the guys she'll be with them in a moment.

I grab my purse and hurry across the bar, turning the

corner down the hallway. Dom stands at the far end, his back to me.

He really does have a nice back. Shoulders. Hair recently trimmed. The guy is not bad to look at.

I don't want to intrude, so I raise my hand to tap him on the shoulder. His words bring me up short.

"...trying to get rid of her. She's annoying, and she has the worst laugh, and she yammers on and on."

My hand freezes in place. Emotions flood my veins, too many to name, and then one comes out the clear winner: *mortification.*

Dom still doesn't know I'm here. His shoulders are loose, his phone held to his ear while his other hand rests in his pocket. "Pretty soon my ears will beg me to pull a Van Gogh and cut one off."

Heat spreads through my body, my toes curling and my skin flushing.

Should I stay? Go? Grab his perfectly intact ear and shake his head? Purchase a billboard ad with his photo and the caption *I make passionate love to inanimate objects*?

"...I'm telling you, she's the worst."

GO. Get the hell out of here and don't look back. I'm good at doing that, and once a person knows they are capable of it, they can do it repeatedly. Roads well traveled, and all that.

I pivot and flee. No looking left or right. I do not pass Go, or collect two hundred dollars.

If Halston caught sight of me, I'm not aware. All I can think about is putting distance between me and the two-faced man back there.

I spill from the restaurant door into the hot evening air. A group of women stand around, all wearing dresses that at one time would've been purchased in the lingerie section. One wears a silk sash and an obnoxiously huge tiara. *Bride,* the sash reads. This is not at all shocking. The pink party bus toting around drunk bachelorette parties is a regular sight on these streets.

My eyes close as I place my hands on my hips and suck in a lungful of hot, Scottsdale air. When my eyes open, I find a few curious gazes from the group.

"Are you ok?" The question comes from a brunette wearing large coral pink hoop earrings. She steps closer, away from her group.

"Terrible date," I answer.

She nods. "Been there."

"We've *all* been there," another girl says, a blonde with a diamond stud nose ring. "What does he look like? That way we'll know to avoid him when we go inside."

I hear Dom in my head. *She's annoying. She has the worst laugh...yammers on and on.*

"Actually," I say, an idea forming. "He hates being told happy birthday. How about—"

The brunette is already nodding. "Oh yes. I'm all over that. We are going to embarrass the shit out of this guy."

I picture Dom confused, struggling to understand why this group of women is telling him something he hates to hear. It makes me feel incrementally better. Sticking around to see it would be entertaining, but that's not happening. I'll have to ask Halston for a play-by-play another time.

I show them Dom's photo from his company website. "Thank you for doing this," I say, feeling genuinely grateful for the show of female solidarity.

The brunette blows me a kiss as her friends hustle her inside.

I hurry to my car and hurl myself in, throwing on the air-conditioning. It blasts my face as embarrassment swirls through me. Was I totally and completely misreading his signals this whole time? I must have been.

I put my hand on his forearm. Leaned in closer. Laughed, and smiled, and *I was having a good time.*

I've never felt like such an idiot.

But it doesn't end there, does it? This isn't a random person I will never have to see again. As long as I'm friends with Paisley, seeing Dom will be a possibility. He will never stop being Klein's cousin.

This was a bad idea. What was I thinking? Men are toads. This has been proven to me time and time again. Klein is a unicorn. My big brother is a good person, too, but even he has one failed engagement under his belt. Don't get me started on my dad.

Angry tears heat the backs of my eyes, but I refuse to let them fall. Instead, I pull my phone from my purse and block Dom.

I didn't think a date could get worse than the klepto, but here we are.

CHAPTER
Four

Paisley: How was it meeting Dom?

Cecily: Fine.

Klein: What did you think of Cecily? She's cool, right?

Dominic: Yeah, she's cool.

CHAPTER 5

Dominic

EIGHT MONTHS LATER

BEING A LITERARY AGENT HAS CHANGED ME.

Where I used to merely enjoy stories, now I live them. I see them in my head, and create them for the strangers I interact with.

The harried barista at the coffee shop on the corner closest to my apartment? She's a young mother. *Of twins!* And she's raising the toddlers by herself, *because her husband abandoned her.* Wait, no. That's too predictable. And it leaves the door open for him to return in the third act, and nobody wants that jerk. *He died! Hit by a bus, the poor fellow.*

On and on I do this. A hefty portion of my job is reading manuscripts, and some days, separating fact from fiction is too demanding. Reality might be tangible, but fiction is a shapeshifter. After a while, when you live story and breathe words as I do, the boundary line becomes permeable.

This (not at all) lauded talent has allowed me to compartmentalize my disaster of a date eight months ago with Cecily Hampton AKA the Wicked Witch of the West. Literally. She lives in Scottsdale, Arizona. The West's Most Western Town. I don't know who appointed it the title, but signs around the downtown area declare it as such.

High on the excitement from having secured Klein a meeting with a publisher, I'd said I wanted to take Cecily out for a drink to thank her for her contribution to Klein's burgeoning career.

Things were going well. Or so I thought. Cecily is beautiful, but she's a lot of other things, too. Witty, which I'm a sucker for, but the kind of witty that calls upon my own cleverness. Her personality sang to mine in the oddest way. Sure, she was physically attractive, but I was mentally attracted to her, too.

And then she ghosted me. I've rewritten the true story of what happened on our date to include sudden onset illness, followed by a head injury on the way home that kept Cecily from remembering we went out. Nothing tidies up plot confusion like conveniently placed short-term memory loss.

What else could explain the events of that evening? We'd been having a good time, I stepped away to answer a work call, and Cecily disappeared. My text messages to her were not delivered. She blocked me.

Was I the only person feeling the chemistry between us? Am I really so out of touch that I detected and defined her facial expressions and mannerisms in an absolutely, totally, unbelievably wrong way? The thought of the disaster tinges my vision red.

Maybe I haven't compartmentalized the catastrophe as neatly as I'd like.

It doesn't matter. Cecily didn't tell Paisley anything

about the date, which means Klein has no knowledge about the date, which means I can go on and lie to myself about the date.

Hello sand, here's my head.

Sally, an associate agent at the lit agency, sails into my office like someone has invited her. She does this often, and she also starts conversations as if we were in the middle of one already.

Her corkscrew black curls bounce around her head as she strides up to my desk in her striped leggings and corduroy skirt, theatrically dropping a coil-bound printed manuscript on my desk. It lands with a dramatic thud, blowing two Post-it notes onto the floor. "It might not be your usual taste, but you should take a look at it." Her arms cross, her gaze flicking down to the stack of paper.

"What is *it*?" I ask. Sally is also known for her use of the unspecified subject. Drives me crazy. I'd like to take a red felt-tip pen to every sentence Sally speaks, marking up the surrounding air.

"The man-u-script," Sally says, looking at me like I'm the one who's hopeless.

I sit back, crossing one ankle over the opposite knee. "As much as I enjoy the syllabification you're doling out, you've made multiple errors, the first of which is walking into my office like you own it."

Sally arches an eyebrow.

Dammit.

She doesn't own anything, but her mother does. Sally is here because her last name is Whitaker, and this is Whitaker Literary Agency.

Nepo baby. And a recent college grad in need of a job.

I tap a finger on my thigh to keep myself from pinching

the bridge of my nose. The last thing I want is to show this near-child she has riled me.

Tucking back my sigh, I look down at the printed manuscript.

Last Things First.

Was I drunk when I requested the full manuscript from the author? That title is terrible.

"A western horror," Sally explains. "Love the concept."

Now I remember this garbage. I didn't make it past page four before I tossed the brick of paper into the slush pile yesterday. But here the manuscript is, pristine and in front of me like it never met the shredder.

I smell a rat.

"The writing is sophomoric," I tell Sally, keeping my tone measured.

Her eyes harden. "It is not. I think it's really good. Maybe you're too old to understand how people of this age communicate."

Now it's my turn to narrow my eyes. Thirty isn't old. I could be offended, but I'm too busy sniffing out a ruse.

"Why did you tell your friend I'd look at their manuscript?" It's a hunch, but I have good instincts. It's part of what makes me a great literary agent.

Sally's lips sew shut. She knows I'm on to her, so I continue. "Why did you print out the manuscript and put it on my desk yesterday?" It's unlikely I would've requested a full manuscript of this book from a query letter. The only way this made it to my desk in physical form is if it was placed there.

There it is. A slight movement in her jaw. A flicker of fear in her eyes.

Now I feel bad. Not *bad* bad, but enough to be done with the accusations.

Pushing the manuscript across the desk, I say, "Tell your friend nobody wants to read that many adverbs and alliteration in the same sentence. The exposition was boring and redundant. Large blocks of text are mentally exhausting for a reader."

Sally frowns. "There is no way you read the entire book."

"Didn't have to. Your friend didn't magically become a better writer on page five."

Her frown deepens. She takes the manuscript, arms dipping with the weight before hauling it up and tucking it into her chest. "You're arrogant."

"Whatever gets the job done," I respond, already turning my attention to my computer screen.

Sally doesn't stomp from my office, because that's not her style, but she mumbles on her way out, something that sounds like *I feel sorry for any woman dumb enough to date you.*

The door closes behind her, and I run a hand over my forehead. I shouldn't allow the opinion of a twenty-three-year-old to bother me, but her comment lands, settling somewhere near my solar plexus.

No matter how many times I tell myself the story I've made up for Cecily, I'm tender. Not for any deep, dark reason other than our connection felt instantaneous and rare, something I would've fought for if given the chance. Cecily got under my skin. The work I've done to pigeonhole her actions that day, and her motivations behind them, was for nothing because I've ended up right where I was at the beginning.

Angry.

And, *ok fine*, hurt, too.

My phone dings with a text message from Klein.

Klein: Vegas, baby.

Dominic: I'm listening.

Klein: Joint bachelor and bachelorette parties.

Dominic: Is that wise?

Klein: Anything else would be unwise.

Dominic: Fair point. Tell me more.

Klein: I'll send you the info. Just be available in a month.

Dominic: You, me, and Paisley?

Klein: No, jackass. A group.

I flop back in my desk chair, pinching my lower lip as I re-read Klein's text.

A group? Will that group include Cecily? I have to imagine it will. She might be Paisley's employee, but from what I understand, they're good friends, too.

I can't ask, because Klein is annoyingly perceptive. He'll want to know why I want to know. And then it will be a whole thing. It does not need to be a whole thing. It doesn't need to be a fraction of a thing. It is, in fact, a non-issue. I can be around Cecily and not demand to know why she ghosted me mid-date.

Dominic: Cool. I'm available.

I'm already bobbing my head in anticipation, drumming my fingers on my desk. I haven't taken a proper vacation in three years, I'm embarrassed to say. A quick trip here and there, usually home to visit my parents and Klein, though probably not as often as I should. It's a long flight from New York City to Phoenix, especially when it's only for a weekend.

Another text comes in from Klein, delivering dates and times. Before I can forget, I shoot an email to my boss, Dee, letting her know I'll be taking a few days off. I'm tacking on some time in Phoenix to see my parents after the weekend in Vegas, since I'll be close by. I reserve a hotel room, then spend twenty minutes searching for the best deal on flights, book those also, and *bada bing* my day is looking up. Dopamine floods my system, as if I'm already walking the casino floor.

Whiny, entitled benefactor of nepotism sneaking a steaming pile of literary muck on my desk? *Gone.*

Stunningly beautiful and charming woman performs a vanishing act mid-date, and now I'll be subjected to her presence? *No sweat.*

The bright, blinking lights of the Vegas strip beckon me, the scent of the perfumed air pumped into the casinos already creating that euphoric cloud.

I text the group chat with my mom and dad, telling them the dates I'll be coming to town.

Dad: We should put some money on the ponies while you're here.

Mom: Ron! Do not say that to your son!

Dad: What? He doesn't care, do you, Dominic?

Mom: Of course he cares!

I sigh. They can't help it. That's what two years of therapy has taught me. Mom will never stop reprimanding Dad as though he is a child, and Dad will never start acting like an adult. He will always be bad with money, chasing the next get rich quick scheme. Invariably, these schemes involve gambling of some sort.

Dom: I won't have time for that on this trip, but it will be nice to see you both.

Clear boundary lines, just like I've learned. They keep me from feeling resentful. I'll have to extend the developed skill to my interactions with Cecily in approximately one month.

Dad: Looking forward to seeing you, bud.

Mom: I'll make your favorite coffee cake!

I huff a laugh at the exclamation point at the end of her sentence. At the end of every one of her sentences. If one of her sentences weren't exclamatory, I'd be worried.

CHAPTER 6

Dominic

I LAND IN DRY, DUSTY LAS VEGAS AND LEARN THE AIRLINE has lost my luggage.

I'm put out for a second, but decide to take it in stride. I'm wearing a T-shirt and soft shorts, comfortable for travel, so I'll need to stop somewhere and buy clothing for a night out. And toiletries. I hate spending money unnecessarily. I make good money now, enough to keep me clothed and fed. Cold on warm days, warm on cold days. But the feeling of never quite having enough is pervasive, a holdover from childhood. Like a weed, the emotions that grow when you come from a place of lack persist. They have roots. Gnarled and stubborn.

I follow the signs for ride-sharing, then the Uber line. It is long, much longer than I anticipated, winding around the covered parking lot. I check my watch and worry my bottom lip. There is no way I'm going to be on time for the dinner reservation in one hour. And no time to buy clothing appropriate for the meal.

I look down at myself, surveying my clothing. I might

be dressed casually, but the fabric is thick, and well-cut. Quality clothing—items that last.

That, too, is a product of my childhood. *We don't have money for that. Money doesn't grow on trees.*

We bounced around the Phoenix area, never staying in one place too long. *The landlord's an asshole*, my dad would declare, indignant. It was always their fault, according to him, but he never provided an actual reason for whatever they had done that constituted asshole behavior.

I send Klein a text and tell him I might be late. He informs me the restaurant won't seat us until we have our full party.

Great. Making our reservation at this fancy dinner hinges on me being on time, something I have zero control over at the moment. I'm already anxious about seeing Cecily, no matter how hard I try not to be. Lost luggage and a long Uber line is not easing my nerves.

By the time the Uber driver deposits me in front of the hotel, I have three minutes to make it to the dinner reservation on time, and zero time to appreciate the surrounding opulence. On the bright side, I don't have luggage to slow me down. Because it's evening, there isn't a line to check in, so the process is quick, thankfully.

I slip my room key into my shorts, shoulder my backpack, and make my way through a busy hotel lobby. It's a little like New York City, and I'm adept at navigating it. But you know who's not great at navigating it? All the people who are not from bustling, walkable cities.

The woman in front of me slams on her heels, spins, and deposits an entire cup of lukewarm coffee on my shirt.

For half a second I'm stunned, then I'm pulling the fabric away from my body, grimacing.

"Lo siento," she cries, her face aghast. It's obvious she feels terrible, and I don't have time to be mad. I nod curtly and move through the crowd, the strong smell of coffee filling my nose. I love an Italian roast as much as the next guy, but I don't want to smell like it. The scent of coffee is so potent it's like I have inserted fresh grounds in my nose, and not even the perfumed hotel air can compete with it.

The thing about Vegas hotels is that they are huge. They go on forever, and in multiple directions. This hotel has an indoor fountain, botanical garden, twenty-foot tall chess pieces covered in moss like a living chess game, and elaborate handblown glass flowers hanging from the ceiling. I'd love to spend a single minute admiring the place, but I can't.

Two minutes late.

I get myself oriented, figure out what direction I'm headed in, and duck into the first bathroom I see, shucking my ruined shirt and tossing it in the garbage. Klein is going to think it's hilarious that the only shirt I have to wear is the one he sent me. Who would've thought when I shoved the package in my backpack this morning on my way out of my apartment I'd be so grateful to have it? At this point, it's either the T-shirt I'm ripping from its packaging, or me parading around half-naked to dinner. Something tells me the restaurant Paisley chose takes 'no shirt, no shoes, no service' seriously.

Seven minutes late.

My phone buzzes in my pocket, but I ignore it. It's Klein, or possibly Paisley, wanting to know where the hell I am.

I pull the new, not coffee-stained shirt over my head

and barrel from the bathroom. By the time I skid to a stop in front of Palm Luxe, I am twelve minutes late.

Klein, Paisley, and a group of people I don't recognize stand in the vestibule.

"There you are," Klein says, relief plain on his face. Everyone turns to me. "I was worried about..." His words die on his lips as he takes in my shirt. Paisley's eyes become saucers, and she snaps a cupped palm over her mouth.

I look at my chest, trying to see what they see. Four words, hard to decipher from this angle. A few disbelieving chuckles sound from somewhere in the group.

"Klein," Paisley hisses, smacking his midsection without looking at him. "I told you to forget the stupid shirts."

Klein's lips press together, suppressing laughter I'm certain would be booming if unbridled. "I'd already sent it to him. I didn't think he'd wear it to dinner."

"*He* is standing beside you," I remind them, irritated. "And *he* has had a hell of a day and doesn't know what the shirt says because—" I point a stiff finger at my cousin "—this asshat chose Old English lettering for the font, and I can't read it upside down."

Klein scratches his thumb over his eyebrow. "Did you wear that on the plane?"

Seriously? What the hell does this shirt say?

This is when I catch sight of dark, gleaming brunette locks. Creamy skin, pink lips. Narrowed eyes shooting death rays my way. *Cecily*.

I force my gaze away from hers, finding my asshole cousin's face. "I haven't been wearing this shirt more than five minutes." Every word slips between gnashed teeth.

"Can you change?" There's a trace of humor in his tone. Beside him, Paisley grips his arm and turns away, like she's struggling to contain her laughter.

"No." My jaw clenches. "I also haven't looked in the mirror since I put it on after a stranger spilled a cup of coffee all over the shirt I wore *on the plane* and the airline *lost my luggage.*"

Klein releases the hold he had on his laughter. Paisley, too. The whole damn group, in fact, save for Cecily. She looks like she'd rather eat her shoe than direct any mirth my way.

Klein's arm goes around my shoulder, steering me toward a rectangular gilt-framed mirror on the wall beside the hostess stand.

He's smiling like a birthday party clown as I read the words.

No Muff Too Tuff.

Klein cackles. The guy is vibrating with laughter.

All this time I've spent making up scenarios for what would happen when Cecily and I saw each other this weekend, and none of them included mortifying myself within the first five seconds.

I give my cousin a quick jab with my elbow. "If I weren't standing in a fancy restaurant in front of a group of strangers, I would punch you in the face. And knee you in the balls, which is a low blow but well deserved."

Klein grunts at the contact my elbow makes, holding his side. "A couple of cocktails will make you forget all about that shirt you're wearing."

"I hate you," I say to him as the hostess leads us to a large table.

"For what it's worth, I am sorry about your bad luck today."

I nod at his apology, my attention snagged by Cecily walking beside Paisley at the front of the group. She's dressed in lemon yellow, the dress hitting mid-thigh. The back is low cut, down to the middle of her back. The front is more conservative. Covertly sexy.

I wish I could say I have no reaction to it, but that would be a flat-out lie. I like the dress on Cecily. I like it very, very much.

Klein double-times his steps, catching up to Paisley.

Cecily glances back at me. Sends me a venomous look. Audacious, considering she's the one who ghosted me.

Maybe it's the day I've had. Perhaps it's the disappointment and embarrassment from being left high and dry by her. It's possible I'm simply out of my mind.

But I raise a hand. Middle finger stiff and punching the air.

Cecily's eyes squint to slits. Her head shakes back-and-forth, a tiny motion. It's the perfect opportunity for her to draw her thumb across her throat, but she doesn't take it.

I have just made myself an enemy. The first one in my life, to my knowledge.

The hostess directs Paisley to a seat wrapped in white silk ribbon. Gold confetti around the table catches the overhead light, glittering. Klein takes the seat beside Paisley, his equally festooned. Cecily settles across from Paisley, and I make my way down to the end of the table, hoping to hide on the corner and do my least favorite activity, make friends with strangers who have already laughed at my expense.

"Dom," Klein says loudly. "Over here." He points at the seat across from him.

Beside Cecily.

I pause, thinking for a moment about pretending I didn't hear him. But he points again, more forcefully this time, and indicates the seat with his chin.

I exhale a slow breath nobody can hear because of the music playing. My hesitation has gone on too long, confusion tugging at Klein's eyebrows.

I don't have much of a choice. Not without causing a scene, and I think I've done enough to draw attention to myself this evening.

I start for my cousin. The closer I get, the more I see, taste, and smell the hatred emanating from Cecily. Hopefully she doesn't order the steak. I don't trust her with a knife.

"Why are you being weird?" Klein asks as I pull out my seat.

"I'm not being weird," I argue.

"You are," Paisley confirms enthusiastically, flicking a piece of confetti at me.

I sit down. Haul my seat in closer to the table. Smack Cecily's ankle bone with the chair leg.

She grunts in pain, reaching down to rub her ankle. It was an accident, I swear, and I'd apologize, but the way she's refusing to acknowledge it happened keeps my apology hovering in my throat.

Klein's gaze darts back-and-forth between me and Cecily. His brain is doing somersaults, cataloging our body posture and microfacial expressions. The guy is always taking inventory of people. Maybe he should retire from authoring and become a detective.

If I don't say something to Cecily in the next three and a half seconds, Klein is going to start asking questions.

I dip my head sideways, closer to Cecily, and open my mouth to speak. But just as I do, the server walks up and begins his spiel, and I'm awash with gratitude for the delay. Never in my life have I been so interested in the preparation of a whole branzino.

He starts the drink order with Paisley, moving on to Klein. When he asks me what I'd like to drink, I look left, to the human embodiment of the word *loathing*, and say the only drink that comes to mind. Just to mess with her. "A blueberry mojito, please."

Cecily's gaze sharpens. So worth it.

"And for you?" the server asks her.

"A Ballbuster," she says, lips forming the word innocently. It's the tiny, nearly imperceptible shake of her head that gives away the attitude lying beneath.

"That's not a drink," I grit, matching Cecily's attitude.

She leans closer to me. A lock of her long brown hair dips forward, tickling my forearm. She smells like she did that afternoon at Obstinate Daughter, like bourbon vanilla and something else, a scent I'm not familiar with. "Pretty sure it is a drink," she snaps, tapping the menu with intensity.

Ballbuster. Right there on the drink menu.

But I'll be damned if I acknowledge it out loud.

I stare down at her.

She glares up at me. We have a hateful conversation with our eyes.

Thanks for taking off in the middle of our date.

You're unbelievably rude, did you know that?

A sneer tugs at the corner of her mouth. "You have a lot of nerve, Dom-in-ic."

It's a murmur. A soft tone with serrated-edge words.

And I very much take umbrage with it. "A lot of nerve doing *what*? Breathing?"

I swivel my upper body enough so I can face her. A mistake, to be sure.

Disdainful pink pout. Shrewd chocolate brown eyes. Taut, carved cheekbones. She'd like to rip my head off. I'm not sure how I know this so certainly, but I do.

She runs a fingertip over her sweating glass of ice water. "Showing up here."

"Oh? I didn't realize you own Las Vegas."

"You know what? I'm not going to say any more to you. Wouldn't want to yammer and annoy you." She enunciates the last few words, adding to the confusion of this interaction.

"What are you—"

"Whose decision was this?" Paisley's yell breaks through my question. Two servers have arrived at our table, both carrying a tray loaded with shot glasses holding clear liquid.

"It was me!" A woman three seats down raises her hand. She has an accent, but I can't tell if it's Spanish or Portuguese.

"Paloma," Paisley says motherly, "you know this means you have to hold my hair later."

The woman, Paloma, wrinkles her nose. "Fat chance. Sounds like a job for your fiancé."

Klein nods and shrugs resolutely. "For better or worse."

Usually, I think his utter devotion to Paisley is something to aspire to, but right now I'm not feeling particularly charitable. "Might want to think twice about what you're getting yourself into."

Hurt flickers through Paisley's blue-green eyes, and I feel like a giant asshole. Klein kicks me under the table. Hard. Without a doubt, my shin will be bruised tomorrow. And I deserve it.

The shots are delivered to each of us, along with a lime wedge.

I'm not typically a shot guy. Under normal circumstances, I'd probably give the shot to somebody else, or only pretend to take it. But today is not a normal day. And it's obvious I need to do something to dull my senses and curb this foul mood I'm in before I do or say anything else I don't mean. And, as an ancillary benefit, maybe the injection of alcohol into my bloodstream will rubberize me enough that I won't feel the pierce of Cecily's poison-tipped dagger she's currently sending my way following my rude comment.

Two salt shakers make their way around the table, and I direct my face away from Cecily when it's her turn to swipe her tongue over her hand and pour the salt.

When everyone is ready, Paloma lifts her shot in the air. "To Paisley and Klein."

We repeat after her. I lick the salt, grimace at the burn of tequila, quickly quelling it with the tang of the lime.

That wasn't too bad.

It's not long after that my limbs feel a little looser. The tension in my neck melts. My molars stop grinding.

Our drinks are delivered, and our food orders are placed. Klein introduces me to everyone around the table. They all laugh at how I ended up wearing this awful shirt.

If I weren't feeling waves of hatred rolling off Cecily,

I'd offer her a conciliatory clink of glasses. I'd love to understand what it is she could possibly be angry with me about, but tonight isn't the right time. Cecily isn't crazy, she must believe she's justified for the way she feels. Or, maybe she is a few bricks shy of a load and I didn't notice because I was too busy appreciating how gorgeous she is.

Wait, I think I figured it out. Cecily likes drama.

Satisfaction rolls through me at my superior sleuthing skills, and I mentally pat myself on the back. I'm a no-drama guy, so if Cecily thrives on drama, I've dodged a bullet.

Those tequila shots were pretty good. We should have another one.

"Are you sure about that?" Klein asks.

Oh. I didn't realize I'd spoken out loud. "What say you, bride?" I ask Paisley, hoping she hears the apology in my tone.

She shrugs, grinning. "When in Vegas!"

The more we eat, the more we drink, the merrier we become.

Even Cecily, to my great shock, is not impervious to tequila. She laughs at a joke told by the person beside her, throwing back her head and swaying closer to me. Her shoulder brushes mine, sending a waft of her sweet scent my direction.

She doesn't speak to me for the rest of dinner, but her demeanor is softer. Looser. More like the woman I first met. I was captivated by her throaty laugh, her slow smile. She was like smoke curling up over a campfire.

What happened?

Maybe I should ask her and stop this angst fest. After

months wondering, asking myself the same question over and over, I'm sick of my whiny ass.

We're paying the bill now, and there's no time to break into a conversation with her. But at least I'm no longer worried she'll stash a steak knife in her purse and stab me later.

Thank you, tequila.

We hit the next place, a club where we have a table and bottle service. I sit back, nursing a drink, pretending to look around but watching Cecily on the dance floor instead.

She's something else. Generous curves, hips that switch, beaming as she dances with Paisley and Paloma. Her shiny brown hair tumbles down her back, catching the pulsing light.

"What's going on with you and Cecily?" Klein yells in my ear.

I pause with my drink at my mouth. "Nothing. Why?"

Klein frowns. "Don't lie to me. I know you better than anybody."

"I don't think I made a good first impression. That's all."

"What? You?" Klein slaps my back, and my drink bounces against my lower lip. "You're a hell of a guy."

I love when Klein has too much to drink. He becomes his cuddliest, softest, most emotional self. I like to give him a lot of shit, but he's a hell of a guy, too. I champion his work because it's my job and I believe in him, but it's a bonus knowing someone as good and hardworking as him is succeeding.

"Cecily is tough," I counter, shrugging as I set my drink on the table.

He nods. "I look at her with two parts awe, and one part fear."

Paisley materializes at the table, Cecily in tow. Behind them, Paloma dances by herself.

"Dance with me, Word Daddy," Paisley yells. Sweat at her temple has captured a tendril of blonde hair, sticking it to her face. Her eyes are bright, exhilarated. Klein grins like the lovesick fool he is, standing up. He's stepping down from the area when he turns around, cups his hands around his mouth, and yells, "She's tough, but you're tougher. No muff is too tough for you, buddy!"

I close my eyes and shake my head. As if I could forget the shirt. How many people commented on it on the walk over from the restaurant to the club? Seven? Eight? Luckily, we found a boutique where I could buy clothes to satisfy the club's dress code, and send my other clothes up to my room. At long last, I'm presentable.

Paisley and Klein move away.

Cecily remains standing, backlit by the multicolor strobing lights. Music pounds in my limbs, vibrating my chest.

I shift right, making space. When she doesn't move, I busy my hands by making a drink for her. We've stuck with tequila. A smart choice, I'd wager.

Cecily settles beside me. I add a lime to her drink, turning so I can hand it to her. I lift my own, offering a *cheers*.

Her fingers brush mine when she takes her drink. Maybe it's the alcohol, but I swear her touch extends beyond my hand. I feel it everywhere.

I look up into her eyes, prepared to say *cheers!* but her expression stops me. Her brown eyes search mine, her teeth catching the side of her lower lip. She releases it, and opens her mouth. This is it. She's going to tell me why she ghosted me.

"Fuck you, Dominic."

Harsh words. Soft tone.

This woman.

"Right back at you, Cecily." I can't bring myself to retaliate with the same sentiment. Nor can I ask why she hates me. Why she ghosted me. I almost don't want to know. By not knowing, I can keep up this game. If I know, I'll have to face it. And then we'll be in a much worse state, an alternative I cannot live with: apathy. Hate is an extreme emotion, and I'm stupid enough to want an extreme emotion from this woman. I've never been much of a masochist before now, but here I am. Welcoming the torment she deals.

Cecily drinks. I drink. We both drain our glasses.

"Do you dance, Dominic?" Cecily arches one eyebrow.

"I'm not half-bad."

"Well, then." Cecily slides her empty drink onto the table. "It's your lucky day, because I love to dance, and you're the only man in this place I'd let that close to me."

I point back at myself. "Me? Are you sure?"

She nods. "Dance with the devil you know, as they say."

"I'm the devil?"

At this point I no longer want to know her reason for leaving me high and dry on our date. I don't even care that she hates me. This woman spars with me on a level no one ever has. And I like it.

Her head tips sideways, considering me. "No. You're only smart enough to be Satan's errand boy."

Ouch.

Fuck, but I like it.

Without a word I stand, taking her hand and roughly hauling her up with me. She tumbles into my chest, catching herself against me. She looks up, quickly replacing that look of thrill with irritation. But I saw it.

Cecily might hate me, but she loves the way we tangle.

I spin without saying a word, winding us through the writhing bodies, finding a square of space. Turning to face her, I put a hand on the side of her head and bring my lips close to her ear. "Should I worry you'll produce a shiv from under that dress?"

I feel her head shake. "Now, Dom, where would I hide a shiv when I'm not wearing underwear?"

Blunt, unapologetic, and setting loose a torrent of vivid pictures in my imagination. How am I supposed to respond to that? How am I supposed to breathe normally after hearing her smart mouth say such a thing? The air between is hotter, heavier.

"Fair point," I croak, stepping back and trying but failing to look everywhere but at the borderline evil temptress beside me.

Cecily watches me with that half-daring, half-amused look that would, if the way I'm feeling now is any indication, drive me wild if we were together. Is she testing me, or just enjoying herself?

She shakes her head and laughs. She turns around, curves her body into mine, throws an arm in the air and palms the back of my neck. Her ass presses against me, hips gyrating, body undulating.

This woman will be the death of me.

CHAPTER 7
Cecily

POUNDING HEAD.

Dry mouth.

Stomach one moment away from heaving.

I've never been so hungover.

Light presses into the slits of my eyes. Fogginess hangs heavy in my thoughts, making them difficult to form.

Slowly I turn my head left to right, my head thumping with the movement. I don't know where I am, but I know I am in a bed. It's soft beneath me, plush. I must have made it back to my hotel room.

My memories swipe at the fog in my brain, revealing bits and pieces of the evening. Tequila. Dinner. Dancing. More drinks. Sweat gathering at my hairline. Feet aching. More drinks. Laughing until tears ran down my cheeks. Paloma and I in the bathroom, pressing a cool wet washcloth to our necks. Waffles dripping with cinnamon syrup. Klein carrying Paisley on his back. After that, a haze blankets the night. The memories are jagged, angular, forming an incomplete picture. Dom appears over and over. Smiling. Happy. Laughing. Staring at me with this look in his eyes, baffled at first, and then later, a look similar to the one from our disastrous date. Back when I thought he liked me.

I rarely drink as much as I did last night, but I was anxious. Nervous. I saw Dom, and he was so handsome, and he looked hurt when he saw me. It was confusing, and I was already a mix of emotions, so it all melded together and turned into outrage. The burn of tequila seemed like the best solution.

Not so much now, especially with—

The bed dips. But I haven't moved.

No. No no no.

There's a soft shuffle of sheets. Horror mixes with the rolling nausea in my midsection. Who is beside me in this bed?

Please let it be Paisley. Please let it be Paloma.

Taking a deep breath, I crack open one eye.

The bed is empty. My other eye opens. The room spins when I push up to my elbows.

There's the quiet snick of a door closing across the space. The bathroom. Slowly, to keep from expediting an almost certain need to vomit, my gaze explores the room. It looks exactly like the room I checked into yesterday, but I know it's not mine. There isn't a black dress draped over a chair, the runner-up in my choice for what to wear last night. No propped open suitcase on the floor. My comfortable sneakers I wore on the plane aren't lying haphazardly after being kicked off.

In fact, from here I can't see anything personal in this room. Not a stray shoe or sock.

Was this a room rented solely for—*NO.*

I can't go there right now.

Panic overtakes me again. I am not in my room. This is the room of whoever is in that bathroom.

A toilet flushes. Water runs.

I need to get out of here before whoever that is comes out. If I never see their face, I'll never have to know it happened. Sound logic if there ever was any.

I attempt to sit up, but the dizziness sends me back to my elbows.

The bathroom door opens.

With all the reluctance I've ever felt in my life multiplied by ten, I force my gaze that direction. A man stands in the doorway. Bare chest. Shoulders that stretch on and on, carved and expansive like he was built to carry the weight of things. Things like furniture, or boxes filled with books, or a wanton woman to his sex lair.

Dom.

Silently, I send a mighty and heartfelt *thank you* to the heavens. It could be so much worse.

But also, *this isn't good*. In fact, this is monumentally bad.

Dom is beautiful, and not in a brooding-for-no-apparent-reason cologne ad way. Not at all. Dom has a brand of attractiveness that begs to be obsessed about later, the kind that has staying power in a woman's thoughts.

He leans a ridiculously muscular shoulder on the doorframe, skin faintly illuminated in the morning light. His hair, normally neat, fluffs up in caramel tufts, suggesting he ran a hand through it.

I look away. Or I try to, anyway. My gaze drags itself back to the cut of his abdomen, the way his shorts hang just a little too low on those hips. Dear me. Send help.

Nope. No. Absolutely not.

I am not about to be charmed by this man.

But my stomach flips anyway.

Just once. Maybe twice.

"Good morning," he says, voice like a rake over hot gravel. "You look—"

"Like a roadkill coyote, I'm sure." I don't need this guy telling me how terrible I look. I palm my hair, swipe under my eyes, discovering the telltale crust of old mascara.

He smirks. Shouldn't he be too hungover to smirk? I know I am.

"I was going to say you look good wearing my shirt."

Stomach sinking, I glance down.

No Muff Too Tuff.

I'd say I've officially hit rock bottom, but I have a feeling the bottom is an illusion at this point.

My head snaps up when Dom takes a step toward me. My hand shoots out. "Stop right there. On a scale of one to ten, how likely is it that you saw me naked last night? Or, this morning?"

Dom pauses. He's wearing shorts, something like what he wore to dinner last night. Probably the same ones, unless the airline found and delivered his luggage.

He stays quiet, evaluating. Then he says, "As much as I would love to tell you something that would make you want to crawl into a hole, I'll be honest. You grabbed my shirt the second we walked into this room, went into the bathroom, and came out with it on."

Hmm. Ok. I can work with that. I'm pleased with hammered-yet-modest past Cecily.

"Did we..." I gesture from me to him.

He shakes his head. Does it not kill him to motion that way right now? "Did we what?"

"Did we...*you know*?" I make a ring with my pointer finger and thumb, poking my finger from the opposite hand through.

His brow furrows. "I'm not sure what you're getting at."

An angry breath streams from my pursed lips. I don't have the patience. I may not have much time before I'm placing my face where faces are not meant to go. "What about that hand motion are you not understanding? Did. We. Shag?"

He grins.

Comprehension dawns. "That was mean."

"That was fun," he argues. "I was wondering how creative you could be while nursing a hangover this atrocious. And no, we didn't sleep together. Not in the way you mean, anyway." He gestures at the bed. "We most definitely fell asleep on that bed at the same time."

He steps closer, cautious, testing the temperature between us. This time I don't stop him. I'm feeling more generous now that I know we didn't do anything totally regrettable.

He pauses, eyes locking with mine. "For the record," he says, voice low but steady, "Enthusiastic consent is a requirement for any woman I take to bed. And you were not in a position to give enthusiastic consent." There's no bravado in his voice, just conviction.

My pulse skitters at the idea of being *enthusiastic* with Dom, but I tamp it down. "You do know the difference between enthusiastic and *my show starts in two minutes that should be enough time for you*, right?"

Dominic nibbles his lower lip while he stares at me.

Shirtless. Ugh. Fuck him and all his muscles. He opens his mouth, pauses, and decides against it. He sinks onto the bed, staying on top of the comforter. I push myself all the way to seated, still fighting the effects of the hardest night of partying I've ever participated in, and drag my knees into my chest. My arms wrap around my knees, and my head leans on my forearms in a way that makes it possible for my eyes to remain on him. Now that he's closer, I see the redness in his eyes, how the hangover tugs at the corners. I am delighted to note he looks a shade green.

"Cecily, you—"

"Dom?" Klein's panicked voice punches through the door at the same time he knocks hard. "Dom, open up. Now."

Dom's eyes find mine briefly before he stands, striding for the door. From my position on the bed, I can't see around the little corner to the door, but I hear it swing open. Klein says, "Please tell me that picture was a joke."

Paisley's higher pitch joins in. "Dominic, I'm going to inflict bodily harm on you. Something creative. You'll never see me coming."

"What are you talking about?" Dom asks. Klein and Paisley barrel further into the room, clearing the corner that was keeping my presence unknown.

Paisley screeches to a halt. She stares, her eyes as bloodshot as Dom's, and probably mine, too. Her blonde bun dangles precariously from the crown of her head. Klein looks like he has aged five years overnight.

The four of us are a motley crew.

"Hey," I say weakly. It's not lost on me that although I'm in front of my friend, I am also in front of my boss. It's not a good look.

"What's going on?" Dom demands in that scratchy voice, sidestepping Klein. He has the sensibility to take a seat in a chair in the far corner of the room, instead of returning to the bed.

Klein and Paisley look at us like we're telling a joke that is not at all funny.

"This isn't what it looks like, I promise," I say, just to get it out there.

Paisley's pulling her phone from her pocket, swiping quickly over the screen and crossing the room in a few steps. She plops onto the bed, thrusting her phone in my face. "This isn't what it looks like?"

Every breath in my lungs disappears. *Poof.* Gone.

It's me.

It's Dom.

We're standing in front of a wall of multicolored fake flowers. Dom holds me by the waist, dipping me backward. My arms encircle his neck, one leg kicked out. Above us is a neon sign that reads *Just Married*.

All the breath that vanished comes rushing back, too much for my throat. I'm dragging it in, holding my chest.

"What?" I manage. "No." Alarmed eyes find Dom, already crossing the room. Paisley hands him the phone. A second later, Dom's looking down at me, eyes wide.

Memories develop like film in a darkroom. Slowly but surely, coming into stark relief.

Dancing with Dominic. My fingernails raking over the back of his neck. The hard press of him against my backside. Him groaning into my neck as the music thumped through us.

Sweaty and loving it, the burn of our muscles matched by the burn of tequila. Dom ceased being the guy who'd said those awful things. He was the same guy from the beginning of our date. The one who had my hopes up, who arrived early and said *She's beautiful* and *Who said I was playing*?

"Dom," I start, at the same time he says, "Cecily."

I feel as he looks, aghast and horrified and confused.

"Do you remember?" he asks.

I nod, only slightly. Any more movement than that and I'll pull an Exorcist all over the ivory comforter.

The roiling in my stomach may have kept the memories of last night at bay, but they are plentiful now, screaming forth with blinding clarity.

How we'd broken off from the group after gorging ourselves on waffles, warbling songs about Vegas as we walked. We'd passed a restaurant where Bruno Mars crooned from the speakers, singing about how he was looking for something dumb to do. Dom had looked at me with a spark in his eyes, said, *What could be more Vegas than getting drunk-married?*

I turn on Dom now, his hair all bouncy and his face not nearly showing enough signs of how hungover he must feel.

"This is All. Your. Fault," I accuse, pointing a finger at him.

He makes an indignant sound in the back of his throat. "Me?" he sputters. "Nobody held a knife to your throat and forced you to say *I do*."

My mouth opens to reply, but Paisley screeches. "What? This is real?"

I wince. So does Dom.

Paisley slaps a hand over her mouth. "Sorry. No more high-pitched exclamations."

"We're married," I whisper, the realization slamming through me. "We're...married." My lip curls on that last word.

Dom's mouth flattens. "Maybe if you keep saying it, it will be less true."

"Shut up." I groan, dropping my head in my hands. How could I have done something this monumentally stupid? I'm never impulsive. I do not make bad decisions. Apparently I was saving up all those small bad decisions to make one really, truly, terrible choice instead.

That's when I feel it. The illness climbing, pushing against gravity. "I'm going to be sick," I moan, throwing back the covers and running to the bathroom.

The door opens a moment after I shut it behind me. I hate throwing up, but it's ten times worse when there's an audience. I'm already emptying my stomach over the bowl when strong, nimble fingers gather my hair.

"Go away," I moan, batting behind me. I don't need to look to know it's Dom. I am acutely aware of him.

He gathers a lock of hair that hangs in my face, his fingertips brushing my forehead. "In sickness and in health."

"Please go," I whisper, humiliated. I throw up again, tears leaking from the sides of my eyes. "I mean it, Dom. I don't want you here."

He hesitates. After a moment's deliberation, my hair falls down my back and over my shoulders. The door opens, then closes. Lying down, I press my face to the cool tile of the floor. The bathroom door creaks open.

"Go away," I croak.

"Hey," Paisley says softly. The water turns on, and then Paisley lays a cool washcloth over my face.

I sigh at how good it feels.

"That's a nice shirt you're wearing," Paisley jokes, rubbing a palm over my back.

"Not funny," I murmur.

"Look on the bright side. At least you have a nice ass."

"Wha—" No. This can't be happening. I'm only wearing underwear beneath this shirt. I lied last night when I taunted Dom by telling him I was going commando. So when I got up to run in here... I was right. Rock bottom was an illusion.

"Don't worry," Paisley assures me. "Klein turned away when he saw you get up. He might love to tease, but he takes pride in being a gentleman."

"Dom did none of that." Dom came in to witness my mortification. *And to help*.

"Dom ran after you. And he asked me to check on you."

I sit up, taking the washcloth and pressing it to the back of my neck. "I can't believe I did something so stupid. I married him." I could say it one hundred times, but it might take double that for me to believe it.

Paisley shoulders me lightly. "Here I thought I was the one headed down the aisle."

"You can't tell Paloma. She will never let me live it down."

Paisley makes a face, one that clearly says *too late*.

"You told her?"

"*You* told her. The same way you told me and Klein."

"I sent a photo?"

Paisley nods in the affirmative. "Don't you remember?"

"Not really. I remember the ceremony"—I stammer over the word—"but I think after that I was so tired I could barely stand up. The alcohol turned into a sleeping pill."

Paisley slips an arm around my shoulders, delivering a reassuring squeeze. "This is a messy mess. But it's fixable. You weren't of sound mind during the decision, so you can get an annulment. It will be like it never happened."

"Like it never happened," I echo.

I climb to my feet, and Paisley slips out. I rinse my mouth and splash water on my face, then brave a look in the mirror. Wow. That's...not at all pleasant. I look like I feel. The best I can do now is a finger comb through my hair and leave the safety of the bathroom behind.

Blessedly nobody looks at me when I walk out. Klein and Paisley sit at the small table, and Dom sits on the end of the bed. He has his phone out, thumb scrolling.

"I'm learning about annulments," he says without looking up.

"Can't we say we had our fingers crossed behind our backs? Or we tripped and fell and *oops we're married*." I climb back into the bed, pulling the covers up around me and my nearly naked bottom half.

Klein looks at me now that I'm appropriately covered. "At least your walk of shame was short. What was it, five feet from the bathroom to the bed?"

"Too soon," Paisley sings.

"Tread lightly, KleinTheWriter," I retort, using his social media handle. Grabbing my phone from the nightstand, I mentally prepare myself to do damage control. *Please tell me Paloma is the only other person I texted that photo.* Taking a quiet breath, I open my messages app. I don't want to look, but I have to face it.

Oh no. Oh no no no.

"Dammit." This is so much worse than I thought.

It gets Dom's attention. "What's wrong? Other than the obvious."

"That picture of me and you under the Just Married sign? Apparently I wanted to share our newlywed bliss." It's so unbelievable it feels like it should be happening to someone else.

Dom's head shakes in confusion. "Who else did you share it with?"

If I weren't already hungover, what I did would make me sick right now. I meet Paisley's gaze as I answer, because she's the only person in this room who will grasp the gravity of what I'm about to say. "My *entire* family."

Paisley's gasp is sharp. She knows what my relationship with them is like, tense and strained, a powder keg of hurt feelings. Kerrigan and my grandma are the only family members I talk to regularly.

The group chat, unused for months, now shows unread messages. I'm not looking. Not yet. Reading those messages is a job for future me. Current me can only handle so much at one time. Kerrigan is going to kill me. Duke, my older brother, will criticize like always. And my parents, well, it's a toss-up between who will notice I exist.

"Why did I do that?" I'm looking at Paisley when I ask, but really I'm asking myself, the universe, anybody who will answer. "Why would I text all of them? Why not just Kerrigan?"

"Intoxication has a way of bringing feelings out of their hiding spots." It's Dom speaking.

"Apparently so," I say meaningfully. "I thought I hated you, but it looks like I can stand you enough to marry you."

"Last night it looked like you could do a lot more than

stand him." It's Klein again, with that teasing tone. And Dominic, smirking.

These damn cousins.

"I like to dance," I say defensively.

Klein stands, placing his hands on his knees and shaking his rear end.

"What are you doing?" Paisley asks.

"Dropping it low," Klein answers.

Dom's laughter fuels Klein's charade.

"You should bring it back up," Paisley says, but I know she's repressing laughter.

Klein sits down, grinning at me like he's waiting for me to say something.

"Thanks for the demonstration," I say dryly.

"You're welcome. It was like hitting replay on the night."

I roll my eyes. Even drunk, I look way better bumping and grinding than whatever Klein just did.

"I'm going to need everyone in this room to get serious," Dom announces, attention on his phone again. "It says here we can't request an annulment until Monday. They are not open on the weekends, which makes sense."

I groan. Loudly. "It's Saturday. And I don't know about you, but I'm supposed to fly out tomorrow afternoon."

Dom's back is to me, but he's nodding. "It says we can petition a court in the state in which one of us resides." He swivels around on the bed to look at me. "Lucky for us, I'm going from here to Phoenix to visit my parents. As long as you're free, we can go together on Monday."

"Great," Klein says, clapping once, loudly, and making my head throb. "Who's hungry? I'm starving, and if

Paisley doesn't get a bucket of coffee soon, she'll turn into a chupacabra."

"He tells no lies," Paisley confirms solemnly.

Coffee sounds good. Food, however, does not. I may never eat again.

Paisley rises, pulling Klein up with her. "Let's leave these two alone. I'm sure they have some big emotions to work through and they don't need an audience."

Klein wraps an arm around Paisley's waist as they head for the door. "Meet us in the lobby in an hour."

"An hour?" Paisley squawks. "But—"

"Don't worry, Ace, I'm going in search of coffee for you right now."

Ugh. Klein is so good to her. Which is great, obviously, but also *ew*. I can't take it at the moment. The hotel room door opens, and they disappear through it.

Quiet falls around the room, but it is so loud, bouncing off the vacated seats, careening from the unremarkable picture on the wall. Finally, I drag my eyes to Dom, still sitting at the end of the bed. Hunched shoulders, hand on his forehead, thumb rubbing circles over his temple.

"So..." I don't have anything else to say. I'm reeling, stunned, stumped.

Dom turns around, propping one bent knee on the bed, eyebrows raised. "Guess you're my wife for the weekend."

Wife.

Absolutely not.

The memory trickles in, making me hot and uncomfortable. *Dom's mouth on mine to conclude the short ceremony. A searching kiss, extracting from me a response I should have been embarrassed by.*

Anger flares, not at the annoyingly handsome face of

the man looking at me, but directed inward. And that anger makes me uncomfortable. Hot. On edge.

"I'm not your wife," I grit.

I know Dom doesn't find this funny, but his good-natured *take it in stride* expression fades. A muscle in his jaw clenches. "You are, actually. That is a fact, plain and simple, and wishing for it to be untrue won't make it less true."

Dom strides, long-legged and lean, to the closet. He opens it and reaches in, producing my yellow dress.

"Did you hang that?" I ask.

"Someone had to," he responds irritably. "You left it in a puddle on the bathroom floor."

Great. My dress is wet. I have to wear that thing out of here. "Why was there water on the ground?"

"Not literally," he mutters. "You took it off and it puddled at your feet." He mimes pulling something down his body and letting it go, and I guess the ending to the motion is that it would *puddle*.

"I'm sure you'd like to go to your room and get ready for brunch," he says, tossing the garment on the bed.

He disappears into the bathroom, door closing softly behind him.

I have been kicked out. Summarily dismissed. I don't blame him. I would've done the same. Still, it rankles me. I want to be mad at him. If I'm not mad at him, I have to look too closely at my part in all this, and I don't want to.

I shuck the shirt, don the dress, and find last night's heels lined up in the closet. Wincing as I step into them, I step jerkily to the bathroom door, saying with a raised voice, "See you at brunch, Satan's Errand Boy."

His answering sigh is so loud I hear it through the door. "Unfortunately so, Menace."

Menace? I like it. Has a ring to it.

Threading my arm through my purse straps, I pass the closet. The shirt Dom wore last night, the one he had to purchase so we'd be allowed into the club, hangs neatly from the rod.

The soft fabric glides smoothly off the wood hanger. I toss it over my shoulder. Behind me, the soft sound of fabric hitting the ground. Then I exit the room, my feet complaining with every step.

This is my first walk of shame, and it is one for the record books.

CHAPTER 8

Cecily

You married Dom. You married Dom. You married Dom.

The refrain is all I think, all I hear, while I get ready for brunch. At this point I can't tell if it's the alcohol making me sick (it certainly is) or my new status as *married* (also possible).

The long, warm shower I took revived me, but only barely. I haven't thrown up again, so I'll take that as a win. I dress in loose-fitting boyfriend jeans and a square neck tank top that is, blessedly, not tight. My hands deftly work my hair into a fishtail braid. It is all I can manage, and given how poisoned my insides feel, I am proud to have managed to wear deodorant and brush my teeth.

My phone charges on the nightstand, but it may as well be a bomb with the amount of hesitation with which I regard it. I've put it off long enough. It's time to read my family's response to my irresponsible and impetuous behavior.

Duke: Are you kidding, Cecily?

Duke: I'm really asking if this is a joke. A
bad one, but a joke nonetheless.

Kerrigan: I have a lot to say about this,
starting with, Paisley better not have been
your maid of honor because that's my job.

Grandma: Well, well, well. The middle
child hits a homer.

Nothing from my parents. *Nothing.*

It makes me sad. And angry. Why would I expect anything different from them?

I thread turquoise studs through my earlobes and dab my smoky vanilla perfume behind my ears. It makes me think about what Dom said on our date, how he had a vanilla upbringing.

Lucky guy. If my family had a flavor, it would be that putrid durian fruit, the one that's visually appealing but stinks like rotting garbage.

It's a good thing I have Paisley and Paloma. Klein, too.

Slipping my phone into my purse, I push the unanswered messages from my siblings and my grandma from my mind. Undoubtedly, Kerrigan will spam my messages in our private conversation, demanding to know what is going on. I don't have the energy for her right now.

If I could choose how I spend the rest of today, it would include pajamas, movies from the '80s, and room service. But then I would be missing Klein and Paisley's special weekend. And what if Dom thinks I'm so upset that I'm in hiding? That's the last thing I want.

I will spend today parading around him with my head held high. I'm going to show that obnoxious, annoyingly tall and handsome man that he hasn't shaken me. Come Monday, we will take an eraser to this mistake, and it will be like it never happened.

CHAPTER 9

Dominic

Not only do I craft backstories for people in my mind, but I know the ending of every book, every story, every movie I see. Sometimes the plot surprises me, but never the ending.

Until now.

The story where I go to Vegas for my cousin's bachelor party? I did not see it ending in *I married the girl who abandoned me on a date and wishes me dead without me knowing why*.

At long last, I'm surprised by an ending.

Great.

Klein, that bonehead, finds this all *hilarious*. Maybe he feels some vindication for how much grief I gave him for fake dating Paisley before they fell in love. Not that I truly tormented him, but there was no way I was going to let that opportunity get away.

Judging from the text he just sent, Klein is enjoying this far too much.

> Klein: This is the best thing that has ever happened to me.

> Klein: I'm really mad I didn't get to be your best man.

> Dom: This topic has an expiration date.

> Klein: Set by me.

> Dom: Absolutely not.

> Klein: Hurry up. We're hungry. Don't make us late AGAIN. And for the love, nobody needs to be reminded no muff is too tuff for you. Have a little class and wear a different shirt to brunch.

A knock on the door interrupts my all-caps expletive response. I swing the door open and find a bellboy, and, blessedly, my missing suitcase.

He hands it off to me, and I heave a sigh of relief when I get it opened. Nothing is missing.

Rifling through the clothing, I find a fresh shirt and pull it on. The shirt I bought so I could continue the night is hung now, but it was lying in the middle of the floor when I stepped out from the shower. Cecily's work, no doubt. Taunting me.

And, as if Cecily removed it and dropped it where she stood, the T-shirt I wore to dinner last night lies on the bed.

Swiping the shirt from the sheets, I fold it quickly and lay it on the table. And ok, yes, I *might* have raised it to my nose. I *might* have inhaled. Cecily can be as prickly as a damn teddy bear cholla, but she smells sweeter than the desert after a rain.

Don't let me get started on those soft little moans I felt in her throat when I kissed her. It's better for both of us if I forget about them.

Cecily, my *wife*, does her best to pointedly ignore me for the remainder of the day.

Once the group gets over their collective shock and awe at hearing our *married in Vegas* story, we become the butt of every joke.

For example: Cecily said she loved the sandwich she had for lunch, and Paloma said *well you can't marry it because you're already married.*

One guy Klein plays his weekly soccer match with asked how long Cecily and I are waiting to have kids.

And on and on. And on.

Somehow, after last night's shenanigans, the group rallies. We end up at the hotel pool, and the drinking continues. Not for me, and not for Cecily, either.

Something about drunkenly marrying someone is quite sobering.

Cecily lounges on the chair beside me, because Klein, who hasn't stopped being delighted by last night's events, insisted newlyweds sit together.

Cecily wears a white bikini with light pink and butter yellow flowers printed on it, the kind of print I'd have expected on someone sweet, not someone who would launch a poison-tipped dart at me if given the chance. The ruffled edge of the fabric flutters with every breath she takes, giving her a delicate, almost fragile quality that juxtaposes with everything I know about this woman.

Is there anything fragile about her? It doesn't appear so, not with the defiant set of her jaw, or the storm clouds brewing in her eyes.

Despite all this, I can't help the way my gaze rakes over her long legs, the curve of her waist. Her skin looks smooth and supple, soft. My imagination runs wild at the thought of gliding my hands over her, but not for long. It's hard to fantasize about a person whose expression is that sharp, pinched and irritated.

She must be mad about more than the fact we're married. Now that the abject horror has worn off, isn't this something to laugh about? There is an end in sight for us, and this will one day become a hilarious anecdote. She'll be at a party, and someone will tell their best drunk story, and Cecily will say *Oh, you think getting drunk and flashing a cop is funny? Listen to this.*

Judging from Cecily's stiff posture and hate-vibes rising off her skin like mist, she's not there yet. She might be lounging in a chair, but her jaw is tight, eyes closed, arms crossed over her stomach. If it weren't for the breeze gently pushing tendrils of dark hair that have fallen from her braid, she could be mistaken for a statue.

I think I'll try talking to her. I am her husband, after all. Pretty sure that earns me the right to address her, however brief our marriage will be. "Cecily—"

"Nope." She enunciates the 'p'. Her eyes remain closed. "Nothing from you, thank you. I'm relaxing."

I lean over the low armrest of my chair, and because she is stubbornly keeping her eyes closed, she doesn't see me coming. Lips an inch from her ear, I softly say, "Hate to break it to you, but you look anything but relaxed, Menace."

It works. Her eyes open, cutting to me with razor sharpness. Something tells me it was the nickname that got her.

I called her that this morning through the bathroom door but didn't get to see her reaction. From what I can tell, it hits the mark flawlessly, making Cecily the perfect amount of intrigued and irritated.

We're close now, and something flares in her gaze. Discomfort, I think, and although I love teasing this woman, I'm not into making her feel uneasy. I sit back.

She sighs like I am an inconvenience in human form and pulls a bottle of sunscreen from the straw bag lying on the end of her chair. She lathers up her legs, and at this point I'm certain the universe is testing my ability to maintain eye contact instead of salivate over the way she smoothes her hands over her skin.

With manufactured disinterest, she says, "Don't you have some errands to run for Satan?"

I am reluctantly impressed by her little nickname for me. It's inventive and has just the right amount of derision. Placing my palm dramatically on my chest, I tell her, "I have no affiliation with the Prince of Darkness, despite your repeated assertions."

Her chin tips up. "Nor am I a menace."

Ohh but you are, Cecily. How could you be anything but a menace with the way you have plagued my thoughts and tormented me daily for months?

"What?" she demands. Challenging me, really. "I can see you're thinking something. Don't hold back."

Why did you ghost me?

It's not the time or place to air our grievances, but I'm tired of waiting. I'm ready to know why Cecily thinks she's justified in hating me. Clearly something occurred, and if I know what it is, I can either fix it, apologize, or move on. Any of the three is better than not knowing.

Cecily's phone rings from her bag. Her brows furrow. "I put it on Do Not Disturb," she murmurs, wiping her sunscreen slick hands on her towel. "The only people who can get through are my grandma and my sister if they call twice." She reaches into the bag, pulling out her phone. "My sister," she says. She taps the screen, muttering something like, "Might as well get it over with." Phone at her ear, she says, "Hey, Kerr."

I look away to give her space. There is no privacy to be had poolside, but I can provide her the illusion of it by not looking at her. Paisley waves at me from the water, where Klein has her scooped up in both arms. Paloma plays pool volleyball with the other guys from Klein's soccer team.

Despite my attempt to give Cecily space, I can't help but overhear her half of the conversation.

"Are you upset because I got married? I promise, it's not real."

Fact.

She continues. "It was a drunken mistake. You've heard of beer goggles? These were tequila bifocals."

Umm, wow. Ouch.

"Obviously, we're getting it annulled ASAP. I need to strike this guy from the record."

Rude.

"I don't know what happened to him in the last nine months, but he has definitely gone downhill."

Ok, now she's baiting me.

And I take whatever it is she's dangling. I can't help it. Adjusting my sunglasses to the top of my head, I say, "Maybe I should ask your sister if disappearing acts are typical for you."

Cecily responds with an impressive stink-eye and rakes her middle finger over her chin.

"Menace," I mouth.

I'm waiting for her return barb, but it doesn't come. She grows serious. "A family meeting? For what?"

The alarm in her tone of voice triggers a similar alarm inside me.

"I'm flying back tomorrow afternoon." Cecily's gaze slides my way. Is that panic in the set of her dark eyebrows? "I can't make any promises, but I'll ask him."

Him? Who is *him*? Me?

Cecily spends a few more moments on the phone, then says goodbye. She replaces her phone in her bag, gathers herself, then turns to me with worry in the crease of her brow. "My grandmother has called an emergency family meeting for Monday morning. As far as I know, she has never done this before. And she has specifically requested I bring my husband."

I nod slowly, letting it sink in. "That's ok, right?"

She looks at me like I've lost my mind. "For you to meet my family?"

"Is it the end of the world? I know I've gone *downhill*"—I narrow my eyes, and she squints back at me —"but I'm not going to disappear into the ether after our annulment. My cousin is marrying one of your best friends. Knowing your family doesn't seem that far-fetched."

Cecily toys with one of her gold bracelets. "My family

doesn't know my friends. My sister, Kerrigan, has met Paloma and Paisley a few times, but that's it."

I want to ask why, but it doesn't seem like the right follow-up question. She mentioned during our disaster of a date that her family is a lot.

"I'll go with you," I offer, fully expecting her to refuse.

"No way."

Oh look. I was right.

I lift an eyebrow. "You're going to let your grandma down?"

She stubbornly crosses her arms. "I'm not above it."

"She's one of two people with the power to get through your Do Not Disturb."

"So?"

I shrug. "That doesn't seem to me like a person you want to let down."

"She's not." Cecily takes a deep breath and blows it out noisily. "Why are you doing this? There's no way you're this nice."

We both know she doesn't know me well enough to make this assessment. She seems hell-bent on flinging insults my way, and I am too tired and hungover to do anything about it. Have I mentioned I will never touch tequila ever again?

"It'll take up a few hours of my day and make it so that I don't have to spend the whole day with my parents." There. I said it.

Cecily's brown eyes widen. "I thought your family unit was vanilla."

I push out a sigh. "Sort of. Kind of. Vanilla adjacent. Compared to how you talk about your family, anyway."

Cecily smirks. "I knew you had a different flavor underneath."

Now I'm the one smirking. "You do realize you're talking about how I taste?"

Cecily angles her body away, adjusting her sunglasses that needed no adjustment. "I hope you bite your tongue the next time you sneeze."

Menace.

CHAPTER 10

Dominic

Cecily pulls up to Klein and Paisley's house Monday morning in a late-model, black Jeep. I catch sight of her from the front living room window, and not two seconds after she's shifted into Park does she lay on the horn. It's not a nice *beep beep*. It's long and mean, indignant. If a car horn could sound like a put-down, this one would take the cake.

I blow out a breath and step outside. Cecily's death glare reaches across the front yard, searing me. I give her a *one moment* finger, then lock up the house behind me. Paisley is at work, and Klein is teaching a creative writing class at the local YMCA. It's only his third week, and the class consists of senior citizens.

Tucking their house key in my pocket, I make my way down the driveway to Cecily's waiting vehicle. Slowly. To annoy her. Apparently, this infuriating woman has turned me into a spiteful teenager.

She has her phone out, tapping away, refusing to look

at me as I approach. From here I spy her light-wash denim jeans, her white top with the V-neck.

Her outfit is visible to me because her Jeep *doesn't have doors*. What's it like to drive this thing when it's pushing one hundred? Degrees, that is. How does she survive Arizona summers in this contraption? It's spring now, that magical period in central Arizona where the inhabitants forget there is a scorching summer on the horizon.

"Would you like a rag?" Cecily asks when I hurl myself into the passenger seat. Because, again, *there aren't doors*.

"For what?" I ask, buckling myself in.

"To wipe that look of disdain off your face."

Plenty of my time is spent around sharp women, but Cecily is different. Cecily has teeth. Claws. She punches straight. And though I'm not much of an antagonizer, there's something about her that makes me want to punch back. Press her buttons. Light that fire in her eyes. It's a pyre burning men. Burning me.

I deliver a light slap to the glove compartment. "Could you have chosen a more impractical vehicle for the climate?"

She stabs the air between us with a red-painted nail. "There it is. I knew you had something to complain about."

"I'm not complaining."

"You are. And just to let you know, I won't tolerate shit-talking about this car. I worked hard and saved up and bought her outright. She's mine and I love her." Cecily shifts into Drive and pulls away from the curb. "Let me know if you'd like me to stop at a surgeon along the way? Get that stick surgically removed from your ass? It's quite large, but I'm sure we can find someone who can operate on you, Dominic."

My full name. She's doing it on purpose. "I'll be fine," I grumble. It's becoming more and more obvious that when it comes to verbal sparring, Cecily is superior to me.

"Let's just get on with this," I say, watching Cecily pull out into traffic. She has a lazy hold on the wheel, gripping at seven and five instead of ten and two. Hell, even nine and three would be better than where her hands are placed now. How is she going to keep control of the vehicle in the event of an accident? She'll be ejected because *it doesn't have doors.*

"You know," I shout above the atrocious road noise, "if you were really my wife, I'd buy you a safer car."

"Good thing I'm not really your wife," she whips back, hair blowing around her face as she picks up speed.

We're quiet after that, not that we could really talk with the noise smashing around us. I want to ask her what happened nine months ago. I'm dying to know why she left me on that date, slinking away while I was on the phone with a client.

She slows the Jeep at a red light, and just as I open my mouth to ask her about that afternoon, she says, "We'll be there soon, and it might be a good idea for me to tell you what to expect from today. Or, what I expect to happen. Who really knows, though, because I've never brought a surprise husband home."

"No? Weird." A car pulls up beside us at the light. I can't get over how close the vehicle feels, how exposed we are.

"They all know about you thanks to my drunken over-sharing text." She taps her finger on the steering wheel. "I still don't know why I did that."

The answer seems clear to me. "Because they are your family, and you wanted them to know you got married."

Cecily shakes her head slowly back-and-forth, as if to say, *absolutely not.* "You see, that's a normal answer for a normal family. The Hamptons are not normal."

"What are they?"

"Abnormal."

I snort. "Such a generic term. And highly subjective."

"Ok, Word Police. Between you and your wordy cousin, I swear..." she trails off, muttering under her breath.

I'm sure she had some kind of creative insult in those quiet words, but I'm curious about her family. "What about your grandma?"

A light smile tugs on Cecily's lips, brightening her face. "My grandma is a character. Her name is Ophelia, but we call her Savage Grandma, and—"

I cough. "What? You call your grandma *savage*?"

Cecily waves off my question. "You'll understand when you meet her."

This family is already shaping up to be infinitely more interesting than my own.

The light turns green. Cecily shouts above the air rushing around us. "My little sister Kerrigan is a character. She'll say the most unhinged, inappropriate stuff."

"Do you call her Unhinged Sister?"

"No, but we should." Cecily signals for a move into the right lane, glancing over her shoulder before completing it. The sun bounces off her dark hair, making it shine. Her sunglasses hide her eyes.

"My older brother, Duke, is"—Cecily pinches her lower lip between two fingers as she thinks—"aloof. He works closely with my dad, and I think he's created a shell around himself to survive."

"Your dad is someone to be survived?" My family might be vanilla, but I know a thing or two about surviving my parents' behavior.

"Yes, just ask my mom." Cecily takes a turn off the busy road, immediately delivering us onto a quieter street. Quainter. Ranch style homes bracket the roads, set back a good distance. A few are outdated, relics of the eighties before the city built up around them. Most have been remodeled, or torn down and rebuilt. The updated homes have brick-lined semicircular driveways, front yards with citrus trees, mature bushes, and flowering vines.

"What's your mom like?" I ask, inspecting the homes as we pass. The further we drive, the more the homes increase in size.

Cecily twirls a lock of hair around her finger, the other hand holding the steering wheel. "She's sort of this blank space of a human. She's the only person I've ever met who manages to be absent while present. If that makes sense."

My mother couldn't be more different, but I'm not going to tell her that right now. "And what about your dad?" I'm expecting her dad to be nothing short of irate with me. After all, I just married his daughter without asking him. Without knowing her. Genuine marriage or not, I'm expecting to do a little apologizing.

"My dad is cold. Unyielding." Cecily turns on her blinker.

Hmm. That's interesting. On our disaster of a date, she described her parents as *a lot*. Not very descriptive, but hearing she thinks of her dad as cold and unyielding? I can't help but cling to that little nugget. It explains more about Cecily's sharp tongue, her willingness to fight.

We turn left, onto what looks like a driveway. It slopes up, and we climb the gentle rise of the mountain. The higher we go, the more confused I become. I know this neighborhood, but only from afar. As a kid, it amazed me that mountains could sit in the center of a city. When we'd drive on the roads that parallel the mountains, I'd point up from our hot, frequently broken-down car that lacked working air conditioning, and say *Richie Rich lives up there.*

I never expected Cecily's grandmother to be Richie Rich.

Without tearing my gaze from the stunning homes we're passing on our crawl up the mountain, I say, "I'm prepared for your dad to read me the riot act for marrying you."

Can a person *hear* an eye roll? No, they cannot. But with Cecily, I swear I can. She injects the sentiment into her tone of voice. "Cool your jets, Rambo. You aren't walking into the lion's den. My dad isn't the protective type."

That's…sad. I have a protective streak a mile wide. I plan to be a terror if I'm lucky enough to have a daughter. Klein's dad left the family when he and his sister were in elementary school, and I watched the way Eden floundered when she was a teenager. I didn't know it at the time because I was a kid myself, but looking back, I see how Eden would've benefited from an involved, loving dad.

Which is how I know that Cecily, despite sounding nonplussed about her dad's lack of interest in taking up a sword for his daughter, wouldn't mind having someone go to war for her.

I won't be telling her though. She's likely to rip off my arm and beat me with it. "Noted," is all I say.

There's only one house in front of us now, and it looms large. The exterior is tan to match its surroundings, as if the mountain yawned and the home sprang forth, settling on a divot of space. A waist-high glass wall porch stretches the length of the home, supported by metal beams that plunge into the packed earth below.

The Jeep clears the last stretch of road, and Cecily pulls up to a brown metal gate. She reaches out, punching in a code on the box. The gate clangs open slowly, revealing more of the house. No, not a house. A mansion. A compound. A place where many people could live for a solid week and never see one another. I hadn't thought about what Cecily's grandmother's house would be like, but if I'd used my imagination, I wouldn't have come up with this. *Richie Rich*.

"Um." It's all I can manage.

Cecily parks her Jeep beside a shiny luxury SUV. On the other side of it sits a blue-green Bentley convertible. I'm not a car person, but even I know that car is unique.

"I know," Cecily says, peering at the home through the windshield. "She won the lottery before I was born."

"Like, the actual lottery?" People don't really win the lottery, do they? I guess someone somewhere does, but it never feels like it, because I've never met someone who knows someone who won.

Cecily nods. "Savage Grandma is loaded."

'Loaded' is a relative term. When I was a kid, I thought it was fancy if someone had a box of tissues. To this day, my parents blow their noses with a couple squares of toilet paper they've torn from the roll. I mentioned it once to my dad, when I was fifteen, and he'd said *It's the same thing, but I can put some toilet paper in a box if it'll make you feel like you're using tissues.*

So, yeah. Savage Grandma is a whole lot more than loaded.

We climb from the Jeep, feet quickly hitting the pavement since there *aren't any doors.* Death trap. I follow Cecily toward the house, cutting behind the Bentley. That's when I notice the personalized license plate. SVGGRMA

"Your grandma likes the nickname," I point out.

"She does," Cecily agrees. She turns to face me when we arrive at the massive front door. "Here's the deal. We're married, but it was a drunken mistake. We're getting it annulled after we leave here. We're here together because my grandma asked us to be."

"Right." I nod slowly, waiting for her to say something I don't already know. "None of this is new information."

Cecily rolls her eyes.

"Careful," I warn, "those might get stuck looking at the back of your head."

She ignores me. "I'm rehashing the details so we're on the same page. Don't go in there and think we're in a Klein and Paisley situation. We are not in a fake marriage."

"Correct. This is a *real* marriage. And I'd like to point out that everything ended well for Paisley and Klein."

"One in a billion chance of it working out the way it did for them." Cecily adjusts her top. "Now, do not, I repeat, DO NOT"—her stiff finger hovers dangerously close to the tip of my nose—"get some wild hair and tell my family you love me and I'm your wife or some other utter baloney. Do you hear me?"

I bristle at her tone, grip her finger, and lower it. "No

problem, *wife*. We'll make sure everyone knows it was a stupid Vegas mistake. I only chose you because I was drunk."

Hurt flares in her eyes for the shortest second, but she covers it nearly as quickly, and now I'm not sure I read the emotion correctly. She's good at regaining control, whereas I feel like a flailing man overboard in a stormy sea when I'm around her.

"Right." She nods decisively. "I need to be drunk to like you."

She's punching back. Hoping to hurt me, because I hurt her. And the only way I could hurt her is if she cares what I think.

Interesting.

She's looking up at me.

I'm looking down at her.

Her rosebud lips, pressed together, slowly peel apart. A flush spreads on her cheeks.

"Are you planning on ringing the doorbell, Cecily?"

Gaze locked on mine, she leans closer. Memories trickle into the moment. Her draped over me, skin warm and eyes glassy, smile spreading lazy and slow as we danced. I like that version of her. Carefree. Happy. Now she draws near to me, chest lightly coasting over mine. The slope of her curves brushes over me. Every part of me is at attention, my fingers longing to reach for her hips.

I only chose you because I was drunk.

I need to be drunk to like you.

Lies, if this is any indication.

Cecily's arm stretches out, reaching past me. She presses her other palm to my shoulder, using me to steady herself. A loud bell sound rings out, playing a melody.

"Down boy," she whispers before pushing off me and bringing herself upright.

A retort springs forth, ready, but the front door opens. An old woman stands there, dramatically dressed in a flowing, brightly colored floral caftan and a large gold necklace.

This must be Savage Grandma.

"Well, well, well," she says, as if she finds everything about this very entertaining. "If it isn't the newlyweds."

CHAPTER 11

Cecily

WITH A FLAT PALM, I GESTURE AT THE LARGE, FROWNING MAN beside me. "Grandma, this is Dominic."

Grandma's raspberry-lipsticked mouth stretches into a wide smile. Her sparkling eyes appraise Dominic, head to toe and back again. "Your husband," she says, like she's reminding me.

As if I could forget for a single second. As if *my husband* hasn't ruled every one of my thoughts since waking up beside him Saturday morning.

"Yes." Even I hear the reluctance in my tone.

Grandma eyes me. Shrewd. Insightful. When I was little, I thought she was a mind reader, and that firecracker of a woman let me believe it. I was eleven when she admitted she's actually just very good at reading people's emotions.

She steps back from the door, inviting us in. When I step inside, I wrap her in a hug. Grandma has always been a fleshy woman. Well-rounded shoulders for me to hold on to, a back with space for my palms to spread. Today, she feels different. I cannot place why. Maybe it is simply a feeling, or perhaps it's anxiety. Maybe I am looking for signs of a problem, an attempt to prep myself for bad news.

I pull back. Her gaze meets mine. Her eyes speak for her. Sassy, as always. *I didn't call you here for nothing.*

"Well, Dominic," she says, turning to him, and away from my silent, raging questions. "Welcome to the family. I am thrilled Cecily has found her other half. Cecily's father, also known as my son, is out by the pool spitting nails about the two of you. He's a little high-strung on a good day, so this should be interesting."

Dominic coughs. "Thank you, Mrs...?"

He looks to me for help.

"Hampton," I answer, but my grandma says, "Please call me Ophelia."

She pivots away from the door, walking ahead with a flourish, tropical-colored caftan swishing.

"Grandma, wait," I say before I can think much more about it. She's special to me. Different from the other members of my family. I want her to hear the truth about me and Dom now, not when I'm announcing it to everybody else.

"Later, dear," Grandma interrupts. "We've got to get out there before they come to find us. I don't want your father's negative energy in here. I just had the place saged. Come on," she trills, an arm held aloft as she beckons us with two fingers.

Dom walks beside me, footfalls measured. This house is a lot for a person to take in, but there's no time to stop. Grandma walks with purpose.

Dom steps into the backyard just behind me, and I hear the intake of his breath. The soft murmur of, "Wow."

It's opulent by any standard. A glimmering pool set atop a mountain, the city awake and thriving below us.

Everyone is already here, seated around an acacia table beneath a matching pergola. Duke is on my dad's right, and really there is no other seat as appropriate. Duke is Dad's right-hand man. Kerrigan sits across from him, and my mom is on my dad's other side. My mother, with her impossibly perfect blonde shoulder-length bob and diamond-studded ears, looks bored. Possibly drunk. She may not know any of us are here. She might not know where *she* is. Her gaze is on me, but she's poised and elegant with a blank expression. I wish I felt as calm and cool as I know I appear on the outside. Situations like this sometimes send me back to my teenage years, and all the angst that accompanied them.

Dad clocks our arrival with a narrowed gaze. Physically, he matches my mother. Well-groomed and tended, stingy with his love. His chair scrapes the floor as he pushes back from the table and stands. His tone is measured when he says, "Cecily, how could you?"

I'm prepared to first tell the truth, then weather the lecture headed my way. For a time, anyway. I'll only tolerate it for so long before I put a stop to it. That's the number one reason I don't live on Hampton family money. My dad can't call the shots when he's not footing the bill. Kerrigan, bless her heart, is content to live the opposite of me.

I open my mouth to speak, but the oddest thing happens. Dominic speaks instead.

"Sir, hello. I'm Dominic Bellinger." He steps up beside

me, reaching across the table with an offered hand. His voice is deep, confident, and respectful. "My apologies for the shocking text you received this weekend."

Nobody needs this song and dance, not when I'm about to drop a truth bomb, but I have to admit, it's nice. Having Dom in my corner feels good.

My dad glares at Dom, reluctantly shaking his hand. "You married my daughter," he accuses.

Dom nods decisively. "I did."

"Do you think that was appropriate? Marrying her without asking my permission?"

My eye roll is one for the record books, but once again, Dom is there. Saying the right thing. "The only person whose permission I need to marry Cecily is Cecily. I most definitely would've asked you for your blessing though, had there been an opportunity to do things the right way."

My dad stares at Dom, gaze shrewd. Calculating. A typical expression for Glenn Hampton. "Who are you? Where did Cecily find you?"

I speak up. I can't help it. He's referenced me directly. And instead of telling the truth about everything like I should, I sass. "The gutter, obviously." I pinch a small square of Dom's shirt and say, "This tight-weave knit shirt screams *street urchin*."

Dom chuckles. He's probably also feeling relief. For the past few days my ire has been directed his way.

My dad frowns, which is yet another typical expression. "I see you haven't lost that smart mouth."

"As intact as ever," I volley, catching my grandma's eye. She nods once, slowly, and I'm not sure if she's telling me she's here for me or giving me her approval. Either way, I'll take it.

"Can we not do this anymore?" Duke finally speaks up. "Cecily, everyone is shocked and handling it their own way." He looks at our dad. "Some better than others."

Dad ignores Duke. He wears a red polo, and it was a bad choice for today, because it makes his red face redder. "You're getting it annulled." He looks only at me as he says this. "Immediately."

I stiffen. Dom and I are headed straight to the court-house from here, but my dad doesn't know that. And if there's anything I hate, it's being told what to do. Especially by him.

My chin lifts. "No."

I'd love to see how Dom is absorbing this exchange, but I can't look. There can be no chink in the armor when it comes to dealing with my dad. He smells weakness. Pounces on it. Manipulates it to get his way.

My mom stands. Demurely brushes a palm over her smart little sweater with the gold buttons. She touches my dad's forearm, as if to say, *My turn.*

Quickly I look at Kerrigan, and find she's already looking at me, expression of disbelief firmly in place.

"Dominic," my mom says in greeting, "I'm Marilyn."

"It's nice to meet you, ma'am."

My mom continues as if she has not heard him. "If you won't get this marriage annulled, we'll have to throw you a reception." There is almost no emotion in her tone. "We need to do *something* to show this marriage has our *blessing.* We'll have to do it quickly though, before you start showing."

Dom makes a choking sound. "No, no. We're not expecting a baby."

Mom looks at me. I haven't seen her in a few months.

We don't talk. We don't text. She is an island, floating off on her own a mile from the mainland.

I shake my head, supporting Dom's denial. "I'm not pregnant, Mom."

She nods. No emotion on her face. She's either wearing a mask, or she's a robot. "We'll throw you a reception then."

Clearly that's not going to work. "No, Mom."

"Annulment," my dad demands. "If you want to marry, fine, but do it the right way. It's bad enough you've embarrassed this family by refusing to be a part of it, but now you've gone and married without anybody knowing. Do you know how that looks? Before this I could pass you off as the rebel child. The one who needs to see how difficult the world can be before she settles down. Wayward, but expected to return. Now?" He scoffs. "Now you're married to someone we've not only never met until today, but never heard of either. He could be a con man, Cecily. Have you thought about that? Plenty of people would love to get their hands on our money."

Dom frowns. Crosses his arms. Does he have super human self control? He must. If the situation were reversed, I'd last half a second under this level of scrutiny before I'd be telling my verbal attacker where they can stick their head.

"Lucky for you, I'm gainfully employed." Dom doesn't sound upset. He has that unruffled tone, the one he used on Saturday morning when we woke up and realized we married the night prior. "I don't want your money."

Dad directs a rigid finger at me across the table, stabbing the air with each word. "You're getting an annulment. Immediately."

I hear this voice in my head. His, but from more than a decade ago, when I was fifteen. We'd argued, and he told me I am not business-minded, like Duke, or easygoing and pliable, like Kerrigan. *You are opinionated and stubborn. You make it difficult to love you.*

I've tried to forget those cruel words, but I've never been successful. They weighed too much, cut too deep. They are likely the impetus for so many of my defiances.

Years later, they are the reason for this defiance, too. I refuse to be told what to do by someone who does not want the best for me, but cares only for the family image.

"Not happening," I say evenly. "I'm married and that's that."

"Cecily." It's Kerrigan, speaking between clenched teeth. "Can you please let Mom and Dad host a reception?" She looks at me imploringly.

I glare at her traitorous face. She knows this marriage was an accident. She knows we plan to get an annulment today. I told her on the phone on Saturday at the pool, sitting beside Dom, and then again last night when she called, after she knew I'd returned from Vegas. "It's just a party. Who cares?"

My dad has always thought of Kerrigan as agreeable, but that's not accurate. She is a peacekeeper, someone who flits around on the periphery of family strife, managing emotions.

Duke sighs. "Can you please choose the easy route for once in your life, Cecily?"

Growing up, this is how it always was. I make a fuss, and my siblings beg me to capitulate. They were never willing to meet my father in the proverbial boxing ring, whereas I was willing to go round after round with him.

Until the day I escaped Olive Township, putting enough physical distance between us that I could breathe.

I look at my big brother. "Oh, are you siding with Dad? That's hardly headline news. It might as well be the Phoenix weather forecast. Predictable, boring, the same every day."

Dad says something else, but I can't hear. Kerrigan is speaking, then Mom sits back in her seat and disappears into whatever realm it is she retreats to when the family becomes too much for her. Duke cuts in with a scathing remark. I'd be embarrassed this is how we're acting in front of Dom, but what does it matter? We're pulling an Uno reverse on our marriage in a couple hours. No need to be on my best behavior.

Insults are flung. There are assertions, declarations, stinging snubs. It's every man for himself, and it's ugly.

And then, in the midst of the verbal rumpus, a quiet voice slices through it all.

"I have end-stage heart failure."

The words perched on my lips tumble off. My grandma sits serenely, hands folded in her lap. The voices around the table recede.

The shock brings me up short. Cuts out the noise. "What? You...what?"

There's a soft press to my lower back. A supportive hand. *Dom.*

"Grandma." I step around the table, crouching at her side. She smells so good, so familiar, like Red Door and cinnamon gum.

"It's ok, my girl." The corners of her lips pull into the saddest smile. "It'll all be ok."

But it won't be. It's not possible, not now. Grandma is

the only person in this family who is squarely on my side. Even Kerrigan, who I know loves me, splits her loyalty. But not my grandma. She is independently wealthy, beholden to nobody, and gave no fucks before it was cool.

When she is gone, I'll be more alone than ever.

"Mom?" To my dad's credit, he sounds appropriately gobsmacked.

"End-stage sounds so final, and I suppose it is." She pats my forearm. Shouldn't it be me comforting her?

Duke is already on his phone, almost certainly looking up everything there is to know about heart failure. Ways to combat it. It's the problem solver in him. "It says there are medications—"

"I'm already on them. Have been for a while. This diagnosis isn't new to me. Only to all of you."

"Mom," my dad says sharply. "How long have you known?"

"A while," she answers, firm. "And I don't want to hear a word about how I should've told you. It's my body and my future and I made my choice."

"Mom—"

"Now," she says, steamrolling him. "That news is only part of why I asked you all here today." She looks at us all in turn. "I have a request."

"Anything," Kerrigan says immediately. "Whatever you need. Right, everyone?" She looks around at us, brown eyes wide. The baby of the family again.

"Obviously," I answer. If Grandma said it was her dying wish for me to crab walk across the Sonoran desert in July, I'd do it.

Everyone around the table nods, except Dom. He looks uncomfortable, wary, like he wishes he could be somewhere else. I don't blame him. After this, he'll think twice about marrying someone in Vegas.

"Great," Grandma beams, clasping her hands together on the tabletop. "Because I already set it all up."

"What have you set up?" my dad asks. There is trepidation in his tone, the same way each one of us would sound if we'd asked the question.

"A road trip, starting next Monday. I can't play fast and loose with time right now. I no longer have that luxury." She nods decisively. "Three weeks in a luxury motor coach. Staying in hotels, cabins, and glamping in various places around Arizona." Grandma looks at each of us, a devious smirk tugging on her lips. "I want my whole family together. Under the same roof, so to speak."

"Are you sure?" My dad looks like he has a lot to say, but the good sense to swallow it down. "This is how you want to spend your..." He struggles for the words. "Your time?"

"No," she answers plainly. "Stuck with you all for days and days on end is not my idea of a good time. You're so dysfunctional someone should put you on reality TV. However." She glances at me before continuing, "You need it. Think of it as an intervention."

"Ophelia," my mother says, looking as if she's swallowed something that tastes bad. "You've found a vehicle large enough to comfortably fit the six of us?"

"Eight," Grandma corrects.

Mom and Dad share a concerned look. Dad gently says, "The five of us, and you."

Grandma shakes her head. "I've hired a death doula, and she's coming with us."

A fresh round of blank stares. Duke coughs into his fist. "A death doula is what, exactly?"

"Just what it sounds like. Rainbow will assist me in end-of-life matters."

Kerrigan, arguably the most woo-woo out of all of us, arches an eyebrow. "Your death doula's name is Rainbow?"

In total seriousness, Grandma replies, "Her mother almost certainly dropped acid. But yes, that's her name."

Duke speaks up. "That's still only seven people, Grandma. Not eight." His voice is thicker than usual. He's trying not to cry.

Grandma pins her gaze on the man beside me. "Dominic makes eight."

CHAPTER 12

Cecily

"I HAD NO IDEA." IT'S THE FIRST THING I SAY THE SECOND I am alone with Dominic.

We're in the kitchen at my grandma's house. After her announcement and subsequent request, she sent Dominic and me in here to get drinks for everyone. Most likely, so she can lecture them about their behavior toward us and our marriage. My head is still reeling from her announcement. My heart is still splintering.

Dominic turns. Looks at me with bewilderment. "Of course you had no idea."

He sounds, well, not mad exactly, but something similar to it as he steps around the room opening cabinets, in search of the custom paneled fridge.

I bristle. "You don't have to sound angry. You're not the one who's heading out on a road trip with the family from hell."

He whirls on me, hand poised on the correct handle. "I'm not?"

My eyes narrow. "Why would you?"

He releases the handle, turning the full force of his blue-eyed gaze on me. "Why wouldn't I? Better yet, how could I not? She requested the entire family, including *your husband*." His voice drops low on those last two words, his tone caustic.

Pinching the shell of my ear, I wiggle it and say, "Did a bug crawl in your ear and eat your brain cells? We. Are. Not. Married. For. Real."

"No, we're not. But you know what is real? An old woman is dying"—I wince at the bluntness of his words—"and her dying wish is for her family to go on a three-week road trip to repair their relationship with one another so she feels more comfortable leaving the physical earth behind. And guess who she thinks is family now? Me."

I cross my arms. Stare him down. "So, what, you're planning to be my husband? Pretend to love me? Go on a road trip with my family?"

He turns back to the fridge, peering in. "You didn't manage to tell your family about us when you had the chance. Are you planning on telling a dying woman who is clearly thrilled and relieved you've *found your other half* that it is really one great, big lie?"

I wrench my gaze away. Damn him. *Damn Dominic.* Damn Paisley and Klein for getting married, and having joint parties in Vegas, and who was it that suggested tequila shots? Paloma! Damn her, too.

I lean my lower back against the kitchen island. Arms still crossed. Gaze pointed out at the valley. From here, the cars look like ants marching through their day. Is Dominic serious about going on this road trip with me? Am I seriously considering allowing Dominic to be my husband for a three-week road trip?

I look at him now, rummaging through the fridge as he tries to locate the bottle of riesling my grandma said was "in there somewhere".

"It might be harder to be granted an annulment if we don't request one right away." I worry my bottom lip as he pulls away from the fridge, hand wrapped around the neck of a bottle.

He makes a motion with his hands, silently asking for a wine opener. "We could go this afternoon like we planned, and I'll still go on the road trip with you."

I retrieve one from a drawer, and hand it over. "Why would you agree to do this? Don't tell me it's out of the goodness of your heart, because I'm pretty sure you don't have one."

That's not true. Aside from the fact Dom's a living, breathing human, I know he has a heart in every sense of the word. The fact that he's standing here right now, in my grandma's kitchen, weathering the hellacious storm that is my family, proves it.

"Granting a dying woman's wish is important." He pauses for a beat as he opens the wine, releasing the cork with a *pop*. "Ignoring it because I simply don't want to isn't something I'd like to have on my conscience. I guess in a way, I'm being"—he shrugs—"selfish."

I eye him until he becomes uncomfortable and smoothes the front of his shirt, then say, "I smell bullshit."

He balks, eyebrows tugging in the center. "Are you kidding? I think that's a very good reason."

I'm not buying it. The man has a job. Not just a job, *a*

career. Across the country, I might add. I don't know much about the responsibilities of a literary agent, but I'm sure he has deadlines. Authors with needs. Foreign translation rights to negotiate. He's going to put all that aside to accommodate the grandmother of the woman he accidentally married in Vegas? Whose request is, let's be honest, difficult and unpleasant. All because he doesn't want to have his refusal on his conscience? And then he's going to claim he's doing something selfless out of his own selfishness?

"I think there's more to the story." I poke the center of his chest. Hard. "You don't know my grandma. What if I told you her most prized possession is a fur coat made from sad puppies?"

"Is it?"

"No."

Dom sighs. Stuffs his hands in his pockets. He's weighing something in his mind. "I don't have a grandma. My mom doesn't have a relationship with her mom, and my dad's mom died when he was young."

A pang of sadness creeps over me. My grandma is the stuff grandma dreams are made of, and I can't imagine not having her. Though I will have to imagine it, something I haven't begun to process yet.

I don't like the shred of softness I feel toward Dom, so I say, "Despite how moving your sob story is, you cannot glom onto my grandma." There. That should do it. No more soft feelings now. Balance has been restored.

Dom, to his credit, doesn't blink at my unkind words. "Something tells me Savage Grandma doesn't get glommed onto unless she decides she wants it to happen."

Ugh. Why does he have to take my meanness in stride? Moreover, why does he have to be right? He's known my grandma for one measly, albeit eventful, family meeting and he's already picked up on her fierce personality.

I cross my arms, ready to try a different tack. "Let's say, hypothetically speaking, I agree to allow you on this road trip. What's to stop you from leaving halfway through?"

Most men would deny they would do such a thing, but not Dom. He says, very practically, "I could leave halfway through, married or not. *Anybody* could leave *anywhere* at *any* point for *any* reason." I like his acknowledgment of the possibility. He adds, "I wouldn't, though." I like that, too.

"You're asking me to trust you?"

"I suppose so."

"Why should I trust you?"

"Have I given you a reason to distrust me?"

"I can think of one."

"That goes both ways."

My lips are twitching with the desire to unload on him. I want to know how he could've said those things about me, been so duplicitous. I won't, because the last thing I want is for my family to overhear us. Also, I'm embarrassed to say the words out loud. Mortified it ever happened, and even more mortified at how deeply it wounded me. What I overheard Dom saying in that hallway at Obstinate Daughter should have lost its power over me as the days grew into weeks and months, but it didn't. I was too fragile, too tender.

If Dominic had behaved in some objectionable way, I could've walked away with my ego intact. But, no. It was Dominic who objected to me.

And isn't that my worst fear? That I will be myself, let down my guard, and get rejected. *You make it difficult to love you.*

"All right, lovebirds," my grandma calls from around the corner, tactfully announcing herself before entering the kitchen. "I think you've taken long enough to retrieve that wine."

She rounds the corner and takes us in. Our lack of flushed cheeks, our clothing in place and our hair smooth. She thought she'd be interrupting a steamy makeout session between can't-keep-their-hands-off-each-other newlyweds.

"Cecily," she starts, pointing at a cabinet. "Grab the glasses and take the wine out. None for me."

"Or me," Dom adds.

The memory of placing my face over a toilet is fresh in my mind, recent enough that I'll be declining the wine as well.

As directed, I retrieve four glasses, snag the bottle, and pause expectantly at the open doorway leading out of the kitchen.

"Go on, hon." Grandma waves me away. "I want to chat with your husband for a moment."

My gaze slides to Dom, who looks nonplussed. Does nothing bother him?

"See you out there," I say, taking one last look at my grandmother before turning away. Her expression plainly says *get out of here so I can talk to him alone.*

If my expression reflects how I'm feeling on the inside, it says *Please don't leave this world, I don't know how to be in it without you.*

CHAPTER 13
Dominic

"I SHOULD ISSUE AN APOLOGY FOR MY FAMILY, BUT I DON'T know if there is an apology big enough." Ophelia settles on a stool on the far side of the island, smiling at me kindly. An elegant bun at the nape of her neck holds her gray and white hair.

I wave off her words. "No need. Cecily and I were..." My mind trips, parsing through my vocabulary for the best fitting word that doesn't give away the truth. "...*hasty*. I expected nothing less than what I walked into."

This is only partially true. I'd anticipated a protective father, thundering at me for marrying his daughter. He delivered on that, but only in part. His blustering was more on his own behalf, or that of his image. He certainly wasn't taking up any swords for Cecily.

It makes me angry, but I'm trying not to show it. It would embarrass Cecily, to know I am disgruntled on her behalf.

"Still," Ophelia insists, "my son made a very poor showing. Not surprising, honestly. He hasn't been himself in years. Not since he became successful. All that pressure, I guess. Sometimes, pressure makes diamonds." She shrugs. "Other times, it crushes you. It doesn't help that his father died when he was nineteen. He could have used his dad to help guide him in his own parenthood. I don't know that my son will ever go back to the person he used to be. And now that I'm preparing to take a dirt nap, I'll never know."

I stare at her, wide-eyed.

She points back at herself. "Savage."

A smile pulls at my lips, but I'm not sure if I should let it break out fully. It's a morbid topic, there is no place for a grin, right?

"Will you be able to join us on the road trip I've planned?"

I'm not sure I have a choice, even though I suppose I do. I could say no. I could choose not to care.

"I'm not sure," I say haltingly. "I need to check with my boss. I'm a literary agent," I explain, before Ophelia can ask. "My work is portable. There are some meetings I would miss, but as long as I have an internet connection or Wi-Fi, I can do them through video."

Ophelia nods slowly, palms steepled under her chin. "Dominic, I realize this is a lot to put on you when you're new to marriage. New to the family." She licks her lips, weighing her words carefully. "My granddaughter is going to need you. She can be, well, I guess you could say she's a bit of a *brute* sometimes. The only way to survive the house she grew up in was to erect a barrier. She developed quite an attitude until she was old enough to put physical distance between her and her parents."

Ophelia's words strike a chord within me, hurtling

down into the depths of my soul. I know what it's like to run away from family. I ran all the way to New York City when I was eighteen, and that's where I stayed.

"I'm aware of Cecily's protective shell," I say to Ophelia. I might be aware of it, but I don't know it. Not really. I don't understand the ins and outs, the nuances, the reasons behind it all. I probably never will.

An unexpected and odd feeling ripples across my chest. Not sadness, because how could that be? If forced to name the emotion, I'd identify it as melancholy. Cecily, it turns out, is a complicated person, and there is nothing I love more than a challenging puzzle.

"I'm worried about Cecily," Ophelia admits. "About how she'll handle my passing. We've always been very close." She aims a wistful smile at me. "Knowing she'll have you in the hard moments is an enormous relief."

Guilt trickles through me, and though I try to hide it, I cannot stop the way I gulp at Ophelia's words. "Cecily will have me to lean on," I tell her, and it's true. Whether Cecily will allow herself to lean on me is a different story.

Ophelia thumbs over her shoulder, saying, "We should probably get back out there. Make sure they haven't torn each other to shreds. Concrete is porous, you know. I don't want bloodstains on my pool deck."

She sees whatever expression is on my face and smiles sympathetically. "You look uneasy."

I'm feeling a lot of different things right now, and uneasy is only one of them.

Ophelia slides off her stool, crossing the kitchen and opening a drawer. From it she pulls a glass canister, and from that she removes a clear plastic bag.

"I pop one of these sometimes, to take the edge off.

Even on our best day, this family is challenging. Why be sober around them when you can be high? Or at least, you know, a little high." She plucks a gummy bear from the bag and tosses it in her mouth. "They're out there drinking wine. What's the difference?"

She chews, and I watch her, unsure what to do. I should say no, but my reason for declining isn't one I can share. *Sorry, I have to stay sober so I can get an annulment from your granddaughter.* I suppose I don't need a reason for saying no, but one gummy won't hurt. How much THC can there be in a single bear? Besides, I'm a big guy. It probably won't affect me at all.

"See if you can make it into my mouth. Just one." I widen my stance, hands balancing in the air at my sides, and open my mouth.

Ophelia fishes a gummy from the bag and takes aim. "Fire," she says, and lets go.

It sails directly into my mouth, and she shouts, "Bullseye!" Her arm lifts in the air, triumphant.

Cherry flavor hits my tongue as I chew. I offer Ophelia a high-five, and she smacks my hand.

Eyes sparkling, she says, "Now we can face my family."

CHAPTER 14

Cecily

"Is this not the best cheeseburger of your life?" Dom points at the gargantuan burger he holds in his right hand. He's nodding vigorously as he chews, answering his own question.

"Hmm." It's all I can manage to say. I am afraid of what might come out of my mouth if I open it. I am furious with Dom. Seething.

"You seem upset." Dom thrusts the paper bag at me across the console of my car. "Have a fry." I ignore him, exactly like I did when we departed the drive-thru at the fast food restaurant and he offered me the first bite of his burger.

My husband is generous when he's high.

I'm not about to tell him why I'm upset when he is currently under the influence of what has upset me. But if I don't offer him some sort of conversation, he's going to be relentless for the next five minutes until we get to Klein and Paisley's house.

Tossing a chicken nugget into my mouth, I say, "Good

to know this is what you're like when you're high." Could be worse. He could become paranoid.

Dom grins. Ketchup clings to the corner of his mouth. "You should see me when I'm drunk. I end up married."

I absolutely, totally, completely refuse to laugh, but that was very funny.

"I really like Ophelia. It's too bad she's going to take a dirt nap."

Before I know it, my right arm has vacated the steering wheel, snapping like a rubber band into Dom's shoulder.

"Ouch," he complains. "Those were her words. Not mine. I would never use that term."

"Do not use her words again. I don't care how well-adjusted she seems about the whole thing. I don't care that she has a death doula—"

"Rainbow," Dom supplies unhelpfully. "Acid Rainbow."

Ok, how am I not supposed to laugh at that?

"Anyway," I say loudly. Forcefully. Enough to banish the part of me that wants to cackle. "There will be no using my grandmother's terms unless they are something you would say to your priest."

"Technically," Dom says, stuffing fries into his mouth, "You should be able to say anything to your priest. The confessional is sealed. You could describe your most recent murder and—"

"That's enough," I talk over him. I grab a napkin from the center console and throw it at him. This is what I get for speaking to someone who isn't of sound mind, a person who is also highly intelligent.

I direct the Jeep onto Klein and Paisley's street. "Here we go," I announce, making sure Dom knows we are almost there. Do I have to come to a full stop? Slowing down and telling him to tuck his chin to his chest should be enough.

Turns out, I have to come to a stop. Obviously I would anyway, but I really, really have to now that Klein, Paisley, and Paloma are standing on the sidewalk. Why are they smiling like that? Their grins are too broad. Too excited. Shouldn't Paisley and Paloma be at the office? The only reason I'm here, and not at work like I should be, is because I took the day off for the emergency family meeting and the trip to the courthouse. Not that there will be an annulment today, because my husband is high.

I pull up to the curb, and shift into Park. "What's up?" I ask the small crowd on the sidewalk.

"What's up?" Dom echoes, turning to me and saying in the loudest whisper in the history of ever, "Don't tell them I'm high."

Behind Dom's head, Klein, Paisley, and Paloma dissolve. Like ice cream in the summer sun, they melt into obscenely loud laughter. Or at least, Paisley and Paloma are loud. Klein, bent over with his hands on his knees, laughs so hard he makes no sound.

Dom unbuckles himself. Climbs out. Then he does the most Dom thing I could imagine. He turns around and methodically cleans up behind himself. I haven't forgotten the comment he made last weekend about my dress puddled on the floor. Then he pulled it from the closet, where it hung neatly on a wooden hanger.

Heaving a beleaguered sigh, I unclasp my seat belt and make my way around the front of the car. "Any reason you aren't at work?" I direct the question to the still-crowing women.

Paisley answers. "Klein called and said you texted him

something unbelievable, but then I said you don't make stuff up the way he does."

"They're called fiction books," he defends, delivering a smack to her backside.

I hurl an accusatory look at Klein. "I was trying to be nice and give you a heads-up."

"Yeah, well, thanks for that. Because then I told Paloma"—Paisley looks at Paloma, who nods in corroboration—"and we decided this wasn't something that could be missed. Mr. Straight and Narrow gets drunk, married, and high in the span of seventy-two hours? Jui-cy," she sings.

Dom looks at me, shocked and hurt. "You told them?"

I heave a second sigh. Gustier this time. I am just about done with this entire day. I'm going to go home and sleep until tomorrow. It's early afternoon, but this has already been the worst day I've had in a very long time. Here I was thinking waking up drunk-married in Vegas was the worst, but no.

"Who did you do this with?" Klein purses his lips, trying not to laugh.

Dom glances at me. Is there gloominess lurking behind the manufactured relaxed state he's in? I'm gloomy, too. Devastated, really, but I've compartmentalized it. I'm waiting until I get home, until I close the door on my one-bedroom apartment, to break down.

"Savage Grandma," Dom answers.

Shared looks of bewilderment pass between the three people who are not under the influence. Paloma asks, "Does High Dom make up stories, too? Or is Savage Grandma a real person?"

Dom's gaze bores into me. His questions, too. I feel

them, pointy and pressing and unwelcome. "Why don't your friends know about Savage Grandma? She's so cool."

"Dominic," I say through clenched teeth. "Do not lecture me while you're high."

He ignores me. "It's weird, Cecily. You said your family doesn't know your friends, and it looks like your friends don't know anything about your family, either."

Paloma and Paisley know I don't get along with them, but I haven't provided all the dirty details.

"That's enough from you," I shout, losing my temper. My patience. My cool. "You got high with my grandma and as a result we can't get an annulment this afternoon. Now I have to spend another day married to you." A snarl inched its way onto my face as I spoke.

"Which is terrible, right? The *worst*." Hurt and annoyance lace through the sarcasm in his tone. His silliness on our drive has disappeared.

But I don't feel bad. I don't feel bad at all.

The emotions from the day, from the past weekend, surge forward unbridled. I want to rage. Scream at Dom for not remaining sober in Vegas. Scream at myself for making bad choices. At my grandma for daring to leave this world, for leaving me behind and alone. "It is the worst, Dominic. Because I loathe you."

Dominic absorbs my words. Nods in slow, slight movements. Bites the inside of his lower lip. Head lowered, he leans his face closer, blue-eyed gaze holding mine as he says, "The feeling is mutual, Menace."

There's a gasp from the trio of onlookers, but I'm not sure who it came from. I drag in a breath, but the air is all wrong. Thick with hate, soured by emotional exhaustion.

"You're not going on that road trip with me." I'm braced

for an argument, but it doesn't arrive. One side of his mouth curves up in a slow, devilish smile. He's enjoying whatever it is he's about to say.

"I'll be there whether you like it or not. And?" He wears a full smile now. I envision smacking it off his handsome face. "I'm not giving you an annulment."

Please tell me this is the THC talking. Except, Dom doesn't seem high anymore. Just hell-bent on making my life hell.

"I'm not staying married to you." I have to ball my fists at my side to keep from assaulting him.

"You will be for the duration of the road trip." He slides his hands into his pockets. Takes a step back. "I can't wait to wish you a happy one-month anniversary."

I growl, an honest to goodness animal sound. Dominic *laughs.*

I hate him. More than I've ever hated anyone. How can it be that I am also married to the man?

"I'll call you later. Get all the details for our road trip. Make sure you unblock my number."

"How did you know—"

"Educated guess." He smiles at me again, then looks at Klein and nods his head toward the house.

They retreat into the home, and I finally lock eyes with the two women standing shell-shocked on the sidewalk.

Paloma speaks first. "Cecily, warn a girl before it gets that entertaining. I like to eat popcorn when I watch soap operas."

Paisley isn't as amused as Paloma. "What was all that?"

I rub my temples. "My life imploding before my eyes."

Paloma and Paisley share a meaningful look. "It's time," Paisley says.

Paloma nods sagely. "It is time."

CHAPTER 15

Cecily

"ARE YOU *SERIOUS*?" I SEND THE OPEN BOX A WARY LOOK. "A voodoo doll making kit?"

The size of an adult male's shoebox, it's overflowing with scraps of felt in all colors and shapes, hats, and various accessories the size of my thumbnail.

"Don't knock it," Paloma cautions, pelting me with a button. It rolls across the wood table of the coffee shop before settling near Paisley's elbow. "And don't call it a voodoo doll. We're not invoking evil spirits. It's just a doll."

"It's not about the doll," Paisley informs me. "It's about the time spent crafting and talking. You have to pay attention to what's in your hand so you don't jab yourself with the needle you're using to sew everything on. Makes it easier to talk when you're focused on something else."

"I take it you're not new to doll construction?" I rummage through the felt, coming up with a tiny bow tie.

"I made one for Shane a long time ago. Paloma and I didn't know each other very well when she suggested it." Paisley laughs at the memory.

Shane was Paisley's college boyfriend who nearly married her little sister. Icky, yes, but if he hadn't done that Paisley might not have run into Klein at her sister's bachelorette party, setting into motion the beginning of their happily ever after.

"She thought I was *louco*," Paloma says, throwing her sooty hair over her shoulder.

"Ooh, you know how I get when you speak Portuguese." Paisley shakes her shoulders, the gold necklace she wears bouncing on her chest.

Paloma throws her head back, laughing throatily. "Stay focused," she instructs us over the table. "We're here for a reason."

Paisley salutes her. "Ma'am, yes ma'am."

A restaurant employee approaches, dropping off our drink order and maple bourbon scones. When they are gone, Paloma begins her instruction. She shows me how to thread the needle and knot the thread. I feel a bit like a malfunctioning human for not knowing how to do this, but Paloma doesn't mention it.

We're hunting through the box, assembling our doll outfits on the table beside our lattes, when Paisley says, "My grandma has this really fun, cute way of dressing. Living, really. We call it 'Coastal Grandma'. You'll meet her at the wedding."

This is Paisley's way of opening up the conversation, letting me know it's time to start talking. We're here for me.

I look up, expecting to be met with two pairs of waiting eyes, but both Paisley and Paloma are intent on their tasks.

I grab the large fabric scissors and cut the edge of what will hopefully resemble a shirt. "She sounds lovely," I start.

"The person you heard Dominic referring to is my grandma. Savage Grandma. She's not mean or anything like that, but she says whatever she feels like saying. She earned the nickname years ago when my little sister wore her hair parted down the middle and gathered it into a ponytail at the base of her neck. Grandma told my sister she looked like a thirteen-year-old Colonial boy ready to start his woodworking apprenticeship."

Paisley sucks air between her bared teeth. Paloma nearly paints our doll outfits in spat-out coffee.

"I know. And the thing is, she delivers these remarks without fanfare or tone." A smile spreads across my face as I think about her. But then a shadow accompanies these memories, passing over each one and darkening it. "The emergency family meeting she called was to let us know she has final-stage heart failure and won't live much longer." My throat clogs. My eyes burn. I'm realistic enough to know everyone must die one day, and naïve enough to think it can't happen to someone I love as much as my grandma.

From Paisley and Paloma are the murmured words *I'm sorry.*

"You both already know my family isn't exactly easy to be around, but it's complicated." I sigh, trying to put it all into coherent thoughts. "Or, maybe it's not complicated. Maybe everyone has childhood trauma sitting in their adult bones." The vulnerability makes me uneasy, so I rush ahead and say, "Grandma's dying wish is for me and my siblings and my parents to go on a road trip with her." I'm too intent on crafting a tiny shirt collar to look up. The focus and distraction make it easier to talk, just like Paisley said. "And my new husband, too. Which, of course, was supposed to be annulled today until Dom accepted the gummy my grandma offered him. And now, apparently, he's going to hold the annulment hostage until after the road trip."

Why? Why would he do that? Why does he want to be married to me, even when it means nothing? It's not as if he cares about me.

"That's a lot," Paisley says kindly. "Thank you for sharing with us. For trusting us."

"Why do you loathe Dom?" Paloma asks, using the same word I chose when things were getting heated between us in front of Paisley and Klein's house.

I wait for embarrassment to fill me like it does every time I think about what happened with Dom on our first date, but it doesn't arrive. Maybe the events of the last three days have diluted what happened nine months ago. There are more pressing things to be upset about now.

I tell them what happened at Obstinate Daughter, about how our chemistry was sizzling. "It was like adding a tablespoon of butter to a hot cast-iron skillet. Crackling. I've never felt that before. Ever."

"What happened?" Paisley asks, dread deepening her tone.

I tell them everything. Every word Dom said, verbatim. My hands work to make Doll Dom's caramel tufts of hair, and I recite everything the real Dom said in that dim hallway.

"He still doesn't know I overheard. He believes I ghosted him. And he has the gall to be indignant about it." Using the fabric glue, I adhere each curl to the light brown sweep of hair I cut.

Paisley says, "Don't kill me for saying this, but it doesn't sound like Dom. Honestly."

"I heard him. Clearly. With my own two ears."

I look over and see Paisley has stopped crafting. Her arms cross over her stomach, teeth nibbling her lower lip. "I know. That's what makes it extra odd. It means he's either the opposite of everything he presents himself to be, or there's an explanation."

"You need to talk with him," Paloma says. She's putting a baseball hat on her doll.

"I know I do."

"It could be a miscommunication," Paisley says hopefully.

"I don't know how it could be." The whole thing is so embarrassing. Pointing at her doll, I ask, "Who is that?"

"Some asshole I saw litter yesterday. Not just a gum wrapper, either. A bag of fast food tossed from his car window." Paloma swipes my needle off the table, thread dangling, and stabs it into her doll's hand.

"Ow," Paisley yells.

Paloma laughs. "Anyway. You need to talk to Dom before this road trip. You need to clear the air before you're sharing the same air for three weeks."

"What if he doesn't have an explanation?" The real reason I haven't forced the conversation over the past few days finally surfaces. I'm afraid. I know what I heard, but I fear having it confirmed. The way he spoke through our text message exchange setting up the date, the way he acted at Obstinate Daughter before the phone call, and the way he conducted himself all weekend and today at my grandma's house does not match up with the man on the phone in the hallway. But I know what I heard. I'd put my hand on a Bible in a court of law.

Paisley asks, "Do you want to spend three weeks in close proximity to him, not knowing?"

"No." I shake my head as I say it. The mature thing to do is to have the conversation, even if it's unpleasant.

Paisley sits back, her doll complete. It's Klein, but she's decorated it with cut out lips all over the body.

Paloma surveys Paisley's work, pointing a long nail at the center of the doll. "You forgot one right—"

Paisley flicks Paloma's fingertip. "That's enough out of you."

Paloma peers at my doll as Paisley pulls her phone from her purse. "You really captured the essence of Dom," she says, grinning at the misshapen shirt, the hair that looks more like a bad toupee. His eyes are two different size buttons. "What's his name?"

Considering the small x's I've sewn for his mouth, I say, "Malibu Dom."

"Hah," Paloma says loudly. "Put some flowers on his shorts and take him to the beach."

Paisley taps her phone screen and says, "Klein says he and Dom are headed to see Dom's parents."

Dom's parents? Hmm. Dom implied his childhood was bland, but at the pool he let it slip he didn't want to spend all day with them. That doesn't have to mean anything, it could be as simple as needing a break from them, but I'm curious anyway.

Paisley slides the phone back into her purse and turns to me. "Your family thinks you're really married to Dom, correct?"

I nod. "Only my sister knows the truth. My dad thinks Dom married me for my family money."

Paisley and Paloma wear matching expressions of confusion. "Do you have money?"

"My family does." I look at Paisley. "You know what I make."

She pulls an injured frown. "I'm very careful to pay you a competitive salary, plus good healthcare and an annual bonus," she defends.

"I'm not complaining," I blurt. "I'm pointing out I'm not rich. Especially not compared to the Hamptons. My dad and brother run the boutique hotel brand."

"What?" Paloma squawks. "Hampton as in *'You're home when you're in a Hampton'*."

"That's the old tagline. But yes."

Paloma frowns. "Why do I feel like I'm just getting to know you even though we've worked together for almost two years?"

Paisley taps the top of Paloma's hand. "I told you she'd share when she was ready."

They've had a conversation about me? Am I really that closed-off? I don't mean to be, but if I think about it, I guess I don't make it a point to share.

I'm not sure what to say now, but Paisley's hand slides across the table, covering mine. "Some people share. Some people don't think of sharing. And some people share way, way too much. Like my mother, who makes sure I know her new husband is the Energizer Bunny. Don't be like Robyn Royce-Patel." The way she says it, solemn and nodding her head, makes me laugh.

"I promise to never, ever share the details of my sex life with you."

Paloma waves a hand. "Whoa there. Don't get the wrong idea. Unless you're morally opposed, we love a good sex story."

"I get that Paisley is your best friend"—I look at Paisley, then swing my gaze back to Paloma—"but she's my boss. I can't go around slinging stories."

Paisley's hand is still on mine, and she squeezes. "You don't have to, but you can. I consider you a good friend, Cecily. More than that, really. You were a big part of helping me and Klein get together."

"I only ran his social media," I argue.

She shakes her head, arguing right back. "You had him taking pictures of me. Presenting our relationship. Seeing it differently. I'm grateful to you, and I'm happy you're my friend. Every day when I walk into the office I'm thankful I get to work with you two."

Her smile is so sweet it nearly brings tears to my eyes.

Paloma huffs an annoyed breath. Emotions tend to make her uncomfortable. That might be a part of why I've not been gung ho to confide much of anything having to do with Dom. That, and the formidable feeling that is embarrassment.

Paisley smiles sweetly at Paloma, and then Paloma gasps. "Ouch." She reaches down to rub her leg. "Did you kick me?"

"No," Paisley answers innocently. "Someone somewhere must have a Paloma doll."

Paloma sticks out her tongue, and Paisley pointedly ignores it. To me, she says, "Here's the summary: I kinda love you, you're sorta stuck with me, and I'm a fantastic listener if you ever need an ear."

"Me too," Paloma says, pressing her chest against the table and leaning closer. "Everything she said."

"I appreciate that." I lift Malibu Dom in the air, shaking him gently. "Don't be surprised if there comes a point on this ill-fated road trip that you receive an SOS. My dysfunctional family and the man I loathe all crammed into one RV. What could possibly go wrong?"

Then I pinch Malibu Dom's head and give it a twist.

CHAPTER 16
Dominic

"You all right?" Klein's eyebrows cinch with concern.

"Yeah," I groan, palming the back of my neck. "Sharp, hot pain. Must've slept wrong on my neck last night."

"One would've thought that edible could've relaxed you enough to loosen up your neck." Klein reaches across the cab of his late-model 4Runner and snaps a finger far too close to my eyes. "You're fully sober now, right?"

I smack his hand away. "Dude! What are you doing?"

His hand settles back on the steering wheel. "Checking your reflexes."

"By blinding me?"

"Seeing how quickly you blink."

"Speaking as your literary agent, I think it's imperative I remind you how much you should want me to have my vision. So I can, you know, *read your books*."

Klein scoffs. "Have you heard me read out loud? I've been told my voice is melodious."

"Only my entire childhood," I mutter. Klein had severe dyslexia, to the point he went to a special school. He struggled to read, but he loved stories. As kids, we'd take turns reading to each other. Sometimes I'd secretly feel frustrated, unable to get into the story because of all the starts and stops when Klein was reading. It was good for him though, and I knew that. Practice using the methodologies he was learning in school was fundamental to his development. Also, my dad promised me my own bag of ranch-flavored sunflower seeds if I'd let Klein read to me as much as he wanted. To many people that might not sound like a big deal, but to me, it was HUGE.

"You really screwed up with Cecily today," Klein says, bopping his head to the beat of a song. "Dearly Departed" by Shakey Graves.

The memory of Cecily, lip curled and abhorrence burning in her eyes, washes over me. The way she leaned closer, though she didn't need to. The sadness that ringed her brown irises, simmering below the surface. Cecily received terrible news today, and somehow I know she is waiting to give herself over to it. I definitely shouldn't have implied that Paisley and Paloma should know more about Cecily, but that's exactly what I did.

She'd said *I loathe you*.

I'd said *The feeling is mutual, Menace.*

It's the truth, but only kind of. From my side, anyway. I loathe her only because she loathes me. Which sounds childish, but it incenses me that she hates me the way she does. Firstly, because I don't deserve it. Secondly, because... Well, I don't have a second reason yet, but I know I don't like it.

"Does she usually hate people?"

"There was a guy she went on a date with who stole a salt shaker. Or was it a pepper mill? I don't remember.

Point is, she really hated him. But she definitely hates you extra."

I sigh, rubbing a circle over my temple. "She's the one who ran out on our date when my back turned."

Klein gawks. "What? Why am I just now learning about this?"

I shrug. "I felt really stupid. And since it didn't seem like you already knew, I assumed Paisley hadn't told you, which meant Cecily probably didn't tell Paisley. Therefore, I didn't tell you."

"Dumb," Klein declares. "File it under 'Shit I should have told my cousin'."

I roll my eyes, and the movement immediately makes me think of Cecily. She performs the motion with gusto. Pizzazz. Like she means it.

"Her family is a disaster," I say, raking my hand down my face. "Her grandma is the only one I like so far, and even she is not totally sane. She's great, don't get me wrong, but she's a handful." Am I going to hell for speaking ill of someone we know is dying soon? I'm not really speaking ill of Savage Grandma. Everything I've said is true.

"Lucky for you, you've signed yourself up for nonstop fun and a backstage pass to the Hampton family circus." Klein speaks jovially, and I bet he wishes he could accompany me as my silent sidekick, taking notes for a future novel.

"Oh, and get this—" I snap my mouth shut. I'd been about to say Cecily's family is secretly filthy rich, but my brain stopped me. Saved me, really. Cecily must have a reason for not divulging this piece of information. The woman drives that death trap of a vehicle when she could be riding around in something that at least has four doors. Four windows. Better air conditioning. Less road noise. Fewer chances of being hit by road debris.

Have I mentioned I despise her car?

"What were you going to say?" Klein asks, taking the second to last turn to reach my parents' house.

"Never mind." I shake my head.

He lets it go, pressing the forward button on his phone to skip the next song. "Why are you refusing to get an annulment until after the road trip?"

"Cecily needs someone on that trip with her. After meeting her family today, that much is obvious."

"Fair, and also very self-sacrificing of you. But you don't need to be married to accomplish that goal."

"Refusing the annulment until after the road trip was really just to piss Cecily off. She rises to the occasion pretty easily, and since she was being unpleasant, I matched her."

"How mature of you," Klein says sarcastically.

"I know, I know. There's something about her that makes me act in ways I normally wouldn't. She gets under my skin."

Klein glances at me, the red light we're stopped at reflecting in his sunglasses. "Cecily gets under your skin?"

"Not like that." Or, you know, *exactly* like that.

Klein chuckles, just once. A smug sound. "A hundred bucks," he says. "A hundred bucks says you fall in love with Cecily on this road trip."

"And Cecily? You don't want to bet she will fall in love with me?"

Klein snorts, open hand waiting between us. "No way. Cecily wishes she'd never met you."

True. But that doesn't explain the way the pulse in her

neck strums faster when she's sparring with me. It's not the adrenaline from arguing, because I'd bet my last dollar Cecily is a calm fighter. Cecily gets under my skin, but I get under hers, too. It's a truth I feel in the marrow of my bones.

"I'll take your bet, Klein, and I look forward to the moment you press two crisp Benjamins in my palm."

"One," he corrects. The light turns green, and he makes the final left turn into my parents' neighborhood.

"Two. You still owe me money from the Paisley bet."

"What bet?" He winks at me, pulling up to my parents' latest home. The playfulness disappears from his face. "You ready?" he asks.

He knows I love my parents. He also knows what it feels like to be conflicted, and resentful, and altogether mutilated by their life choices.

Klein gets to send his complicated feelings toward a ghost shaped like his father. But not me. The people who raised me, who sent me out into the world with baggage, are still present. They want to see me. They expect to see me. And despite it all, I love them.

One isn't better than the other. In fact, they are equally disturbing.

As is Cecily's family. All the money in the world, and though they're as different as night and day from mine, they have one common denominator: dysfunction.

The house smells like my parents, but also like fresh cleaner. Pine-Sol, the original scent. I've been here once before, on my last visit. They signed a one-year lease, but that doesn't mean much to my parents. Or my dad, at least. If my mother didn't have my dad, she might be more stable. Long-term home, and job.

"Dominic," my mom says, smiling at me. Her hair is almost entirely gray. Early, I think, and probably due to stress. She wraps me in a hug, and mostly I feel love for her. But there's that old flash of resentment, and the guilt that attaches itself to the resentment like a barnacle. My mom was always very good at loving me, but not so great at creating security.

The same is true for my dad.

I kiss my mom's temple and step back. She greets Klein with the same warmth.

"Domino!" My dad's booming voice reaches us before he does, using a nickname he has called me my entire life.

"Your dad's been very excited to see you." My mom pats my cheek. "Go easy on him."

Klein and I meet eyes briefly. *Go easy on him* really means *He has a business venture and he's looking for investors.*

My dad walks into the living room holding a glass of water. I got my height from him, but that's about it. I closely resemble my mom, from my light brown hair to my bright blue eyes. Ciarán Bellinger stands one inch shorter than me, with a mop of cinnamon hair perpetually in need of a trim from my mother (his one and only barber), and covered in freckles. His Irish name is pronounced Keer-awn, but because in English it's pronounced nothing like it's spelled and nobody gets it right, he introduces himself as Ron. If he ever makes it to

Ireland, he'll be in heaven hearing his name said correctly.

"Hey, Dad." Affection swells in my heart at the sight of him, but like my mom, other emotions press in. It used to be that I couldn't name the various feelings, but now I can. I hope the next step is a decrease in all the less-than-pleasant emotions. Baby steps, I guess. A process.

My dad's gaze bounces back-and-forth between me and Klein. "How was Vegas?"

I let Klein answer, since the celebration was for him. "Full of mostly-clean fun. Nothing anyone regrets." He glances at me, eyes mischievous. "Your son came away with an unexpected party favor."

Dad's eyes widen, but Mom steps in. "There's medicine for that. Pills." Her eyes drop briefly to my groin before looking up again. "Something topical, maybe?"

Klein laughs way too hard while I shake my head so vehemently it sends another hot pain through my neck. Rubbing at the angry muscle, I say, "Nothing was transmitted, sexually or otherwise."

My mother's eyebrows pull together in confusion. "Well then, what happened?" She sits back on the arm of a threadbare upholstered chair.

I pause a beat, deciding how to say it, then decide to forgo fanfare and put it out there. "I had far too much to drink and got married."

My dad's head tips back with a jolly laugh, something one of my authors would call a *guffaw*.

My mom, to her credit, is appropriately horrified. She presses a palm to her neck, taking a deep breath.

"We're going to get it annulled, but not for about a month. I have to spend a few weeks helping her out."

Good thing Cecily isn't here. Something tells me she would not agree with my use of the words *helping her out*. She'd say my attendance on her family road trip is a unique brand of torture.

"Help her out *how*?" my mom asks.

I explain it all to her, and Klein interrupts to tell them of my choice to accept a gummy from Cecily's grandma. "Thanks," I say to him. If there was any part of the whole story I was going to leave out, it would've been that.

"You were being polite," my dad says, winking at me. I cannot count the number of times I suspected he was high when I was a teenager. I never asked, because how do you pose that question to your parent?

"Moving on," I say sternly in Klein's direction. He takes my cue and shuts his trap.

"Does this lass have a name?" my dad asks.

"Cecily Harmon," I lie smoothly. I hate it, the way I have to lie. If we'd had this talk yesterday, I wouldn't have known to protect Cecily's real name. But now, after seeing Ophelia's home and learning Cecily's dad's company owns a portfolio stuffed with ultra-luxury boutique hotels, there is no way I can be honest about her name. My dad might be gullible, and fiscally irresponsible, but he's not stupid. He can make use of the internet the same as anybody else. If he finds out Cecily's family is wealthy, he'll be first in line with a list of *investment opportunities*.

Klein doesn't appear to notice the fib. No elbow nudge, no confused micro-expressions. He's been around my whole life. He's seen it all. He knows. We might give one another a healthy amount of ribbing, but we're more like brothers than cousins. There's nothing I wouldn't do for the guy.

"She works with Paisley," Klein offers, lending Cecily credibility.

My dad grins, showing a mouth full of crooked teeth. "Gotta tell ya, Domino, you don't seem like the Vegas marriage type. Bit of a serial monogomer, aren't you?"

Klein shows zero reaction, but he's a wordy guy, and I happen to know he's cringing on the inside at my dad's invented word. *Monogomer.*

My dad's right. I've had two relationships, and both lasted approximately two years. They both ended because neither felt right.

"What could be more monogamous than marriage?" I ask glibly, spreading my arms wide.

Mom makes a disbelieving sound with her lips. "Pshh. I wouldn't call this a marriage. It's an oopsie."

It's foolish, but I bristle. Nothing related to Cecily could ever be termed an oopsie. Even if this marriage is, in fact, an accident, I'm opposed to calling it an oopsie.

"An accident, yeah," I say smoothly. Arguing, but not really. My specialty when it comes to my parents.

"Maybe we should meet her," my dad suggests. Alarm bells scream inside my chest.

Not a chance in hell is Cecily meeting my family. I don't care that I met hers.

"Why make it messier than it already is?" I ask, clapping once to signal the end of the conversation.

"Right." Dad nods quickly. "Yeah, sure. No problem. How about we go get something to eat?" He pats my shoulder. "I have a new business venture I want to bring you in on." He cuts the air between us with a flattened palm. "Ground floor."

"Let's grab dinner. Pitch me." Anything to not have to

talk more about Cecily. She might despise me, but I want to keep her tucked away from my family.

Mom's relieved smile is all I need to see to know I've made the right choice.

In the end, I pay for dinner. I knew I would. I'd do it no matter what, because I make more money than them, and they're my parents. I even listen to my dad's Rent-a-Raptor business idea.

Thanks to a quick internet search, I'm able to avoid it by informing him it's illegal to rent protected species. And, because he planned on having bald eagles be his big ticket item, I have also managed to save him from himself.

For now.

CHAPTER 17

Cecily

I did not expect to still have a husband on Wednesday. Or, I at least expected to be in the process of canceling the whole marriage thing.

Paisley invites me to grab dinner with her after work.

I should've known better.

Klein and Dom sit at a table when we walk in. Dom's back is to the door, but Klein waves at Paisley.

"Smooth," I tell her.

"I wasn't trying to trick you, per se, but I didn't want to give you the chance to invent something pressing to do."

"Like organize my spice drawer?"

"Exactly."

"Scrub behind the toilet."

"Right."

"Clean the soles of my shoes with a toothbrush."

Paisley side-eyes me. "All things you'd rather be doing?"

"Precisely."

"Lucky for you, I have your best interests in mind."

I groan, and she steers me toward the table where the guys are waiting. "You and Dom need to have a heart to heart before you're stuck together, and you're running out of time."

She has a point. Dom turns as we approach. It's the first time I've seen him since I left him in front of Klein and Paisley's house. He looks good, of course, and probably without trying. A light blue shirt. Gray shorts.

"Menace," he booms happily, mouth curving into a slow, wicked smile. "You here to ruin my day?"

My acknowledging nod is clipped, like I can hardly be bothered. "Errand Boy."

"Satan's Errand Boy," he corrects. "You don't know me well enough to shorten my name. Too intimate."

"I will soon, apparently." I stab the papers lying on the table between Klein and Dom. In all-caps bold font it says *All About Me*. Below that is a list to be filled in, starting with *Name*. "Did you two rob a kindergarten class?"

Dom and Klein slide over, making space for Paisley and me to sit. I would complain about being forced to sit next to Dom, but what's the point when living a shared life for three weeks looms on the horizon?

Dom sits back against the wall at the far end of the booth, putting as much space as possible between us. "Robbing a kindergarten class was one of my tasks for the day, directly below throwing nails in the street to cause chaos for unsuspecting drivers."

"Hard day's work," I murmur, picking up the laminated menu.

"The Prince of Darkness never rests."

A pink-painted fingernail appears at the top of my menu, tapping to get my attention. Paisley's eyes glow with mirth.

"What?" Her delight makes me suspicious.

"I cannot tell if you two want to rip each other's throats out, or rip each other's clothes off."

Dom and I turn sharply to each other, gazes colliding. I grimace, and his face, well it's hard to say what it's doing. Aside from looking stupidly handsome, which he can't help. It's not as if he chose that face. That hair. Those shoulders.

"The former," Dom confirms, at the same time I say, "The latter."

His eyes widen, and I realize my mistake. "I mean, the former. Obviously." Heat flushes on the back of my neck. I spent a nanosecond thinking about Dom's good looks and got tripped up. That's all.

"Freudian slip," Klein proclaims, smacking his menu on the table.

"It was not," I argue.

"It was not," Dom repeats, providing backup in my assertion that I am against getting him naked. How gallant of him.

"Cecily loathes me," he reminds Klein.

Hmm, ok. Pretty sure he's teasing me, but I'll go with it. "Yep," I say with finality.

For the record, neither of the beautiful people sitting across the booth from me show any signs of believing us. Doubt rides in the lifted corners of Klein's half-smile, and dubiousness sits squarely in Paisley's eyes.

"Moving on," I say, like it's a command.

The server shows up, takes our food and drink order, and hightails it away. Maybe she spotted the childish printouts on the table and took them for the harbinger of absurdity that they are.

Klein and Paisley turn to each other. She leans her head against the back of the upholstered booth, and he lays his hand on her thigh. They spend a few moments exchanging details about their day. She smiles softly while he speaks. He asks her questions about our lunch meeting with a new account.

Maybe it's the intimacy of their moment, or the glimpse into their private little world, but there's a pinch in my chest. Longing, I think. What would it be like to have a person my heart and soul settles into?

"I'm happy for them," Dom says in a low voice.

"They're annoying," I respond, lowering my voice to match his. *Annoyingly amazing.*

"Without question," he agrees. His forearms balance on the edge of the table, fingers intertwined.

We aren't looking at each other, but our chins tip toward the shared space between us. Questions burn in my mind, and I choose the one most pertinent to our current situation.

"Why are you making me stay married to you until the road trip is over?"

"Two reasons," he says, accepting the soda water the server slides in front of him. I've ordered the same, our fingers brushing as we reach for a lime wedge from the ramekin placed on the table.

The incidental touch shouldn't mean anything, but it does. Brief but warm, and I know, *I just know*, Dom let his hand linger an extra second. Almost certainly to aggravate me.

"What are those two reasons?" I finish squeezing the lime in my drink and bring the glass to my mouth. I'm not thirsty, but I need something to do. He's sitting too close for us to talk face to face.

"For one, it irritates you, and I've found I'm partial to irritating you."

"Thanks for that," I say dryly. "What's your second reason?"

He takes a deep drink of his water, ice gathering as he nearly finishes it. His Adam's apple bobs when he swallows. Then he turns to me, and now I'm looking into unfairly blue eyes. Dark like denim in this warm-lit restaurant. "That is for me to know."

My gaze narrows. For the life of me, I cannot understand this man. He said all those awful things about me, but now he's voluntarily throwing us together for three weeks? We need to get to the bottom of all this, and I'm done waiting for the right time and place. If the past five days are any indication, it's never going to arrive. So, here we go. "Why go to the trouble when I'm annoying, and I have the worst laugh, and I yammer on and on? Don't you want to pull a Van Gogh and cut off your ear?"

Dominic's eyebrows tug together so quickly it's like they were threaded and cinched. "What are you talking about?"

"Don't even think about gaslighting me," I warn, pointer finger suspended between us. "I heard you on the phone in the hall at Obstinate Daughter."

The tip of his tongue pokes at the corner of his mouth while he pretends to work through everything I've said.

Across from us, Paisley and Klein discuss wedding details. They are either truly in their own world, or giving us space to hash out this long-standing grudge.

"Cecily," Dom says through clenched teeth. "I am going to need you to walk me through it all like I'm an idiot. Because I truly, from the bottom of my heart, do not understand."

To his credit, he looks genuine. Could he really fake the confusion? The discomposure?

I huff an aggrieved sigh. "I came to find you, to ask if you wanted another drink. You were in the hall, and I overheard your phone conversation. I didn't make all that up, Dominic. You said those things about me."

Dom spends a few seconds quiet, letting what I've said sink in. Then he laughs.

My stomach muscles clench. "In case you're wondering, this is exactly how you earned the nickname I gave you."

"I'm not laughing because this is funny, Cecily. I'm laughing because it's preposterous."

Then Dominic Bellinger, my husband for the next month unless I can get him to stop being enamored with irritating me, nudges my knee with his. Twice.

"Stop," I snap.

"Please get up."

"Why?"

"Because I said *please*."

"You don't get what you want because you say please. *Cecily, run over that group of baby ducks, please.*"

"Brood." He nudges me again, harder this time.

"Huh?"

"A group of baby ducks is called a brood. Now, please

get up." He says it through tight lips. Is he going to be sick?

I hustle up, lest I become a human barf bag. Dominic stands, looks down at our confused dinner mates, and announces, "We'll be back. Maybe."

Before I can say another word, he threads his fingers through mine and marches me out of the restaurant.

CHAPTER 18
Cecily

"WHAT THE HELL, DOMINIC?" I YANK MY ARM AWAY.

We come to a stop in the parking lot beside my car. The last rays of the sun filter through towering palm trees lining a nearby children's splash pad, sending odd-shaped shadows across our faces.

Dominic clears his throat. "I think I know what happened."

"Glad to hear it. So do I." I lean against my car.

Dominic fishes his phone from his pocket. "I have a feeling you won't believe me unless I do this."

"Do what?" I ask, watching him navigate his phone with his thumb.

He leans against my car too, a solid two feet from me. "Call the person I was talking to that day."

I pale. "You want me to speak with the person you were shit-talking me to? That's like...like...asking a cow if he'd like to eat a hamburger."

"It's not remotely the same." Dom holds the phone out between us. It begins to ring. And ring. The smug look on

Dom's face slides away. Mine turns triumphant for a reason I don't understand. Pure spite, I think.

And then, the ringing ceases. A voice, male and enthusiastic, surges into the Arizona evening. "Dom, hey, how are you?"

"Miles, hey. This is random, but do you remember when you got stuck in the plot on Post Rising? And we went through an exercise to help get your wheels turning?"

"Of course. I thought my ship had *sunk*. Good thing I called you before I set fire to my laptop."

This guy, Miles, sounds grateful. Happy. I know Dom is a good literary agent, I saw what he did for Klein. Hell, his bio on the Whitaker Literary Agency website makes it sound like the sun shines from his backside. He and Miles clearly have good rapport.

"I'm happy you didn't do that. It's a great book." The smug look is back on Dom's face. "Remind me what exercise we used?"

Dom watches me listen, so intent on my face. He's waiting for the moment he receives vindication. I can tell.

"The inverse scene, you called it. Saying the opposite of everything. You used yourself as an example. You were at a bar. Something with an ironic name. And you were on a date, which before I started whining about my plot problem you'd said you were having a great time. I still feel bad about interrupting, by the way."

"No sweat," Dom answers automatically. "Keep talking."

"You showed me how the exercise works. You took everything you thought about the woman you were with, and said the complete opposite. She has dull hair, she's boring, she's annoying with a bad laugh. Oh, and you told me to spitball, too. Lay it on thick. Be outlandish. You said something about Van Gogh and his ear."

Dom's palm performs a celebratory slice through the air, as if he's a maestro. His face says *Hah!*

"Pipe down," I tell him, though he's said nothing. I need quiet so I can concentrate on how wrong I was, even when all signs pointed toward an obvious conclusion. Realization snakes through me, my memories of that day shifting in real time. Heat steals over my cheeks as the scene in the hallway replays, but differently this time.

"Who is that? Why am I supposed to pipe down?" Dom's author asks, confused. "You called me, asking questions."

"She's talking to me, Miles. Thanks for all the info."

They say goodbye. I kick at a pebble with the toe of my sandal.

Dom tucks his phone in his pocket and slides closer to me. "Satisfied?"

"Is satisfied the best-fitting word to use right now?"

Dom crosses his arms, squinting against the early evening sun. The deepening golden rays darken his butterscotch hair, turning each lock molten. "How about you describe how you feel," he says, voice dry, "since I'm apparently inept?"

"You don't have to sound like this irritates you, Dominic. Why would you be skilled in guessing my feelings? You hardly know me."

His mouth tugs into a smirk. "Other than being married to you, of course."

"Obviously."

"Alright, Cecily. Tell me how you feel, now that you've been proven wrong."

"I don't know that I was proven *wrong*. I just wasn't proven *right*."

Dom shakes his head slowly. He shifts, but not away from me. Closer. He's not touching me, but I feel it anyway. His nearness. His intense gaze. The air between us tightens.

"I've never met anyone like you." His voice is a murmur, but there's something in it that's rough, too.

My chest heaves with a raw breath. What is this between us? The push and pull, the scramble for words, it's almost painful. Getting my bearings, I say, "You can blame your cousin for that." It would've sounded better if my breathy, soft voice hadn't betrayed me.

Dom's gaze roams my face as he sucks his lower lip between his teeth. "Believe me, I do."

We stare each other down. A face-off in a restaurant parking lot with distant sounds of kids squealing at the splash pad.

"Your turn," Dom finally says.

"My turn for what?"

"Tell your side."

"There's nothing to tell. I overheard you, and I got the hell out of there."

"Explain why I was paying the bill with the bartender who, by the way, became very hostile in my absence, when a group of young ladies crowded around me and began belting out Happy Birthday."

Before I realize it, I'm laughing. Giggling, really, and I don't giggle.

Dom narrows his eyes, pushing off my car and stepping in front of me. He doesn't lean closer, doesn't take up any more physical space, but somehow he envelops me. His smell. His persona. His emotions.

"What's funny, Menace?" A line of consternation forms between his eyebrows. His lips are full and upturned enough to let me know he is amused.

"Halston's hostility was out of female solidarity when she saw me leaving. She didn't know what happened until the next time I was in there. But the singing girls was absolutely me."

A flash of appreciation crosses his blue eyes. "You're diabolical."

Is this *praise*? A warm glow spreads through me. *Absolutely not.* No. There's no way I *like* it. Unacceptable. To neutralize the fuzzy feeling, I place my hands on my hips, ratcheting up the belligerence in my tone when I say, "I'd overhead you saying terrible things about me, and it was made worse by the fact that you otherwise appeared to be having a good time. What else should I have done?"

"I'd expect nothing less. Not from you."

"Not from me? Why does that sound like an insult?"

"It's not meant as one. Given what I know of you, the reaction was appropriate."

"We've already established that you don't know me."

He arches a brow. "But that's going to change, isn't it?"

"How so?"

"Have you forgotten the road trip in our near future?"

With Dom standing this close to me, I've nearly forgotten my name. "Of course not."

"I'm flying back to New York tomorrow afternoon. I'll be there for a couple days, replenishing my wardrobe and getting what I need from my office so I can work on the road."

"You sure you can work from the RV? What if there isn't Wi-Fi? What if there's an author emergency? What if the motor home Savage Grandma booked is actually a piece of junk and the folding table collapses and your laptop falls and breaks and makes you miss a meeting and your boss is furious and then you get fired?"

Dom spends a few seconds letting my fatalistic mono-logue sink in, then says, "It will take a lot more than that to get rid of me."

My head dips sideways. "Like, how much?"

"I'm not telling."

"The threat of losing your job won't stop you from coming on the road trip?"

He shakes his head.

"What about..." I search my memory. "If every restau-rant we go to I tell the waitstaff it's your birthday and they sing to you?"

A second shake of those butterscotch waves. Maybe I'm misreading it, but is that a look of challenge I see in his eyes? It's as if he's saying *You can do better, Menace.*

And I can. I can do so much better. "Dom," I say, imparting a breathiness to my voice. I press a fingertip to his stomach, just an inch above his navel. Jutting out my bottom lip, I walk my pointer and middle fingers up the midline of his body. His throat bobs with a hard swallow. His hands, hung loosely at his sides, form fists.

My gaze lifts, and there he is, staring down at me intently, lower lip pulled away from top. Hunger burns in his eyes, carving out his breath until it's shallow.

This was supposed to be about torturing Dom, but

dammit if I'm not aching now. His eyes tumble over my face, and I feel it like a caress.

I hate this man. I really do. *My husband.* I loathe him. Even if he does have an excuse for everything that happened. I loathe him on principle. I loathe him because otherwise I might—

NO.

I take back my hand as if scorched and rip my gaze away, forcing it out across the parking lot.

"Dom?" A voice calls.

"Cecily?" A different voice.

Dom takes a wide step sideways, making it easier for Klein and Paisley to see him. I stand up straight, smoothing out my hair and my clothes. I don't know if they're rumpled, or why they would be, but it feels like the right thing to do.

"Here," Klein says, looking at us with suspicion. He's holding two takeout containers. "Your dinners."

"Thank you," I say, avoiding Paisley's gaze. I can practically taste the curiosity rolling off her.

"Everything all good out here?" Klein asks. "I was worried we were going to find you two in cuffs on the curb."

Dom chuckles. "All good. We avoided a domestic disturbance."

His eyes find mine. I don't know about him, but I am plenty disturbed.

CHAPTER
Nineteen

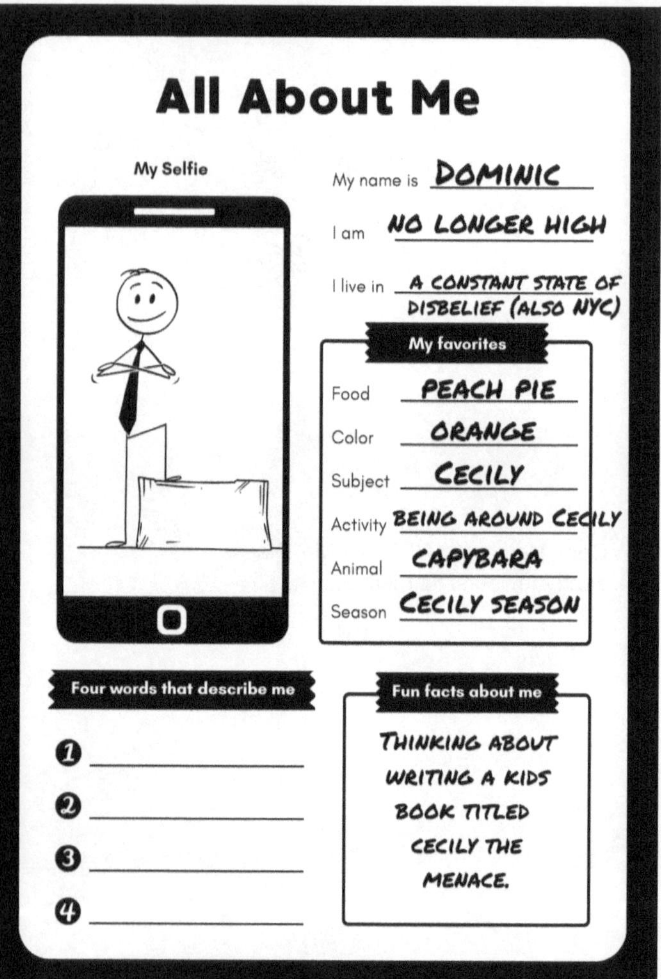

Cecily: You forgot to use four words to describe yourself.

Cecily: I took the liberty, I hope you don't mind. Insufferable, pompous, fancy-pants, buffoon.

Dom: Someone used a thesaurus.

Cecily: Let's get this over with. Here's mine.

Dom: You also forgot to describe yourself.

Dom: I took the liberty. Vexing, bratty, witty, gorgeous.

Cecily: Seriously? What is wrong with you? We're being mean, Dominic.

Dom: I guess I'm not as mean as you.

Cecily: Guess I married the insufferable buffoon with the heart of gold. Great.

Dom: Even better, you get to spend three weeks in his constant presence.

Cecily: Your boss didn't put the kibosh on that?

Dom: Ki-boss?

Cecily: No.

Dom: That was funny.

Cecily: Not even remotely.

Dom: She approved my trip, with the caveat that I answer emails and call in to meetings. Sorry to disappoint you.

Cecily: Are you?

Dom: Nope.

CHAPTER 20
Cecily

Ugh. Why do I find Dom's All About Me kind of cute?

CHAPTER 21
Dominic

I LOOKED IN THE MIRROR AFTER I READ CECILY'S ALL ABOUT
Me. Can confirm hearts decorated my eyes.

CHAPTER 22

Dominic

CECILY HAS BEEN RADIO SILENT SINCE THAT EVENING IN THE restaurant parking lot. Mostly, anyway. We exchanged our All About Me's, and earlier today, when I was on my way to the JFK airport in a torrential downpour, she answered a FaceTime call I hadn't meant to place. She was at work, sitting at her desk eating a salad she'd brought from home. Her hair rode high on her head in a ponytail, cheekbones prominently displayed.

"What?" she'd snapped, looking irritated.

It had rankled me, though I didn't know why. Shouldn't I be used to Cecily being generally displeased at my existence? I guess I thought we'd made progress after our talk, even more so after the All About Me pages we'd exchanged.

I guess not. Cecily seems hell-bent on keeping me squarely in the category of People I'd Kill If I Had A Get Out Of Jail Free card.

I'd told her I didn't mean to FaceTime her, and she'd said *K bye* and hung up. The Uber driver's sympathetic look pierced me through the rearview mirror. I offered a perfunctory smile and looked out my window, watching the rain pelt the glass and bounce off.

I spent most of the flight thinking about what I'd gotten myself into with this road trip, but I kept from letting my thoughts stray too far into the *why*. What I told Cecily is true. I've got a dying woman's last wishes on my conscience, and pissing off Cecily is more fun than I've had in a long time. There's something more there, though, something deeper, and I'm unwilling to dig. Shovels down, blinders on.

Klein's waiting for me at the arrivals curb at Sky Harbor International Airport. The trunk of his 4Runner is open wide, waiting for the large duffel I checked.

"I've seen a lot more of you since you got married," Klein jokes, taking the duffel from my hands. He hoists it into the back. "Hope there wasn't anything breakable in there."

"Laptop's in my backpack," I say, dropping it from my shoulder and onto the floor of the passenger side.

"You ready for Monday?" Klein asks, navigating into the sea of airport traffic.

"As I'll ever be," I answer. There's an edge in my tone.

"What's wrong?"

"I'm tired. I'm hungry. Long travel day." The heavy rain caused a two-hour delay. I'd sat at the airport, reading the manuscript one of my newer clients sent over. A tell-all from her time working in the restaurant industry.

Klein gives me a knowing look. "That's it?"

"Yeah," I answer, tight-lipped. The truth is, the longer I thought about Cecily on that flight, the more a leaden sensation gathered in my stomach. Apprehension, if I had to name it.

Could Cecily and I have been something, if not for the misunderstanding that took on a life of its own? Am I signing myself up for a world of pain, just to keep Cecily from going through this alone?

The amount of angst I'm experiencing over this entire situation is exhausting me. At this point, I am sick of myself.

Klein and I make a supermarket sweep through a local grocery store, picking up enough to last until Monday morning when I'm due to meet Cecily and her family at the closest coffee shop to Ophelia's house, where the motor home will be waiting.

Though Monday morning approaches like a freight train barreling down the tracks, Cecily remains quiet. In my stomach, the uneasiness grows. It was painless to confidently announce my attendance when the trip wasn't staring me in the eyes.

For a guy who usually knows how stories will go, I don't have a clue how this will end.

CHAPTER 23

Cecily

Monday morning arrives swiftly, bringing with it a sense of foreboding. I've heard of dry drowning, but is dread drowning a thing, too?

As previously instructed, most of my family shows up to the parking lot at nine. My parents and Duke stayed the night at a hotel nearby, and the hotel van drove them over. Klein picked me up with Dom this morning, and dropped us off. I planned on getting a ride over, but Dom texted last night and offered to have Klein pick me up. Good thing he did, because it would've invited questions if we showed up separately. Not having rings is bad enough, and when I thought about it yesterday, I decided not to mention it to Dom. Wearing rings would take this situation that is already bad and make it worse. If anyone asks, I'll say I haven't found the right one yet.

For now, we are waiting for my grandma and Rainbow. They are running late, so we've all popped into the free-standing coffee shop beside the busy road, placing orders for large coffees.

Through the store window sits the shiny black, gargantuan motor home. The man who drove it here is waiting inside the vehicle for everyone to be present, at which point he will give us a lesson in how to operate the thing. My plan is to not listen, so when it comes time to be my turn I can claim I lack the skill to safely drive us.

Dom, bless his heart, makes small talk with Duke while we wait. They gesture with their coffees while they speak, and Dom holds a paper bag in his other hand. Kerrigan pushes her oversized sunglasses onto her head, surreptitiously glances at Dom, and, sipping her iced vanilla latte, says, "Don't take this the wrong way, but your husband is a dime."

I sip my own hot latte, just to buy a few moments before saying, "Are you calling Dominic a ten?" Not that I don't agree, because unfortunately, I do.

Since that night in the restaurant parking lot I have done very little but think of Dom. The way he showed me I'd misunderstood his half of the conversation instead of telling me. The fact that he's here on this road trip with my family simply because my grandmother has requested it. How many men would do those things?

And, worst of all, is the gall my body has to be attracted to him. The way he looked when he FaceTimed me in that cab, wearing a gray hoodie and his handsome face. How dare he wear his handsome face? All these years together, and my body betrays me the second she fancies a tall, broad-shouldered, kind-hearted man. Somebody should have told me to keep dating low-caliber men. They're safer. No chance of losing my heart to a salt shaker thief.

My sister snaps her fingers in my face. "Hello? Where did you go?"

The same well-worn road I've been traveling the past four days. A little town called Dominic Bellinger. Population: two.

"Sorry," I say, knocking my sister's hand out of the way. "I was just thinking about how Dominic is a ten."

"Don't lose sight of that universal truth," Kerrigan says matter-of-factly. "You know who else likes tens?"

My eyebrows lift as I shake my head. "Who?"

"Everybody," Kerrigan says, like *duh*. "Literally everybody. So maybe refresh yourself on how to throw a punch." She jabs the air with only her right hand. In the other hand, she holds fast to her iced coffee. Priorities.

Cool. I can't wait to box someone to protect my claim to my temporary hubby. "Doesn't matter. We're not for real." I'd told Kerrigan everything about the way Dom is holding the annulment hostage, but she insists on talking about Dom like this isn't the real life equivalent of a punchline to a joke.

Dom stands beside the large coffee shop window. The shopping plaza in the background brims with fancy boutiques and boozy brunch spots. The white T-shirt Dom wears makes his tan skin appear darker. He has paired it with drawstring shorts in a tawny color, and a brown leather backpack.

Dom catches my gaze and excuses himself from Duke. "Ladies," he says, stepping over to us. "Cecily, I got this for you." He presses the paper bag he'd been holding into my hand. "It's a blueberry muffin. You mentioned in the car on the way here that you didn't eat breakfast this morning, and I noticed you didn't buy food for yourself. The barista swore it's the best muffin you'll ever have in your life. Specially delivered from a small town up north once a week."

The kindness of his gesture steals my breath away. I genuinely don't know the last time somebody was this considerate toward me.

Dom looks at Kerrigan and asks, "How are you this morning?" It's as if he knows I need the spotlight taken off me so I can absorb his gesture sans audience. He's right, I did skip breakfast, and now that I know what's in the bag, I'm starving for it. Removing the muffin, I peel the liner and take a big bite, trying not to groan at how delicious it is.

"Well," Kerrigan launches in, "I'm sure you already know how Cecily is, but I'm sad."

"Why is that?" Dom asks politely.

I've already heard all this, so I settle in for take two and eat the rest of the muffin. Kerrigan lives for dramatizing her life, but she tones it down for me because she knows I won't have the response she prefers. Dom, however, is fresh meat.

"First off," Kerrigan begins theatrically, "I had to leave Moose at the boarding facility, and he hates it there."

"Moose is a dog?" Dom asks.

Kerrigan nods. "He's the sweetest Golden Retriever in the world—"

"Dumbest," I cough into my hand.

Kerrigan shoots me an affronted look. "Moose is a very smart boy."

"Moose chased his tail so exuberantly he knocked himself off the stairs and smacked his head on the corner of a brick paver and needed stitches."

"He was committed to his task," Kerrigan defends.

"He steals food off your counters and hides it under your pillow." I look at Dom, who's laughing. "He has yet to realize he never gets to eat what he steals."

Kerrigan rolls her eyes. "Any-*way*," she says with emphasis. "Moose was very upset this morning. Even though I booked him the biggest room with the best bed and his own television. And daily spa treatments."

Dom blinks hard, and me? I watch it unfold. Kerrigan has no idea how bougie this dog boarding facility is, so she talks about it as if TVs and spa treatments are common-place for dogs. Don't get me started on the continuous livestream the owners can join to watch their dogs.

"I kept telling Moose he was going to have the best time in their pool, but"—dramatic sigh—"he wouldn't listen." Kerrigan shrugs. "I wish I could've brought him on this trip with us, but Grandma said no."

I snort. I can't help it. "Just what we need to add even more flavor to this road trip. A seventy-pound shedding machine whose two brain cells randomly knock into each other."

Kerrigan sticks her tongue out at me. "You love him, and you know it." Then she marches to the coffee shop door and steps outside.

Dom sinks into a chair at an open table. I do the same, sitting opposite him. "Thank you for the muffin. I needed it." Are we being nice to each other now? Because it feels weird.

Dom crosses an ankle over the opposite knee. He pinches his lower lip between two fingers like he's consid-ering me before saying, "I know you prefer to think of me in a negative light, so don't worry, buying you that muffin was for my self-preservation. You're meaner when you're hungry."

My mouth drops open. I can't believe I tiptoed around the possibility of maybe being nice to Dom.

"Do you dislike dogs?" Dom asks, moving us swiftly away from the topic. He removes the lid from his coffee, bringing it to his lips and blowing gently across the top. It's distracting, and I'm grateful when he keeps speaking. "If so, it wasn't on your All About Me, and it's an important detail to know."

"Lest you think I'm a monster, let me stop you right there. I love Moose. When Kerrigan had the flu last winter, I showed up twice a day to walk him. He stole a kid's ball when we passed a park, and deflated it. I handed twenty dollars to the crying child and apologized. He also nabbed a cinnamon roll from a man sitting on a bench. That walk ended up costing me twenty-five dollars, not including the value of time spent." I picture Moose's face, his tongue lolling out one side of his mouth. "It's impossible not to love a goofy boy who smiles when he's being dumb and naughty."

One side of Dom's mouth curves upward. "Noted. To make you love me, I must act goofy and smile while being dumb and naughty."

My laugh sticks in my throat, making it sound deeper, sexier than I intend. "I suppose it doesn't matter, because you have no interest in making me love you, right?" My volume decreased while I was speaking, ending on a whisper.

Dom holds my gaze, a hundred words floating in those blue irises, before simply saying, "Right."

The coffee shop door swings open, and Kerrigan

announces loudly, "Grandma's here." Several strangers turn and look before resuming their activities.

We all file out, Dom stepping in behind me. Is he going to put his hand on the small of my back, guiding me out the door? Isn't that something a husband would do for his wife? Do I want him to? He did it that day Grandma called the family meeting, but maybe that was only because I'd received awful news. Maybe it was only empathy he was showing me, and touching me right now would be something else.

The seconds tick by, and Dom doesn't place his hand on my back. I'm so sidetracked by the thought I don't notice what everyone else has picked up on already.

Kerrigan, astonishment rounding out her voice, says, "Grandma, are you giving Cecily the Bentley?"

My attention snaps to where my grandma stands beside the person I'm assuming is Rainbow. She wears bell-bottoms, and a large Nirvana T-shirt with a fringe cut into the bottom. Her midnight black braid curves around her head like a horseshoe. She's beside my grandma, who stands next to her prized Bentley convertible, top down.

Before I can begin to understand what is happening here I pull my grandma into a hug. There will only be so many more times I can do this, and I don't want to miss the opportunity.

"I'm sure you're wondering what Kerrigan is talking about," my grandma says, patting my cheek when I let her go.

"You never know," I whisper. "It could be the shrooms talking."

Grandma cackles. "Not this time." She pokes the end of my nose. "Go around to the trunk."

I back up until I see what she is talking about. Written on thick white poster board in black marker are the words *Just Married.*

"What's going on?" I look to Dom, checking to see if he is in on whatever this is, but he only shrugs.

"Being stuck in a motor home with your family is not conducive to"—Grandma glances at my dad before continuing—"*marital relations.*"

My dad's lip curls. Duke's, too.

"What?" Grandma asks, drawn-on eyebrows raised in challenge. "How do you think you got here?"

My dad shakes his head but says nothing. Clearly he wants no part in furthering this conversation.

"Anywho," Grandma says, waving a hand in the air. "It's not for the entire road trip, because that would defeat the purpose. It'll be for the first half. You'll leave the car in Sierra Grande, and I've scheduled to have it picked up and driven back to my house." She claps once, loudly, moving on before I get the chance to utter a word. "This brings me to my next two orders of business. First." Grandma gestures to the woman beside her. "As I'm sure you've already guessed, this is Rainbow, my death doula. There will be no, and I mean *no*, belittling or diminishing her important job." Grandma levels her steely-eyed gaze on Duke and my dad. "I'm talking to both of you when I say that." She glances at me. "And you a little bit, too."

I clutch my chest, slightly offended but also aware of why she'd call me out. I point at my sister. If I'm going under the bus, she's coming with me. "What about Kerrigan?"

Grandma gives me a look. "She sends Moose on a

doggy bus to have playdates. Does she sound like a person who is opinionated about the work of a death doula?"

I know better than to ask why my mom wasn't called out. Savage Grandma would answer in a way that is, well, savage. She'd probably say something like *your mother left the building a long time ago and hasn't returned.*

"Fine," I answer. I step closer to Rainbow, and my nose is hit with a mixture of essential oils. Patchouli, and definitely lavender. Something else, too. It's not bad-smelling, but it's strong. Ten bucks says she has a tincture in her beaded-fringe purse. "Rainbow," I greet, sticking out my hand. "It's nice to meet you. Welcome to the shit show."

Rainbow smiles warmly, placing her palm in mine. She has a weak handshake, but maybe it's more charitable to call it a *gentle grasp*. "Cecily," she says, and my spine stiffens at her admonishing tone. "We're looking for fewer curse words. It's important to create a calm atmosphere for Ophelia."

My smile flattens. The only words floating through my mind now are all the ones I've been instructed to use fewer of, but I press my lips together and make a noise that sounds something like, "Mmm."

Grandma has already moved on, introducing Rainbow to the group. Rainbow creates a mnemonic device for each person, and says it out loud as she shakes their hand.

"Duke is handsome like royalty. Like a duke."

"Kerrigan who looks like Nancy."

Grandma arrives at Dom, saying, "This is Cecily's husband, Dominic."

Cecily's husband. The words, the concept, the truth is still so new. Impossible, except it's not.

I wait for Rainbow's wordy trick to remember Dominic,

but it doesn't come. Perhaps she has run out of creativity, because all she says is, "Nice to meet you."

Dominic politely greets her.

"You're not cool enough for a mnemonic device," I murmur.

"I'm devastated," he murmurs back.

Grandma takes charge, marching us to the massive motor home. The man who drove the behemoth steps out. He spends ten minutes walking us around the RV, pointing out the retractable awning, the outdoor lights and water hookup, the slide outs and stabilizer jacks. When he gets to the part about operating the vehicle, I tune in despite having decided I wouldn't. For the good of the group, I should probably know. The most important considerations are a wider turning radius, increased braking distance, and relying on mirrors. Despite understanding all this, the idea of driving such a large vehicle terrifies me. Like kickball in elementary school, I hope I am chosen last.

When the man finishes explaining everything to us, he walks to a nearby vehicle, where someone sits in the driver's seat, wearing the same collared shirt as him. Both men wave at my grandmother, and the car pulls into morning traffic.

"We're almost ready," Grandma says, excitement lacing through her tone. "Let's go inside and get ourselves oriented, then I have something I want to show you."

CHAPTER 24

Cecily

"I wasn't expecting it to be so big," Kerrigan says when we walk into the motor home.

There is a collective pause as we try to figure out if we're supposed to capitalize on the obvious opportunity to make a joke.

"For the love," Grandma huffs. "Someone say it."

"Not me." Duke points at himself. "I'm not saying that to my sister."

"Daughter," my dad explains, shrugging. My mom looks away, lips pursed.

Everyone glances at Dominic, who does a half eye roll and reluctantly says, "That's what she said." He glances around. "Can we move on now?"

Grandma starts pointing out shelves and various features.

"What's wrong?" I ask Dom in a quiet voice, jostling him with my elbow. "You don't like dick jokes?"

"A good dick joke has a time and a place."

"And this?" I circle a lone finger in the air.

He frowns disapprovingly. "Neither."

"Interesting. Who knew you had strict parameters for jokes about schlongs? I didn't. It wasn't on your All About Me."

Dom bites the inside of his lower lip. I've come to learn this means he is holding back a laugh. "Weird," he says, "Isn't that considered basic information about a person?"

Now I'm the one trying to hold it together. "I thought so."

Is this...*flirting*? It might be. In fact, it's feeling a little like the first time we met. Easy. Playful. Enjoyable.

Wow. Ok. I need to be careful. Dom is dangerous.

Dangerous Dom. My mnemonic device.

"What's going on in that head of yours? You're smiling at something." Dom traces a fingertip against my head, around my ear. A shiver rolls through me.

Dangerous Dom.

I have to be careful. We're only keeping this up for a few more weeks. He'll return to New York City, a recently annulled marriage tucked into his memories. We'll be a cautionary tale. The punchline of a joke.

I clear my throat and turn my head away from his touch. His hand drops to his side, all traces of flirtatiousness disappearing from his face.

A terse breath of air streams from his nose. "You know, Menace, with you it's always two steps forward, and one step back."

I should step away, pretend I didn't hear him. It's impossible, though. There's something in me, mulish and masochistic. If I can't have the last word, I at least need to say one more thing.

I look up at him, at the hard angle of his jawline. Those

blue eyes that look just a little bit defeated. I say, "Even at that pace, you're still making progress."

Before he can respond, I turn away, allowing Kerrigan to pull me into her *oohs* and *ahhs* over the hidden compartments in the kitchen.

"This expandable pantry," she says, pulling out a vertical drawer. It bumps my mom's backside, and she takes a step away. "Sorry, Mom. Check out this cutting board," Kerrigan practically squeals, extending a board from below the counter. "The motor home is basically a treasure hunt."

Kerrigan is enjoying this more than any other member of my family, but everybody is making an effort. Duke is poking through the bedroom at the back, remarking how much space there is. My dad has located a cabinet stocked with games, and he's already pulled out three and placed them on the dinette. Rainbow stands alone next to the door, hands clasped and hanging loosely in front of her.

In the middle of it all, stands my grandma. And she is beaming. There is nothing Savage Grandma loves more than the successful execution of an idea.

"Ok, everyone, listen up," Grandma says. She waits as Duke filters in from the bedroom, and then looks at Rainbow. Rainbow bends, rummaging through a ditzy-flower printed oversized tote at her feet. She comes away with a shiny white three-ring binder.

Grandma takes it from her outstretched hands. She holds it aloft, showing it off like a line judge in a tennis match.

Slipped into the clear plastic sleeve on the front of the binder is a piece of paper, a full sentence printed in bold, black font.

We're going to have fun, DAMMIT.

"This is our trip guide," Grandma says. "Travel schedule, destination information, booking confirmations, everything. You have a question about this trip? Look in here. If you ask me a question that can be answered by looking in here, I'm going to tell you to quit being an idiot and look in the binder. And"—Grandma glances at me and Dom—"I had a separate one made for you since you won't be traveling with us at first."

Rainbow, ready like an assistant and not a death doula, hands over an identical binder.

"Thanks," I murmur. I open it an inch, but Grandma snaps it shut.

"No time for perusing," she announces. "We're already behind schedule. At this rate we won't make it to Tucson until the middle of the afternoon."

Tucson? Tucson is our first stop? I was assuming we'd head north, but Tucson is in the southeastern corner of Arizona.

"Shoo," Grandma says to me and Dom. Rainbow takes the binder from her hands, present and ready like a third hand.

Hands-free now, Grandma makes the shooing motion. "Get on the road."

We back up. Dom bumps into the fold-out table, and my calves hit a chair. Looking around at the faces of my family, I suddenly feel extra grateful to be using the Bentley to start the road trip. Duke's face looks pained. He's already pulling his laptop from his bag, ready to work. My dad looks bereft, a king without his proverbial castle. He is always the boss, the ringmaster, running the show and ordering around everyone in his vicinity. But not now. He's here for the same reason as the rest of us, and he doesn't get to tell everyone what to do. He's our equal, and it's obvious he has no idea what to do next. Kerrigan retreats to the bedroom, flopping down onto the bed. She props her head on her hand so she can still sip her latte.

"You're driving this thing," Grandma says to my dad. "You look like you need something to do."

My dad probably has a response, but he holds it back. Wise man.

"And you." Grandma points at my mom. "You're riding shotgun."

I'd be shocked if my mom knows the term 'riding shot-gun'. But, apparently she does, because she dutifully walks to the front of the massive vehicle and drops into the passenger seat.

"Settled." Grandma nods, pleased. Like a mother duck getting her *brood* in a row.

Dom and I step down from the motor home, blinking into the bright sun. We turn around when Grandma says, "You'll need this." She reaches into a hidden pocket in her caftan, coming away with a key and tossing it at Dom. "Treat her well."

Dom catches it. "I won't treat Cecily with anything but the utmost care."

He sounds like some kind of earnest superhero. My heart smacks my breastbone. *Traitor*.

"That was sweet," Kerrigan yells from the bedroom. She's probably already watching the Moose-cam.

Grandma beams and grips the doorframe. The sun glints in her eyes, her excited smile. "You're a good man, Dominic. But I wasn't talking about my granddaughter."

She waves behind our heads to the Bentley. "I was talking about my car. Bernice. She gets premium fuel only."

"Of course." Dom nods, hiding his smile. "I'll take good care of Bernice."

"You'll make it to our first destination before we do. I've already arranged for an early check-in."

"Thanks, Grandma," I say, holding the binder to my chest.

We turn for the car, but Grandma calls my name. Dom doesn't turn back with me. He keeps on walking to *Bernice.*

"Yeah?" I ask. She has a sly look on her face.

"You're going to get there *first*," she repeats, emphasizing the word.

"I know," I drawl.

"So," she says, "It's a lot to ask of your new husband to go on a road trip like this. Make sure you properly thank him. That's the best marriage advice I can give. Keep him *properly thunked.*"

My face heats, and I know it's not the sunshine pouring down on me. "I'll be sure to say thank you."

"You'd better do more than that, Cecily." Grandma grins. She turns her midsection in a circle, but the boxy caftan keeps it from appearing too suggestive. "Give him the old razzle dazzle."

I swear I hear Dom cough lightly behind me. And me? I'll never forget the sight of my grandmother gyrating her hips in the doorframe of a motor home.

"Safe travels, Grandma," I say pointedly, refusing to acknowledge her lascivious suggestion.

She laughs and steps back from the door. Rainbow appears, leaning out and reaching for the door handle. Her eyes meet mine briefly before the door closes, and I fight the urge to shout a curse word at her.

Dom places our bags in the car's trunk. He lays the handwritten Just Married sign on top.

"What are the chances you didn't hear that last part?" I ask.

"Zero," he says, stepping back and closing the trunk. Then he, and I wish I were kidding about this, walks the length of the car, fingertips caressing the frame. When he gets to the side mirror, he cups it like a boob.

Crossing my arms, I exhale a gusty sigh. "Are you about done fondling Bernice?"

He yanks his hand back like he's been burned. "That was not fondling. That was called *appreciating*."

"What's that, Bernice?" I cup a hand around my ear and stretch toward the car. "You'd like to report an assault?"

Dom shoots me an annoyed glare, but there's something softer hiding behind it. He steps around to the passenger side, his movements slow, deliberate, his arm brushing softly against mine before coming to a stop in front of me.

He opens the car door with a small, almost reluctant smile, eyes locked on mine as our bodies brush once more just before I slide inside. I pull my seat belt around me, clicking it into place, and hope Dom doesn't notice the way he throws me off my game.

Dom folds his big body in the car. My purse goes on the floor beside my feet, and the binder finds a safe home on my lap. Dom looks over at me through the open space between us. He reaches into his pocket, produces a pair of brown aviators, and slides them on.

Lethal. Dom in sunglasses should be illegal.

I'm doing everything I can to school my reaction, but it's a lot of work to keep my libido from overtaking my body. That amorous floozy wants out.

"You ready to hit the road with the top down?" Dom asks, blessedly unaware of the meltdown I'm having.

"Ready," I answer, digging through my purse and coming up with a brown hair tie. Fingers working deftly, I thread my hair into a braid and tie off the end. I slip on my own sunglasses and turn to Dom. He has been watching me, one hand on the wheel, the other forearm resting on the center console.

"Don't mind if I speed," he says, smirking. "I've got some razzle dazzle in my future, and the prospect has given me a lead foot."

I flip him the middle finger, even as an ache blooms low in my belly. He laughs, buckles up, and presses a button. The car roars to life. I've been in Savage Grandma's Bentley a hundred times, but it's no less impressive today. Bernice is a babe.

Dom looks around the car, orienting himself. He pokes at the console, turns knobs. He palms the steering wheel, hand gliding in one full circle, and *why is that hot*?

His gaze snags on mine across the small space, and the way I like it infuriates me. "If you're finished making sweet love to Bernice, can we get on the road?"

Dom tosses a reproachful look my direction. "Careful, Mrs. Bellinger. I won't suffer an accusation that I've plea-sured any woman but my wife."

I melt, right into my plush leather seat. My form remains, but my substance is gone.

That's when I know, with total clarity, I won't survive these next three weeks with Dom if he's saying things like that. It's critical that I push this man away, or I will combust. Right in front of my family, on this road trip from hell. "Dominic Bellinger." I flick one of his knuckles. "I. Loathe. You."

He shows no response, to my flick or my pronouncement. "Do you?"

"With a passion."

"Passion, huh? Interesting word choice."

I'd love to volley a response, but I don't. I can't show Dom how deeply he affects me, in all ways.

Dom shifts into Drive, and eases us onto the road.

The start of our road trip. I glance down at the binder in my lap.

We're going to have fun, DAMMIT.

CHAPTER 25

Dominic

CECILY IS A STATUE. OTHER THAN PUNCHING OUR destination into the maps app on my phone and showing it to me, there's been no talking. An open-top convertible doesn't make for great conversation anyhow. We've been driving an hour, and I've just exited the Phoenix city limits. Slowly, the city transformed, the homes giving way to farms, and farms giving way to desert. It's nothing but teddy bear cholla and saguaros as far as the eye can see, interrupted only by mountains jutting up from seemingly nowhere.

It's been a while since I've lived here, and last night I took time to learn about the growth and changes around the state in the last few years. I don't know our route yet, and until I look through Ophelia's binder, I still won't. From memory, I know there isn't much between Phoenix and Tucson except a couple towns and gas stations. Other than that, it will be blowing winds and tumbleweeds.

We drive on, and when the fuel gauge needle reads one

third of a tank, I take the next exit for a gas station. I've never run out of gas, and my first time won't be with Cecily in the car.

The road noise quiets with every mile we decelerate. Cecily runs her hands over her head, smoothing her braid.

"You look good," I tell her, and when her eyebrows raise I hurry to add, "Your hair. It's windswept, but not in a bad way." Sort of in a romantic, older movie type of way, but I'm not going to say that.

Cecily eyes my hair. "Well, you, Dominic, should have chosen a braid, because you are giving the Bride of Frankenstein a run for her money."

I go still as her hand reaches for me, fingers running through my hair. Swallowing a groan as her fingernails lightly scrape over my scalp is probably the hardest thing I've ever had to do.

She takes back her hand, and to save myself from putting my head in her lap and begging for more, I tell her, "I spaced getting a haircut before leaving New York City a few days ago." I've been seeing Natty the barber ever since I landed in the Big Apple, and the idea of trying a new barber puts fear in me. How could anybody else do a good job with these waves? Natty knows just what I want, to the point that I no longer have to utter a word. A man's relationship with his barber is not easily replicable, but three more weeks of this rat's nest might have me desperate enough to go for it. I can't walk around having bad hair day after bad hair day. Not when...what, exactly? Cecily doesn't care. I'm almost positive Cecily is physically attracted to me, but she doesn't *care*. About me, or my hair.

"I'm thinking of growing it out," I say, bringing the car to a stop.

Cecily turns to me, her first full-on gaze since we left Phoenix. "You should grow it out so long that it tickles your ass."

Stone-faced, I say, "I do enjoy ass-tickling."

Cecily's eyes crease like she wants to laugh, but she's so good at remaining stoic. Too good. I've learned the best way to infiltrate these walls of hers is to surprise her. With words. With touch. I nearly put my hand on the small of her back when we were leaving the coffeehouse this morning, but decided against it. It felt natural to reach out and touch her, something I would do if she were really mine.

"I guess I know what to get you for your birthday," Cecily says, flipping down the car's visor.

"A voucher for a session of ass-tickling with none other than yours truly?"

Cecily wipes under her eyes, unperturbed. "If you present your bare ass to me, tickling will be last on the list of things I'll do."

My eyebrows bounce twice, for good, pervy measure. "Kinky."

She blows a hard breath and makes a sound like she's had it with me. "You're disgusting."

I resist the urge to celebrate. I finally got her. Lifting my hands in innocence, I say, "You're the one who said—"

"I know what I said," she mutters, throwing open her car door. "Come on, Errand Boy."

Back to Errand Boy? Interesting.

Grabbing the pump for premium fuel, I insert the nozzle into the car. Cecily waits for me beside the trunk, examining her nails. Without looking up, she asks, "Do you want to grab a snack or drink inside? Road trips aren't complete without snacks."

"Sure. Let me put Bernice's top on."

Cecily laughs.

I palm my chest. "Forgive my heart attack. I wasn't expecting you to permit yourself to laugh at a joke I've made."

Cecily's head cocks sideways, a tendril of escaped hair sweeping the creamy expanse of exposed neck. "When something is funny, Dominic, I laugh. Perhaps you're simply not as funny as you think."

"Perhaps," I concede. "Or maybe you're too fucking ornery to let me think making you smile is in the realm of possibility."

Instead of waiting for a response from her, I slide into the driver's seat, locate the convertible top switch on the center console, and hold it. When the top is secure, Cecily and I walk into the convenience store that appears to be in the middle of nowhere.

"This place is cute," Cecily says when she finds me standing in front of a wire display rack of desert-themed postcards.

The place is kitschy, the walls decorated with old license plates from various states and Mexico. In the spaces where there aren't license plates, there are shiny silver hubcaps.

Cecily lopes across the place, stopping in front of a wall of machines churning bright, artificially colored Icee drinks. My eyes remain on her. She wears cut-off jean shorts, frayed at the edges, and a white tank top. On her wrists are those gold bracelets she favors. In her ears, she wears simple gold hoops. Yes, I studied her on the drive. I can't help it. She's gorgeous.

I glance away, in case she catches me staring and gives me grief about it, and my gaze lands on a man walking through the glass double doors. I watch him register Cecily's presence. Watch his eyes indulgently peruse her body. My blood heats the longer his eyes remain on her. Back turned, she is none the wiser.

The man is average height, soft around the middle, a sweat-stained trucker hat clinging to his hairless head. I'd place him in his mid-forties. I'll also place him in a grave if he does anything to hurt Cecily.

"Pretty little car for a pretty little woman," I hear him say. He sounds as slimy as he looks.

Cecily's head snaps to the man, now only a few feet from her. She clocks him, gazes at him with a face full of disinterest for a solid two seconds, then looks away. I know what it's like to be on the receiving end of Cecily's glares. It should be enough to send a man scurrying.

But of course, this is not just any man. This is someone who believes he is entitled to Cecily's attention. He grins at the side of her face, and it's downright lecherous. Well, damn. I've never killed a man, but I suppose there is a first for everything.

"Sugar, how'd you know I like it when women play hard to get?"

The muscles in Cecily's back bunch, and then her shoulders square. "Just yesterday I was thinking about how it's been too long since the human equivalent of a foul stench hit on me. Thanks for bringing me up-to-date."

Her voice is jaunty and laced with venom. It takes the man a moment to process what she has said, but not me. I hold an advanced degree in Cecily's razor-tongued remarks.

His face turns from ugly to uglier.

My feet are moving, apparently of their own volition because I don't remember thinking about walking. I'm in motion, skirting the end of an aisle with a large candy display, and then I'm there, at Cecily's side. Wrapping an arm around her trim waist, I press a kiss to the side of her head. Somewhere in the back of my mind I register how good she smells, but I can't spend more than a nanosecond on the thought.

"Hey, babe," I say against her head. "Which flavor did you decide on?"

Cecily melts into my chest. She fits me. So perfectly. Her dips, my curves. Concave and convex.

She looks up. A soft breath comes from her parted lips. Her brown eyes hold gratitude, and then give way to something else. Something stronger, less inhibited. Something I know she does not want to feel.

"A fire drill," she finally answers. "A little of every flavor."

"I hope you plan on sharing." I drag two knuckles along her jaw.

The tiniest hard breath escapes her, and if I weren't this close, I'd never hear it.

"Twenty on pump three," I hear from somewhere behind me. The lecher, I'm assuming. The bell above the door dings, signaling his exit.

I step away from Cecily. Not that I want to, because I absolutely do not, but Cecily's already dealt with one asshole thinking he has a right to her space. She doesn't need a second man trying to take what isn't his.

"Thank you," she says, grabbing the largest plastic cup from its sleeve under the counter. "He was going to be a handful."

"I am your husband," I remind her, palming the very beginning of stubble that runs over my cheeks. "I promised to protect you."

"You sure did," Cecily murmurs, stepping up to the first nozzle and positioning her cup beneath. She goes down the line, creating a layered drink that likely tastes like sweetened battery acid.

When she finishes securing the top, we make our way to the cashier. Cecily snags two more items just before we get to the checkout counter. I do the same. A bottle of water and Corn Nuts.

The cashier says very little other than a mandatory and lackluster greeting. I press my credit card to the reader, and when we step out into the midday sun, Cecily stops out of the way of the door and says, "Thank you. We should probably take turns paying. Unless we're in front of my family, then you can pay, and I'll pay you back."

I'm already shaking my head before she finishes her sentence. "No. Sorry. I'm old-fashioned."

"Are you sure about that?" She nods her head at Bernice. "Don't I appear to have deep pockets?"

"Are you flush with cash?"

"No. I don't accept money from my parents. Or my grandma, though I will admit she loaned me the money to put a deposit down on my apartment."

How do I explain to Cecily that although she is my wife in name only, this is important to me? Tightening my grip on my bottle of water, I say, "I didn't grow up with a lot, and it embarrassed me. Not that I didn't have things, but that I couldn't invite a friend out to dinner." Never mind how infrequently we went out to a restaurant. *Overpriced*, my dad would declare. *Shit service, shit food, and tiny portions.* I remember wondering why he would want bigger portions of shit food.

Cecily's face softens. Her head tilts. She's listening intently.

"It matters to me that I pay for you, ok? Whether that's wrong, or right, I don't know." I shrug. "I only know that it matters to me."

"Ok." Cecily nods. "I was trying to buy a present for your heroics in there, but since you paid for it, I guess I'll say that I picked it out for you."

She holds out her hand, and in her open palm lies a rectangular-shaped yellow lollipop. Suspended in the center of the candy is a small scorpion.

"The choices in there weren't exactly robust," Cecily says, offering the kind of smile I've yet to see on her face before now. Bashful.

"I love it," I tell her, taking the treat. "Even if it is disturbing." Sunlight beams through as I hold it up by the stick, revealing tiny striations in the candy.

It's only a piece of weird candy, but the gesture brings a tightness to my chest, my throat. It's so sweet, so unexpected. "Thank you," I tell her, forcing the emotion from my voice.

"You're welcome," she says. "Thanks for saving me from having to remember my old Krav Maga lessons."

She heads for the attention-getting ride that nearly prompted my first murder, and I follow, holding on to that little martial arts tidbit she offered. I disconnect the nozzle from the car and secure the gas cap, then slide into the car where Cecily waits. I point at the top, wordlessly asking if she wants it retracted.

"No," she answers. "It'll be harder to eat our snacks." She pulls a bag of Bugles from the thin plastic gas station bag, passing me the ranch-flavored Corn Nuts I snagged in haste.

"Are you well-trained?" I ask, ripping open the bag like a caveman and tossing back a handful. I'd never eat these if Cecily and I were really together. Too much garlic.

"In Krav Maga?" she asks, opening her bag of snacks. "I was. I'm not anymore."

I nod, watching her pluck out a single crunchy corn snack and, instead of eating it like a normal person, places the cone-shape on the pinky finger of her opposite hand.

"It's probably something that comes back to you when you need it," I say, mesmerized by her process. Cone-shaped corn snacks now adorn every finger on her right hand.

She nods sagely. "Very true. And you'd do well to remember that for the next three weeks." She leans closer. Taps the end of my nose with the tip of a Bugle. "It's a bad day to be a Bugle," she says, biting one snack off a finger.

"It appears so," I answer, throwing in another handful of Corn Nuts so I don't say something I regret. Namely, *Can I be a Bugle?*

I shift into Drive and make my way back to the freeway.

Cecily proceeds to demolish the other four. She washes them down with her fire drill Icee.

Wordlessly she offers me the drink. "I already drank from it, so you know I didn't poison it."

I take it from her, grimacing at the injection of sugar when I take a sip. She smirks, and I pretend I'm not thinking about the way my lips were on something that was in her mouth only a moment ago.

CHAPTER 26

Cecily

I OPENED THE BINDER WITH ONE HOUR REMAINING IN THE drive. I wish I hadn't. I am officially freaking out.

Page one. Stop one. I didn't make it past the first page. The first reservation, even.

Cecily and Dominic - King bed.

"You ok over there?" Dom asks, sending me a worried gaze before returning his eyes to the road. "If you're going to be sick, let me know. I'll pull over."

Do I look green? Maybe I am an unflattering shade of putrid, but it has nothing to do with the Bugles I powered through.

"Dom," I begin, tone serious. "Please stay calm when I tell you this." Deep breath. "My grandma has booked us a room that only has one bed."

How in the world did I not see this coming? I look at Dom, ready to see my alarm mirrored in his expression. But, no.

He's making a face that can only be described as *Yeah, well, what did you think was going to happen?*

"Hello?" I ask. "Feel free to join me in the tsunami of dismay I'm experiencing over here."

Dom rubs his cheeks with a palm. "I admit I hadn't thought about it, but now that I am, it makes sense. From her perspective, why wouldn't we sleep in a bed together? We're married."

"*We're married*," I parrot. "Dom, how are we going to share a bed?"

"We've already shared a bed once," he points out. "In Vegas."

"Yes, but I didn't know I was sharing a bed with you. I was drunk, remember? This is vastly different." My breath comes faster. I cannot share a bed with Dom. It'll be too much. Too difficult. This is really asking a lot of my self-control. My brain hates him, but my body is being very stubborn about receiving that message. "When we go to get an annulment, what if they ask us if we've been sleeping together?"

"I don't think sleeping in a bed at the same time is what they mean when they ask that question. If they ask it at all."

I sit up in the seat. "Will they?"

"I'm assuming so, but I don't know for certain," Dom says, patience sounding forced. "You're my first annulment."

I drop back into my seat. "I don't see a way around this. Unless you sleep on the floor."

"I will not sleep on the floor."

"Why?"

"I like my back, thank you very much. If I'm going to be driving to different destinations until we give Bernice back, I prefer to keep my back pain-free."

"I guess." I cross my arms as hare-brained ideas pass through my mind. "Maybe we could find an empty room and con one of the hotel staff into letting you use it. You could put that pretty face to work." As soon as the words leave my mouth, I know I'm in for it.

"You think I have a pretty face?" Dom asks.

I sigh, long and loud, to let him know how obnoxious I find this. "You are mathematically good-looking."

"Explain."

"Your face is symmetrical." I gesture around my face. "Your nose has a pleasing slope."

"Careful, Menace. You know what they say."

"What's that?"

"Compliments lead to softened feelings, and that's a threat to all that loathing you feel for me."

"Don't you worry, Errand Boy. My hard feelings are in no jeopardy of diminishing."

"Good. For a second there..." He trails off, leaving my thoughts flailing like a trapeze artist suffering a malfunction.

This is his way of communicating that although he is gallant, and likes to flirt, and is extraordinarily caring, he has no interest in me beyond surviving these next few weeks and annulling our marriage. It's imperative I keep that top of mind.

Oddly, it makes the whole only one bed scenario more palatable. The only feelings I'll be fighting in bed at night will be mine.

"This forces a conversation we need to have anyway," I declare, composing myself. "What are the parameters around public displays of affection? We're not selling this relationship, so it's not like we need to go hard."

Dom nods, quietly focused on passing a semi-truck. When we're cleared, he says, "I'll follow your lead. I'm still not sure why you didn't tell your family the truth from the beginning."

"Because I hated the way my dad assumed he would control what was going to happen. How he instructed us to get an annulment, without asking questions. How could he assume I would blindly follow his directive?"

Dom's phone belts out an instruction to exit the freeway at the next ramp, and he complies. "Probably because a lot of people do." He leans forward to check the traffic from the left before easing the car right.

I scoff. "His employees, sure. But not me."

Dom only nods, and it makes me realize we have not talked about his parents and if he told them what we did. "I'm sorry I didn't think to ask about that night you had dinner with your parents." I was busy making Malibu Dom, but that probably doesn't need mentioning right now. "Did you tell them what we did?"

"Yeah." Something in his demeanor changes. Perhaps it's his shoulders, the way they curl in a degree. For reasons I do not understand, his parents are a touchy subject. "My dad thought it was hilarious. He asked if he can meet you. My mom had a far more expected and appropriate reaction."

"Horrified?" I ask.

"She called it an oopsie." His jaw clenches.

"To be fair," I point out, "I called it an oopsie that first morning, too."

"I recall," he says dryly. "It was a poor decision, sure, but an oopsie is when you throw a football to a friend but it sails through their hands and hits someone nearby in the head. It's unintentional."

I look out the window, getting my bearings. The University of Arizona campus is on my right, the first building a terra cotta brick structure lined in tall, skinny palm trees. A metal sign reads Architecture & Landscape Architecture.

"If an oopsie is unintentional, and you wouldn't call us an oopsie, does that mean you intended to marry me, Dominic?"

We slow for a red light. The car in front of us has a bumper sticker that says Free Hugs.

Dominic presses his forearm on the center console, leaning over it to capture my gaze. It's like he wants to make sure I see him when he says, "In the moment, yes. I did."

CHAPTER 27

Dominic

Hand to God, I do not know if I should have told Cecily that.

It takes our actions and removes every shred of *we were drunk and didn't know what we were doing.*

For me, anyway.

Cecily grew quiet after that, and I don't blame her. I know she wrestles with everything that has transpired between us. The good date that soured, that night in Vegas, waking up to find out we'd married. And now this road trip, underscored by the certain loss of her grandmother in the not-too-distant future. It's a lot to handle.

The city of Tucson, with its traffic and restaurants and people, yields to desert scenery. Bigger homes, spaced further apart. A wildlife center. When Cecily was in the bathroom at the gas station, I took a minute to tap on the map she'd text me and look at where we're staying and the surrounding area. There wasn't enough time to look at street views of anything, so I have only a basic idea of where we're headed.

It's a two-lane road all the way there, interrupted once in a while by a yellow road sign showing a man on a horse. It's not as if I've never seen these signs before, some parts of Scottsdale still have them, but it's a reminder of how far out of Phoenix we are.

"Almost there," I tell Cecily.

She reaches for the binder, flipping it open to the first page and reading from a printout. "Nestled among the Rincon Mountains and adjacent to Saguaro National Park and Coronado National Forest, Tanque Verde Ranch is one of America's old-time cattle and guest ranches." Cecily looks up, an excited twinkle in her eyes. "It's a dude ranch."

A dude ranch? I could get into that.

My phone, propped up in the center console, spouts a direction I no longer need. "I'll close out the map," Cecily says, grabbing my phone. Finger poised, she pauses. Her eyebrows tug together. "My grandma sent you a text."

"Read it, please."

Cecily taps the text notification, and our conversation opens. "She says they are an hour away. Kerrigan refused to use the bathroom in the motor home, and it took everyone a long time to choose snacks at the convenience store."

"I wonder if Duke had to defend anybody's honor while they were at it." We come to a fork in the road, and I go right, following the unassuming wooden sign for Tanque Verde Ranch. "This is—"

"You talk to my grandma?"

"What?" I come to a stop in the parking lot for a family to walk past. They wave a hand in thanks, and I wave back.

Cecily's finger drags the length of the screen. "Dominic, you talk to my grandma! Enough that I had to scroll three times to reach the beginning."

"Of course I talk to her, Cecily. She's my supplier."

Cecily turns her head to me slowly, sending me a look that could curdle milk. "No getting high on this trip. I need you on your A-game."

"It was a joke," I mutter, making my way to the far end of the parking lot. I don't want Bernice next to any cars, or more accurately, car doors.

When we're in Park, I turn to Cecily. "You can read every text I've exchanged with Ophelia, ok? It's not like I've said anything bad about you, because there is nothing bad to say about you. And I haven't told her about our marriage, because that's our business. She asked me for my number that day at her house because she wanted to include it in the information she was putting together for the trip. And then she sent me a message the next day, asking about food allergies and preferences." I gesture at the phone. "Look for yourself."

Cecily skims the phone. "You asked her how she was feeling."

"Should I not have?" I'm so confused.

Emotion floods Cecily's voice. "It was nice of you. Thank you for doing that. For checking on her." She takes a deep breath and replaces my phone in the console, then looks around. "Why are we parked so far from the entrance?"

"Away from cars that could dent Bernice, but also where there's enough space so that giant motor home can park near us."

We get out of the car, and Cecily meets me at the back. I

pop the trunk, hand Cecily the Just Married sign, and grab our luggage. We both brought soft-sided bags with handles, not a rolling suitcase in sight. Cecily places the sign on the now-empty floor of the trunk, then shoulders her purse and larger travel bag, binder clutched to her chest. She reaches for her luggage, but I shrug her off. "I've got it."

She gives me a look. "Are you going to carry my bag for three weeks?"

"No. Sometimes I'll set it down."

She turns away to keep me from seeing her smile. Too late. I glimpsed it.

We check in at reception and are led down a cactus-lined path to a group of muted salmon-pink casitas. Each one has a seating area out front with a rough-hewn wood overhang. It's charming and western and our home for the next two days.

The receptionist opens the door with an actual key, which she places on the small table inside the door. "Let us know if you need anything. Please enjoy your stay."

Then she's gone, and there's nothing in the room but silence and a massive bed.

"Do you feel like it's staring at you?" Cecily asks, eyeing the bed.

"Sort of, yeah." I walk over, giving it a hip check. It doesn't budge. The frame is made of solid wood. "Maybe if we lie on it, we'll take away some of its power."

Cecily saunters over. She slides the hair tie from the bottom of her braid, positions it on her wrist, and runs her fingers through her hair. The gold bangles tinkle, ceasing as they fall down her forearm.

I swear I try not to stare at her, but her eyes are closed

while she massages her fingers over her scalp, and the motion lifts her chest, pushing it out a bit, and, yes I am a nice, respectful man, but I am also human. Humans like pretty things. I don't make the rules.

Cecily finishes her post-braid ritual. She hoists herself onto the tall bed, lying back on her elbows. Her legs stretch out, sleek and tan and toned in those denim cut-offs. "Let's get this over with," she says, patting the empty space beside her.

I'd love to, but now I have a bit of a problem. If I lay on that bed, Cecily is going to see how very much a certain part of my anatomy enjoyed watching her not-intended-to-be-sensual bedside grooming.

I roll back on my heels. The move is really just a covert way for me to place my hands in my pockets and tent the front of my shorts. "I'm going to freshen up first."

Cecily's eyes squint in confusion. "You know it was your idea to get on this bed, right?"

"Mm-hmm," I say, trying to see but not see Cecily's shape on that bed. Her dark hair wavy from her braid, spilling out behind her.

People chewing with their mouths open.

How hot dogs are made.

In-grown toenails.

Nothing is working. That fucker is still punching the front of my shorts.

Cecily frowns and rolls over onto her side. She props her head up on her hand, arm bent. Gravity does its job, weighing down her breasts. They are round and full and there's now a deep line of cleavage, reducing me to a pubescent male. Fuck you, gravity.

"Dominic—" My name is all that Cecily can get out,

because her eyes are level with my crotch. And, despite my best efforts at concealment, Cecily has clocked my raging erection.

"Oh," she says, the blush on her cheeks instantaneous.

It cannot be any more crimson than the heat I feel rushing over me. Is it possible for the entire body to blush, and have it not be from excess niacin or an allergic reaction? Because, damn, do I feel hot all over.

She sits up quickly, cross-legged on the printed bedspread. "I'm gonna—" Her eyes flash around the room. She must decide on something, because she launches herself off the bed. "Take a walk," she says, with too much gusto. "You, uhh—" She pauses to slide her feet into the shoes she discarded by the door. "You do you. Literally."

Cecily flees.

My head drops. Perhaps, when I step through the bathroom door, I will be thrust into a different world. I'll even take a sinkhole.

I'm a grown man. Persistent and unrelenting hard-ons should be something I can handle. I step into the bathroom (no sinkhole, no portals), and close the door behind me. Gripping the edge of the bathroom sink, I force my gaze to the front of my shorts.

Wow. No wonder Cecily escaped. This thing was pointed right at her.

I take so many deep breaths, I lose count. In for four, out for four. I should be the most relaxed man in the desert southwest, but I'm not. This thing will not go down. I turn around, and face the door.

At this point, there is only one solution. I have to act fast, because who knows how long Cecily's walk will be?

Turns out, that's not a problem. With my left hand

pressed against the wooden door, I take matters into my own, ahem, hand. Closing my eyes, I chase the edge of something sharp and carnal and necessary. Too much of Cecily lingers in my system, and in a shockingly short amount of time, I am relieved of my problem. When it's over, I rest my forehead against the door, heart rate lowering to a steady rhythm.

The alleviation is tantamount to the realization quickly soaking through my post-orgasm stupor. What just happened does not bode well for the next three weeks. All it took was Cecily to shake out her hair and I was a goner. What am I going to do, dissolve into a puddle when I see Cecily in her pajamas? What if I catch a glimpse of her changing? It's very possible that for the next three weeks I'm going to have to add *rub one out* to my morning routine. Not even for pleasure, but for survival.

What have I gotten myself into?

CHAPTER 28

Cecily

I TURNED MY WALK INTO A PERUSAL AROUND THE GROUNDS OF the ranch. There's a pool I'd love to put to use later, a spa, restaurants, and endless tiny lizards darting across the paths. I lost count at twenty.

Why am I spending time counting lizards? Because there was a lizard of a totally different variety back in my room. I'm nearing death just thinking about it. About Dom. The way he tried so hard to keep me clueless, and then once I clued in, the way he blushed like he'd experienced a wardrobe malfunction. If it hadn't been for the way he reacted, I would've made light of the situation, or reminded him it's simply blood flow. I can't deny the knot of pressure I felt low in my belly at the sight of him. A teeny, tiny part of me entertained the teeniest, tiniest, most fleeting thought of helping him relieve it. But that didn't come to me until I'd stepped out the door and made my way under a palo verde tree.

So. Here I am. Sitting on a bench near the Dog House Saloon. Trying and failing not to think of Dom's bulge.

It sounds like the name of a landmark. Dom's Bulge.

I laugh to myself. I can't help it. That was funny.

"Are you smiling for the reason I think?" Dom's voice comes to me, timid. I don't think I've heard him sound that way before. It's...endearing.

Gripping the edge of the bench with my hands on either side of my leg, I lean forward and peer left, watching Dom walk up. "Yes, but only because I made myself laugh."

"That's not awesome," Dom says, walking closer. "That is, in fact, one of the worst things I could hear."

He is so embarrassed, it makes me want to hug him. But what if I hug him and it happens again? Is that a thing? Can it happen in succession? I'm assuming he tired the fellow out, but what if he only willed it away?

No touching, then.

"Not laughing at you," I clarify.

Dom stops in front of me, blocking the sun from shining in my eyes. It makes the outline of his body appear to shine, like the world's hottest, most mortified angel. "Should I ask what made you laugh?"

"That depends."

"On?"

"On whether you agree to stop feeling embarrassed and laugh with me."

"Easy for you to say. You weren't the one with a *physical response* to something."

I pretend to be scandalized, leaning forward and holding onto the bench on either side of my thighs. "What was it exactly? The rustic, western vibes? The framed wall art of the old cowboy in the bathtub?"

Dom narrows his eyes. "You know what it was. I'm sure your ego is feeling very stroked right now."

I raise an eyebrow.

He huffs. "I heard it."

"My ego isn't supersize now, if that's what you're implying. I didn't presume it was me who made you have a *physical response*."

He looks at the ground, and then bumps my sandaled foot with his sneakered one. "It was the way you ran your fingers through your hair," he admits.

I flinch. That's not at all what I was expecting. No mention of breasts, or me bending over to pick up something, or any other low-hanging fruit.

"It was pretty," he adds, like he needs to explain what he liked about the motion. "Feminine." He sighs. "I don't know. But that's what started it. And I could've dealt with it, but then you got on the bed, and, yeah."

I'm nodding, listening, absorbing everything he has to say. "Dom," I begin, folding my hands in my lap and sitting up primly. "I feel in this situation you are due some recompense. So, I promise you, at some point in these next few weeks, I will get a violent lady boner for which I am in agony over."

His mouth tugs up in a grin. "How can you promise such a thing?"

"It won't be without work on your part." I shrug. "But I volunteer as tribute."

He offers a hand. I place my palm in his, and as we're shaking, I say, "Did you use this hand to—"

"This conversation is over," Dom declares, dropping my hand. "Let's go see if your family is almost here."

We make it one minute down the path when Dom says, "You didn't tell me how you made yourself laugh."

"I was thinking Dom's Bulge sounds like a landmark, but now I'm thinking it's more of a roadside attraction."

Dom laugh-coughs. "You know, Cecily, since we're making this a joke. Bulge can be turned into the anagram *bugle*."

I'm rearranging the letters in my head and seeing the truth to his statement when he says, "And we both know how much you love Bugles."

Dom spotted the motor home at the back of the parking lot before me, but I recognized my sister's happy shriek before Dom registered that a woman was not, in fact, being kidnapped. "That's the sound she makes when things thrill her," I warn Dom.

He frowns. "I wonder what sound she would make if she needed help."

"One would hope she'd yell *help*."

He ignores me. "Sounds like they're checking in."

We wander into the reception area and find my family straddling the tall, gleaming check-in desk. The young woman who walked us to our room an hour ago is most definitely checking out Duke. Gross, but objectively, I get it. Growing up, all my friends wanted to come to my house because they were hoping to catch a glimpse, or maybe even a frown, from my broody older brother.

From across the room, I lock eyes with my dad. He

dips his chin in greeting. My mother, standing beside him, must recognize his motion, because she follows where he's looking. A feeling resurfaces, niggling and insistent and so very unwelcome. A desire for her to smile at me. To acknowledge my existence. She doesn't, of course. She stares for a beat, then looks away.

I expected nothing more of her, and by doing so, her lack of acknowledgment doesn't hurt.

"Cecily!" my sister hollers. "Was that not the ugliest drive? Nothing between here and Phoenix but U-G-L-Y."

I give her a look, hoping to communicate her comment could be offensive to people overhearing her, and how could they not, given the yelling? She makes a face.

"But it's gorgeous in here!" she trills, hand gesturing around. She comes closer, wrapping me up and whispering in my ear, "So fugly, though, right?"

"Not pretty," I whisper back.

Grandma steps from the manager's office behind the check-in counter, her caftan swaying. Rainbow, whose name might as well be Shadow, follows. Mom, Dad, and Duke make their way over to us so we form a group. Grandma looks at me and Dom, bopping her shoulders a couple times before saying, "Did you two settle in ok?"

"We did, thank you," Dom answers smoothly. I try not to smile. Any expression of mirth will be perceived as recent razzling and dazzling.

"I was speaking with Garth, the manager." Grandma indicates behind her. Garth, a man in his fifties, gives us a perfunctory wave and smile. He might be the manager here, but I'm certain Savage Grandma is the boss right now.

"We're happy to have you all here with us," he says,

slipping into hospitality mode. "Please let our staff know if we can make your stay more enjoyable."

Kerrigan plucks a trifold brochure from a table and peruses it. "Does the trail ride come with this cowboy?" she asks, to nobody in particular. I lean over, finding there is indeed a handsome cowboy positioned on a horse in that cowboy way, hand perched on his thigh and reins loosely held in his grip.

The manager smiles knowingly, like this isn't the first time he's been asked the question. "That particular cowboy will not be leading the trail ride, but I'm sure you'll find Quint a satisfactory replacement. He's extremely knowledgeable about the area."

"Great," Kerrigan chirps. She replaces the brochure in the sleeve. When she sees me looking at her, she juts her lower lip out, whispering with certainty, "Quint is most definitely a grizzled old fart."

I do my best not to laugh, but beside me, Dom's shoulder moves.

Likely scared of more questions, Garth beats a hasty retreat into his office.

"Good job terrifying the manager," Duke says to Kerrigan.

"If he scares that easily, I don't know how much hope he has in this life."

Duke sends her a derisive look. "He is twice your age. I think he's doing just fine."

"Enough," Grandma says, and we all know when Grandma uses that tone of voice, we're teetering on thin ice. "I know Dom and Cecily have been here for an hour, but I'm ready to have a little alone time in my room. You all can do whatever you want, just don't be late for dinner."

"When is dinner? And where?" Kerrigan asks.

Rainbow answers for Grandma. "The primary restaurant on the property. Six o'clock."

At first I feel cross at how Rainbow is speaking for my grandma, but when I look closer at my grandma's face, exhaustion sits heavy in her eyes. Rainbow must know this, must understand when it is ok for her to step in.

"We'll be there at six, Grandma." I lean over, lightly kissing my grandma's cheek. It's the same cheek I've been pressing my own against during a lifetime of hugs. How can this be a last hurrah road trip for her, when she feels the same to me?

A ranch attendant hovers near the door, waiting to show Grandma to her room. Rainbow escorts her, not holding onto her exactly, but very present nonetheless.

"I wonder how Rainbow knew the details of dinner?" Kerrigan asks. "Grandma must've told her."

"The binder, Kerrigan." Duke's tone of voice gives away the eye roll he's holding back.

"Right. I should go get that from the motor home." Kerrigan sends us a quick wave and sails out the front door of the reception area.

"Mr. and Mrs. Hampton?" An employee approaches my parents. "Are you ready to see your room?"

My parents follow after, and then it's only Duke left standing with us. Not for long though, because the woman who showed us to our room strides up. Her hair is shinier, her lips slicker.

"Can I walk you to your room?" Her voice is pleasant, but she has lost the saccharine tone, the manufactured smile she used on us. In its place is something deeper. Less eager, more sultry.

If Duke notices, he doesn't make it known.

They go off, and now it is just me and Dom. "Pool?" he asks.

I nod, and we make our way back to our casita. He sits on the bed while I take my bathing suit into the bathroom, and when I'm out, he takes a turn. For someone I claim to loathe, we get along well.

At the pool, Dom swims laps while I lounge in a chair and thumb through emails. Or, at least that's what I am pretending to do. It's hard to focus on emails when Dom's cutting through the water, powerful arms producing rhythmic strokes. His head is down, and I am free to stare without fear of being caught. Is it healthy for a male to be this attractive? Shouldn't there be a physical fatal flaw somewhere? I'd settle for a nubbin, but no. Dom is flawless.

He surfaces, hair slicked back, and my attention snaps down to my phone. Paisley told me she'll try to keep her emails to me at a minimum, but I know there's no way I can be totally off-grid when it comes to work. There are some accounts for which I am the only contact, and even though Paloma has said she'll monitor my email to make sure there isn't anything I might be missing, I don't want to depend solely on her. Technically, I'm not taking vacation time for this road trip, and since it was sprung on us with very little time to prepare, I wasn't able to manage projects like I would have had I known I would be gone for three weeks.

"Working?" Dom asks, settling himself on the lounge chair beside me.

"Mm-hmm," I answer, not because I'm busy, but because he looks so good in those bright blue swim trunks it should be criminal. He hasn't dried off, and rivulets of water stream down his toned torso. My lady boner is peeking her head up from dormancy, but thanks to my anatomy, hiding it isn't a problem. "How about you?" I ask, hoping work talk will be the equivalent of a cold shower. "Have you had to work yet?"

Dom checks the time on his phone. "There's a three-hour time difference. Or is it two right now?"

"Two," I answer. "Daylight savings was last weekend. You missed the turn of the clock."

Dom tosses his phone at the bottom of his chair, near his feet. "I didn't notice. It's nice not having to change a clock."

"One of the perks of living in Arizona," I say, setting my phone down as well. "The extreme summer heat in the lower half of the state isn't awesome, but in exchange our time is consistent."

"Very true." Dom nods. A bead of pool water slides off his shoulder, traveling down his arm.

I will not watch that water travel any further south.

"Do you miss living here?" I ask, desperate for a distraction.

Dom wraps his hands behind his head, tipping his face to the cloudless sky. "Yes, and no."

When he doesn't say anything more, I prod him. "Care to elaborate?"

"I loved the energy of the city when I first got there. I moved for college, and never left. But lately"—he shrugs —"I've lost that lovin' feeling."

I smile at the old-timey song reference. "What are you working on right now?"

"Klein is working on the idea for his second book. And I've signed an author who's writing a tell-all about her years working in the restaurant industry. I think it'll be successful." Dom runs his hands through his hair. "I love my career. It means a lot to me. The authors I work with, the new ones at least, they have stars in their eyes. A dream in their heart. I'm part of making it come true." His eyes flicker to me. "Like you, I suppose. Your marketing plans help business owners' dreams come true."

"That's the goal. But don't try to switch the focus to me. You do that a lot."

His eyebrows raise. "Do I?"

"Mm-hmm. Keep going. Why have you lost that lovin' feeling?"

"I don't know that I have a real grasp on the way I feel yet. All I really know is that when I walk into the office, when I sit down in my office chair and look at my desk and my computer, I don't feel the thrill I used to."

My heart twists. A person trades a good portion of their lives for time spent nurturing a career. For so many, it's how they measure themselves. For better or worse, it can be how a person defines their existence. When someone asks, *What do you do?* they mean *What do you do for work?* They're not asking if you topped your toast with butter or jam that morning.

"What do you think would give you that thrill?"

"I'm not sure," he says, grabbing for the towel folded at the end of his chair. He runs it over his head, drying, then drags his free hand through his mop of gently sloping curls.

Oh. My. Watching someone you're physically attracted to drag their hands through their hair is highly underrated.

He continues, unaware of my invisible *physical response.* "I know I'm not disenfranchised with the work, so I guess I'll have to determine if it's the company, or the city, or something else entirely."

"That must be tough," I say sympathetically. "Wrestling with something like that."

Dom gestures around. "On the bright side, I'm currently poolside on a perfect seventy-five degree day." He grins, and it's like the sun chasing away mildly threatening clouds. "With my wife."

I wait for the customary annoyance at the reminder, but it doesn't arrive. Hmm, that's odd. There's probably a traffic jam inside me, caused by the rousing of my nether regions.

Dom closes his eyes, tipping his head back against the plastic chair. "There's a siesta in my immediate future."

I wake up my phone and return to my emails. "I'll make sure to punch you if you start snoring."

"I don't snore."

"That remains to be seen."

CHAPTER 29

Dominic

THERE WAS NO POOLSIDE PUNCHING, SO I GUESS I DIDN'T snore.

This family dinner, though? It's making me wish Cecily had delivered a swift jab to my nose. It would've given me a reason to hide out in our room.

Duke and Glenn haven't looked up from their phones once the entire dinner, unless it was to confer between the two of them. I'm no stranger to things at work taking a nosedive and needing to divert all my time and energy, but the Hamptons overlook their behavior as if this is a frequent occurrence. Kerrigan is on her phone watching Moose on the pet resort's in-room camera.

My family isn't great, of course, and my dad is always half a hard thought away from a Ponzi scheme at any given moment, but at least they interact.

I shouldn't judge the Hamptons too harshly. They rode in a motor home for more than two hours today, I'm sure they've had plenty of togetherness. My job isn't to judge them, anyway. If anything, I should study their dynamics for a future book idea for Klein, or let myself be entertained by them like an exhibit at the zoo.

I sit back, malbec in hand, and observe the space. The lighting is warm, emanating from elaborate candelabras hanging over the large tables. The walls are wood planked until chair height, when they turn into a decorative stained concrete. A scent of cedar runs through the restaurant. Even the stemless wineglass I'm holding is sturdy and thick, well made.

The Hamptons don't look appreciative of this. They don't look unappreciative either, and therein lies the problem. *They don't notice it at all.* Delicious red wine, glistening grass-fed beef filets, linen napkins, none of this earns their attention.

It's not totally their fault. They are so used to these fine things, they don't know how fine they are. I'm guilty of the same, in other ways. I don't spend any time thinking about the coffee shops I stop at on my way to work, or the place on the corner where I buy gyros twice a week. I put my head down and grind through my day and when I pick my head up again it's time to go home.

Cecily's elbow sits near the edge of the table, chin propped in her hand. She'd gone back to our room to get ready this afternoon after the pool, and I'd hung back, using work as my excuse. And, yeah, I have plenty of work to do. But really, I didn't want to be in the room with Cecily, hearing the shower running and knowing she's in there sans clothes. And what would happen next? She'd walk out in a towel? Grab her clothes from her bag? Would her underwear fall from her hand, some tiny lace scrap of cloth that will haunt me for the rest of my days? No thanks. Hiding out poolside was safer. I know the shower situation will have to happen sooner or later, but I'll avoid even a single instance of it if I can. By the time I returned to the room, Cecily was sitting out front of the pink casita, working her way through a word search.

Cecily's chin tips toward me now. "Penny for your thoughts," she murmurs. The low, warm lighting does pretty things to her skin tone, bringing out the tans and pinks. Her chestnut hair and brown eyes, too, as if there is a filter over her. A powerful urge to lean closer, to press my lips to her shoulder, rises in me like a tide. That damn casita smelled like smoked vanilla when I returned to it. Cecily sat out front with her puzzle while I was inside trying to pretend the scent wasn't driving me to the brink of insanity.

"Just appreciating the scenery," I tell her. "No thoughts in this head."

She squints, seeing through me. She knows I've thrown her a softball, served her up an easy chance to deliver one of her patented barbed remarks. The pad of her pointer finger presses to the square between her eyebrows. "You were cinching your eyebrows, Dominic. So don't tell me there were no thoughts in your head."

The servers arrive, setting down everyone's dinners. Different cuts of meats, roasted vegetables, cast-iron mini-crocks piled with saucy potatoes.

Ophelia requested a different preparation for her potato, and the server announces it by saying, "Your loaded baker, Mrs. Hampton."

Everyone's gaze is on the monstrosity, a pile of bacon and cheese and sour cream.

"Is there a potato under there?" Cecily jokes.

"That spud is a stud," Kerrigan says.

"Ophelia," Cecily's mom says reproachfully, when Ophelia sinks her knife into the little dish of butter. "Do you think you should be eating like that?"

Ophelia doesn't halt her motions, her hands working and her eyes downcast, as she says, "I'm dying. Who the fuck cares?"

A quiet extends around the table, nobody sure of what to say next. Ophelia has done nothing but tell the truth to a table full of people who haven't yet figured out how to handle what's happening.

The quiet presses on painfully for another moment, and then Cecily says, "Why does Grandma get to curse but the rest of us have to watch our mouths?"

The question, though not directed at Rainbow, implicates her. Rainbow is either very good at ignoring, or is slicing into her steak with such enthusiasm that she has not heard Cecily.

Ophelia, fork loaded with buttery, cheesy, bacon baked potato, takes a bite and offers a heartfelt middle finger around the table.

Judging by the tinkle of cutlery, the scrape of knives on plates, the family receives Ophelia's message loud and clear.

There is no more talking, only awkward silence while people eat. I feel a second, odd pang of missing the climate of dinner with my parents. At least they speak. I'm not sure this family knows how to be together.

"So, uh, what are we doing tomorrow?" Kerrigan asks, the first person to finally talk. "I don't know about you, but I'd like to sleep until noon and then get a massage."

Grandma pushes her plate away. "Quit being an idiot and look in the binder."

Hurt softens Kerrigan's features. "What?"

Grandma looks around the table. "Do any of you know what we're doing tomorrow?"

There is a collective shaking of heads.

Rainbow says, "If you bothered to look at the binder, you'd know."

Duke glares at her. "What exactly is a *death doula*?"

Rainbow, her serene mask growing tight around the edges, says, "I provide emotional, spiritual, and practical support to a person nearing the end of their life."

"Sure," Duke says, in a tone that really says *give me a break, con artist.* "But what does that really mean?"

"It means I am helping your grandma plan for her passing, and I ensure a peaceful environment for her as she navigates the many emotions that accompany preparation for death."

"You sound like you're reading from a brochure." Duke slices into his steak, the knife sinking in with minimal effort. He stabs the piece with a fork, pointing it at her when he says, "Don't think I'm not looking into you. You show up when a rich woman is on her deathbed?"

There's a collective inhale around the table. Except for Glenn. He doesn't look at all surprised by this.

"You all are a bunch of assholes on a good day." Grandma eyes Duke. "But this is extreme, even for you."

Duke sighs. "I'm trying to protect your interests, Grandma."

She makes a disbelieving face. "You mean *your* interests."

"The family," he insists. "I'm planning to look into Cecily's husband, too."

Cecily sputters. "You're looking into Dom?"

"For the same reason," Duke defends. "You and Kerrigan bop around like there isn't a family to protect."

"I do not bop," Kerrigan argues, but only half-heartedly. I barely know Kerrigan, but bopping feels like the right word to describe how she lives.

"Fuck you for looking into Dom," Cecily snarls. Hackles up, claws out. *For me?*

"Fuck you for not thinking about this family before bringing a random person into it." Duke's eyes blaze, but behind the fire, there's hurt. "Fuck you for not thinking about this family *ever*."

Rainbow, looking as if she might regret saying yes to this job, chooses this moment to say, "Please remember how important it is to your grandmother's health that we be as stress free as possible."

Cecily's head rears back. "Says the interloper who chided us for not looking at the binder when she just as easily could have told us what we're doing tomorrow."

"Enough," Ophelia barks. Palms flat on the table to steady herself, she pushes to standing. "Read the binder, you entitled bunch of assholes. Read the fucking binder. And when you're done, I expect you to get your act together."

Rainbow is already up, a cupped hand on Ophelia's elbow. Ophelia shakes her off. I cannot tell whether she does not need, or does not want, the assistance.

Ophelia stands tall, chin regal, and says, "I did not expect better from any of you."

Savage.

Everyone stays silent as Grandma sweeps from the dining room, Rainbow in tow.

After a moment, Duke says, "I didn't mean to offend

you, Dom. There are certain responsibilities that come with family wealth. Managing it, and the like."

I wave off his apology. I don't care that he plans to look into me. I'm a literary agent who lives in an apartment the size of a shoebox. I drink black coffee, buy my lunch from street vendors, and I haven't been on a date since the disastrous one with his sister. There's nothing to find.

Duke looks tired. Exhausted, actually, and I find I feel bad for the guy. I've never been responsible for generational wealth. I don't know what kind of pressure or resentment that brings. Maybe that's why Cecily's dad is the way he is. Years upon years of pressure, chipping away at his civility, his familial tenderness.

Not an excuse, of course, but a reason. People usually have one.

Cecily turns to me. "Are you done? Unless you'd like dessert or more to drink, I'd like to leave."

"I'm all set," I respond, placing my napkin beside my plate. I get up first, pulling Cecily's chair back for her as she stands.

"I suppose I'll see you all tomorrow, for whatever it is Grandma has planned," Cecily addresses her family. Kerrigan blows her a kiss, her mother waves, and Duke and Glenn dip their heads at her.

If Cecily is hurt by Duke's harsh assessment, she doesn't say on our walk back to our casita. It isn't until I'm turning the key in the lock that Cecily says, "At dinner Kerrigan pointed out that we aren't affectionate. She called us 'hands-off' newlyweds."

I push open the door, allowing Cecily to step in before me. "What do you think about that?"

Cecily collapses onto the bed, her gaze stuck on the

ceiling. "If that dingbat sister of mine noticed, then so did my grandma."

I'm toeing off my shoes, depositing my wallet and lip balm on the nightstand. "And how did you feel about that?" I sound like a tired therapist falling back on the most basic question.

Cecily massages her knuckles over her eyebrows. "I don't really know. A lot was said, or not said, or intimated, at dinner. It's hard to pick one topic to turn my attention to first." As if she's thought of something, she sits up. "I'm sorry about Duke. I don't know what's wrong with him, other than that he's turning into my dad."

I'm dying to take a hot shower and trade these jeans for sweats, but Cecily has an air of fragility about her right now, and it's becoming increasingly obvious the glimpse of it is rare. There will be no hot shower, or comfortable clothing. Cecily needs me.

"I think," I start, taking a place on the bed across from her, "that Duke feels he's solely responsible for the continuation and future success of the Hampton family, and its business interests. Something like looking into someone, which sounds insane to the common individual, to Duke feels normal in the course of life. To him, it's simple due diligence. If *this*, then *that*."

Cecily nods like she's considering. "Like, *if* he found something, *then* he'd reveal it and provide grounds for an annulment."

"Exactly."

A muscle twitches in her cheek. It's the tiny movement that precedes mischief, usually of the verbal variety. "Well, Errand Boy, tell me, do you have a history of con artistry?"

"Hate to disappoint, Menace, but you've married a man as straitlaced as they come."

Cecily holds my gaze, eyes darkening, chest expanding with a slow exhale. "Probably not straitlaced at all times."

I could do it, right now. Scoop her up, the heat of her surprised gasp on my shoulder, and put her on her back.

I want to. Dying to, really.

But then a thought occurs to me, and I'd really like to dropkick it from existence. *There won't be an annulment if we've consummated the marriage.* I learned about it that first morning when we woke up married, when I was figuring out what's considered justifiable grounds for an annulment.

The seconds tick by. Three, four, five. The spell breaks. Cecily gets off the bed, pulling the binder from her bag. "I need to look this over," she says. She collapses into the leather chair in the corner, light from the low lamp beside her illuminating her face. She scratches a hand over her collarbone, something innocuous but somehow sexy.

I suppose when a man is starving, like I am, even tofu starts looking like a steak.

Forget the hot shower. Better make it a cold one.

When I'm finished in the shower, I find Cecily still seated in the chair. She snaps the binder closed when I walk out. Her gaze starts at my head, dragging down. "I was wondering if you'd pull one of those obvious man-moves where you only wear a towel and force me to look at your bare upper half while you rummage for clothing."

I run a hand through my wet hair. "Uh, no. I'm not interested in making you uncomfortable."

"Speaking of uncomfortable," she says, tossing the

binder on the table. "We need to talk about what level of physical affection you're comfortable with."

"Because of what your sister said?"

"Because I read the binder!" Cecily gestures frenetically. "My grandma put an unreal amount of work into this trip. Hotel rooms, dude ranches, glamping tents? Booked. Excursions? Booked. Dining reservations for certain nights? Booked. Desert stargazing? Booked. All she wants from my family is three weeks of being in close proximity and not acting like we did tonight. And we are going to give that to her." Her pointer finger jabs her opposite flattened palm. "Grandma deserves it. She needs it. From here on out, this road trip must be ideal. Even if it means opening up old wounds with my parents and having to sit there with the pain. I can handle feeling hurt if it means bringing relief to my grandma before she's"—Cecily's voice catches—"gone." Tears flood her eyes, and my heart lurches. I want to take her in my arms, console her, dash away her tears.

Cecily extends a hand, like she's stopping me from something. "Let me guess, you expected me to cry tears of blood or some other heinous substance."

My mouth opens to object, but she forges ahead. "By coming on this trip you have gone above and beyond for my grandma. I didn't realize how entitled I was acting until now when I saw that binder and understood the amount of work it took to plan and execute a road trip like this."

Her lower lip trembles. Not a lot, but enough to pinch my heart. I wish I could take away what's upsetting her. I can't, of course. In fact, I can't do much of anything for her. The lack of control makes me uncomfortable. I'd love to be her knight in shining armor, slay her dragons. All I can do is be there for her.

"Do you want to tell me what's on the agenda for tomorrow?" I ask gently.

She sniffles. "It's a sunrise trail ride to a breakfast somewhere else on the property."

"An early wake up, then?"

She nods. "Looks like it. I texted my family. I told them I read the binder, and they better have, as well." Her gaze slides past me, to the bathroom. "I guess I'll get ready for bed."

I step aside, motioning. Cecily escapes, while I set up my phone charger, then settle into bed with my laptop to work until Cecily is ready for bed. Cecily's phone vibrates numerous times, likely her family responding to her text.

My fingers falter over the computer keys when I hear the snick of the bathroom lock. The opening of the door. Cecily steps tentatively from the bathroom wearing an oversized plain peach-colored T-shirt.

"Cute," I comment, "but I think I prefer you in *No Muff Too Tuff.*"

"Satan's Errand Boy forgot to deliver T-shirts to me today, so"—she pinches the fabric between two fingers and holds it away from her body—"I'll have to settle for this."

Sliding my laptop off my lap, I stand and cross the room to my open bag. "Here," I say, handing her my softest heather gray T-shirt, the one with the V-neck. "Satan's Errand Boy might be late, but he never no-shows."

Cecily laughs. *Two in one day? I'll take it.*

She twirls a circle in the air with a lone finger. "Turn around."

Dutifully, I pivot. Close my eyes against the soft swipe of fabric. She is so close, an arm's length away.

"Ok," she says, and I turn back around in time to see her throw her shucked shirt into her bag. She faces me, and I'm pretty sure everything in the world disappears.

Help me. Cecily's nipples welt beneath the thin fabric, and I swear, *I swear*, they are calling to me.

She gives me a droll look. "Yes, yes, I have nipples. They are erect. Changing in a room with the air conditioning blasting will do that to a girl."

Summoning all my strength, I force my gaze to remain on Cecily's face, which isn't exactly a hardship because she is so, so lovely. "Is that your version of a lady boner?"

Cecily smirks, sliding past me to the bed. She pats my chest on the way by. "Nope."

I rake a hand down my face and follow her to bed. Setting my laptop on the nightstand, I climb in beside her. She snuggles down, eyes on me. Reaching behind my neck, I tug off the T-shirt I wore out of the bathroom.

"Whoa, whoa," Cecily says, alarmed. "Why are you undressing?"

"Calm down. I realize my naked torso is a lot for you to handle, but let's be adults about it, alright?" It's possible I'm enjoying her perusal of my chest and torso equally as much as I enjoyed it at the pool this afternoon. "Besides, this is more than I usually sleep in."

"You sleep naked?"

"Sure. Things need to breathe."

Cecily's eyes narrow. That playful sparkle enters those brown irises, and I know, *I just know*, I am in for it. Her hands disappear under the bedding, she wiggles, and out from under the sheets she produces a black thong. She positions her fingers in the scrap of clothing, and sling-shots it across the room, where it lands softly beside my bag.

Here lies Dominic Bellinger. He died bravely.

Cecily grins, a menace in every sense of the word. Leaning back on her elbows, she glances at me, all inno-cence and wide eyes. "Things need to breathe." Then she flops over, stretching out to turn off her lamp.

I do the same, feeling as if all the blood has been sucked from my body. Into the darkness, I say, "I better not find you on my half of the bed."

She snorts. "Oh, please. With the look you just gave me? I won't be surprised if I find you draped across me by midnight."

I'd like to do far more with her than that, which means I need to change the subject. "You don't like Rainbow, do you?"

Cecily yawns. "Her face is so punchable."

I laugh. "Have you ever punched someone?"

"No. But when I do, I'm going to do a really good job. Closed fist, follow through."

"Remind me not to get on your bad side."

"You've been on my bad side since the day I met you."

"Have I?"

Long pause. "Yes," she finally says.

But she doesn't mean it. I know it, but more impor-tantly, she knows it.

"I'm comfortable with PDA," I tell her, remembering what she said when I stepped from the bathroom after showering.

"Huh?"

"Public displays of affection. You said we needed to

talk about what level of physical affection I'm comfortable with."

"Are you saying that because it's an opportunity to touch me?"

"Sort of sounds like you're accusing me of being a creep."

"I am not."

For a woman who claims to have never punched anybody, Cecily spends a lot of time with her fists in fighting stance.

Staring up at the dark ceiling, I say, "You asked a question, and I'm answering it. All typical levels of PDA are fine. Holding hands, light touches, chaste kisses."

"Light and chaste. Got it."

"Try not to attack my mouth, ok, Cecily? Once my lips are on yours for that chaste kiss? I didn't bring the right tool to fend you off, and menaces are *very* hard to get rid of."

The bed dips. Cecily flips over. My eyes have adjusted to the darkness enough that I recognize her dim outline.

She kicks me. Hard.

I grunt through the pain, rubbing at my calf. "Good night, ornery wife."

Cecily rolls over, back facing me once again, and doesn't say another word.

CHAPTER 30

Cecily

M̲Y̲ B̲L̲A̲D̲D̲E̲R̲ W̲A̲K̲E̲S̲ M̲E̲ F̲I̲R̲S̲T̲, B̲U̲T̲ I̲ R̲E̲F̲U̲S̲E̲ T̲O̲ O̲P̲E̲N̲ M̲Y̲ E̲Y̲E̲S̲. I'm too cozy.

Fancy hotel pillows really *are* better. Especially this pillow. It smells incredible. And it's like one of those bears you put a heart inside before stitching it up, except this one has a little battery-powered motor inside it giving it a realistic-sounding heartbeat.

I burrow my head, and the hard plane of the pillow registers in my sleepy brain. Pillows cannot be hard and soft at the same time.

The real world crashes in on me at the same shocking moment. I smell Dom. I feel Dom. Oh my goodness, I am *on* Dom.

My eyes adjust to the darkness in the room, the muted light from the ajar bathroom door giving me just enough to see Dom sleeping soundly beside me. A sigh of relief slips between my lips.

The last thing I need is that man knowing I made myself into a blanket and draped across him.

My bladder pokes at me more urgently. I carefully roll away from Dom and rise from bed, peeking at my phone. Two in the morning.

Again, I glance down at the man I've been spending all my time with lately. He's pretty cute when he's sleeping, arm stretched across the bed like that. No wonder I snuggled into him. I can't believe it's only been a few hours since he instructed me not to attack his mouth when he kisses me.

So arrogant.

As quietly as possible, I close the bathroom door. Taking great care to move like a ninja around the small room, I lift the toilet seat lid inch by inch and make no noise when sitting down.

Chaste kisses. His words, and—*something touches my ass.*

"Ahhhhhh!" It's a scream and a cry and a choked sob in one petrified sound. I'm up from the toilet, tripping forward, catching myself on the wall.

The door flies open, hinges protesting. Dom, hair flat on one side of his head, fixes me with wild eyes. "What is it?"

His gaze rakes over me, searching for an obvious problem. His T-shirt hits me at mid-thigh, but does he remember I'm not wearing underwear? I feel more exposed now, being upright and without the protection of bed covers.

"Eyes up here," I hiss. "There's something in the toilet. It"—my eyes squeeze closed before popping open again —"touched my butt when I sat down to pee."

Like a deflated balloon, the fight leaves his body. His relief is obvious, and then something else makes its way into his expression. Amusement.

"Just go." I point at the bed beyond the bathroom door he barreled through.

"Nope." He takes a step closer. "Let's see what we're dealing with."

"I can look," I argue.

He raises his eyebrows. "Sure about that? You're plastered to the wall."

I look down at my body, the way I'm pressed against the wall like I could become a part of it. "Fine."

Dom peers over, straightening up after only a second. "It's a cricket."

I shudder. They're harmless, but the way they jump unnerves me.

Dom unrolls a handful of toilet paper, using it to urge the insect down further in the bowl, and once it's in the water, Dom flushes. "Safe to use," he says, gesturing at the toilet before stepping from the bathroom and closing the door behind him. As if it never happened.

My bladder yells at me, and I lock the door since Dom is awake out there. I double-check the toilet, just in case the cricket had a buddy. It's clear, and when I finish up and wash my hands, I slink out of the bathroom hoping Dom is one of those people who fall back to sleep the second their head hits the pillow.

No such luck.

"Don't say a word," I mutter. I'm so embarrassed. I want to crawl into the nearest abandoned copper mine and die there.

"Wasn't planning to," Dom answers. His voice sounds rich, and I know it's because he's holding back laughter.

After a few minutes, I say, "Thank you."

"For what?" Dom asks.

In the darkness, a smile spreads across my face.

CHAPTER 31
Dominic

CECILY LOOKS LIKE A DREAM ATOP A HORSE. LIKE A MODERN, western version of Xena the Warrior Princess. I might, and I stress *might*, have had a thing for Xena when I was younger. Those after-school re-runs were something to behold. Was it Xena's powerful thighs, or her villain redemption arc that spoke to me? Not sure, but it had me feeling things.

Today I am wearing compression underwear underneath the jeans required for the trail ride. They won't stop me from having another unfortunate situation in Cecily's presence, but they might give me a fighting chance. I'm going to need it, after our middle-of-the-night cricket fiasco. Cecily didn't realize how much her shirt had ridden up, how the fabric had gathered at her hips and lifted the hem. I didn't see what a bikini bottom hides, but knowing it was right there, not covered by fabric or a sheet? The memory played on a loop in my mind, unsettling me enough that it took an hour for me to fall back to sleep. I'm convinced that woman might be the death of me.

She was awake and in the bathroom before me, emerging wearing skin-tight blue jeans tucked into tan and turquoise cowgirl boots, tan tank top knotted at her lower back. And the braid, tossed over her shoulder. May the good Lord help me when she brushes out that braid. Help me, or knock me dead.

Quint the cowboy is not a grizzled old fart. He's not a young stud either, much to Kerrigan's chagrin. Ranging somewhere from forty to fifty-five (hard to tell with the cowboy hat and sunglasses), Quint wears the typical cowboy getup: jeans, boots, and a button-up long sleeve shirt. And, most notably, a simple gold wedding band.

We ride in a line through the desert, with me bringing up the rear and Cecily directly in front of me. Before we climbed on our horses, we stood in a semi-circle and listened to Quint's lecture on what to do and what not to do. I overheard Kerrigan say to Cecily, "Isn't it weird to see Mom in this setting?"

"Like putting an alien in Sweet Nothings," Cecily agreed.

Kerrigan had looked at her with surprise, and Cecily said, "Stop it, Kerr. I can talk about home."

"Not fondly," Kerrigan countered.

"Get on your damn horse," Cecily responded, and that was that.

Surreptitiously, I typed the name of Cecily's hometown and Sweet Nothings into the internet search bar on my phone. Turns out it's simply the name of a bakery in Olive Township.

I am, by nature, curious, but there was something else driving me, a desire to glimpse anything having to do with Cecily. I want to know her. Her backstory. I'm learning her preferences by being around her, but I want more.

The sun, heavy in the east, peeks over the tops of the mountains ahead and sends a glow around Cecily. Her braid shines in the sun, a loose tendril floating in the slight breeze. Her posture is relaxed, hands loosely holding the reins. Surrounded by outstanding desert scenery, yet Cecily is the most breathtaking view of all. Sliding my phone from my pocket, I snap a photo of her. I'll send it to her later.

The trail is a wide swath of dirt, flanked by cacti that look menacing despite the bright flowers unfurling from them. In the distance, a large bird of prey swoops and soars.

Quint talks loudly to the group, but I can't hear most of what he's saying. That's just as well, because I don't care. Between the desert landscape and Cecily, there's too much beauty around me to pay attention to much else.

Eventually we arrive at The Outpost, the building where the ranch serves the sunrise breakfast. Ophelia and Rainbow are already there, having been driven over by a ranch vehicle. The Outpost is an ivory stucco building with a decidedly Spanish feel. A splintered wagon wheel leans against one wall, prickly pear cactus growing around it. Written on the wall in bright orange-red lettering are the words The Outpost. An honest-to-God hitching post runs half the length of the front porch, and Quint shows us how to safely tie up the horses. The entrance to the place appears to be nothing more than antique saloon doors, and when I push through, I find there's a proper door on tracks that has been rolled open.

"This place is so cool," Cecily says. Her touch runs over

my shoulder, trailing down my arm. It's not as if she has never touched me, but this time feels different. Slower, lingering. Affectionate.

It's not, though. Ophelia's looking on. The rest of her family, too.

A long picnic table occupies a majority of the open room, candelabras much like the one at dinner last night hanging above the table in three foot intervals. Behind the table is an open style kitchen, men and women walking quickly back-and-forth.

"Breakfast is being cooked out here," Quint says, leading the group through a door on the opposite side of the building. "Come out and take a look."

Cecily and I are standing closest to the exit, so we are the first to follow Quint. I motion for Cecily to step in front of me, and without thinking too hard about it, I place my hand on the small of her back. She has a deep curve there, and my hand fits inside it perfectly, my fingers evenly splayed. Cecily tosses me the briefest of glances before we step out of the door into the bright sunshine.

I could probably drop my hand by now, but, well, I don't want to. Instead, I let my thumb inch over the skin of her lower back, left bare by that knot in her tank top. Back-and-forth, my thumb drags on, and it cannot be more than five seconds, but those five seconds feel *right*.

Dropping my hand should be a decision I make without consideration, but not right now. I have to, quite literally, force myself to discontinue contact. My fingertips meet the air, and I have the irresistible urge to say *fuck it*, to bend her backwards and kiss her like there's no tomorrow.

I won't. I can't. Not in front of her family. I know we

agreed on chaste kisses, but the first time I put my sober lips on hers cannot be in front of her family. She deserves more, and I don't know if I'll be able to stop myself. A taste of Cecily, and I'll become a man crazed.

Quint shows us the flat-top griddle, and one by one the men and women from the kitchen walk out, arms laden with everything needed to prepare a breakfast that more closely resembles a feast. Blueberry pancakes, scrambled eggs, ranch potatoes, and thick, hickory smoked bacon. Salty ham, fruit, sourdough toast, juices and coffee.

The Hamptons behavior is vastly improved this morning. Perhaps Ophelia scared them straight, or maybe it was Cecily's text to the sparsely used family group chat last night. Whatever it was, they seem to have taken it to heart. Even Marilyn, usually absent while present, compliments the crisp bacon, the fluffy pancakes.

When she thinks nobody can see, Kerrigan mouths to Cecily, *What the fuck?*

Cecily smiles slowly. She wraps an arm around Ophelia's shoulders, and says, "Thank you for arranging the trail ride and breakfast. It has been an amazing experience, and I would've never thought to plan it for myself."

Ophelia harrumphs. "You are only saying that because I got mad at everybody."

Cecily laughs. "That is one hundred percent not true."

"Sure it is," Duke says, popping a piece of cantaloupe in his mouth. "Cecily sent out a group text last night and threatened everybody within an inch of their lives."

Cecily makes an aggrieved sigh, but Duke winks at her, and her bluster dissipates.

We stack our plates for the staff, carrying them inside despite their protestations. Even Glenn carries empty coffee mugs on his fingers, earning a second murmur of *what the fuck* from Kerrigan.

I'm starting to think watching this family interact might be better than prime-time television.

Everything is going well until we reunite with the horses. I'm standing beside Cecily, and the natural thing to do would be to plant a kiss on her before we part to mount our horses. She seems to know this, understand this, and tips her face up to mine.

Two opposite and distinct thoughts swell inside me. Devour her mouth because I cannot imagine doing anything less, or settle for a chaste, underwhelming peck.

Or there's option three, which is what I end up choosing. I lean in...*and rub the tip of my nose against hers.*

Cecily pales. Hurt fills her eyes, followed closely by fury. I wish desperately for the packed Arizona clay earth to crack open and swallow me down. How am I going to recover from a gaffe of this magnitude?

Cecily shoves her foot in the stirrup, swinging her other leg up and in the direction of the horse's backside. And also, directly into my crotch.

"Oof." I breathe hard, knees knocking together as the sharp pain boomerangs around a part of me I'm quite fond of.

Cecily glares down at me, deliberately rearranging her face into one of apology. "Oops," she says, adopting an ultra-feminine lilt. She guides her horse away, leaving me there. Forcing myself upright, I look into the curious gazes of the Hampton family.

"She's a pistol," I say, retreating to my own horse.

"Probably should have figured that out before you married her," Glenn responds.

I stiffen. Turn around woodenly. "I wouldn't have her any other way." There's challenge in my tone. Defiance.

Glenn has nothing to say, and that's a damn good thing. Cecily and I might be headed for an annulment at the end of this, but for now, she's my wife.

I need to catch up with Cecily, explain myself. I've hurt her feelings. I mount my horse, using the reins to urge his turn, and startle. Cecily has not gone far. In fact, she's hardly gone anywhere.

"Thank you," she says softly.

I pull my horse up beside her, her booted foot bouncing against my tennis shoe. Impractical footwear for a trail ride, but all I had.

I look at her full on, hoping she can feel the strength of my gaze, an apology without words. "You are sacred ground, Cecily. I won't allow anyone to speak badly about you in my presence."

She smiles, but it's not exactly happy. More like melancholy. "Because I'm your wife?"

I long to reach out, lift her chin with a fingertip. "Because you're *you*."

CHAPTER 32

Cecily

I was livid.

LIVID.

Until I heard what Dominic said to my dad. The way he defended me. Who in my life has ever done that? Nobody.

My anger melted away, leaving behind confusion and heaps of mortification. Little is worse than tipping up your head for a kiss, and receiving a childish nose nestle. It's like the participation trophy of kisses. *Thanks for coming, now go away.*

I did everything I could to put Dom out of my mind on the return trail ride. Spring in the desert is impossibly beautiful. Needle covered cacti make room for bursts of vibrant flowers, hot pinks and bright purples, vivid orange and lemony yellows. A sunrise represented by flowers.

No matter how hard I tried, I knew the warmth on my cheeks was from more than the midmorning sun. Dom and I are going to have to talk about what happened, even though I don't want to. If it were possible, I would simply ignore him for the next three weeks. Fake an illness. Cut off my ears. Almost anything to avoid the conversation I know we must have.

We arrive back at the dude ranch, and Quint hands everybody brushes. He shows us how to properly care for the horse after a ride. When that is done, Kerrigan asks Grandma if she would like to go for a walk in the meditation garden. Rainbow, everyone's favorite (but not really) interloper tags along.

Dom is looking at me with reluctance. When I incline my head away from the others, he nods, a silent agreement that his thoughts mirror mine.

"We'll be at the pool later," I tell the remaining members of my family, not that they care. Duke's fingers are itching to work. He's literally twitching, probably envisioning all the bossing around he needs to do.

Dom falls into step beside me. "Cecily—"

"Not yet," I interrupt. "I'd like to be out of earshot of my family."

He nods. We arrive at our casita, and I tell him I'll only be a moment. "We're going for a hike," I say, switching out my boots for tennis shoes. I hand him one of the two water bottles housekeeping has left on our nightstands. "We shouldn't be gone long, but it's the desert."

"Better safe than sorry."

We set out, me in the lead. I'm trying to get a handle on the way I feel, but it's tough. Emotions are high and intense, and I'm starting to not know up from down. I went from hating Dom, to begrudgingly being apathetic about him, to wanting him to kiss me and feeling devastated when he didn't. Add to that the way I feel about my family and how much I love my grandmother, and it's a tsunami of chaos in my mind. My heart.

Dom, thankfully, stays quiet as we walk deeper into the desert. I like that about him, the way he is ok with not talking.

The sun rises higher, and the trail gradually becomes less manicured. Rockier. Large boulders accumulate at the base of the mountain, balanced on each other. We stop for water, Dom's eyes watching me even as he tips up his water bottle to his mouth.

"You ready to talk, Menace?" He wipes the back of his hand across his lower lip.

I twist the cap on my water, squaring my shoulders. "You said last night you were ok with chaste kisses. Has that changed?"

"Not at all."

"Then please help me understand that stupid nose thing you did." The mention of it has my body warming again.

Dom sets his water on the ground and takes a step closer to me. I'd take a step back, for the sole purpose of being petulant, but there's a boulder behind me. "I panicked," he admits.

I'd seen an emotion in his eyes when I tipped my face up, but I hadn't labeled it as panic. To me, it was horror. "I suppose the thought of kissing me is panic-inducing." Sarcasm as a salve isn't as soothing as I'd like it to be. Dom's rejection of me refuses to stop stinging.

He's only a couple feet away from me now. There's dust on his right thigh, as if he brushed his hand off on the fabric. "It wasn't about you," he says.

It is without a doubt one of the worst things I could hear.

It wasn't about you, Cecily. Today was about your sister. Today was about your brother. I missed your orchestra concert because I had to work late, it wasn't about you.

Nothing in my family was ever about me, no matter how hard I tried. Until I got older, and stopped trying.

I wish I could cry about this. I wish I could scream into the desert, frighten away the hapless bunnies, send the pack rats scurrying to their middens. I'd choose crying over the reaction that comes naturally: mean.

I lift my chin. "Why do you think I said nothing more than modest kisses? It's because I find you repulsive. I'd rather lick the bottom of the shoes I wore when I married you than have your tongue in my mouth."

A muscle in his jaw twitches. His voice, deep and gravelly and curling low beneath my belly, warns, "Careful, Menace. I like it when you're mean." He takes another step into me, and now I'm bad-tempered enough to move back.

The boulder is closer than I realized, and my back presses against it. My water bottle drops and my breath hitches, a touch below ragged, my pulse thrumming as electricity zips through my veins. "I bet you only like girls with daddy issues."

He takes another step, dropping his lips to my ear, caging me in with his hands on either side of my head. He smells of salty sweat, cedar and orange. "Watch what you say about my wife. She has daddy issues."

His audacity draws a gasp from me. The words are on-target, as accurate as any arrow hurtling toward a bullseye. I don't like them, but they're not wrong.

The front of my thin tank top grazes his chest when I

drag a much needed deep breath into my lungs. "You seem protective of your wife," I sass, but the effect is lackluster. Thanks, hormones.

Dom runs the tip of his nose over the shell of my ear. Chill bumps break out over my forearms, even as the sunshine streams over us.

"I'll protect her from villains of all forms. I'll even defend her against herself."

I whimper. I don't mean to, and I hate the sound. His words have pierced my chest, landed in the center of my heart.

Dom pulls back, but only a few inches so he can look at me. "I couldn't stand the thought of the first time I really experience kissing you to be in front of your family, or for show. It's personal, and private, and I demand it be genuine."

I want to give in. I want to wrap my arms around his neck and lose myself to his mouth. Closing my eyes, I tip my head back until it meets the hard surface. "We have to stop at kissing," I tell him, even as my lady part is nearly pulsating at the top of my thighs.

"Of course," he agrees. "You deserve a lot more than a dusty, sweaty fuck in the desert."

It's startling, hearing it come from his mouth, but in the best way. A way that makes me squirm, sending heat up my thighs. Projecting images into my brain of precisely what it is he says I deserve more than.

Dom's hand works its way behind my head, cupping me. His other hand slips over the small of my back. "What I want from you right now is the kind of kiss that would make your family blush."

My eyes open, and I take him in. His angular jaw, the

plains of his face, his denim eyes and the way the sun lightens them. "Yes, please."

I meet him halfway, because I am as ready as he is.

Dom is not gentle, or rough, but lands at the sweet spot between. Hot and light against my mouth, and then deeper, fuller. Desire races through me, pinpricks along my skin as if I've tangled with a cactus. I reach for his shirt, fisting the fabric, drawing him closer to me. His hand leaves my back, gliding up my rib cage. At my neck, he swipes his thumb over my jaw.

He leans into me until I'm against the boulder once more, the hard cold of the rock cutting through my shirt, the knotted fabric at the bottom pressing into my lower back. I sigh into his mouth. Perhaps it's a groan. His kisses turn deeper, rougher, less contained. My hands run over his shoulders, his back, his waist, pulling him closer to me.

I don't know when the last time was that I felt this way. Maybe never. This need, this want, this urge to lose myself entirely to this man.

His touch drifts lower, feathering over the top of my chest, left bare by the cut of my shirt. My hands rake through his hair, and I arch into his touch. He cups my chest with one hand, his other hand still protecting the back of my head from the unforgiving boulder we're leaning against. I groan into his mouth when his thumb brushes over my shirt, pressing myself into him, willing our clothes to melt away.

He breaks the connection of our mouths, spinning me until my hands are braced on the rock. His lips skim my upper back, his teeth combing over my skin, and a hungry groan lifts in his throat. He flattens against me, his hand snaking around my midsection, dipping under my shirt. My backside presses into him, his hardness. Heat floods the tops of my thighs.

We haven't spoken, we are simply a hurricane of craving and yearning, ache and thirst. How can one kiss be enough? Kisses this hot can never satisfy. For the rest of my life, all kisses will be compared to this.

His hand finds my bra, slips into it. My flesh fills his palm, his thumb stroking my nipple. "Cecily," he says my name roughly into my hair. "This is—"

He cuts off. What was he going to say? This is bad? Good? Wrong? Stupid?

"I know," I say, hoarse. This kiss is a combination of many things, and I don't think I want to hear him name them.

I'm so delirious, so crazed for this man, that I'm considering suggesting we go back to our room. Will it really make it that much harder to get an annulment if we give in, just this once? Can we lie? I'd known I was attracted to Dom, but this physical response to his hands, his mouth, is beyond what I knew to be possible for me. I want him, plain and simple.

"Dom—"

A loud yell sounds from the distance. We freeze, dragging in heavy breaths. I look down at my breast that has popped out from my shirt, held in Dom's strong hand. "What was that?" he asks, lips at my ear. His thumbnail scuffs my nipple, back and forth, making my legs a little less sturdy.

"I don't know," I whisper, and the sound comes again. It resembles a greeting, a *hey* or *hello*.

Then a splash. Dom lets me go. He steps back, and I straighten myself up. Back into my bra goes my breast.

"Are we close to the pool?" Dom asks. "I thought we walked in a straight line, but maybe we were in more of a circle than I realized."

"I'm positive we walked away from the ranch." I turn around. Meet his eyes. He looks ragged. Out of sorts. He looks like he wants me, like we were interrupted.

His eyes rove over my face. He reaches out, runs his thumb across my lower lip, and I find my face lifting into his touch, wanting it so desperately. "You're swollen," he husks.

"I was properly kissed," I say. "In a way that would make my family blush."

Dom's eyes heat. "As you should have been."

My heart pinches. When he says things like that, it makes me feel uncomfortable in a good way. I don't know how to grapple with someone who makes my experience, *me*, a priority. But Dom does, unfailingly.

"Do you want to go see what the ruckus is about?" He offers me a hand.

I nod. "Yes." I place my hand in his, expecting him to walk us toward the sound, but he hauls me into him, taking me by surprise.

"One more," he says, "because I'm not sure there will be another." He captures my mouth, holds me to him, molding against me. My arms wrap around his neck, holding on, riding the high. With the way we respond to each other, perhaps it is better if this is it.

When we've stepped away from one another, attempting to get our bearings, he says something that takes me by surprise. "I looked up the official definition of menace, and after today I am more convinced than ever that it is the right word to describe you."

My eyebrows lift, urging him to continue.

"A person or thing that is likely to cause harm." His head shakes slowly. "You, Cecily, could not be more of a menace."

CHAPTER 33

Dominic

I'VE NEVER KISSED ANYBODY LIKE THAT. I'VE NEVER BEEN kissed like that.

Earth-shattering. If I read that in one of my authors' manuscripts, I'd accuse them of using hyperbole.

But that kiss *did* shatter my world, never to return to precisely the position it was in prior. I'm just a man, knocked off his axis by an earthquake named Cecily.

She leads the way now, to the sound of water and chatter. She peeks back at me, eyebrows furrowed. I feel the same way. Have we stumbled upon an oasis in the desert?

We round the base of the mountain, where the barely marked path drops in elevation. There, in a copse of trees, the sun glints off the surface of a small body of water.

Cecily pauses, turning back to me. "What if they are desert dwellers?"

I do my best to take her seriously, but it's difficult with the taste of her lingering in my mouth, the feel of her seared onto my fingertips. "Are you referring to people who live in the desert? If so, that includes you."

"No," she whisper-hisses. "I mean, what if they are a band of people who live in the middle of nowhere, subsisting solely on rainwater and desert creatures?"

I do my best not to laugh at her serious expression. "I think they are too close to civilization to be considered such."

Cecily nods her head in agreement after pausing to consider it. I must not have done as good of a job holding back my mirth as I thought I did, because she says, "I suppose you don't believe in ghosts, either?"

"I do not," I respond, but the laughter in her eyes makes me wary. "Why?"

"We're staying at a haunted hotel in Flagstaff." She grins broadly, accompanied by a sassy shoulder shake, and all I want to do is take her mouth one more time. I know we said only one kiss, but maybe we could extend the parameters. Kiss until we get back to the ranch? Kiss only for the duration of our hike?

"Ho there," someone calls to us. A man.

Cecily's eyes widen, remaining on my face. "I think he called me a ho."

"I'm positive he was talking to me," I joke, but I step in front of Cecily so half my body shields half her body.

The man, who looks to be sitting in the water, waves us over.

"We either say hi, or make a run for it," Cecily says. "Although, it's never a good idea to run in the desert. Too many loose rocks, uneven ground. At best, you roll an ankle. At worst, you fall into a cactus."

I'm not sure which of those misfortunes I would rather experience, but for now it appears we're going to make a new friend. The guy is still waving, but his hand has changed from a motion of *hello* to one of beckoning.

"Unbelievable," Cecily mutters, as I make my way down to where the trees provide shade. "Here I was thinking deserts were deserted."

We make it fifteen more feet before we see everything the trees hid. And when I say everything, I mean it.

Several more people sit in the water, men and women, and from what I can tell, their upper halves are not clothed, leading me to believe their lower halves aren't either. Cecily gasps. "Are they *nude*?" she whispers.

"I think they might be," I say under my breath.

"Nude desert dwellers," Cecily says against the fabric of my shirt. My abs contract with the effort it takes to hold in my laughter. Cecily grins up at me, holding fast to my bicep.

Yeah, I love it. The way she clings to me.

Closer now, I see the man who called out to us is at least sixty. He is mostly bald, with just a handful of hair neatly combed over the top of his head. His generous belly rises out of the surface of the water like a landmass in the ocean. His thick chest hair swirls this way and that.

"You and the missus look shy. Don't be," he says jovially. In an odd way, he reminds me of my dad.

Shy isn't the word I would use to describe us, clinging to the safety of land ten feet away from the bank. More like *petrified*.

"Remember, all comfort levels are welcome at Buena Mesa," he says, with an air of friendly leadership. "Clothing is optional, so you can wear your swimsuit. Though I will say, the hot spring is better when you're in a state of nature." A murmur of agreement winds through the group.

I'm going to make the leap that *state of nature* equates to *naked*. "We're ok, thank you for offering." Not only am I uninterested in sitting in nature's bathwater with a bunch of naked strangers, I don't want to invite conversation. It's obvious this man thinks we are guests of whatever Buena Mesa is, and who knows what will happen if he finds out we stumbled upon them. The last thing I need is to be chased through the desert by a sixty-year-old man and his flaccid penis.

Cecily draws in a shocked breath. Her gaze is locked on somebody in the water. "Mrs. Abbot?"

A woman turns. She is older too, her hair a blondish-gray, and clipped on top of her head. "Hello, dear," she says, voice warm with recognition. "You're not the first former student I've run into at Buena Mesa." She smiles serenely and adds, "Don't even think of asking me who, because we believe in everybody's right to privacy. Just like I won't be repeating that I saw you."

"Thanks?" Cecily's voice shakes. She pinches my arm, and I take it as a distress signal.

"We're going to continue our nature walk," I tell the group.

This is when the friendly leader takes it upon himself to be unnecessarily friendly. He lumbers up out of the water, marching toward us. Cecily squeaks and ducks behind me. The friendly leader is undeterred.

"Johann Bradford," he declares, extending his hand. Water drips from his fingers, from his entire body. He's close enough now that I can only really look into his eyes, and thank goodness for that. His trek over to us will be burned into my memory for the rest of time.

Swallowing my horror, I place my hand in his. How long will it be before I can douse it in soap and place it under scalding water? Longer than I'd like.

"Klein Madigan," I lie. I hope they mean what they say about privacy, because if Klein's career skyrockets the way I hope it will following his book release, we're going to need that discretion.

"Nice to meet you, Klein," Johann says enthusiastically. He leans left, to look at Cecily. "And you are?"

She leans over also, sending him a small wave. "Mrs. Madigan."

He nods. "You're new here, aren't ya?"

"What gave it away?" Cecily asks.

"I can always spot the first-timers. One of my jobs is to serve as an example of how to live nude without embarrassment." He takes a step back. Opens his arms wide. "It's ok to be shy, but you don't have to be. We're a wholesome place."

I will never hear the word *wholesome* the same way again.

"Don't miss the pickleball tournament this evening," he adds. "It's always a good time."

"Ok, well, thank you for the warm welcome," Cecily says, wrapping her hands around my arm and tugging. I offer a wave, and Mrs. Abbot merrily obliges.

Cecily and I beat a hasty retreat, or as hasty as we can be without rolling our ankles or falling into cacti.

When we are a safe distance away, Cecily says, "I did *not* see that coming."

"Did you see it *going*?" I am referring to the unfortunate sight of Johann's rear end.

"He made quite an exit."

"You have to hand it to them. Those nudists were a happy bunch."

"I can't imagine doing that."

"Being naked in front of a bunch of people? Yeah, me neither."

"That, too, but also, being that vulnerable. Every flaw on display." Cecily shakes her head. "The nudist life is not for me, for many reasons."

"Flaws are on display all the time, whether you realize it or not. Not physical flaws, necessarily, but the others. Flaws in personality, for instance. And what is seen as a flaw for one person, might not be seen as a flaw for the next person."

"Sort of like saying beauty is in the eye of the beholder?"

"In a way."

Cecily turns around suddenly. Pokes me hard in the chest. "Sounds to me like you're trying to get me to go tits out with Mrs. Abbot."

"Never," I say solemnly. "Nobody sees my wife's tits but me."

Cecily blushes.

I like it, the way the red spreads over her cheeks. "Or at least one, anyway. I've seen one."

She plays with the end of her braid, fighting a smile. "The other one looks just like it."

Knocking her hand gently aside, I toy with the braid. "I'll be the judge of that."

"We said we'd kiss once, Dominic."

Ooh. She full-named me. A sure sign I'm making her feel something.

Her grin turns mischievous. Her eyes, too. Her whole damn face. With two hands she reaches for the hem of her shirt, pulls it up, stopping for a short second to gather her bra. Up, and away.

She's beautiful. Perfection. I want her.

Too soon, she lowers her top. Wiggles her eyebrows.

I point a stiff finger her way. "Menace."

"I might not mind that nickname after all," she says, continuing the walk like she didn't just flash me. "In fact, it has a ring to it."

It's late afternoon when we make it back to the dude ranch. Cecily tells me we're ten minutes late for a cookout, according to the binder. There is no time to change, to clean up. I've been in these clothes all day, and I've been dreaming about a shower.

We walk into the outdoor pavilion, locating the Hampton family at a large table under a mesquite tree. The place smells of charcoal briquettes, open flame, and barbecue. Thank goodness for the country music blaring from the speakers, because my stomach is starting to talk. I didn't realize how long we'd been gone. Time with Cecily passes differently.

Two plastic folding chairs are vacant between Rainbow and Duke. Forced by our tardiness, we will have to sit next to Rainbow. I remember what Cecily said last night about Rainbow having a punchable face, and slide to Cecily's other side, placing myself between her and the death doula.

The Hamptons stare at us, agog. We must be a bedraggled, dirty sight.

"Where have you been?" Ophelia asks.

Cecily tosses her empty and crushed bottle of water on the table and sits heavily in her seat. "Let it be known that today is the day I saw my high school principal's fun bags."

Duke spits out a mouthful of amber beer, attempting to catch it in a cupped palm. "Mrs. Abbot?" he sputters. Beer seeps through the cracks in his fingers, absorbing into the front of his shorts.

Cecily nods. "Old Abby," she confirms.

"I never liked her," Marilyn announces. "She held a grudge against our family for no reason that was discernible to me." She lifts her glass of white wine in the air. "Tell us everything."

Duke and Kerrigan stare at their mother. Cecily stiffens, what can only be shock running through her. She recovers quickly, grabbing a full goblet of water and sucking it down. I do the same. I'm positive we are both dehydrated. It wasn't nearly as hot as it will be in the summer months, but the dry heat can be misleading.

"Well, Mom, thank you for giving me the floor." Cecily glances at me. "Have we got a story for you."

Cecily wore her own pajamas to bed tonight. She placed a pillow between us on the bed, and still she hugged the edge of her side.

A week ago, I would've said she's doing these things because she loathes me.

But now? I know better.

CHAPTER 34

Dominic

WE SPEND ONE MORE DAY AT THE DUDE RANCH BEFORE WE SET off for Tombstone. Ninety minutes southeast, the Town Too Tough To Die promises a Wild West atmosphere and gunfight reenactment.

Yesterday, during some downtime between morning ax throwing and the afternoon falconry demonstration, I compiled a road trip playlist.

It was a huge miss not to have one ready for the drive down from Phoenix. No road trip is complete without a playlist.

The music is queued up and ready to go the moment we pull out of the dude ranch. My finger hovers over the play button, but I think better of it. I have an idea.

"Have you ever kept a journal?" I ask Cecily. Not gonna lie, she doesn't seem much like the journal type.

Cecily's hands clasp and she holds them next to her face, her expression taking on a dreamy quality. "Dear Diary, yesterday Satan's Errand Boy kissed me."

We're back to the original nickname. We have been

since yesterday. It doesn't take a rocket scientist, or even someone with above average intellect, to know what Cecily is doing. Pushing me away. Because in Cecily land, anything is better than letting me get close. Or, said better, than letting *herself* get close.

I deepen my voice as we return on the dirt road we traveled over two days ago. "Dear Diary, last night Chestnut moaned in relief when she took off her bra."

Cecily pokes my shoulder. "Who is Chestnut?"

"You."

"I like Menace."

"I'm sure you do. But I need another name for you."

"Cecily works just fine."

We come to a four-way stop, and since nobody else is around, I take my time, reaching over and fingering a handful of her dark, shiny hair. "Chestnut it is."

She grumbles, something that sounds like *so fucking annoying*, but that woman likes her new nickname. The rising corners of her lips give her away.

"I do not moan in relief when I take off my bra."

A vehicle approaches from behind, and I make my way through the stop.

"You did last night," I point out.

"I'm not positive you are right, but let's say, hypothetically speaking, you are. *If* I made such a noise, it was due to all the activity yesterday. Ax throwing and underwire do not go together."

"Help me understand the negative relationship between the two."

Cecily's arms cross. She stares out the window.

The moments pass, and I say, "That's what I thought."

"You didn't think anything. Your brain is too small."

For a man who had such a cutting remark tossed his way, I'm grinning broadly. Cecily doesn't mean it. "A *journal*"—extra emphasis on the word—"might be something you'd enjoy reading later. After the trip is over."

"After my grandma is gone, you mean."

I wince. "I was trying not to say it quite like that, but yes."

Cecily is quiet, tracing an unknown design on her thigh. "She was short of breath yesterday. Did you notice?"

"Yes." It's what prompted me to think about a journal. "You don't have to do anything you don't want to do. Obviously. But you're in a unique position. Even taking a note on your phone would suffice."

"True," Cecily says, a lone fingertip swirling over the fabric of her yellow pants. They are paired with a small top, something that shows off an inch of her midsection when she's standing. "Sometimes loved ones die suddenly, and you don't get to say goodbye. Or I love you." Her voice softens. "Or thank you." She looks at me. "Has anybody you loved ever died suddenly?"

"No. I have very little experience with death." Other than what's happening now, anyway. To be here, firsthand witnessing a family scrambling to get their act together as their matriarch prepares to leave them behind, is an honor. Mostly. It's weighing on me, too, on a much lesser scale. "What about you?"

"Not really. Maybe tangentially, when I was younger. Growing up in Olive Township, a friend of Duke's lost his father. He was murdered, and the crime went unsolved until recently."

The story sounds familiar, and then I remember why. "My parents watched the news when that happened. It was all over every channel." Specifically, I recall sitting in the nurse's office and seeing it on the small TV that sat on the corner of her desk. It was the first time I understood such violence could take place outside of a book, fiction or otherwise.

"I was too young to understand it, but I grew up alongside the family. I watched how it devastated them." Cecily resumes tracing her thigh. "A journal is a good idea. Thank you, Dom, for suggesting it."

My eyebrow crooks. "Are we back to *Dom*?"

Cecily presses her fingertips to her mouth, making an *oops* face. "My apologies, Satan's Errand Boy."

Two steps forward, one step back.

The last time I said that to Cecily, she informed me it meant I was still making progress. She was right.

I have never expended maximum effort for half the reward. Yet, here I am with Cecily, eager to net a single step of progress. I don't care how much work it takes. How much work *she* is. I want it. I want her.

Maybe it's crazy. Maybe I'm insane. What I know more than anything is that I cannot tell her, not yet. Cecily's priority must be her grandmother. Her family.

And there it is. The second reason I came on this road trip. I knew Cecily would need a friend, even one she loathed. What I think I hid, even from myself, was that I needed to be that friend. I could not, would not, allow anybody else to take that spot. I could have given her that annulment. Quite simply, I didn't want to. My heart knew what my brain did not.

I want the woman sitting beside me.

I chance a glance at her now, the dark hair that slips

over her shoulders, the way her teeth strum at her lower lip.

Our eyes meet briefly before I turn back to the road. "Are you ready for that playlist I made yesterday?"

"I reserve the right to veto."

"I reserve the right to block your veto."

She huffs, pretending like this irritates her. It doesn't, and I know it. Everything about her demeanor has shifted, even if her words are as sharp as ever. Her arms are not crossed in front of her, a place where they were previously glued. Her shoulders no longer hover near her ears, back muscles bunched and ready for a fight.

I hit the play button on my phone, and the first song on my carefully curated playlist fills the car. The rowdy notes bounce around, the song easy to identify.

"Viva Las Vegas" by Elvis Presley.

Cecily rolls her eyes. "Veto." She taps my phone screen, and I press my lips together because I know what's coming.

"Marry You" by Bruno Mars.

"Dom!" Cecily leans on the center console. Her face is a few inches from my arm. I can't look, I'm too busy navigating the road. I feel her eyes. Her breath. And then she bites me, teeth sinking into the outside of my bicep, not hard enough to cause real pain, but it takes me by surprise.

Bruno Mars croons about getting married, then waking up and breaking up.

Cecily isn't biting down anymore, but her lips are still on me. "I'm not sure why I did that," she murmurs against my arm. "It was"—a long pause—"*Oh.*"

I don't have a hope of hiding it this time.

"You like being bitten?" Cecily asks. She sits back in her seat, positioning her body so she can partially face me.

"Not historically, no." *Not before you.* "Do you like biting?"

There's a hitch in her breath, and she says, "Not historically, no."

The car cabin is too small for me to do any effective adjusting to the front of my pants, but I give it a go.

"Oof," I grunt, when I hit my head on the hard top. "Awesome," I mutter, sulking. "I guess we're 2-0 on the *physical response* scale."

"We-ell, maybe not."

The exit for Tombstone comes up, and I navigate the car onto the next road in our journey. It's paved and deserted, cacti growing wild on both sides. "Keep talking," I instruct.

Cecily's lips vibrate as she blows out a reluctant breath. "I told you that you were due recompense—"

"Your exact words were 'violent lady boner'."

"Did you get that tattooed somewhere on you?"

"Keep talking, Chestnut."

"Where did Chestnut come from?"

"Your hair color. Now, stop trying to change the subject."

She's back to tracing designs on her thigh. "I currently have a violent lady boner."

I glance at the apex of her thighs. I can't help it. "Lucky for you, nobody would know."

I really should receive a commendation medal of some sort for keeping my voice steady. It's no easy task when every part of me is screaming to go on an hours-long tour of Cecily's body.

"This sucks," Cecily pouts, crossing her legs. "We're married, but we can't have sex because consummating the marriage means we can't get an annulment."

Bruno Mars stops singing about getting married. The next song begins, and now Riley Green sings about wanting someone in the worst way.

Cecily smirks. "Fitting."

"Cecily Menace Chestnut Hampton, did you just say you want to sleep with me?"

She bites down on her lower lip. "I do believe that's what I was getting at."

My heart lodges in my throat. The side of my thumb taps the steering wheel. My brain trips over itself thinking of the way she just said that, like it was the most natural thing in the world. "This is a conundrum."

"The thing is, I don't know if I'm going to survive eighteen more days of this." She motions between our bodies. "It's possible I'll spontaneously combust."

I can't imagine a person more in need of a release than Cecily. A little relief of the pressure valve inside her would be beneficial, possibly for everybody.

An idea strikes. "How about you tell me when you're nearing combustion, and I'll make sure it doesn't happen?"

"How could you possibly—"

I turn up the music. Drown her out. She bites back a smile.

I like the idea of Cecily sitting there, thinking about how I'll keep her from combusting.

CHAPTER 35

Cecily

Dom is trying to kill me quietly. Softly. Without the use of violence or weapons.

How about you tell me when you're nearing combustion, and I'll make sure it doesn't happen?

What does that mean? And why does it seem like he wants me in a silent tizzy, mulling over his intentions until I collapse?

The man is diabolical.

There's no time to think about it now, because the gunfight at the O.K. Corral is underway. Wyatt Earp and Doc Holliday jump and roll, shoot and stagger. It's the lawmen versus the outlaws, hollering and leaning into their questionable and campy but altogether fun accents.

We're sitting in the stadium-style stands, watching the popguns smoke and the booted men kick up dust. Duke sits on one side of me, Kerrigan on the other. Dom is between Rainbow and my grandma. My parents are one row above us. I split off from Dom when it came time to take our seats. I've been mentally agonizing over what he said in the car, and standing beside him smelling his cedar scent was too much for me. I needed a break, hoping distance would break the spell I fear I'm finding myself in.

Dom is, well, a lot of things. Great things. And I can't think this about him while simultaneously smelling his delectable scent, or feeling the warmth of his arm when it brushes mine. It's too much.

Dom catches my eye during the ending scene, where guns blaze and men give their all to the reenactment of the famous gunfight. He makes a finger gun, points it at me and shoots, blows on it, and pretends to holster it.

I shake my head at him like *What a nerd I cannot believe you did that*. What I think, but do not dare reveal, is *Nerds aren't supposed to be so hot*.

The show wraps up, and my mom says she'd like to wander through the town. "I want to buy kitschy shit."

Duke starts to disagree, but my dad talks over him. "Ok, Mare. Let's go buy kitschy shit."

They walk off. My dad reaches for my mom's hand.

Like Kerrigan and Duke, I stand agape. "When was the last time you saw Mom and Dad holding hands?"

"Probably around the last time he called her Mare," Duke answers.

"Grandma," Kerrigan says. "Did you sprinkle something on Mom and Dad's oatmeal?"

"That was me," Rainbow chimes in. "My famous Reconnection powder."

"Famous to whom?" Kerrigan asks.

"I'm only joking," Rainbow says when she sees Duke's stormy expression.

He glowers. "Don't make jokes that could be taken as truth."

"Or as poisoning," I add.

Rainbow steps away, suddenly very interested in the chalkboard menu at a nearby soda fountain.

"Quit being so nice to her," Duke says to Kerrigan through clenched teeth.

"Quit being so mean to her," Kerrigan volleys. "She's doing a nice thing for Grandma." Kerrigan looks to me for backup, but she won't find it.

"Sorry, Kerr. I'm with Duke on this one."

"You two are so cynical. I actually feel sorry for you."

Duke shrugs. "And you're too trusting." A buzzing sound emerges from his pocket. "Excuse me," he says, smoothly stepping away.

Kerrigan looks put out, so I suggest a treat from the soda fountain. Grandma perks up at the idea.

"Nothing better than eating your feelings," she announces, jostling Kerrigan with her elbow.

Grandma orders a sarsaparilla float and swears it tastes just like the one she used to get at the ice cream shop in Olive Township when she was a teenager. "That was where I met your grandfather," she tells us, dipping the long-handled spoon deep into the tall glass.

"What did he look like?" Dom asks, taking the spoonful of chocolate ice cream and caramel sauce I scooped. Just when I think he's going to place it in his mouth, he feeds me instead. The sweet sting of sugar, the burst of cold from the spoon, and Dom's warm eyes on mine. Heady combination. Surrounded by my family, but still my toes curl in my sandals.

He slowly drags the spoon from my mouth, scoops up a bite for himself, and places it upside down on his tongue. I look away. I cannot watch that spoon slide from his mouth. Combustion will most certainly occur.

"Your grandpa worked there," Grandma says, launching into her story with that fuzzy look of nostalgia. "Wore a pageboy cap and vest. It was their uniform, but it looked better on him than it did on the other employees. I went in when I knew he'd be working, but Tessa Bredesen was already there. She liked him, too."

"What did you do, Grandma?" Kerrigan asks around the extra-wide straw of her chocolate malt.

"What any self-respecting young lady of that era would've done. I yanked that bitch back by the scruff of her neck and tossed her out." Grandma jerks her chin and thumbs sideways. "Louis was mine, and that was that."

"Grandma, are you telling the truth?" Kerrigan asks, wide-eyed.

Grandma winks. "Anything can be true, as long as you tell the story with your chest."

"So it's not true?"

Grandma shrugs. "I didn't say that."

We're laughing when Kerrigan turns to Rainbow and says, "Sorry about my brother. He doesn't mean to be so rude."

"Sure he does," Grandma argues. "He could really use a woman. Someone to put him in his place once in a while, and provide him with an outlet, if you know what I mean."

"He had Daisy," Kerrigan points out.

"Daisy was Duke's fiancée," I explain to Dom. "They broke up at the wedding. It was super dramatic."

Dom blinks. "That's terrible."

"Objectively, yes," Kerrigan says. She wipes at the corner of her mouth. "But there was someone else for

Daisy, and it would've been a mess if they didn't realize it first."

Rainbow nods sagely. "Duke's bad energy is making more sense now. He had his heart broken."

"I don't think so." Kerrigan shakes her head. "Daisy was a good match for Duke on paper, but they were more like friends than lovers. The Hamptons and Daisy's family go back a long way. Like, *generations*."

"Don't get me started on my father-in-law's—*God rest his soul*—childish feud with Byron St. James." Grandma rolls her eyes. "Those two families were always going at it. It was entertaining."

Dom's phone rings, and he looks around with an apology. "It's one of my authors. I need to take this."

He steps onto the old-timey Tombstone street, phone against his cheek.

"He's a doll, Cecily," Grandma says, watching him through the large front window. "It's obvious he loves you."

"Oh yes," Rainbow chimes in. "You can feel it in his energy."

"Sort of how you felt Duke's broken heart in his energy?" Kerrigan teases.

"Say what you want, but that man has a sadness about him," Rainbow defends. "If it's not from a broken engagement, it's from something else."

She and Grandma share a look, one that says they've discussed this before. What else do they discuss? Is Rainbow my grandma's confidante? Does she know her secrets? Her fears?

Big Nose Kate's Saloon is where Grandma chose to end our day in Tombstone.

The floor is a warm-colored parquet, with a bar running the length of one wall. Colorful strands of Christmas lights shine off bottles of booze. An old man wearing a red bandanna around his neck plays the harmonica in the corner. His setup is simple, just a chair and microphone.

The hostess leads us to a table in the back, and we wind around seated tables to get there. The place is cramped in that way that doesn't feel like an annoyance, but more of a shared understanding between the patrons that we are all here to partake in something.

The hostess snaps our menus down on the table and tells us Queenie will be with us shortly.

"That's it," Grandma declares, smacking the plastic menu on her open palm. "I'm changing my name to Queenie."

"Sort of feels like it should've been your name all along," my dad says, a note of fondness in his voice.

I sit up straight, the words *what the hell* hovering in my throat. Where is my indifferent father?

A warm hand presses against my back. Rubs a gentle circle. *Dom.* His lips meet my shoulder. He says nothing. He doesn't have to. The communication is received. *I'm here.*

Queenie ends up being an inch below five feet tall. She

is ghostly pale, with jet black hair in a pixie cut. She wears dream catchers as earrings, and earns a compliment from Rainbow.

We order two pitchers of beer, one a fruity cider and the second a stout I want no part of. Duke does an internet search trying to learn the story behind Kate with the Big Nose.

"A soiled dove of the American West, and on-and-off girlfriend of Doc Holliday," Duke reads theatrically as Queenie arrives holding two pitchers in one hand and a sleeve of cold glasses in the other. Dom reaches out to offer help, but she's faster, moving with the grace of someone who has performed the maneuver countless times. Duke continues, "While the dance hall girl was attractive, she did have a prominent nose."

"She also had a temper that matched Doc Holliday's," Queenie adds, pouring a beer. "And she was tough and stubborn."

"Sounds like someone else I know," Dom says in a voice meant only for me.

I reach for the cider, bringing it to my lips. "Don't even think of calling me *soiled dove* as my third nickname."

Dom's thumb grazes my thigh under the table. Around my kneecap. Back up the inside of my leg. Hot sparks of desire shoot through my chest.

"You're looking piqued," Dom says, bringing his beer to his lips with the hand that is not currently tormenting my leg. He takes a deep swallow, throat bobbing.

"I'm fine," I insist. I'm not. I'm anything but.

Back down my leg he goes, and this time when he gets to my knee, his fingers slip into the crease. His grip on me tightens, and in his grasp I feel one word: *mine*.

It makes me think of our kiss two days ago, the way the boulder dug into my skin and Dom's lips teased my mouth open, the swipe of his tongue and the way my breast looked in his palm.

I suck down half my beer. Fan myself. Who turned on the heat in this place?

"Hot, Menace?"

I turn to look at him. He wears a smirk. And in his eyes, a hunger.

"I've noticed something interesting."

"What's that?"

"You call me Chestnut when you want to be sweet." My voice lowers, and he leans in, a lock of his hair falling over his forehead. "And you call me Menace when you want to fuck me."

Muscles along his jaw tense. "Wrong."

My eyebrows lift. "How so?"

His fingers flex on my leg. "It doesn't matter if I call you Chestnut, or Menace. I always want to fuck you."

His words send a current of electricity straight to my core. "Combustion imminent."

Understanding filters through his eyes. Grabbing my hand, he hastily hauls me up from the table. My family watches us, waiting for one of us to explain our behavior.

Dom is quicker than I am. "Cecily and I are going to check out the gift shop. I'm sure my parents would love souvenirs from here."

"Do you want to wait until we place our dinner order?" Mom asks.

I'm still getting used to the fact that my mother has returned from her years-long hiatus. "Two pulled pork sandwiches. Coleslaw. Fries. Thanks." I don't have a clue if

Dom likes to eat the foods I rattled off, but that's what he's getting.

Dom pulls me in the direction of the gift shop attached to the front of the store. He leads me directly through it, and out the front door. We spill out onto the main street, where a hot pink and orange sunset streaks over the western sky.

Dom pulls me in close, running his fingers through my hair. "I have a plan."

"I don't have one, so I guess we're going with yours."

Dom walks me down the dirt street, to the parking lot beyond. I put on the brakes, shaking my head. "I don't think Bernice—"

Dom tugs me harder, urging me to keep pace. "I have the keys to the motor home."

"Why in the world do you have the keys?"

"I have one of three."

I could ask how Dom ended up with a key, but I don't really care.

All that concerns me now is getting my hands on my husband. And his, on me.

CHAPTER 36

Dominic

The door of the motor home opens, the automatic steps extending. In the distance is a low thrum of music, the melody pierced every few seconds by voices.

Cecily peers up at me. Her cheeks are flushed, like they were in the restaurant. I've seen her flushed before, from anger and from embarrassment. But this? This is different. A pink hue with eyes that soften, corners creasing. Vulnerable. Open.

For me.

My heart lurches. I like Cecily a lot more than I've allowed myself to realize. I can't have her all the way, not fully, not the way I truly want her. But I'll be damned if I won't make this her best experience.

Stepping closer, I grip the bottom curve of her ass and lift. She follows the movement, wrapping her arms and legs around me. She snuggles in close as I navigate the metal steps and doorframe of the motor home. Stopping once I'm inside, Cecily leans around and reaches for the door, slamming it closed. She slides the lock across.

Sitting up, arms casually draped over my shoulders, she licks her bottom lip and asks, "We're alone now. What are you going to do with me?"

In two strides, I have her on the counter of the kitchenette. There's a loaf of bread behind her, a box of powdered donuts.

Her chest, daintily covered by that yellow top, heaves with her heavy breath. Pressing my fists on either side of her thighs, I take a moment to look at her. Let my eyes wander. Her shoulders. Her collarbone. The top swell of her breasts. I'm dying to put my lips on every inch of this woman.

Using my hips, I urge her knees to part. The fabric of her pants swishes around us, and I step between her thighs, briefly meeting her eyes before I press a kiss to the pulse fluttering in her neck.

"My wife told me she needs my assistance." My tongue drags over her throat, and she whimpers. "I took a vow to care for her, and that's what I will do."

"Your wife is a lucky woman," Cecily says, and I feel the way she swallows.

My hand slides up her neck, gently gathering her hair. I pull, guiding her to look up. "My wife's pleasure is a priority."

Cecily breathes a tiny groan as my lips meet her jawline, feathering kisses over the delicate ridge. She reaches for me, wrapping her arms around my back. Her nails drag lazily over my shirt.

She turns her mouth, capturing mine. Once I'm there, it's electric. My whole body zings, the attraction something that doesn't feel like it's safe to exist. It should be contained somewhere, buried a mile underground. How are we supposed to successfully walk through daily life when there is this much chemistry between us?

Cecily arches into me, her head pressing into the cabinets. Her chest grazes mine as our tongues tangle, her flavor a fruity apple, mixing with the thick bitterness of the stout. She lets go of me, and when the kiss breaks, I see the thin straps of her top dangle off her shoulders. "More," I demand, and she eagerly complies, probably for the first time since I met her. She pushes down her top, no bra, and her breasts spill out. Full, heavy, and so fucking perfect.

My head dips, and I take a hardened peak in my mouth. Cecily's nails drag through my hair. "Dom," she says, drawing out the *m*. The same sound she would make if she were eating something delicious.

I give her other nipple a pinch with my finger before dragging my touch down the center line of her body. Stepping back, I give myself room to work.

"We probably don't have time," Cecily protests throatily when she sees my fingers flip open the top button on her pants. "I'm sure my family is wondering where we went."

"There is time, Cecily." Her zipper slides down smoothly, revealing a line of light pink silk underwear. "There is always time to make my wife come."

My gaze snags on hers. Hair a little wild, eyes borderline frenzied. Will she regain her composure? Change her mind about us?

I see in her eyes the way she's fighting herself. How hard she is working against whatever it is she's feeling for me. So, I give her an out.

"This doesn't have to mean anything, Menace. Look at it as me doing you a favor." Her hips thrust the tiniest bit, and maybe she didn't consciously do it, but I take it as the invitation I know it is. My fingers slip under the pink fabric. "Doing us all a favor, really."

Her eyes darken, and my touch finds its way south.

Eyelashes fluttering, she says, "As soon as this is over, I will go back to loathing you."

It's a stilted response. She wants me so desperately she can barely get the words out.

It makes me hungrier, mad for this woman. The pad of my finger finds the jackpot. Slips inside. She groans. Loudly.

"You can loathe me right now for all I care. It won't stop me from doing what I intend to do." I lean forward to her chest, fill my mouth with her rounded flesh. Suck hard. Her nails scratch over the back of my neck. She mewls, legs lifting like she wants to brace them against something, but she finds no purchase.

Gently I ease her off the counter, turning her over. I reach around, filling my hand with her breast again, nibbling at the juncture between her shoulder and her neck. It's just like it was two days ago during our kiss, with the addition of my hand between her legs.

She groans so loudly a passerby would think she's receiving the real thing. Cecily needed this. Wanted it, as badly as I did.

The *real thing* is currently furious and painfully engorged.

I drop my hand from her breast and direct it around the front of her, using it to flick over her while my other hand keeps up the task. Voices come from somewhere outside the RV. People walking past.

"Dom," she whimpers. "Are we making"—a pause to convulse, and I know she's close—"a bad decision?"

"Shh," I tell her, bringing her to the edge. Her legs begin to stiffen, center contracting. "You better be quiet while we're making bad decisions."

The hand she's using to brace herself against the cabinet moves, fingers splayed and knuckles white. She's not quiet. Not at all. She comes like it's been a long fucking time, yelling my name.

My name. With that long *m* sound.

Keeping one hand wrapped around Cecily's hip, I pull myself from my pants before I make a mess of my clothing. "Bend over," I command, and she listens without hesitation.

What a picture she makes, ass up, dark hair spilling across her back. She reaches back, nails scoring my thigh.

Two quick seconds and I'm finishing, too. I was closer to ruining these shorts than I realized. Cecily's back moves with her heavy breath, still coming down from her own high. "Don't move," I tell her. The last thing I want is my spend on the countertop her family makes sandwiches on. We could sanitize it, but it would never really be clean again.

I tuck myself back into my pants and reach out for a paper towel.

"It's almost a shame to clean you up," I tell her, admiring the mess I've made of this woman who loves to drive me crazy. She looks back at me over her shoulder. "You look like every fantasy I've ever had."

"I'm sure that's not true," she argues.

It is, though. It is. Because anything I dreamed of before Cecily has ceased to exist. Erased from my memory. I don't want to imagine a time when it won't be Cecily I'm talking to, trying to make her smile, laugh. Cecily I'm endeavoring to win.

Am I trying to win her? I don't know. At this point, all I'm trying to do is not lose her.

I finish cleaning her up, carefully folding the paper towel into a second, clean paper towel, which I deposit into my pocket to get rid of in a different trash can.

Cecily turns around. She looks like herself again, but different. Slightly drugged, maybe. Relaxed. Calm.

She zips up her pants, threads the top button. When she goes to fix her top, I push her hands aside. "Allow me."

She smirks, but she lets me get one last nuzzle of each before I tuck them into her top and replace the straps on her shoulders.

"You seem to have a preference for my breasts."

"Nope," I tell her, placing my hands on her cheeks. "I have a preference for you."

Her eyes search my face. Emotion roams through her gaze. "I don't think I loathe you anymore."

I chuckle. I can't help it. "I know."

"How do you know?"

"In the last few days I realized you lacked conviction." Before she can argue, I kiss her. Lightly. "*I loathe you* stopped sounding like you meant it."

She wraps a hand around my wrist. "What does it sound like?"

"I'm not sure. I only know you don't mean it."

She nods slowly. "We should go. The food is probably at our table by now. There's no way we can hide this from my family, we were gone far too long."

"That's the beauty of being recently wed," I tell her as we lock up the motor home and walk away. The sky is darker now, burnt orange in the west and navy blue in the east. "They'll blame it on newlywed bliss."

She grins as we round the corner back onto the dusty main street. "You're telling me we can do"—she points back at the parking lot—"*that* over and over and have it be excused?"

"I suppose," I answer, more thrilled about the idea than I should be. "It would be a true test of our self-control." My hand finds her lower back, staying there as we navigate the wood plank sidewalk.

"It's only two and a half more weeks," Cecily reasons. "We could do it, don't you think?" She looks up at me with the most innocent expression, a juxtaposition to the subject matter.

"You're telling me you want to fool around, but not consummate the marriage?"

"No," she answers matter-of-factly. "What I want to do is fuck like bunnies and still be able to get an annulment. But that's frowned upon."

I'm shaking my head at her audacious mouth as we push into Big Nose Kate's Saloon. In our absence, a fiddler has replaced the harmonica player. She wears a corset and skirt, and a small hat with netting that swoops over her eyes.

"There you are," Kerrigan yells as we approach the table, hands around her mouth. "How long does it take to buy souvenirs?"

Cecily glances at me before nonchalantly saying, "They have a large selection, and Dom is very particular."

"Mm-hmm." Kerrigan crosses her arms. "So, what did you choose?"

I take my time pulling Cecily's seat out for her, then my

own. Even after the forced delay, I can't think of anything better to say than, "I didn't hear you. Can you please repeat yourself?"

Kerrigan's chin lifts. She knows we were up to something. "What souvenirs did you choose for your parents?"

I grab my beer. It's warm now, not at all appetizing, but it gives me something to do after I say, "I couldn't find any."

Kerrigan grins knowingly. "Even with a selection so large?"

Cecily shakes her head. "Nope," she lies even as she beats back a smile. They're on to us, and we both know it.

Duke grumbles and takes twenty dollars from his pocket. Kerrigan extends her flat palm, and he slaps it into her hand. She folds it in thirds and tucks it into her bra. "Nice doing business with you, Big Bro."

Our dinner arrives at the perfect moment, two younger guys placing a pulled pork sandwich in front of each person.

"Everybody got the same thing?" Cecily asks.

Grandma shrugs. "Queenie said it was what they're known for." She picks up a fry, pointing it from me to Cecily. "It's good to see you two finally acting like newlyweds."

Cecily's gaze slides guiltily over to me. I'm half-frozen, pinching my lower lip. I'll be honest, I have no idea how to proceed. Finally, I say, "This is pretty awkward."

"It's not pleasant for the rest of us, either," Duke announces, and Glenn laughs.

Cecily gapes at her dad. From the short time I've been around him, I've noticed Glenn does not laugh, or smile. But today, he has done both. Maybe Ophelia knew all along that this is what her family needed. I was certain that at worst they would fail her, and at best they would fake it. But this banter, this playfulness, these smiles, they seem genuine.

"Get used to it," Grandma says, turning her pointed fry in Duke's direction. "They are leaving Bernice behind in Sierra Grande and joining us on the motor home."

"We've renamed it the Road Kraken," Kerrigan tells us. There's a smear of barbecue sauce on her cheek.

"You have sauce on your cheek," Cecily tells her, and she replies, "I don't care."

Using my napkin on my face in case I'm suffering from a similar affliction and nobody is telling me, I ask, "What's with this family and naming vehicles?"

Duke drains his beer. "I have an idea. Dom, you should name Cecily's Jeep."

Glenn scrunches his nose like he's smelled something unpleasant. "Death trap," he says. "There, I did it for you."

"Wind tunnel," Duke says.

Cecily looks like she's trying not to care what they say, but I see the way she stiffens. A few weeks ago, she probably would have told everybody what they could do with their joke, but she's trying so hard for Ophelia's sake.

Last I checked, my last name isn't Hampton. I am not here to mend fences. I'm here to be Cecily's husband, and that's what I'll be.

Curling a lock of Cecily's hair around my finger, I say, "My wife's Jeep is named Miss Independence."

Game stymied, Glenn and Duke fall quiet. Neither expected my response, but I'm not done. "Cecily worked hard to buy that car. She saved up her money, and bought it outright." Casually, I look at Glenn. "What kind of car do you drive?"

He shifts uncomfortably. "A Mercedes."

"What is your monthly payment?"

"It's a lease."

"So then, you pay monthly."

"I suppose."

"Does your car have a name?"

Glenn shakes his head. *No.*

"May I?"

Glenn motions with an open palm, giving me the go-ahead. But then he crosses his arms in front of his chest, a sign of nervousness he's trying to conceal. He doesn't know what I'm going to say, but he does know that I'm ready to throw down for his daughter. He should appreciate my willingness, and if he doesn't, it says a lot more about him than it does about me.

"Your car's name is Teenager. It'll only be around awhile longer, it costs a lot of money, and it thinks it's better than everybody else." I wink at him, and smile good-naturedly, just to soften the blow.

The table is utterly silent. Even Kerrigan, who almost always has something to say, is shocked into quiet.

I put a hand on Cecily's knee. Squeeze gently. She covers my hand with her own, running her fingertips over my knuckles.

Marilyn picks up her half-full glass of cider. Lifts it in the air. "To Miss Independence," she says, her eyes directly on Cecily.

CHAPTER 37

Cecily

WHEN I WAKE UP THE NEXT MORNING, I FIND MYSELF DRAPED over Dom's chest. We'd gone to sleep on opposite sides of the bed, but during the night I gravitated toward him. It's not him on my side, or even in the middle. It is me, firmly on his half.

He breathes deeply, evenly, my head rising and falling on his chest in a peaceful rhythm. I should move, shimmy over to my half of the bed, but I fear moving will wake him.

My mind wanders to last night. The way he defended me. *My wife's Jeep is named Miss Independence.* And then earlier, when we'd snuck off to the motor home. *There is always time to make my wife come.* The man seems awfully preoccupied with calling me *wife*.

I don't hate it. Not one bit. Not like I did that first morning in Vegas, or the week that followed. Could Dom and I be something? In another life? In another world where he lives in the same city as me, where we weren't already married and could date like two people who meet under normal circumstances. If we hadn't gotten drunkenly married in Vegas, we could've talked about our first date faux pas. Laughed about it. Instead, we're here, thrust into this alternate universe where we're married and on a road trip with macabre undertones.

Still, Dom has found ways to be what I need, when I need it. A friend. A listener. A protector. A semi-lover. I want to thank him. I want to tell him what it means to me that he's here. It's just so damn hard to get the words up out of my throat.

Beneath me, Dom shifts. Makes a sound like a brief sigh that sticks in his throat. My eyes track his hand that reaches down into his sleep shorts, adjusting himself. Lazily, he gives it a half-hearted tug. I don't think he's fully awake, but his morning wood is at attention, still within the confines of his shorts.

Before I can think much more about it, I slide down his body. If I can't get the words out of my throat, I can put something else down it.

Dom stirs when I pull him from the soft shorts he wore to sleep. "Cecily, what—"

Heavy in my palm, I stroke my hand over him, making my intentions clear. Just a few seconds spent on this and I'm already squeezing my thighs together. I want him in a way that's foreign to me.

I take him in my mouth, and he goes quiet. His hand finds my hair, slipping through the strands until he gets to a tangle. His hand leaves my hair, moves to my face. A contented groan trickles from him. I peek up. His eyes are locked on me, deep blue and half-lidded.

"You're beautiful," he murmurs, voice husky with sleep and pleasure. "My Menace. My Chestnut."

My heart gallops in my chest. I love his nicknames for me. Far more than I should.

He groans, louder now, the sound coming from deep in his chest. His eyes do not stray from me, and I find it intoxicating. It's like he doesn't want to miss a moment of it. So I lean into that. *Perform*. Drink him down while my watery eyelashes flutter. His chest heaves, his jaw locks tight. He loves it.

So do I.

His fingertips brush over my face, thumb curving along the apple of my cheekbone. His fingers find my hair again, tightening on my scalp with the perfect amount of pressure.

"Cecily," he husks. "I'm close."

I nod in understanding, but I keep him where he is. I've never swallowed before, but with Dom, I want to.

Dom's fingers curl, pulling my hair in the best way, and he tips his head back and shuts his eyes tight. He's doing his best to be quiet, but he can't help the groaning grunt that vibrates from his throat.

"Your parents are on the other side of this wall," he says when he opens his eyes. "You have no idea how difficult it was to be quiet."

I sit back on my knees, demurely dabbing at the corners of my mouth. Swallowing wasn't that bad. "Wouldn't want Mommy and Daddy to know I gave you the old razzle dazzle."

The corner of his mouth tugs into a slow grin. He's still dazed, but he reaches for me.

I roll off the bed, wagging a finger at him as the ache between my legs yells at me. "No, no, no, mister. Keep your hands to yourself. We have places to be."

Dom follows me into the bathroom. He is sleep-rumpled and recently orgasmed, his shorts cinched low on his hips. I run the tap, tossing a handful of water in my mouth and swishing.

He runs a hand over the back of his neck, watching me in the mirror. "Not that I'm complaining, but what was that for?"

I spit, grabbing the hand towel and wiping my mouth. "I couldn't depart Tombstone without the opportunity to become a soiled dove."

Dom chuckles. I could leave it at that cheeky remark, and that would be it. But maybe I shouldn't. Maybe I should be brave. "I have a hard time verbalizing my appreciation of you. I thought I would show you instead."

Dom grips my hips, digs his fingers into me with the perfect amount of roughness. "I wouldn't mind spending some time appreciating you." He presses a kiss between my shoulder blades, his mop of messy hair toppling with the angle of his head.

"You did," I remind him. "Last night." The thought of it sends a bolt of heat to my core.

"Wasn't enough," he complains, almost pouting.

He looks so cute like that. It's enough to make a girl want to hop up on the countertop and spread her legs.

But I know better.

"No more funny business," I tell him. "We have a long drive today. Five hours to Sierra Grande. Plus, it's our last time traveling in Bernice. We need to make the most of it. Copious roadside stops. Many bags of Bugles. The most disgusting assortment of Icee flavors."

"Ugh," Dom groans. "I can't kiss you if you taste like Bugles and swamp water Icee."

I turn around, pressing my palms firmly against his hard chest. "That's why you need to eat Bugles and drink swamp water Icee with me. If we taste the same, we won't know the difference." I push him lightly, attempting to urge him out the bathroom door, but he doesn't budge. "I need to pee," I tell him, pushing him a little harder this time.

He shrugs. "So?"

My mouth drops open. Gross. "So, *go*. I need to pee."

"Then *pee.*"

"Do you have a urination fetish, Dom?"

"Married people pee in front of each other."

"That's nice, but no. The first time your eyeballs are on my lady part won't be when I'm doing that."

He ignores me, tugging at a lock of my messy hair. "It won't be much longer before I'm up close and personal with what you have between your thighs, Chestnut."

I swallow. Hard. Dampness spreads over my underwear. Clearly it's my vagina crying.

"Go," I command, pointing out the door to the rest of the room.

Dom grins and backs up. He points at the part of me that's sobbing between my legs. "Her days are numbered. Not even days. *Hours.* She has hours until I ruin her."

My knees weaken, but I force myself to stay standing. Who is this man with this mouth? And why *why WHY* do I love it?

Dom smirks and closes the door. I turn around, sinking back against the solid wood. In the mirror, a woman I don't recognize stares back at me. Pink cheeks, hair swirling around her. She is free of makeup, one of her pajama top straps lying haplessly against her shoulder. It's her eyes, though. Unguarded. At ease. Happy.

Dom's work, surely.

And maybe this road trip, too? This chance to see my family outside the roles we usually occupy? We are so far from being in a better place, but we can't get there unless we start somewhere.

This trip might be our first step.

CHAPTER 38

Cecily

WE'RE THREE HOURS INTO OUR DRIVE TO SIERRA GRANDE when Dom exits the highway to refuel Bernice. We've been listening to his playlist on repeat. His Vegas-themed songs make me smile, and his addition of "Bad Blood" by Taylor Swift made me laugh. My favorites are the road trip classics, Bob Seger and Lynyrd Skynyrd, Bruce Springsteen and Fleetwood Mac.

Dom navigates Bernice off the dusty road and into the asphalt parking lot. I peer through the windshield at the gas station that, if it weren't for the fuel pumps, looks nothing like a gas station. "Are you sure this is a gas station?"

"There are pumps and people parked at them." Dom is looking too, trying to make sense of what we're seeing.

The gas station convenience store is called THE THING. The building is long and low slung, bricks painted in mustard yellow with ketchup red lettering. The vibe is slasher flick meets Ronald McDonald.

Dom eases Bernice into a spot vacated a moment ago

by a van big enough to seat twelve, with windows tinted dark purple and faded lettering on the sides. It adds to the ambience of the place, and not in a good way.

Dom gets out and begins the refueling process, while I do a quick investigation on my phone.

"It looks legit," I tell Dom when he opens my passenger door. "This place is associated with a museum that claims to have mummified remains of a mother and her son. The Internet calls it a roadside attraction."

Swinging my legs from the car, I blink into the bright sun and stand. Tenting a hand over my eyes, I say, "No shade to mummified remains, but as roadside attractions go, I prefer Dom's Bulge."

Dom moves in closer, palming the side of my head. Lips hovering near my ear, he murmurs, "Funny thing about that attraction, it only appears for a certain person."

I pull back, feigning shock. "Hugh Jackman?"

Dom shakes his head and laughs, pulling me back in and pressing a light kiss to my lips. Thrill shoots down my spine. Look at us, kissing in public for no other reason than that we want to. What is happening?

"You are a very funny woman," Dom says, threading his fingers through mine. "Let's go into that weird place and see what we can find."

Turns out, THE THING is as odd as it sounds. Wood paneled walls make it more gift shop than convenience store, but it still offers a large selection of snacks and a refrigerated section. On every available surface is a tchotchke of some sort, and the walls have taxidermy animals with signs around their necks. *Don't touch, I bite.*

Dom picks up a stuffed jackalope. "I've never seen your apartment, but I strongly feel this guy has a home there."

I snag a navy blue hat with THE THING embroidered in bright yellow stitching. "Only if you promise to proudly wear this on your way to work."

Dom points behind me to a display with the same colors and theme. "Shot glasses, bumper stickers, coffee mugs, I could go all out."

In the end, we chose against the stuffed creature and swag. I opt for a crisp bottle of Coke, and Bugles, of course. Dom goes hard with a Gatorade and shelled pistachios.

"Turn your back," I tell him, when it's time to check out.

He frowns and gives me a look, but I show him my sternest eyebrows and he listens.

I grab a bag of candy rocks at the register and add them to the purchase, looking at the cashier and pressing my finger to my lips. The cashier winks and rings up our things.

"I'm turning back around," Dom warns, while he's already spinning.

"Go for it," I say, as the cashier hands me the thin plastic bag containing our items.

"Would you like to purchase tickets for THE THING museum?" She asks the question in the resolute tone of someone who is required to query every customer. "They are one dollar each."

There is no way I'm saying yes. That is exactly how people in horror movies die. This is the desert roadside equivalent of *let's check out the sound we heard coming from the basement.*

"Is that where the mummified people are?" I feel bad for the cashier. How many times in a day is she told no?

"Sure is," she answers.

Dom takes the bag from me. "Thank you for offering, but—"

"He's afraid," I tell her, taking the bag back from him.

"He looks afraid," she volleys, leaning around me and signaling for the next person in line to step up to the counter.

It's not until we're back inside Bernice that I reach into the bag and give Dom his silly present.

"It's no scorpion lollipop." I press the bag into his hand. "But it is a desert delicacy."

Dom turns the bag of speckled and muted tone chocolate rocks over in his hand. "These aren't really rocks, are they?"

"I'm not sure, but I don't think so. That would be pretty mean."

"Thank you." He gives the bag a shake. "I think you might be sweeter than you act, Cecily."

I gasp dramatically. "Blasphemy."

He reaches into the back seat for his backpack, tucking the candy rocks safely into a zippered pocket where he's been keeping the scorpion lollipop.

His bicep flexes when he replaces the backpack. Something akin to delight passes through me. I had this man in my mouth this morning. *And he wants me.* He's made it abundantly clear.

He starts the car and shifts into Drive. "The lollipop was a gift for defending you. And you already thanked me this morning in a way that was very generous and"—he pauses, thinking—"*fucking lovely.* What are the rocks for?"

I lean on the console, using my forearm for leverage to reach his cheek, where I plant a kiss. "For the way you defended me last night. I thought you hated my car."

He navigates to the freeway and picks up speed. "I do hate your car."

"That's what I thought! You were horrified that first day I picked you up in it." I cross my arms and nod, so proud to have been right about how much Dom hates the newly minted Miss Independence.

"I couldn't sit there and listen to them talk about a car you worked hard to get. Even if they were just teasing you, there was an undertone of mocking. I didn't like it." He rubs a hand over his jaw. "I thought maybe they didn't know about how you ended up with that car, and if they didn't, they should be told."

"You named my dad's car *Teenager.*" I snicker. "It's so accurate."

"He took it well," Dom says. "Your mom stepped in and shaped the conversation from there."

"She did," I say, toying with the hair tie on my wrist. "Every day of this trip she shocks me. It's like I don't know her. Like she was black and white, and slowly she's coming into color."

"You sound melancholy about it."

"I don't feel melancholy about it." I don't think so, anyway. "Maybe I'm adjusting to this new side of her. Who knows how long it will be around. Maybe forever. Or only the duration of the trip."

"You don't want to get attached to the new version of her, because you don't trust it has staying power. If you let yourself care, it'll hurt when she goes back to who she was before."

Oh. Wow. Ok, yes. That's exactly how I feel. "How did you know that?"

Dom taps the steering wheel with the side of his

thumb. "I have firsthand experience, unfortunately. Also, therapy."

I remain quiet, hoping this will be the moment Dom finally talks about his supposedly vanilla family.

"My dad is a character. In both good and bad ways. He calls himself a showman, but it's just a gilded word he chooses because he can't bear to accept the truth about himself. My childhood..." Dom trails off, and I'm so worried he'll stop talking. I've been waiting for him to open up, and now that the moment has arrived, I realize how badly I want to know him.

"I'm listening," I say quietly.

He glances at me, breathing a hard, closed mouth breath. "I love him, you know? But I don't understand him. Growing up, things were never stable. I wasn't sure if I would come home and find my stuff in the back of his truck, because we had to move again. Another fight with another landlord. It could be as simple as them asking my dad to mow the lawn more frequently. It would set him off, and that was that. My dad's a nice guy, but he can be a hothead. He's calmed down since he's grown older." Dom reaches out to adjust the air vent, angling it away from him. "Kids need stability. I know things happen, and people move, but it happened too many times. It didn't take long before I saw he was the problem. I promised myself I would do whatever it takes to not be like him. I worked hard in high school, I did everything I could to get as far as possible from that mentality. I was always afraid it was transmissible. I couldn't believe it when I got a scholarship for college in New York. It didn't cover everything, and every second I wasn't studying, I was working. But I did it. I made it happen. I'm nothing like him, which should make me happy, but really, it just confuses me. It's hard to love somebody who is so deeply flawed. It's even more difficult when it's your parent."

"What about your mom? Where does she fit into all this?"

"It would be easy to let my mom off the hook for everything because she is a really nice person. But she enables him. She never seems to mind the way he lives life. As a kid I wished for her to take a stand on my behalf. I wanted her to do what was best for me, but she rarely did. It was hard to let myself acknowledge my disappointment in her, because I know she loves me. Our parents can love us, and still hurt us, and that's a difficult concept to grapple with."

"You are so much further than me in your childhood trauma repair journey. You've realized your flawed parents are still lovable. I haven't reached that point yet. Instead of doing the work, I ran away."

"Sometimes it's safer to do the work from a distance."

"You're very wise."

"I am older than you by two years."

"When is your birthday? I only know you hate it. I need to know the date you hate."

"October first."

I grab my phone and enter the date in my calendar. "Why do you dislike your birthday?"

"It's not something tragic, if that's what you're thinking." He shoots me a wry smile. "My dad isn't big on birthdays. He thinks they don't matter, and celebrating them is silly. So my birthday was just another day. Again, nothing truly tragic, but as a kid, it's hard to watch your peers be celebrated. My elementary school teachers always knew when it was my birthday, and they had these paper crowns they would make for every child when it was their special day. I kept all of them, but they're packed away in a box now. So there you have it. That's why I don't like my birthday." He shrugs.

My heart lurches. I wish his birthday were tomorrow. I'd find a cake and candles and make him a crown. I opt for running my fingers over his forearm.

His playlist plays quietly in the background, and he says, "Tell me about the next place we're going."

It's his way of saying he's done talking about his parents.

We're Going To Have Fun, DAMMIT is in the bag at my feet. Spreading it open on my lap, I read from the Sierra Grande section.

"A classic western town, Sierra Grande is home to the largest cattle ranch in Arizona, the Hayden Cattle Company. The walkable main street will transport you to the Wild West. Grab lunch at The Orchard and watch bull riders try their luck at The Chute." I turn the page, continuing to walk Dom through our next week of destinations. "Sedona. Glamping. The haunted Hotel Monte Vista, in Flagstaff." I flip to the information printout with our reservation and schedule. "Considered one of the most haunted hotels in Arizona, inhabited by several spirits, including a bellboy, two prostitutes, and the Meat Man."

Dom reaches over and playfully chucks my chin. "Good thing I don't believe in ghosts."

"I do, until I'm proven otherwise. Best believe I will glue myself to your side all night while we sleep."

"I could think of far worse experiences."

After that, I let the ghost discussion die (no pun intended). We stop once more at a rest station to use the facilities, and when I exit the ladies' room, I see Dom has Bernice's top down. He leans against the car, one leg crossed over the other at the ankles, his arms folded in front of his chest. With his wavy hair, flopping lawlessly about his head, he resembles a literary James Dean.

A pair of older women walk out of the restroom behind me, and one of them says, "Dear me, look at that man. If I were thirty years younger..."

Her companion snorts. "You'd what?"

"Teach him a few things about life."

I press my lips together to keep from laughing, but then decide *fuck it*. I turn around. "My husband is hot, right? But he's also really smart, and very kind."

They blink in shock, but I smile and say, "Safe travels."

And then I practically float to where Dom waits for me. I don't know what that was about. My actions, my words, I don't know how to explain them. I only know I wanted Dom to be mine in that moment. I wanted him to belong to me. What the hell is going on in my head? In my heart?

"You ready?" Dom asks when I get closer. I don't say a word. I step into him, wrap my arms around his neck, and pull his mouth down to mine.

Mine.

Surprise suspends Dom's response, but only for a second. He eagerly snakes his arms around my waist, hauls me flush against him, and kisses me like we aren't in a dusty parking lot in the desert.

When the kiss breaks I pull back, but not too far. I can't stand the idea of not touching him, so I cup his cheek. "Sorry I attacked your mouth in public."

Dom tucks my hair behind my ear. "For the record, I like being attacked by you in public."

My fingernails lightly scratch over his stubble. "There were two women talking about how hot you are."

He crooks an eyebrow. "Feeling jealous, Chestnut?"

"Possessive."

Confusion blooms in his gaze even as he holds me fast to him. "What is it you want, Cecily?" His eyes search my face, looking for an answer.

"I'm not sure," I admit. "I've had so many different feelings toward you, and now I'm here with my family and my sick grandma. This experience is ripe for big emotions."

He nods like he understands. "You just tell me what you need from me, alright? I'll give it to you."

My head bobs in agreement. "Thank you for telling me about your parents."

A neutral smile tugs up one corner of his mouth. "You're the first person I've talked to about them, aside from my therapist. It only seemed fair, given that I have a front row seat to your family dysfunction."

I breathe out a laugh at the same time my heart does a twisty motion in my chest. "I appreciate that you trust me."

He traces my lips with a fingertip. "You are something else, Cecily."

"You too, Dom."

He drops his head for another kiss, something sweet, and small. Then he walks me around the car and opens the passenger door.

When we're back on the road, I hit play on Dom's road trip playlist, and we spend the remaining drive in companionable silence.

CHAPTER 39

Cecily

GRANDMA HAS US BOOKED INTO A CUTE HOTEL, THE SIERRA. The manager tells us it was renovated in the last couple years, and Tenley Roberts, the retired actress who lives in town, sometimes stops into the bar for a cocktail. I would never approach a famous person in the wild, but Kerrigan would have no qualms.

On the way to the rooms, Kerrigan says, "If we see her, I'm gonna ask her to sign my boob."

I smack Kerrigan's chest lightly. "Nobody wants to sign your tit."

"It's a signable tit," Kerrigan defends.

"Yeah, yeah," I say, shooing her down the hall to the room beside ours.

She waggles a finger at me and Dom. "I don't want to hear you two having sex."

"You won't," I promise. "We can't do that, remember?"

Kerrigan turns her attention to Dom. "I'll tell you what I told her right before your doomed first date. *Your mouth can't get pregnant.*"

Dom coughs out a laugh. "Uh, thanks for the advice."

"You're welcome. Guess what your mouth can get no matter what you use it for? An annulment. Bye." Kerrigan twirls her fingers at us and disappears into her room.

"I apologize for her," I say to Dom, stepping into the room with him.

"She's the quintessential baby of the family," he says, setting his backpack on a chair.

"I suppose we all play our birth order roles. Me, the difficult middle child. Duke, the overachieving first born."

"Hey." Dom snags my wrist. "That's not what I meant."

"It's ok," I say, quickly. "It can be true."

"You're not difficult, Cecily."

"Oh, please." I give him an imploring look. "This morning's *service* may have blown your mind, but I know it didn't erase your memory. You disliked me at the beginning of this as much as I disliked you."

His fingertip finds the underside of my chin, lifting, forcing my gaze to meet his. "No matter what transpired between us, it would be impossible for me to dislike you."

Salty heat pricks the backs of my eyes. I don't know why. "I really did dislike you."

Laughter tugs at his cheeks. "Fair. You thought I said terrible things about you."

"Technically, you did."

He runs his knuckles over my jawline. "Chestnut, I will wake up every morning, roll over and call that author, and make him tell you over and over what happened on that call."

"If you did that, you'd probably find yourself with one fewer client."

"Then I'll get him to record himself saying it, and send me the audio."

"You're very creative."

"Part of the job."

"Is it wrong that I wish we weren't having girls' night tonight?"

"Don't tell anybody, but I'm not exactly stoked to have dinner with your dad and Duke."

"Might want to brush up on your hotel chain acquisition talking points." I snap my fingers, realizing something. "Duke likes to read."

He winks at me. "I can hold my own. Nestled among the emotional wounds given to me by my father is the ability to find common ground and make conversation with just about anybody."

"A highly sought after trait to have." I don't want to step away from him and start to get ready, but I need to. The hotel car is waiting downstairs to drive us to the bull riding bar I read about on the drive.

Locating my jean skirt, I stand in the middle of the room, and when I'm certain Dom's gaze is on me, I unbutton my shorts. Slide them down my legs. Step out of them, and kick them aside.

Dom takes a step closer to me. My arm shoots out.

"No, no, no," I say playfully. "We need to get ready for dinner."

"I know what's on my menu," he all but growls. I love it.

"Later," I tell him, stepping into the jean skirt. I locate my cowgirl boots and stuff my feet into them.

Stepping into him, I run my hands through his hair.

"Don't stay out too late, Cowboy." I'm two paces away when he smacks my ass.

"You're lucky I'm letting you leave this hotel room at all," he says, his tone thickened by a kind of arrogance I have a hard time leaving behind.

I stand in the open door and look at him. He's tall, and big, and I want to know what it feels like to be under him. To have him inside me. Next door, the sound of a door opening. Kerrigan will be here any second to walk downstairs with me.

My gaze travels south, down Dom's body, to the place where I started our day. Then I meet his eyes, lick my lips slowly, letting my mouth shift into a smile and a wink.

Dom palms his chest. Strides forward. I know what he's going to do. Haul me in and lock the door. Sink to his knees.

Just before he gets to me, I step backward and close the door.

"Hey, Cecily," Kerrigan says from two feet away.

"Hey, Kerr," I say, loudly.

Kerrigan eyes me like a police investigator. "Why do you look like that?"

"Like what?"

We start for the elevator at the end of the hall. "You're breathing heavily. Did you—"

"No. You know we can't have sex."

"There are a lot of stops between point a and point z. I know something went down in the motor home last night. Probably Dom from behind, if the crushed loaf of bread on the counter was any indication."

I remember the bread, but I have no memory of what precise moment I squashed it. "Oops."

"I knew it," Kerrigan says loudly, victorious. "What a hussy."

I lift my nose in the air. "I prefer the term 'soiled dove'."

Kerrigan hits the button for the elevator. "Help me understand. You and Dom like each other, that's clear. I can smell the attraction coming off the two of you. It's like a master class in sexual tension."

"What is it that needs understanding?" I ask, as the elevator doors open. We step on, and I press the button for the lobby.

"Dom has you feeling all kinds of ways, your chemistry is undeniable, and he can stand to be around your family for long stretches. If you try to explain that to a stranger, they would probably tell you it sounds like you've been dating for six to twelve months and are thinking about getting serious."

"Except for the teeny, tiny fact we are already married."

"And that's where I need help understanding. What are you going to do, get an annulment and never see this guy again? Dom's great, Cecily. Like really, *really* great. Rare." The elevator door opens, delivering us to the lobby. Rainbow, my grandma, and my mother stand near the doors leading to the street. "All I'm saying," Kerrigan says in a low breath as we walk over, "is that you need to adjust your camera lens. Pan out. What does life look like for you and Dom once this is over? Is it an annulment and you two return to opposite sides of the country? Or do you think you might have a shot at something great?"

"Um," is all I manage to say. Kerrigan has given me a lot to think about.

She waves her hand. "I know, I don't usually have that much wisdom. It's disorienting."

Her sentence makes me pause. I hear myself in it. The way she makes fun of herself before I can. I don't typically make fun of myself, but I have other defense mechanisms. Most notably, staying away from my family and approaching every interaction with my fists raised.

"Kerr," I say, my arm shooting out to stop her. "You have plenty of wisdom. And I appreciate you sharing it with me. What you said was very insightful, and you've given me a lot to think about."

She's quiet for a long beat, then says, "I'm not sure how to respond. I'm not used to you being this nice."

"Credit should probably go to Dom. He gave me one hell of an orgasm last night."

"Poor loaf of bread didn't stand a chance."

"Girls," Grandma hollers. "Get your asses over here. The driver is out there waiting, and you're standing there talking about bread."

CHAPTER 40

Cecily

I grew up in small-town Arizona, but this? It's night and day different. With an olive grove and a thoroughbred farm, Olive Township is a charming town with a decidedly Spanish flair. Sierra Grande is as cowboy as it gets, especially this bar we're in. The Chute has neon bar signs, a wooden dance floor, and an outdoor bull riding arena. A full band plays on a stage, with a crooning country singer. It smells of beer and barbecue, leather and cologne. I love it here.

We've finished dinner, and now we're on our third round of margaritas. Except for Rainbow. She's sipping soda water with an orange slice. She frowned when my grandma accepted a margarita, but said nothing. Secretly, I was hoping Rainbow would attempt to tell my grandma not to have a drink. Listening to Savage Grandma tell Rainbow what to do with her disapproval would've been superb entertainment.

"What do you think, Grandma?" I yell over the lively

song. Bodies crowd the dance floor, everybody in cowboy boots, a cowboy hat atop every man's head.

"This place is fucking fabulous," she yells back. Her eyes are twinkling, and she shimmies her shoulders. Tonight she's wearing her signature caftan, but this one is turquoise and fringed. She wears three strands of silver bead necklaces, and chandelier earrings that catch the light.

How can she be so sick? Look at her. Vibrant, smiling. Sipping a margarita. She turns to chat with my mom, and Kerrigan pulls me up to dance.

"I know your toes were tapping," Kerrigan says as we weave closer to the dance floor. "You love to dance."

"Busted," I trill.

Kerrigan and I find a little corner of the dance floor and plant a flag in it. It's not the same music, or even close to the same venue, but it reminds me of that night in Vegas with Dom. My hands holding onto his shoulders, the way he gripped me as we danced.

Kerrigan's questions from earlier come back to me. *What does life look like for you and Dom once this is over?*

I don't know what's possible for us. Dom lives across the country. A different life awaits him, a career, a clock that will never read the same time as mine.

"Hey, pretty lady," a deep voice says, too close to my ear.

I stop dancing, and so does Kerrigan. Cowboys stand on either side of us. The man beside Kerrigan offers her a hand, asking if she wants to dance. I nod at her, telling her to go for it if she wants to. She places her hand in his waiting palm, and he pulls her deeper onto the dance floor.

"I think I'll sit this one out," I say to the cowboy still standing there, eyes on me.

"Come on, sugar. It's just a dance."

"I'm married."

"An empty ring finger on your left hand says otherwise."

I glance down at my hand. "I forgot to wear it tonight."

"Forgot," the cowboy says, making air quotes.

I'm out of what little patience I had for this guy. "Bye," I say, pivoting on my heel. I'm brought up short by a sound at the bar. A yell, but more of a screech. The protest of barstools scraping the floor. More yelling. Pushing, now. Adrenaline slips through me. Will I get to watch my first bar fight tonight? I take a step toward our table, ready to pick up my margarita and pull up a chair, but I'm frozen in place when I see the blonde bob in the middle of the fray.

My mother.

Her forearms lift to protect her face, and she tries to shoulder her way out of the bodies. There are too many, the crowd is too thick, outliers being pulled into the scuffle by wayward arms and elbows.

I hurry that direction, prepared to extract my mom. But then a woman pushes her, two-handed while she does nothing but try to protect herself.

Is someone seriously trying to rough up my sixty-year-old mom?

Looks like tonight will be the first bar fight I've ever witnessed, and joined.

I charge in, head ducked, flattened palms held above my eyes like the bill of a hat. Someone knocks into me, and I stumble but remain upright. In the middle of it all, my mother shakes like a leaf.

And that bitch who pushed her once? She does it again.

I wind up and throw my first punch. Closed fist, follow through. It catches her in the jaw. My aim could use some work, but it gets the job done. The woman stumbles back against the bar, laid out but looking at me. I'm on her again, pressing my finger into her chest.

"Don't touch my mom," I yell in her face. Then I add an extra *thwap* to the top of her head. She deserves it. Grabbing my mom's hand, I tell her, "Keep your head down."

We duck low, sliding parallel to the bar. The fight has moved away from the stools, out into the center of the room. Two men wearing tight Security T-shirts and built like brick walls rush in from the arena behind the building. The fight is as good as over, but the second we're back at our table, I tell Rainbow and Grandma it's time to leave. Kerrigan shows up, too, eyes bright.

"I kicked someone," Kerrigan says breathlessly. "Right in the babymaker. It was easy to hit the target because his jeans were so damn tight. Can't miss what's on display."

We grab our purses and march out the door. We're only a few feet from the entrance when it opens and two women walk out. One is older, and holds tight to the upper arm of a girl who cannot be more than eighteen years old.

The woman looks ready to fly off the handle. She passes a few feet away from us, and I catch her mid-sentence "...showing a fake ID in this town? I'm not sure you can be more of an idiot. Everybody knows who you are, Peyton."

"Aunt Jessie, please don't tell my dad."

"I'll tell your dad what I damn well please."

And then they're gone, swallowed up by the night. A

minute later I hear the roar of a truck engine, and the rig passes under a parking lot lamp, a decal on the driver's door that says HCC.

"The hotel van is on its way to pick us up," Grandma says. "I called them the second I watched Cecily jump into the fight."

Kerrigan smacks my arm. "You jumped into the fight?"

My adrenaline still flows at top speed, blood pounding in my ears. "Didn't you? You said you kicked somebody."

"Yeah, that stupid cowboy who wouldn't stop grabbing my ass."

"She saved me," my mom says, leaning back against the front wall of the bar. Her hands are on her knees as she catches her breath. "I thought for sure I was going to end up in a heap on the sticky floor."

"There's no way I would ever let that happen, Mom."

Mom pushes off the wall, steps in front of me, and wraps me in a hug. At first I'm too stunned to move, but then I thaw. I let her hold me in a way she hasn't in years.

"Thank you," she whispers against my head.

"You're welcome," I whisper back.

Headlights swing into the parking lot. It's the van, come to return us to the hotel.

It's a loud ride, everyone telling their version of what they saw.

"Cecily went in there like a bowling ball," Grandma says.

"Your aura was red," Rainbow adds.

"I didn't see any of the good stuff," Kerrigan whines. "I was too busy fending off the cowboy with arms like an octopus."

"Does this mean you're officially over your fixation with cowboys?"

"Don't be silly," Kerrigan responds tartly. "I refuse to let one bad apple ruin the whole bunch."

When we arrive at the hotel, we find my dad, Duke, and Dom in the bar. Three longneck beers sweat on coasters, a basket of chips with a salsa trio on the bar top.

Dad and Duke are seated, but Dom stands, a forearm on the bar. He sees us first, and a smile lights up his face.

I float into his side, tucking myself there. It's like there's a blank space my exact shape and size waiting to be filled against him.

Mom, with unfettered pride, announces, "Cecily punched someone for me."

Dom jerks in surprise, leaning back so he can look down at me. "Closed fist, follow through?"

"Obviously," I say with a smile, accepting a glass of water from the bartender. My mom and Kerrigan order margaritas.

"Before you get to regaling everybody with your story," Grandma interrupts. "I'm going to call it a night." She sends us a wave and air kisses, and Rainbow assists her from the room. I don't know how much assisting Rainbow's doing, but she's there in case Grandma needs her.

"What happened?" my dad asks my mom.

"I was at the bar getting another round for us when people around me started fighting. I don't know their reason, but suddenly it was a group of people, and some woman pushed me. Twice. Cecily saw it happen, and she rushed in and punched the lady. Then she yelled at her. *Don't touch my mom.*" Mom reenacts it, leaning over a phantom person at the bar, finger pressing hard the way mine did.

It's the most animated I've seen her since I can't remember when.

"Did anybody know who you were?" Duke asks, alarm and worry creasing his tone. Always thinking about the family image, like my dad when we were young.

I frown at my smart-yet-dumb brother. "We're not famous, asshat."

"Don't make her mad," my mom warns, swiping a chip through the salsa. "She can throw a punch."

Duke looks at me with, *say it isn't so*, a morsel of respect. He offers me a fist bump. "Good work defending Mom. Didn't know you had it in you."

I bristle. "Did you think I would leave her to fight it out herself?"

Duke picks up his beer, closing his eyes briefly like he's trying to get control of his emotions. "No, Cecily, that is not what I thought."

"You just said that you didn't know I had it in me to defend Mom."

"I meant I didn't know you had it in you to fight. Of course you would defend Mom."

"Oh." I really read that one incorrectly. "Ok. Thanks."

Duke offers the bottom of his beer, clinking it against the bottom of my water glass in a reconciliatory way. I return the gesture with a small smile.

The bartender drops off the margaritas and another round of beers.

Mom takes a healthy sip of her margarita. "You should have seen Cecily," she says, drink aloft. "Everyone in that bar was afraid of her."

This couldn't be more untrue, but I don't correct her because she's doing something new. *Bragging.* About me. Not openly complaining about how I'm argumentative, or ungrateful, or disinterested in our family. She's saying something complimentary.

"I'm sure the security guards who came rushing in at the end were not afraid of me, but I wasn't sticking around to see." I grab a chip and drag it through the brightest of the salsas. "Holy—" I press a hand to my mouth as fire consumes my tongue. "What is that?" I ask, pointing at the orange-colored salsa.

"Habanero," Dom answers, pushing my water into my hand.

"Your husband has been eating it all night," Duke says. "Apparently he is impervious to spicy food."

Beer poised at his lips, Dom says, "I like spice." His fingers, splayed against my lower back, dip a half inch into the waistband of my denim skirt. He drags them back and forth across my skin, lighting a fire in my belly as hot as the residual burning across my mouth.

The family makes small talk, asking Dom about a day in the life of a literary agent, and I bide my time, waiting for Dom to finish his beer. I want to get out of here, now. I want Dom in our hotel room.

With only a few sips remaining in his beer, I turn my face into Dom's chest and murmur, "Let's go."

I hear it in my voice. The sex. The desire. The need. Consummating this marriage is starting to look like an eventuality.

Kerrigan's questions from earlier this evening pound in my head, a drumbeat.

What does life look like for you and Dom once this is over?

Is it an annulment and you two return to opposite sides of the country?

Or do you think you might have a shot at something great?

"Well," Dom says, pushing his empty beer to the far edge of the bar. "Cecily and I are going to hit the hay."

"Is that what the kids are calling it?" Kerrigan asks.

My dad groans. "We get it, Kerrigan. They're newly-weds. They're...*active*."

Kerrigan grins at me and sips her drink.

We say good night and step away, and I'm just about to walk through the bar and into the hotel lobby when my dad says my name. I pivot, and Dom walks to the elevator bank to wait for me.

"Yeah, Dad?"

He shifts uncomfortably, an uncharacteristic move. "I want to say thank you for how you protected your mother tonight. She's not bar-fight material." He chuckles to himself. "Not like you."

"I'm not sure if that was a compliment, but I think I'll take it as one."

"It was a compliment, Cecily. You're tough. You always have been."

You make it difficult to love you.

I hate it, but it's all I hear.

Even now, as he tries to compliment me, I only hear the most damaging sentence he's ever spoken to me.

"Thanks, Dad." I step away. "Good night."

CHAPTER 41

Dominic

CECILY STEPS UP BESIDE ME AT THE ELEVATOR. I'VE BEEN thinking of her all night, the way she teased me in our hotel room and then left, jean skirt hugging the curve of her backside.

I hit the button for the elevator and curl my pinky around hers. She looks at me, the expression in her eyes reflecting exactly how I feel. Hungry.

I have to keep my hands in my pockets to stop myself from pressing her up against the wall, right here in the lobby within eyeshot of her family.

The elevator dings, the doors sliding open. "After you," I say, and Cecily steps on.

I push the button for our floor, and Cecily says in the sultriest voice I have ever heard, "I hope you have wicked plans for me."

I reach for her wrist, brush my thumb along the sensitive skin on the inside. "I plan to be so good to you that when you think about me tomorrow, you'll blush."

A tiny moan escapes that perfect mouth.

That's when I decide I don't want to wait. I want her, I need her, immediately. The door is closed, and the lift rises. I give it three seconds before I hit the emergency button. Cecily and I catch ourselves as the car comes to an abrupt stop.

"What—" Her question cuts off when I drop to my knees, pushing her against the mirrored elevator wall. Leaning in, I nibble at her mid-thigh, wrapping a hand around the other thigh.

"Dom," she says, breathless, as she realizes my plan.

"Just want to be certain you understand my definition of wicked."

"I think I do," she replies, running her hands through my hair.

"You teased me." I nip at her skin, nosing the hem of her skirt. "And now I'll be teasing you."

"Mmm," is all she can say.

I work my way higher up her thighs, swiping my tongue over the soft skin. Her skirt is too tight, a hindrance. "Pull up your skirt, Menace, I have work to do."

Cecily's nails brush my forehead as she hoists the fabric up to her hip bones. And there she is, covered in baby blue lace.

My finger dips under the fabric, running along the edge. "This fucking thong is what started this."

"You started this, Dom. You, and me, and hard feelings, and tequila."

I look up into her eyes, her heated gaze staring back at me. She's right.

Truth be told, I don't know how elevators work. Is there an intercom system? Can somebody's voice penetrate this moment? Ask us if we're ok, why we've stopped the elevator? Someone somewhere must have been notified the emergency button was pushed.

As much as I would love to settle between Cecily's legs, worship her the way I want to, there isn't time.

Hauling those criminally sexy underwear aside, I'm met with my first full glimpse of a part of Cecily my hand is well-acquainted with. She's lovely, and later, when she's on her back in bed, I'll learn every inch of her. Right now is about going from zero to one hundred.

I lean in, pressing my mouth to Cecily. She moans indecently. I don't know where our elevator has stopped, but if it is anywhere near a floor opening, somebody would know precisely what we're doing.

Hitching one of her legs over my shoulder, I make another pass over her. Once. Twice. She's so responsive, so ready, fingernails dragging over my scalp. I love how open she is, how much she's enjoying it. Making Cecily lose her mind is extra-special, she's—

"It's hot," Cecily says.

"I know," I murmur against her. If I get my way, I'll be coming up with more hot shenanigans for the two of us for the duration of this trip.

"No, no. Dom." Her panicked voice has me pulling away. "It's *hot*."

She's pointing down at herself. I look at her center, glistening and perfect, calling my name.

"Burning," she explains, pain in her voice.

"How—"

She gasps. "You were eating habanero salsa."

I pale. No. That can't be. But I was. Despite what I told Cecily about being able to make conversation with anybody, I was nervous to be at dinner with Glenn and

Duke without Cecily as a buffer. I ate copious chips and salsa.

Letting go of Cecily's underwear, I cover her back up, tugging her skirt down. She's biting the side of her lip, pressing her legs together.

I feel terrible. All I wanted was to bring her pleasure, and instead I've brought her pain.

I hit the button for our floor, and the elevator moves. Problem-solving mode activated. "We need milk," I tell her, already thinking about the store I saw earlier. A quaint place called Mercantile.

"What the hell am I supposed to do with milk? Drink it?"

"Sit in it. It counteracts the capsaicin from the pepper."

The elevator opens, and Cecily steps off. "Are you coming?" She's grimacing, her knees pressed together.

"I'm going for milk. Lots of milk." I hit the down button. "Get undressed and wait for me in the tub."

It feels like forever, but it's probably only ninety seconds before I'm out front of the hotel and jogging toward Mercantile.

The place is still open. There is a refrigerated section in the back, and I hustle toward it, grabbing as many handles of gallon-size whole milk as I can carry.

"You're either having an emergency with a calf, or a cookie party," the woman at the register deadpans.

"I can neither confirm nor deny," I say with a tight smile as I pay with my phone.

"Good luck," she says.

I thread my fingers through the handles and thank her.

Bringing my arms into my chest as if doing a bicep curl, I hurry back to the hotel. If it weren't for the group of people gathered near the elevator, I wouldn't have to put on the brakes.

"Dom, are you aware you're carrying"—Duke stops to count—"six gallons of milk?"

"Cecily was thirsty," I explain, trying not to meet Glenn's shrewd gaze.

"For six gallons of whole milk?" Kerrigan joins in, picking up on the type of milk.

"I prefer whole," I lie.

"The rooms don't have big enough refrigerators," Kerrigan presses.

"Why is the elevator taking so long?" I ask, trying to keep frustration from my voice.

"There's only one elevator working right now," an employee says, coming up from behind us. "I had to call maintenance for the other one. We're not sure what happened."

I know exactly what happened. That elevator didn't stand a chance against a sex-starved married couple trying valiantly not to consummate their marriage.

Without a word, I stride toward the door labeled *Stairwell.*

All six gallons of milk are in the bathtub. Cecily scrambles in, wearing only a soft-looking bra that more closely resembles a sports bra. Her eagerness makes me feel worse about the situation. If Cecily isn't arguing about something as absurd as sitting in milk, it means she's truly in pain.

And it's my fault.

"Make room for me," I tell her, pulling off my shirt.

She finishes tying her hair into a knot on top of her head. "You want to sit in milk?"

"Not particularly." I drop my shorts. "I'd rather go through something unpleasant with you than watch you go through it by yourself."

Cecily leans forward, giving me space to slide in behind her. When I'm situated, she leans back, her legs long and running parallel with mine.

"I'm sorry," I whisper in her ear.

"Ten out of ten I do not recommend cunnilingus following hot pepper ingestion." She cranes her neck to look up at me. "But the milk bath is nice."

I trace the curve of her jaw with my knuckles. "Are you getting some relief?"

She nods.

"You wouldn't believe how bad I feel."

Her eyebrows lift. "Have you ever seen the movie Inside Out?"

"Yes."

"Do you remember Anger?"

When I nod, she says, "He gets angry, and fire shoots out of his head? That was my vagina."

I chuckle at the image. "She was angry and on fire? Deadly combination."

"Just on fire. Not angry. Before the burning, she was quite happy."

I feel myself stir. I can't help it.

Cecily notices. "You are very responsive to me."

My fingertip dips into the milk, and I drag it over her stomach, watching a drop slide down to the 'v' between her legs. "I've never been this attracted to anybody. There's something about you, Cecily."

"People don't say things like that to me, Dom."

A swell rises within me. I want to travel back in time and punch the face of every man who didn't recognize Cecily for what she is. I press a kiss to her shoulder. Maybe I won't be punching anybody. Maybe I'll sit here and be silently grateful for their mistake. "Every person you come across all day long should be telling you how great you are."

Cecily's body moves with a soft laugh. She's quiet for a moment, and then she breaks my heart by saying, "When I was a teenager, my dad told me it's not easy to love me. His exact words were *You make it difficult to love you.*"

I hate the way Cecily's voice has shrunk, lost its characteristic strength. I hate the way she carries those seven words around in her heart, in her mind.

A lie. Cecily believes a lie. How can I show her how wrong her dad was back then? And still is today?

I hold her until her skin pebbles and I realize she's cold.

"How are you feeling down there?" I wince at the words. My fault, my fault. I'll make it up to her.

"Better," she says. She sounds tired.

"We should rinse off the milk. The sugar in it will make us sticky."

Cecily sits up, removing the stopper from the drain.

"No," she says when she sees me getting out of the bathtub. "Stay." She pulls the bra over her head. "Shower with me."

"Ok," I agree quickly. I'd never pass on the opportunity to wash her. To hold her under the warm spray.

It's precisely what I do. I'm gentle with her, and even

more careful of the tender space between her thighs. She lays her head on my chest while I run soapy hands over her back, and my heart pulls a cartoon character move and beats a heart-shape straight out of my skin.

Cecily is opening up to me. This infuriating, sexy, stubborn woman is letting me in.

I know what it's like to earn my way. I attended college with kids who didn't need a job to pay for books, who weren't taking on debt to get an education. My collegiate strides pale in comparison to the satisfaction I feel at earning Cecily's trust. Her vulnerability.

I turn her around. Run soap slickened hands over her breasts. She arches into me. Moans. Nipples need extra cleaning. I don't make the rules.

When I'm finished, Cecily steps behind me. "My turn," she says, husky.

She runs her hands all over my body, with a reverence I can barely comprehend. This is a side of Cecily she keeps locked up tight. Caring. Sweet. I like when she's spicy, but I like when she's sweet, too. I fear I may like when she is *everything*.

Between the elevator before I knew she was in pain, the milk bath, and washing Cecily, I am painfully hard. Cecily's touch slides over my stomach, then lower. She grips me with one hand, dragging me. So slow. My head tips back, eyes finding the ceiling.

"Cecily." Her name pours from my lips, a groan. "Not fair, after what I did to you."

"It's not about fairness." Her words are soft against my back. The warm water hits my chest, and her hand continues to work. "It's about giving you what you need, when you need it."

Add generous to Cecily's ever-growing list of attributes.

I look down at Cecily's hand, watching her movements. "I can't believe I ever thought you were mean."

She smiles, and I feel the curve of her lips. "I'm still mean. And you know you like it."

I jerk in her hand. She's right. I fucking love it when she's mean. "You can do what you want, Chestnut, but when you're feeling better, I'm going to be so nice to you."

"Is that right?"

"I'm going to fuck my wife the way a husband should."

The words are out of my mouth before I consider them. I wait for her to falter, to chide me, to remind me what it is we're really doing. But it only spurs her on. She grips me tighter, pumps faster. Finally, she says, "You can't say stuff like that right now."

"You're right, you're right, I—"

"The blood flow hurts," she interjects.

The blood flow... *oh.*

"Sorry," I murmur, feeling bad but not for long because the pleasure is coiling tight, and then bursting, and my eyes squeeze shut.

"Fuck," I groan, bracing my arm on the wall.

Cecily lets the water run over her hand, washing away my spend. I turn off the shower, and we both climb out. Grabbing a fluffy towel off the rack, I dry her off first, then myself. Cecily pulls on my T-shirt, and when she brushes her teeth once, I do it three times. Anything to get the habanero out of my mouth.

She laughs at me, and waits for me in bed. When I pull on my pajama pants, she crooks an eyebrow and says, "I'm surprised you're not taking this opportunity to sleep naked."

I pull back the covers and slide in beside her. "I noticed you put on underwear. I figured if you were erecting a barrier, I should, too."

Should we talk about what I said? *I'm going to fuck my wife the way a husband should.* It would be easy to talk about, if I didn't mean it. But I mean it.

Cecily snuggles into my side, her head on my bare chest. She has unwound the knot she put in her hair, and now it flows like a river over my arm and the bed. While I rub her back, her fingers turn circles over my chest.

"Kerrigan asked me some questions tonight that made me think." Her tone is contemplative.

"What kind of questions?" I ask, my thumb stroking over her shoulder blade.

"She wanted to know what life looks like for me and you once this is over. She asked if we're going to say our goodbyes and retreat to opposite sides of the country." Her voice sounds despondent. Fearful.

It's exactly what we talked about. What we planned. But... "Is that what you want?"

Cecily pushes up onto an elbow, her face a handful of inches from mine. "What if I said no?" Her head shakes, just a little. "I don't know how it all works, Dom. I don't know the details. I only know that you going back to New York feels like losing you. And losing you feels like"—she shrugs—"*loss.*"

The soft glow of the nightstand lamp reveals the sorrow etched on her face, matching her tone. Perfectly matching how I feel inside.

"I don't want to lose you, Cecily."

She lays her head back down on my chest. "I don't want to lose you either."

We leave it at that. When Cecily's breath becomes rhythmic, I stretch out my arm and turn off the lamp. Even then, I cannot go to sleep. I stare at the ceiling, Cecily wrapped in my arms sleeping peacefully, and think about her admission in the bathtub.

For years, Cecily has carried around the idea that she is difficult to love.

I cannot imagine anything easier than loving this woman.

CHAPTER 42

Cecily

AFTER A DAY SPENT EXPLORING SIERRA GRANDE, WE SAY OUR official goodbyes to Bernice and climb into the Road Kraken.

Following a unanimous vote, Dom is driving the motor home to Sedona. Like the good little wife I am, I grab the passenger seat. Dom, sexy as hell in his aviators, does not look like he should be operating this gigantic vehicle. That role belongs to middle-aged and above dads wearing T-shirts from the places they've visited tucked into jean shorts pulled up too high on their waists, and blindingly white clunky tennis shoes.

I'm sure everybody passing us as we climb north on the interstate is doing a double take.

Dom's playlist blares from his phone, grabbing the interest of my dad.

"Classic rock guy, Dom?" Dad stands between our seats, one hand on each to brace himself.

"Uh, yeah," Dom answers, briefly glancing up at my dad before returning his gaze to the interstate. "My dad was always listening to classic rock when he repaired our car. I guess it stuck with me."

"We should meet your parents when this road trip is over. Maybe we'll be one big, happy family." Dad laughs.

I try not to stare at him. One big, happy family? Who is this man standing beside me? First, my mother, and now him. "Have you been micro-dosing with Kerrigan?"

Annoyance passes over his features. "No, Cecily, I haven't."

Duke walks up behind my dad, staring out the windshield the same way.

"I thought one rule of the motor home is that everybody is supposed to be seated while it's operating?" I ask.

"Kind of surprised you care about rules," Duke says, blank-faced.

I sigh, irritated. Unbuckling my seat belt, I stand up. My dad and Duke step aside, letting me through. "I'm going to chat with the ladies."

My grandma, Rainbow, Mom, and Kerrigan play Scrabble at the dinette.

"Hey." I pull over a folding chair tucked between the couch and kitchen counter.

"You're not allowed to help anybody," Grandma informs me, finger pointed in my direction.

Leaning left to look at Kerrigan's letter board, I ask, "What if I help *everybody*?"

Grandma smirks. "We'll let you help us if you tell us why your husband walked into the hotel with six gallons of milk after we thought you two had gone upstairs."

My arms cross. "Absolutely not."

Grandma shrugs. "Then I guess you don't get to help."

She knows how hard this will be for me. I've been dominating Scrabble boards since I was a kid.

The game continues, and I help myself to an eyeful of everybody's letters.

Is my mom seriously going to place an 'e' at the end of that word? She could put her 'x' below the 'o' and get a triple word score.

On and on, almost as if they're playing like fools to annoy me.

"Fine," I bite out. "We had a sexual mishap." I rearrange the letters on Kerrigan's board, and she looks up at me in surprise. "I would have never put that together," she says.

"I'm aware," I deadpan.

Grandma lays down her word and asks, "What was this sexual mishap?"

"I am not telling."

Kerrigan nods sagely. "Did he come in your eye?"

Instantly the table falls silent. All eyes are on Kerrigan.

"No," I answer, horrified. "I think something might be very wrong with you."

Kerrigan lifts her hands in innocence. "I didn't say I know what it's like. But that would be a terrible sexual mishap." She flicks her hair over her shoulder. "I noticed the absence of moaning last night."

My gaze snags on Dom in the driver seat. The shower water had drowned out his moan.

From nowhere, Rainbow adds her two cents. "I suggest you make your vagina a more inviting space."

"There is nothing wrong with my vagina," I protest. The effect of the habanero is long gone, thankfully.

"There are crystals, specifically a carnelian," Rainbow presses, nodding eagerly. "You put them in—"

I hold up a hand. "Thank you for the suggestion, but there will be no crystals entering my hoo-ha."

Mom laughs. "Cecily, please hand me the folder." She points to an open bookshelf lining the top of the kitchen cabinets.

I retrieve it and hand it over. "What are you doing?"

She flips it to the back, where a pen waits in a little sleeve. "We've been writing funny things down. "Quotes and such. What you just said has to go in here."

It's similar to Dom's suggestion that I keep a note in my phone to record these memories. I've been doing it when I remember, typing snippets of our days.

"No way," I say in a rush, because writing down what I just said is too far. Nobody will want to read that later. "Absolutely not."

Everybody around the table is giving me a look that clearly says *stop being a poor sport.*

"If you're going to write down what I said"—I point back at my chest—"then you have to write down what Kerrigan said, too."

"The difference between me and you," Kerrigan starts, tapping the end of my nose, "is that I don't care. And you do."

"Fine." I extend an arm. "Write it down. Write it all down."

Grandma smiles. "It's good to have you in the Road Kraken, Cecily. We've been missing you."

"I'm sure you're the only one," I say, peeking at Rainbow's letters. There's no helping this woman. I hope she's better at being a death doula than she is at spelling or vocabulary.

"I'm happy you're here," my mom says.

"Me too," Kerrigan adds.

"Same," Rainbow says.

I give the still-an-interloper a look. "I am," she insists. "Your grandmother's energy is much more peaceful when you're around."

"You can feel her energy?"

"I see it," Rainbow corrects, fully serious. "As an aura. Your brother is restless nearly all the time, he is very blue. Your husband is green. He is loving and compassionate. Very nurturing."

This gives me pause. Dom is all those things. "For the record, I think this is horseshit. But do me."

"You and Duke have made it clear you don't care for my work," Rainbow says, not a hint of hurt feelings in her tone. "People like you often don't."

"People like me? What does that mean?"

"Those with a red aura. You're very intense and passionate."

"Ding ding ding," Grandma says, miming the ringing of a bell.

I exaggerate a sigh. "First the vagina carnelian, now the aura. What's next?"

Rainbow presses her palms on the table like she's going to stand up. "Let me get my sound bowls."

"No," everyone shouts in unison, arms extended to stop her.

Mom flips open the binder to the back, finger sliding down the paper until she finds what she's looking for and taps it twice. "No sound bowls in an enclosed space."

Everyone laughs. Everyone but me.

I would not trade traveling alone with Dom in Bernice

for anything, but I wouldn't mind understanding these inside jokes.

"I bet you're looking forward to this afternoon," I say to Rainbow. "The binder says we're spending time in Sedona with vortexes, aura readings, and crystal stores."

"I lived in Sedona for a long time," Rainbow answers. "It'll be nice to be back, but what I'm really looking forward to is the glamping tonight."

"Speaking of," Kerrigan says. "How much *camping* is a part of *glamping*? Because I'm too delicate for tents and such."

I snort. "Delicate? Or bougie?"

Grandma says, "You'll be pleasantly surprised, but if I think you're being an entitled brat, I'll have them move you to the woods away from everyone else."

"Nature's corner," I say, nudging Kerrigan. "You face away from everyone. And we confiscate your phone so you can't watch the Moose-cam."

Kerrigan sticks her tongue out at me.

Rainbow bows out of the next round of Scrabble, and I sub in. And then, in a move very uncharacteristic of me, I lose on purpose. Kerrigan wins. Under the table, my grandma affectionately squeezes my thigh.

The red rocks of Sedona come into view, and though I've seen it before, that doesn't stop it from being stunningly beautiful.

Our first stop, according to **We're Going To Have Fun, DAMMIT** is Airport Mesa to feel the vortex.

When the motor home is parked at the far end of the lot because that's the only place with enough space for this behemoth, Rainbow scoots out of the bench. She stands at the ready for my grandma, should she require assistance. I fold up my chair and replace it where it goes, then stand at the counter and pretend I'm busy with something so my grandma doesn't feel like I'm watching her. But I am, in my peripheral vision. I haven't been privy to the ins and outs of her day on this trip, seeing her only in chunks of prescribed time. Aside from the shortness of breath that is not constant, it's hard to believe she's ill. Until now. Until her caftan sways just so as she slides from the booth, lifting enough to reveal a swollen ankle.

I glance at my mom and Kerrigan, expecting to see their alarm, but there is only sadness across their expressions. Ten minutes ago we were laughing, but reality has swooped in and smacked us across the face.

I excuse myself to the small but surprisingly nice bathroom, splashing a little water on my cheeks and forehead. I can do this without falling apart. Falling apart is for later, when she is no longer here.

I leave the bathroom and find everybody has walked outside. Dom waits for me, leaning against the open door with his phone in his hand.

"Is work ok?" I ask.

He nods. "I have a meeting tomorrow morning I'll have to call in for."

"Sure," I answer, my thoughts drifting to my job. The meetings I'm missing. It feels odd not to go into work every morning, coffee in hand. I'm not on vacation, but I'm not going to work, and I'm not at home. I'm in limbo, in an alternate universe where all I do is road trip around the desert.

Dom motions for me to go first. When my feet hit the pavement, I stare out across the red mesa, piñon trees growing wild from the canyon walls.

"I feel it," Duke says dramatically, shaking his arms. "The vortex has taken hold."

"Me. Too." I twitch my hands, enjoying the way my big brother laughs.

Rainbow pointedly looks the other direction.

Grandma smacks both of our arms. "Quit being assholes."

She steps away to talk to our dad. Duke and I share a smile, and he asks, "Hey, why did your husband buy a bunch of milk last night?"

"He was thirsty," I answer, turning on my heel. No amount of sibling bonding is worth answering follow-up questions.

Dom leans against the motor home, eating a protein bar. "How many of those did you bring on this trip?"

"A lot," he answers after he swallows. "I knew I'd be eating on other people's timetables, and I figured it was a good idea to have easy food that would keep the blood sugar up."

I tug at his sleeve and bring my lips to his upper arm, saying against the fabric, "My grandma and Duke both asked why you were buying so much milk last night. They saw you?"

"Not your grandma, but the rest of your family was standing next to the scene of the crime when I walked in with the milk. I guess word got around. What did you say?"

"I ended up telling my grandma we had a sexual mishap."

Dom's eyes widen, and I hurry to defend myself. "I know, I know. I wouldn't have said anything, but my grandma is diabolical. She knew just what to say to get me to talk."

Dom presses the last bite of his bar into his mouth. "Which was?"

"She said I couldn't help with Scrabble if I didn't tell them why we needed milk."

He finishes chewing, nodding acceptingly, like *that'll do it.* "How did you avoid telling them what really happened?"

"The conversation moved on to semen in the eye, and carnelians in the vagina."

It takes a few moments for my words to penetrate before Dom asks, "Carnelians like the crystal?"

I nod. "Supposedly they will make my vagina a more inviting space."

Dom blinks twice. Steps closer, voice low. "As the man lucky enough to spend a few glorious minutes between your legs, I can personally attest to how *invited* I feel."

My eyebrows raise, my heart beating erratically. "And how invited is that?"

The look in his eyes, hungry and downright devious, softens slightly. His lips part, and I wait for his next words. But they do not arrive. Whatever he was going to say, he folded it back, tucking it away.

I want to know what he was going to say, but maybe it's better if I don't. We're precariously walking a tightrope, dancing on it, while lust and attraction reaches for us, trying to pull us under. How much longer before we succumb?

Dom's hands slip into his pockets, his shoulders straightening as he regains control of himself. "I missed you in the passenger seat today."

My hands run over his shoulders. I do not feel compelled to exercise such control, considering he is currently a bastion of it. "I missed being there."

"You didn't get Bugles."

I pout. "I didn't get to pick out a weird little treat for you."

"There will be other opportunities. I still have my scorpion lollipop and questionable rock candy should we get desperate." A gust of wind sweeps over us, and his hands leave his pockets to push my hair back from my face, his fingertips blazing a trail of heat down my throat. Two knuckles drag across my collarbone. Maybe he's not as in control as I thought. "I can't wait to get you alone later," he says, a groan but also a growl, something that reaches deep into my belly and takes hold.

My mind fills with memories of last night in the elevator, before my nether regions caught fire. Before that pain, there was exquisite pleasure. I want more, and I want it delivered by this man, with his strong hands and nimble fingers. "I cannot wait to be alone with you." I look over at my family, standing around at the start of the trail.

"Can you hurry up?" Kerrigan yells when she sees me looking. "The vortex is closing."

Rainbow shakes her head. "Vortexes don't close, though their energy does fluctuate."

To Dom, I murmur, "How do you feel about making them think we're walking with them to the vortex, but then we double back and hide out in the Road Kraken?"

"I feel great about it, but Savage Grandma looks like she's pretty serious."

I look back, finding my grandma. Fisted hands rest on her hips, eagle eyes on us.

Dom takes my hand, and we head for the vortex.

CHAPTER 43

Cecily

The glamping portion of the trip is my restitution for putting up with hours of listening to Rainbow wax poetic about auras and gemstones and vortexes.

Kerrigan needn't be worried, there is no real camping to be found here.

Sky Island Glamping is a place you'd expect to find a celebrity who calls themselves 'down-to-earth' in an interview. The tents are not called tents, but *suites*. Made of thick, sturdy canvas, the freestanding *suite* is large enough for a full bathroom, king-size bed, and a sixteen-foot long floor-to-ceiling window to show off a panoramic view of the Ponderosa pine forest beyond. The suite also has air-conditioning and heating, and as the perky employee who showed us to the suite reminded us, "It's that time of year where you never know which one you'll need."

"This is probably the coolest place we've been so far," Dom says, lying back on the bed and looking up at the skylight where, when it's dark, we should be able to see millions of stars from the comfort of our plush bed.

"I can't get over this view." I'm standing beside the windowed wall, staring out at the dense forest, the clouds hanging low above the treetops. In the distance, the clouds are heavy and dark. "It doesn't seem real."

"It's stunning," Dom agrees.

I look back to say something, but the words die in my throat. He's not looking outside at the natural wonder. His gaze is locked on me.

"Come here," he says, his voice vining around me, pulling me in. I should be ashamed of how quickly I go to him, but I can't muster the indignation. The man I recently loathed has become someone I'm growing addicted to. Maybe there really is a thin line between love and hate.

I tuck in beside him, lying on my back so I can look up at the darkening sky. Watching an afternoon thunderstorm from the safety of Dom's arms, cocooned in this soft bed, sounds like paradise.

"How are you feeling?" Dom's question rolls over me.

He's not asking how I'm feeling in this moment, at least not directly. He wants to know how I'm feeling about listening to Savage Grandma struggle for breath on the short, easy, flat walk to the vortex.

"Like a part of my heart is being slowly ripped from my body."

"Yeah," he says. There is sorrow in his tone. "That was hard."

"She got so mad when we asked her if we should turn back."

"What did she say?" Dom had taken a position at the front of the group, the leader setting the pace after Duke's long-legged strides proved too strenuous for Grandma.

"My dad offered to carry her, and she told him she

would ground him if he touched her." It took her a long time to say it, each word buffeted by breaths dragged into her throat.

I look up at Dom and find him looking at me. "Savage," we say in unison, smiling in that way that's not actually happy, but we're both desperate for an ounce of reprieve from the gloom that hangs heavy in our hearts.

A crack of thunder rings in the distance.

Dom gets up from the bed, going to stand beside the window. "That storm is headed right for us."

"It appears so."

"Everyone else said they were going to take a nap." He turns back to me. His eyes are as dark as the incoming storm. "Maybe we should, too."

I pop up to my elbows. "You want to take a nap?"

Hunger floods his eyes. Heat. "A very specific kind of nap."

My teeth skim my bottom lip. "Does this specific kind of nap have a name?"

He considers. "Active nap."

I pretend to deliberate, tipping my head back-and-forth. "I suppose I could be convinced."

Dom presses the button on the wall, and the automatic shutters lower. Bit by bit, the room darkens. The only light is from above, but even that grows darker by the minute as the storm approaches.

Dom walks closer. Stalks, really. A predator. I lift my chin. He smiles, wolfish.

Climbing onto the bed, he grips my knees and spreads my legs apart, settling between them.

He palms my thighs. "I told you I was going to be so nice to you."

You also said you were going to fuck your wife the way a husband should.

I loved it in the moment when he said that. So strong, so certain. I felt like I was his. His wife, but for real.

Dom reaches for my calves, bending my knees and placing my feet on the bed. My dress falls down to my hips. Dom lets out a moan of approval as his eyes rake over me.

"Another one of these pretty silk thongs," he comments, finger tracing up the center of the fabric.

I say nothing, hips bucking at his touch. I suppose the motion speaks for me.

He hooks his finger around the side of the silk, pulling it aside like a curtain. "So fucking inviting." He drags a finger along me, teasing. "Am I invited?" His eyes remain fastened to me.

Half-drunk for this man, I say, "Not if you've been eating spicy peppers."

He grunts a laugh. "I won't eat spicy food ever again."

"You don't have to give up your favorite food for me."

He leans down suddenly, pressing his mouth to me. The comforter bundles in my grasp as I search for something to hold on to.

He drags a slow circle over me, then lifts his head and says, "I have a new favorite meal."

I am done. *Done.* My hands reach down, fingernails raking through those caramel curls. Thunder overhead, the *tip tap tip tap* of raindrops hitting the canvas.

Dom teases me relentlessly, lapping at me, drawing it out. "Please," I finally whisper, and Dom immediately listens. Slipping his hands under my backside, he lifts me, like I really am a meal.

My eyes have been closed, but I allow myself a peek. Dom's eyes are shut, mouth pressed to me. He works me over with fervor, with passion, as if he loves it there. As if it matters to him. He desires my body, sharing an intimacy. Dom is a real man, the kind I thought existed solely in women's fantasies.

Seeing him like this, intent on bringing me pleasure, sends me over the edge. The rain picks up, and my pulse pounds.

"Dom," I whisper, fingernails scraping his shoulders.

"Mm-hmm," he groans against me, telling me he knows. He's meeting me where I am, giving me what I need. He's telling me he's here for it. Here for me. He has been all along.

I shatter. Dom holds me steadfastly, keeping me in place as I writhe. His ministrations change in pressure, becoming softer, looser, lazier. Almost adoring.

He lowers my backside to the bed, pressing a kiss to the inside of my thigh. He lets go of my underwear he had held to the side this whole time. Curtain closing.

But I don't want it to close.

I want him. I want my husband. I don't know what that means, or will mean to us in the future. I only know that I need him. I need Dom. In so many ways, but right now, in this way.

"Take them off," I tell him.

He looks down, his lips and chin shiny with remnants of me. "Are you sure?" he asks.

"Last night you said you'd fuck your wife the way a husband should. The way you said it, it felt like a promise."

Still between my legs, he hesitates.

CHAPTER 44

Dominic

I STARE DOWN AT CECILY, TRYING TO FIGURE OUT HOW I GOT so lucky.

She is pink-cheeked, her dark hair a shiny ring around her head. And she wants me.

Apprehension filters into her eyes. Only a minute ago, those eyes were in the back of her head as I spent time being the reason for it.

"If you think it's a bad idea," she says, still breathless from coming.

"No," I practically growl. "I've just been given every-thing I could possibly want."

A smile breaks onto her face. "Then what are you waiting for?"

She sits up and gathers her dress, daintily lifting it over her head and tossing it. She's not wearing a bra.

"I wish there were some way to show you how I feel when I look at you." The words are out of my mouth without a second thought, but I'm not sure there was a first thought. I don't remember thinking them, did not consciously decide to speak them.

"I looked at you while you were—" Cecily glances at her center, currently covered by underwear I'm seconds from tearing out of my way. "You looked like you liked it."

"Love it," I correct. Present tense. "Unless you tell me otherwise, I'll be down there daily. Like you're a fucking vitamin."

Her mouth drops open, and I smile proudly. It's not easy to shock Cecily.

"But right now," I tell her, reaching behind myself and gathering my shirt. I pull it off and fling it aside. "Right now, I need to fuck my wife like I *promised*."

Slipping my hands into Cecily's underwear, I slide them down her legs. Cecily, using her foot, reaches for the waistband of my shorts. I pinch her toe and move it, shucking my shorts.

Cecily's eyes grow with need. We've been dancing around this, saying we absolutely cannot, then fighting how much we want it. I'd hate for her to regret this later. Or worse, to blame it on a moment of passion.

"Cecily," I start, fisting myself. "We—"

"Should date," she interrupts. "When we get back. When this road trip is over."

"I live across the country." Fuck. I hate that I had to say it.

"Long distance," Cecily replies, sitting up. She wraps her hand around mine. Lifts it up and down. My teeth clench.

"No annulment?"

"I've never met anybody like you, Dom, and if our first date hadn't gone so terribly wrong, we might have wound up right here, on this road trip together anyway. We probably wouldn't be married already, but that's beside the point."

She's right. "I care about you, and the idea of hitting the delete button on everything we've been through, I don't like it. I don't know what the future holds, but I'm not interested in erasing us, Cecily."

"I don't want to erase us, either, Dom."

"So we're not getting an annulment?"

Thunder smacks the suite, reverberating around the room, Mother Nature in agreement with our choice.

Cecily shakes her head. "No."

Every tether on my composure fractures. My mouth seals over hers, my exhale heavy and full of relief. The wall I had to put up between us simply for the sake of surviving the force that is Cecily has crumbled.

She rises onto her knees, nipples trawling my chest. Her fingers slide up into my hair, tugging. She bites at my lower lip, running her tongue over the indentation her teeth leave behind.

My hands splay against her lower back, holding her in place as I devour her mouth. She kisses me like she needs me, like she has needed this for so long. She pours herself into me. Physically, emotionally, mentally, Cecily brings it all. It's everything I want from her. Every last drop. I give it all back, and I hope she can taste how badly I wish we could go back in time, rewrite our history.

We can't, of course, and maybe we shouldn't. Maybe we wouldn't have ended up right here, and if that were true, I would do this all one hundred times over.

Cecily breaks our kiss. "Now, Dom. I need you now."

"Lie down," I instruct. She listens promptly, and it

reminds me of the elevator when I told her to pull up her skirt and she complied.

I look down at her, beautiful and naked and mine. "Have you realized the only time you listen is when you think there might be an orgasm in it for you?"

"I can't believe it took you this long to figure out how to properly persuade me to listen." Her dark lashes drop low over her cheeks as she bats them.

I breathe into a smile and come up over her, resting a palm on one side of her rib cage. Cecily mewls as I drag myself slowly up her. "Are you going to listen?"

"Only if you make me come," she shoots back, but the retort doesn't have teeth. She's too breathless. Too needy.

I run myself through her again, as if conversation is normal while I make the motion. "Baby, you're going to come so hard every person in one of these fancy-ass *suites* is going to hear you through the rain."

Her eyes sparkle with challenge. "Make me."

I glance at my bag. "I should grab a condom."

Honestly, I don't want to. I don't want a barrier between me and Cecily.

Cecily grabs my hips, fingers digging in. "I'm on birth control."

"Bare?" I have to ask. It needs to be clear.

She doesn't answer, at least not with words. She thrusts up with her hips as she holds mine in place, catching me, notching me inside her.

I grunt at the feeling. My Cecily. My wife. Of course she didn't wait for me to push inside her. She took me for herself.

Triumph burns in her eyes. Not hubris, but a quiet

victory. She's not celebrating that she got me, but that she allowed me in. In more ways than one.

"Menace," I say, jaw clenched as I sink into her warmth. "My Menace."

Her arms circle my neck and she urges me down, bringing me to her mouth. "Yours," she says against my lips, trembling.

"Mine," I echo, rough and reverent, the word breaking my throat. I move inside her, savoring and memorizing. Slow and deliberate, plunging into every one of her soft gasps as we find our rhythm.

She purrs in satisfaction, wrapping her legs around my lower back, anchoring me to her. To this moment. I've touched her, and tasted her, but this? It's something else. Trust. Vulnerability. Nose to nose, heart to heart. This is Cecily, laid bare.

Her body moves with mine, soft and sweet, so damn responsive. Slow thrusts graduate into something more feral.

Her hips lift to meet mine, and she clings to me. I brush hair from her face, and gaze into her pretty eyes, my lips brushing over hers with every pass.

"So fucking gorgeous," I whisper, rugged and broken. A sheen of sweat mixes with her moaning *oh yes* and *right there* and *don't stop* and me losing my mind, groaning *you feel so good* and *perfect for me.*

My hips slam into hers harder, faster. Her nails dig into my back, and I'm filled with need. Desperate, aching need that's been mounting from the first moment I touched her.

We're wild, urgent, like we're trying to crawl inside each other just to feel more.

"Cecily..." My voice is raw. I'm close. So close. But I

don't want to finish without her. "Come with me," I rasp, pressing my forehead to hers. "I need you to."

And she does.

Cecily's head tips back as her body heaves, pulsing, pleasure ripping through her. I let go, warmth spreading through my body, legs tightening. My hips jerk as I bury my face in the crook of her neck, her name on my lips like yet another promise between us.

We are quiet for a few moments as I lay on top of her, inside her, both returning back down to earth, to this luxury tent in the middle of a pine forest, where raindrops continue to pelt the skylight above us. Cecily lightly scratches her nails over my back. I feather kisses over her jaw until she turns her face into me, presses her mouth to mine.

"That was new," she says when she pulls away. "The goodness of it. It felt raw. Slightly unhinged."

I run my thumb along the sweat that has gathered at her temple. "I loved it."

She cups my cheek. "Me too."

My forehead rests against hers, my heartbeat trying and failing to return to normal.

"Cecily?"

"Hmm?"

"You've ruined me."

She's quiet for a moment, then says, "You're welcome."

CHAPTER 45

Cecily

I don't mean *you're welcome* as a response to *thank you.*

You're welcome, as in, you are welcome to have me. My heart. Anything. Everything.

CHAPTER 46

Cecily

AFTER OUR PHYSICAL EXERTION, DOM AND I REALLY DID TAKE a nap. No alarm, cozy sheets, and Dom's hard chest beneath my head. I don't know which I enjoyed more, the pitter-patter of the rain, or Dom's heartbeats.

I woke to Dom's hand running up the inside of my leg, and I scrambled on top of him. We slept naked, and it was too easy, too convenient.

"I can't pass up the chance," I said to him once I was fully seated.

"I agree with your choice." He spoke roughly, voice thickened by sleep and other things.

Afterward, I took a quick shower, washing the stickiness from my thighs.

We're walking to meet my family at the Sky Island restaurant on the property when Dom reaches for my hand. I love the gesture, tiny, but still satisfying.

"The pines smell amazing after a rain." I take a deep breath, letting it fill my chest.

"That's what I miss most about living in the desert."

Dom does the same, dragging in a breath that is deeper, fuller. "The smell of the creosote after it rains."

"What does the city smell like after a rain?"

Dom shrugs. "Trash. Asphalt."

"That can't be true."

"It is true," Dom insists. "I'm sure people have different opinions, and it probably depends on where you are in the city. A walk through Central Park after a rain smells great. Walking to work after a rain, not so much."

"Sounds...delightful."

The Sky Island on-site restaurant looms ahead, all glass windows, and outdoor seating. Two employees dry off rain-soaked tables and chairs.

Dom stops suddenly.

"Everything alright?" I ask.

"I have an idea," he says, palm connecting with my waist as he pulls me closer. "What if I could make it so that we didn't have to be long distance? We could date like normal people. We could—"

He cuts off.

"Finish that sentence, Dom."

He shakes his head. "I don't want to scare you off."

"I'm not going anywhere." My head tips sideways and I give him a sassy little look. "I'm already married to you."

"I was going to say that we could fall in love like normal people. A natural progression."

I poke at one of the buttons on Dom's shirt. "You want to fall in love with me?"

He stares down at me, small smile tugging up one corner of his mouth. "I do."

Dom's words make me happy, sublimely so, but

dammit if I don't hear that old refrain in the back of my mind.

You make it difficult to love you.

Anger sparks deep in my belly. I do not want to think of my father right now. I do not want this childhood wound to exist in my present life. I push it away, somewhere down in the depths, locking it up, right where I've kept it for so long.

Dom's blue eyes search my face, and it's like he knows the way I hear my father's hurtful words.

"Cecily," Dom says, capturing my face in his strong hands.

"Yes?"

"I'm going to tell you something at the risk of scaring you away, because I think you need to hear it."

I nod, waiting, hanging on this man's every word. The person I was three weeks ago would be disgusted at how eager I am to soak up everything about Dom.

Tenderly, Dom's thumb strokes my cheek. "You are far too easy to love. You are so easy to love that I have to remind myself to slow down. Give us the proper time to coalesce." He smiles crookedly. "The fact that we're already married notwithstanding."

A searing ache hits my chest. Dom wants to fall in love with me, and in fewer words, he said he's already falling. Do I feel the same?

Yes. Yes a thousand times.

My arms wrap around his neck. I press my face up to his for a kiss. "I want to fall in love with you, too."

"I don't know about you, but I felt the vortex today." Kerrigan pokes at the crackling fire with a stick.

We declined dessert at the restaurant, opting to roast marshmallows over the campfire instead. My parents stayed at the restaurant bar to have another cocktail, and Dominic retreated to our tent to prepare for the work meeting he has tomorrow morning.

I scoff at my sister's insistence. "You did not either, you liar."

Kerrigan throws a marshmallow at me. "I totally did."

"Not," Duke adds. "You totally did *not*."

Grandma yawns. Exhaustion pulls at her eyes. Has she been looking more tired the last few days? Is it the travel, being on the road constantly?

"I think it's time for me to turn in," Grandma says, her hands finding the armrests on her chair. She pushes up to standing, and Rainbow, present like a shadow, is there to assist.

"Good night, Grandma," we chorus.

"Love you, kiddos," she replies. The three of us share a look. Grandma is many things, but emotionally demonstrative is not one of them. Unless we're counting fiery retorts, and putting somebody in their place.

Rainbow pats Kerrigan's hand as she passes, mollifying her. "Some people are more sensitive to the vortex than others." Her gauzy skirt flows with her retreating steps.

"See?" Kerrigan says, childishly sticking her tongue out

at me and Duke. "People with blue or red auras get left out in the cold."

Duke rolls his eyes. "I thought you gave Mom and Dad the last of your shrooms."

I gasp. "I knew they were acting different."

"They only took them once," Kerrigan replies. "They're acting different because they're much calmer now that they're away from the stress of their lives."

I pierce a marshmallow with the pronged end of my poker and hold it over the open flame. "The rest of us deal with stress the old-fashioned way."

Kerrigan makes a face. "Like getting drunk-married in Vegas?" Her eyes widen as soon as she says it. Hand snapping to her mouth, she squeaks, "I'm sorry."

My lips press together as I avoid my big brother's judgmental gaze.

"I knew it," he says triumphantly, drawing my attention. "Your favorite thing to do is to not be a part of this family, but I knew that even you would not get married without telling us."

I sputter, offended and outraged. "Even me? Go fuck yourself, Duke. You were all set to marry Daisy even though it was obvious you weren't in love with her."

"Guys," Kerrigan hisses, playing the role of peacekeeper. "Please remember how important it is for Grandma to see us all getting along. We've been doing really good so far."

"Yeah, because everybody is on their best behavior." My marshmallow catches fire, and I quickly blow it out. "Imagine if we weren't."

"Bloodbath," Duke says, sipping his drink. He has

forgone a s'mores making kit and elected for a tumbler of whiskey.

Assembling my s'more, I say, "I think what Grandma would prefer is for us to actually get along."

Duke taps the side of his glass. "That would require the help of a professional."

Kerrigan's laugh is hollow. "Getting this family to hash it out. Can you imagine? We never talk about anything."

"I suspect that's what Grandma wants from this road trip."

Kerrigan sighs. "Well, we can't always get what we want."

Wiping marshmallow from my chin, I say, "I triple dog dare you to go up to Grandma and say that to her face."

Duke rubs his palms on his jean-clad thighs, as if the idea excites him. "Make sure I'm there when you do it because I want to watch."

"Shut up," Kerrigan snaps.

"Very peaceful," he says, flames dancing in his eyes. "Sometimes I think I'm the only person in this family who cares about its future." He zeros in on me. "And then I receive confirmation that I'm right."

"I care about the future of our family, Duke."

"Sure you do," he says. "That's why you married someone none of us knew anything about." He stands up quickly, tossing his last sip of whiskey into the fire, and strides off to his tent.

CHAPTER 47

Dominic

Cecily wakes me at four in the morning.

"I can't sleep," she whispers.

"What's wrong?" I ask, reaching for the bottle of water on the nightstand. Cecily scoots aside so I can sit up and take a drink.

"Nothing." She falters. "Other than my grandma is dying, and every day I spend with her makes that reality come into sharper focus."

I recap the water bottle and set it aside. This whole thing, from accidentally marrying me in Vegas to facing her grandmother's imminent death, must be a mindfuck for her. I can't think of anything to say to make her feel better. Is feeling better the point? Maybe she just needs somebody to sit with her in the mess.

I place my hand on Cecily's knee, not for any reason other than to let her know I'm here for her. I'm listening.

Cecily looks outside, a swath of moonlight cutting across her face. We'd opted to open the blinds after turning off the lights at bedtime, readying ourselves for a spectacular Arizona sunrise. But now the moon glow on Cecily's features is giving the sunrise a run for its money.

"I was looking outside while you were sleeping and thinking about how pretty it is here, and how Sky Island is the perfect name for this place because it's like the sky goes on forever out there, nothing to halt the view. Then I thought about how Grandma brought us all on this road trip, planned it carefully and thoughtfully. We've been making an effort to get along to make her happy, and obviously that's great, but I think what would make her happiest is if we'd figure ourselves out." Cecily fingers the edge of the blanket. "She has been our common thread for so long. Once she's gone, what will keep us together?"

Cecily tucks her knees into herself and places her chin on her knees. Her dark hair spills down her back. "When I left Olive Township, I knew I was breaking ties with my family, but I still had my grandma. She was that connection to them, keeping me from truly being no contact. A passive string remained. Without her, it's going to take more effort on my part. And theirs, too. Do they even want that?" Her tone shrinks. "I hate that I have to wonder. It seems wrong for a person to ask themselves if their parents will want to put in the work to repair a relationship."

I move closer to her on the bed, pressing my lips to her shoulder. "It's wrong that so much has been broken."

Cecily's head turns toward me, her profile backlit by the cool light of the moon. My heart twists at her beauty. At the pain that tugs at her cheeks.

She shrugs. "All families are some degree dysfunctional."

"Just because it's normal, doesn't make it right."

I picture my therapist sitting across from me, saying those exact words. At the start of my sessions, I defaulted to defending my parents, even when I was in the middle of talking about what they had done.

"Did you learn that in therapy?"

I nod. "One of my biggest strides in therapy was learning how to let myself feel love for them while also feeling negative emotions."

"I think that's something I could stand to learn."

"If not for them, at least for you."

"Yeah." She snuggles down into the covers, and I follow, tucking her into my chest. "I wonder if there will be a time I help you with your parents. Or will it always be me needing your coaching?"

"If I need an ear when it comes to my parents, it'll mean my dad has been up to his old tricks."

"I want to meet them."

"Sure," I say, but the thought causes panic to rise in my throat. "We'll make it happen sometime."

Cecily drifts off to sleep, and I'm not too far behind her.

Early morning sun soaks our room, soft and warm and fuzzy. Cecily sleeps soundly, even breaths setting a rhythm in the rise and fall of her chest.

A midmorning meeting on the East Coast is early here in Arizona, so I roll out of bed carefully, keeping my foot-falls light. In the bathroom, I change into the clothes I hung from the towel rack last night while Cecily roasted s'mores with her siblings.

There isn't Wi-Fi in the suites, but it's available at the main lodge. Early morning dew gathers on my shoes, darkening the tan leather as I make my way through the grass.

In the lodge, an employee sets up grab-and-go breakfast items for the guests. I help myself to a mason jar with a label that reads *apple pie overnight oats* and pour myself a cup of coffee from the steel canteen.

"Thank you," I tell her, passing her on my way to the small room marked *business center*.

In it I find two separate workspaces, which are really just two desks, and two chairs. A framed piece of paper on the wall provides the Wi-Fi name and password.

I take a couple bites of the oats, wash it down with a big slug of coffee, and log into the meeting. The faces of my colleagues appear, looking no different than they did ten days ago when I left the office to pack and head for the airport.

"Nice of you to join us, Dominic." Sally greets me first, drawing attention to the fact I am two minutes late. Of course she could not allow me to quietly appear on an all-agents call.

I say nothing, addressing Sally's mother, also known as my boss. "Hello, Dee. Apologies for being tardy."

Dee's face gets too close to the screen. She squints. "Where are you? That looks like an office."

I swivel my chair and look behind me. I hadn't noticed the single bookshelf, decorated with books that have probably never been read, and a potted faux plant. "I'm in the business center where we're glamping."

Sally snorts. "Glamping. Never thought I would hear that word come out of your mouth."

I say nothing. Again. Sally does not know me, we are not familiar enough with one another to determine what the other might say. What is the nepo baby playing at?

"Glamping," Dee repeats, pulling back from the screen. "That sounds delightfully rugged."

I do my best not to scoff, or tell her otherwise. If I were to explain that last night I had the best halibut of my life, slept on Egyptian cotton, and stargazed from my bed, she might hop on the computer and book herself a stay.

Dee starts the meeting by asking everyone to give a brief summary of the project currently taking up most of their time.

John speaks first. I've never disliked the guy, but I don't like him either. He used to be a literary snob with strong opinions about commercial fiction, but in the last year he has adjusted his position and rebranded himself a 'man of the people'. *People* being anyone young and trendy. "I've just signed a debut author." He rubs his hands together, sending a brief glance at Sally before saying, "A western horror titled Last Things First. It's gonna be great."

The manuscript I discarded? Declined?

I have to say something. "John, if I may—"

"You may not," Sally snaps, crossing her arms. I would never hit a girl, but maybe I could recruit Cecily to slap the haughty look off Sally's face. Given what happened with that woman in the bar in Sierra Grande, Cecily would be up for the task.

I look to Dee, waiting for her to interject, to tell her daughter to pipe down, but she says no such thing.

Ignoring Sally for the third fucking time in this meeting, I say, "I declined Last Things First because the writing is bad, and—"

"That is your opinion," Sally interrupts.

"That would be most people's opinion after reading the first five pages." I do not want to argue, I do not want to stoop to this child's level, but how am I supposed to help the company if I don't tell them what they're signing up for? *Who* they are signing. Sometimes there are books an agent thinks will be great, but they are duds. For whatever reason, the market doesn't like the story. And then there are books that an agent knows will be a dud, and *surprise surprise*, they publish and flop.

"Sally," I start, doing my best to keep my irritation from seeping into my tone, "signing books you know won't do well as favors to friends harms the reputation of the agency." It's also a great way to make your colleagues find employment elsewhere.

Dee steps in. "Dominic, how about you give us an update from your side?"

"He's too busy *glamping*," Sally mutters, and finally earns a look of reproach from her mother.

I wish there were a remote control capable of muting Sally.

"I have Klein Madigan working on his second concept to present to his publisher, and Veronica Fisher on second round edits for Dirty Restaurant."

"Dirty Restaurant is going to be good," Dee says, tapping her chin. "Salacious."

"It has tremendous commercial appeal," I start, but Sally raises a hand like she is in a classroom.

Phone in hand, she holds it out triumphantly. "Klein Madigan is your cousin."

I can't see what's on her screen, but it doesn't matter. My eyebrows lift. "So?"

Sally stares me down with wide eyes like she is trying to prove a point. I'm not sure what point that might be.

"I thought signing books as favors to friends harms the reputation of the agency?" She has a *gotcha* tone, but she's cherry-picked the words I spoke a minute ago.

"I said signing books you know won't do well harms the agency." Klein's writing speaks for itself, so there's no need for me to defend my representation of a relative. But Sally? Her insistence that this pile of horseshit book get published is suspicious. My attention switches to John, who has officially lost all my respect. "Have you read that manuscript?"

"Of course he's read the manuscript," Sally bulldozes. "He signed the author."

John shifts in his chair. Fidgets with his paper cup of coffee on the desk in front of him. "Yes." The way he says it makes it sound like an admittance. John knows the book is terrible, and he knows precisely what he has signed up for. "I was planning on working with the author. Developing her." He clears his throat. "Him, I mean."

"Great," Dee says. "Let's move on."

The other agents take a turn, but I tune them out. There's something more to Sally and her determination to publish this book, and as much as it piques my curiosity in the same way it would any normal observer, all I want is to be away from it. For the first time since I started at Whitaker Literary Agency, I picture life beyond it. What would it look like if I didn't work there anymore?

Someone on the screen drones on, but all I see is Cecily. Sly grins, quirked brows, and a heart that has so much love to give. She's witty, and daring, and stubborn. Intelligent, too, with a smart mouth, and so beautiful it makes me rethink anything I thought of as beautiful before her.

Right then and there it comes to me.

I know what I'm going to do.

CHAPTER 48
Dominic

I EXIT THE LODGE TO FIND THE BRIGHT SUN CLIMBING UP THE eastern sky. My steps are certain, and quick, my mind filled with the look on Cecily's face when I tell her—

"Dom."

I pull up short, whipping around to find Duke seated at an outdoor table. He does not have a phone, or coffee, or anything to suggest he just happened to be sitting there when I walked out.

He was waiting for me.

"Good morning," I say in a clipped voice. Whatever he has to say to me, I hope he makes it short. Cecily is probably warm in our bed, and I'm anxious to return to her. I want to tell her my idea, and then I want to have a private celebration for two.

Nowhere in my plans for this morning was *chat with Cecily's big brother*.

"I learned something interesting last night." He crosses an ankle over the opposite knee. His posture is relaxed, casual, but it's only designed to look that way. So far I've thought of Duke as a nice guy, but he was raised by Glenn Hampton. Nature might be strong, but nurture is tenacious. There is no way Duke has escaped his father unscathed.

"Yeah?" I ask, schooling my voice into polite interest. Duke pushes aside the only other chair at the small table, a silent offer for me to take it.

Stowing my sigh of irritation, I sink down. I hope he makes this quick. I have big plans to make his little sister's back bow off our bed.

"Let me spare you the trouble." I meet his gaze. "I understand that if I ever do anything to hurt your little sister, I'll have you to answer to."

Duke chuckles dryly. His hair, equally in need of a haircut as mine, swoops sideways. In another conversation, where the tone isn't mildly threatening, I might ask him what he uses to deep condition. The guy has the hair of an early 2000s Abercrombie & Fitch model.

Duke looks out at the sweeping expanse of Sky Island. There's movement in the distance, a guest on the lake in a canoe. "Presently, you have a lot more to answer for than my little sister's future heartbreak."

The sentence grips me, and not because it's the kind better found in a suspense novel. I don't know what Duke's talking about, but in the back of my mind, I am afraid I do.

"Please do me the favor of cutting the suspense portion of this talk. Tell me what it is you think I have to answer for."

"Last night, my sister let it slip that your Vegas wedding was something you did while under the influence of alcohol."

I try not to show how much this surprises me, but it's not without difficulty. Cecily made it very clear from the beginning she did not want the rest of her family knowing this truth. Why tell them now?

"I found that very, very interesting. So I made a call and looked into you." He glances my way briefly. "Like I told you I would."

"I didn't care then, and I don't care now." I open my laptop, input my password, and turn it to him. "Look through it. Look through every single file. My personal email, and my work email too."

"That won't be necessary," Duke says smoothly. While I might never lay a hand on Sally the nepo baby, I have no qualms about punching my brother-in-law in his square jaw. "Your dad is not the cleanest of *showmen*."

His sentence is enough to disorient me. Duke's use of that fanciful term my dad prefers makes my blood run cold. "What are you talking about?"

"Are you working together?"

There's no schooling my reaction anymore. I am fucking furious. "Working together on what?" My molars bite together. I wish it were only Duke's accusation making this fury roll through my body, but there's a second emotion riding the coattails of my anger. *Fear*. It takes these already unpleasant feelings and adds acid to them.

My dad would never outright do anything criminal, but he is foolish enough to be unwittingly dragged into something.

I moved all the way across the country to put distance between myself and my dad's antics. I went to therapy to deal with the emotional fallout of an unstable home. But here I am, years later, still dealing with the ramifications of my father.

I close my laptop. "My dad isn't a bad man, but he is an idiot sometimes. He means well, but the shiny idea of getting rich quick has always lured him in. I distanced myself from him a long time ago, and even though I still see him, I am not privy to what he does on a day-to-day basis. So, Duke, while I understand you are motivated to protect your family's interests, please hear me loud and clear when I tell you to fuck off."

My heartfelt expletive does not shake Duke. "Do you want me to tell you what I found?"

"I do not. My dad can tell me himself, or, you know what? Not at all. Because it has no bearing on me, or my life, or what I do." Without additional fanfare, I stand up and walk away. On the outside, I am calm. On the inside, I am enraged.

What has my father done now?

CHAPTER 49

Cecily

DOM HAS BEEN ON THE PHONE SINCE HE RETURNED FROM HIS meeting. I stayed in bed while he was gone, hoping he would slide in beside me and ravage me when he returned.

No such luck.

He walked into the suite with a furrowed brow and air of frustration, kissed my temple, and told me he needed to call his dad. I watched him step out onto the little outdoor covered porch, back muscles taut and posture stiff.

Lustful plan delayed, I rise from the obscenely comfortable bed and use the en suite coffee maker. To grant Dom privacy, I keep my back to him. Considering I keep peeking over my shoulder to check on him, I give myself a solid grade of C in the privacy department.

When my first cup of coffee is drained, I make a second and, thanks to my bold peeking, see that Dom is off the phone.

"Hey," he says, poking his head around the open door. "Do you want to drink that out here with me?"

Relief fills me. He doesn't sound upset.

I follow him out, settling into the chair beside his. Early morning birdsong reaches us from the pines, and larger birds swoop over the glistening lake, looking for breakfast.

"Is everything ok?" I ask without looking at him. Like me, Dom's feelings when it comes to his parents are complicated.

"Yes, but for a moment I wasn't sure it was," he says haltingly.

His tone draws my gaze to him. He sits back in his chair, an ankle crossing over his opposite knee. Far more relaxed than when he first stepped out here.

"Do you want to tell me about it?" I sip my coffee.

"I ran into Duke this morning. Sort of. He was waiting for me after my meeting."

My eyes narrow. "Why?"

"He looked into me, like he said he would. He said you told him we were drunk when we got married." Dom's gaze briefly meets mine, confused but not accusatory.

"Kerrigan let it slip."

Dom thinks about this, nodding his head slowly. "That makes sense. Duke said *my sister told me*. He was talking about Kerrigan, not you."

"An assumption he knew you would make." I can't help my harsh breath of disgust.

Dom turns his body so he's facing me, looking me in the eyes with such intensity. "Do you want to know what he found?"

I gaze back into that face, those earnest blue eyes, the arched eyebrows and light scruff cheeks. Do I want to know what Duke found?

The answer arrives swiftly.

"You can tell me if you need someone to listen. I already know there's nothing about you to find, so I'm guessing he learned something about your dad."

Dom nods.

"You telling me what your dad did will not change how I feel about you, Dom. So tell me only if you want to. My decision about you has been made."

Dom takes the cup of coffee from my hands, setting it on the small table. Then he gathers up both my hands in his, rubbing his thumbs along my knuckles. "If I hadn't been watching your family misbehave for the past week, it would be more embarrassing to admit this." He half-smiles. "My dad is very good at making friends. Sometimes, he attracts the wrong people. The kind of people who take advantage of him. This isn't an excuse, but he has never been very good at seeing someone's motivations. Anyway." Dom sighs. Lightly squeezes my hands. "My dad became friends with some guy who said he had collected used items to sell, but wasn't sure where to sell them. My dad saw an *opportunity*"—Dom rolls his eyes —"that's always the word he uses. He told the guy he would take care of selling everything for a cut."

My heart makes its way into my throat. I know where this is going, and it's not good.

"The goods were stolen. Electronics, high-end tools, things like that. Someone responded to my dad's for sale post, and when my dad went to meet him, the guy said it was his generator that had been stolen out of the back of his truck the week prior. There was a serial number on the bottom that matched the serial number on the paperwork the guy had. The police came, and my dad cooperated. He gave them his new *friend's*"—Dom's jaw tightens on the word—"name and number, but it turned out the guy was using a fake name with my dad. The guy claimed to have never seen my dad before and had no idea who he was."

I feel terrible for Dom. My parents have embarrassed me plenty of times, but never like this. "What happened to your dad?"

"The police said this isn't the first time something like this has happened in recent months, and they'll be looking into the man who gave my dad a fake name. So, my dad's not in trouble exactly, but he's not in the clear yet, either."

I take my hands from Dom, only so I can place them on his shoulders. "I'm sorry Duke forced you to have this conversation with your dad today."

"I understand what Duke was doing. Why he was doing it."

I open my mouth to speak when Grandma and Rainbow appear around the corner.

"Knock, knock." Grandma wiggles her eyebrows. "I hope we're not interrupting anything."

I drop my hands from Dom's shoulders. "Not a thing. Everything alright?"

"Have you looked at the weather for today?"

I shake my head. "No." Currently the sky is a perfect blue.

"Looks like our next destination is going to get a late spring snowstorm. We need to get on the road."

"Wha—"

Grandma gives me no time to process. "I'm going to the lodge to grab a bite to eat and sign the bill. I need you to make sure your parents and siblings know we're leaving as soon as possible."

"No problem." I glance at Dom, who's nodding like he's

prepared to be a part of the roundup. "Do I have time for a shower?"

Grandma looks at Rainbow. Rainbow says, "There's a shower on board the motor home."

I want to tell Rainbow that does not answer my question, but in an effort to make everything as easy as possible for my grandma, I nod my head in compliance. "We'll see you at the motor home."

Grandma and Rainbow walk away.

Dom stands, pulling me up with him. "If it's not one thing, it's another."

CHAPTER 50

Cecily

With Dom's help, every member of the Hampton family is at the motor home within the hour.

"It's just a little snow," Kerrigan complains, rubbing the sleep from her eyes. "It probably won't be enough to make a snowball. You know how the Arizona weather forecasters get about a little precipitation." She rolls her eyes. "So dramatic."

"A bit like somebody else I know," Savage Grandma volleys.

Kerrigan gasps, pretending to be offended. "Shots fired."

Dom and Duke load everybody's belongings into the RV. They are both quiet, their body language stiff.

"It's Cecily's turn to drive," Grandma says when we load into the vehicle.

"Absolutely not." My head shakes vehemently. "I have no intention of driving this thing at all, but especially in snow."

"I'll take her turn," Dom offers.

"Nope," Duke says, domineering as ever. "I'll drive."

"Whoever is driving, put your ass in the driver's seat and drive," Grandma commands, officially out of patience. "There are a few things I'd like to do before I die, and being stuck in snow is not one of them."

Duke takes his place as the driver. Dom and I sit at the kitchenette table, both working on our phones. I peek at his screen. It holds an email with nothing in the body or subject line. The recipient name is dee@whitakerlitagency.com

Duke nibbles at his bottom lip, lost in thought.

Gently, I elbow his ribs to get his attention. "You doing ok over there?"

With only a few inches between our faces, he lets his eyes travel over me. "Just fine. How about you?"

I nod, letting him know I'm ok. Better than ok. As I laid in bed this morning, waiting for Dom to return, I replayed our middle of the night conversation. Nothing monumental was revealed or said, but I came away with a feeling that was more important than anything else. Strength.

For so long, I thought my parents behaved the way they did in reaction to me. Even if I knew the way they acted was wrong, I saw it as actions that were brought about because of me. Last night was the first time I considered that their behavior belongs to them, and only them. Putting this together was freeing and empowering. I haven't forgiven them because they haven't asked for forgiveness, but one day it might be something I do on my own, for me.

Dom flicks on the light fixture attached to the end of the table. Grandma goes back to the bedroom to lie down, and Rainbow accompanies her. My dad has taken the passenger seat, and my mom and sister sit in the swivel bucket chairs on the opposite side of the RV. The further we drive, the darker it gets. The winding road gives way to towering pines with skinny trunks. We pass a yellow caution sign warning us of elk crossings.

"Snowflakes on the windshield," Duke announces.

Like the snow-starved desert inhabitants we are, everyone is out of their seats and crowding around the front of the RV to see the sight. Everybody except Dom, who probably views snow as a nuisance after spending so many winters in the city.

"It's so cute," Kerrigan says, wonder in her voice.

I go back to Dom, snuggling into his side. "You don't want to see the snow?"

"I've never liked snow, here or anywhere else."

"I think you might live in the wrong place, Dom."

Dom gazes at me. "I think you might be right about that."

As we drive, the landscape turns into a winter wonderland. Grandma comes out from her rest, peering out the windows in awe like the rest of us.

The snow falls heavy now, in thick, wet clumps. The RV inches along, the visibility going from bad to worse.

Duke does his best, I'm sure, but we are no match for the snow in our giant, heavy vehicle. He guides the RV to a shoulder, not bigger than a small clearing, right off the road.

"I'm not sure this is a good idea," Dom says loudly, so Duke can hear. "We're going to get stuck."

Duke turns around, glaring at Dom. "What is it you think we should do?" he asks.

Dom motions outside, where the white falls in sheets. "It's probably too late."

"What does that mean?" Duke asks through clenched teeth.

"It means we are probably already stuck."

Duke turns to face front again, staring out the windshield. Hands on the large steering wheel, he presses a foot to the gas pedal.

And then comes the sound nobody wants to hear. The rev of the engine, followed by the spinning of tires.

We are stuck.

I share a look with my mom and Kerrigan. Mom, always useless in a crisis, retrieves a bottle of champagne from the fridge. She pops the cork, sips, and hands it to Kerrigan.

Duke and my dad open up the door and step out, a blast of cold air whipping through the RV.

"I better go see if they need help," Dom says.

I scoot off the bench so Dom can follow. After a few minutes, I make a decision. "I'm going to go, too," I say, grabbing a sweatshirt and threading my head through. Somebody has to make sure Duke and Dom don't end up in fisticuffs.

The three of them stand at the rear of the RV, examining the way the tires spit snow as they spun. Tension rolls off Duke, his jaw set tight.

"How's it going?" I ask, because I don't know what else to say.

Duke explodes. "What kind of stupid fucking question is that, Cecily? How does it look like it's going?"

Here we go. Looks like it'll be me and Duke going round for round.

But I didn't account for my husband.

He steps in front of Duke, big and broad-shouldered and defensive. "You might be her brother, and you might have a problem with me, but you watch your tone when you're talking to my wife."

Despite the cold, I've never felt warmer. More safe. More loved.

"Oh shit," Kerrigan sings. I didn't know she and my mom followed me out, but there they are, huddled together and snuggled up with their bottle of champagne. Grandma and Rainbow stand beside them.

Duke sneers. "Your wife? Don't you mean the person you got drunk and convinced to marry you in Vegas?"

"Thanks a lot, asshole." I turn to Kerrigan. "Thanks a lot to you, too, big mouth."

"Sorry," she hollers.

"You said you got married in Vegas," my dad says.

Oh goody. My dad has decided to be flabbergasted.

"I did," I grit out.

He sends an accusatory look at Dom. "You made it sound like Vegas was where you chose to get married, not that you got drunk and then got married."

Snow trickles into my sandaled feet. "It's Vegas. Alcohol consumption is implied."

He rubs his hands together, presumably for warmth. "I guess we're back to the beginning."

Snow falls, and I square off with my dad. "What does that mean?"

"You're getting an annulment, just like I told you to from the very beginning."

"First of all, no. Second of all, an annulment is not an option."

"Why, because you've slept together?" Duke scoffs. "Who cares? Lie."

I take Dom's hand. "An annulment is not an option because we want to be together."

Duke blows out a harsh breath. "You won't want to be with him when I tell you what I found out about his father."

Dom cuts in. "I talked to my dad this morning, Duke. He explained everything. And I told Cecily everything, too."

"And I don't care," I say to Duke, chin tipped high.

"Un-fucking-believable," Duke yells up at the sky spitting snow on us. "Of course you don't care. Why would you? Why would you ever lift a finger for this family?"

I open my mouth to respond, but Duke is on a roll. "You left," he spits at me. Then he points at Kerrigan, who at this moment is drinking champagne. "She runs around doing God knows what. Who does that leave? Me. I'm left doing everything for this family. I've been left to deal with him." He points a stiff finger at our dad, who pales. "And her," he says, pointing at our mom, who is now holding the champagne Kerrigan pawned off when Duke called her out. "You left, Cecily. You abandoned me."

"Kerrigan comes home," I say, defensive but not really.

"But not you," he says. "You never do."

Something in my chest fractures at the sight of my big brother breaking down. He's not angry, even if he sounds like it. He's *hurting*. And he has been, for who knows how long.

A loud engine roars from the other side of the RV, and we scamper around, our fight momentarily forgotten.

Duke throws up his arms at the sight of the snowplow. "Fucking figures. The snowplow was behind us."

"Great," my dad says. "Gives us time to figure out what you meant when you complained about being left behind to deal with your mom and dad."

Duke looks at him, and for what is probably the first time in his entire life, he simply says, "No."

Dad sputters. "What do you mean, *no*? Don't tell me you're going to start acting like your sister."

Duke strides over and swipes the bottle of champagne our mom holds by the neck. "Which sister?" he asks, tipping back his head and finishing the bottle.

Dad stares at him, not speaking.

Duke steps closer to me. Kerrigan steps forward, flanking me. Our dad looks us over, unsure of what we're doing. I'm not sure of what we're doing either, but we're together.

Another sound comes from the road, the rumble of an engine. Around the crest of a turn appears a giant four-door pickup truck. The vehicle pulls off the road, coming to a stop near us. A man hops out and walks our way, a cowboy hat on his head. He's tall and lean and, most importantly, not a grizzled old fart.

"Hello there," he calls, in that cowboy way. "Do you need some help? I have a chain. I can tow you out."

Kerrigan turns her lips to my ear. "I can think of some ways he can help me."

My lips press together to keep from laughing.

"That was louder than you think," Duke mutters. But there's mirth in his tone, and that's what matters.

The cowboy introduces himself. His name is Christopher, and he works at a ranch not too far away from here. "Quite a snowstorm," he says. "It came on hard and fast."

Kerrigan elbows me. "Who knew paradise was a freak spring snowstorm in Arizona? Can I borrow the gem from your hoo-ha?"

"No, it's mine," I say.

"There is something wrong with both of you," Duke mutters, stepping away to introduce himself to Christopher.

Dom wraps his arms around my waist. "Nobody is allowed to see your carnelian but me."

Kerrigan looks at him in shock, but it quickly changes to a bark of laughter. Then she throws me a wink and lopes off to make sure the cowboy gets an eyeful of her.

With the aid of Cowboy Christopher's kind heart and massive truck with a tow hitch and chain, we are towed out of the snowy mess.

My dad offers to pay Christopher for his trouble, but he waves off payment. "I knew there'd be folks stranded out here. Just came to see if I could be of service."

I glance at Kerrigan, waiting for her to say it. She knows I'm waiting, so she whispers, "He can service me."

Christopher offers a friendly parting wave and walks toward his truck. He's halfway there when he throws a glance over his shoulder at Kerrigan.

"That's all the encouragement I need," she says, hustling after him.

"She's a trip," Dom says. He pulls me in close. "Do you have a thing for cowboys?"

"Who doesn't?" I tease.

His eyes narrow, leaning close until his breath streams

against the shell of my ear. "Do you think you're funny, Mrs. Bellinger?"

A shiver trips down my spine, and it's not from the snow. "I do."

"We'll see how funny you can be later when your mouth is too full to make jokes."

I pat his chest playfully. "Promises, promises."

We load up into the RV, Kerrigan the last person in. Her cheeks are pink, and when I catch sight of myself in a window, I see mine are too. The cold, probably.

"Did you give him your number?"

"Yes," she answers, flinging herself into a chair. "It wasn't until I opened my mouth to talk to him that I considered he might have a girlfriend. But I figured, what the hell? I'd regret it if I didn't shoot my shot."

"It seems like it went well," Dom says. We're back in the same spots we vacated when we got stuck.

Kerrigan pushes her hair off her face. "I told him if it all works out, it would be a great story to tell our grandkids one day."

Dom coughs on the bottle of water he grabbed from the fridge before sitting down.

"Kidding," Kerrigan adds.

Duke's driving again, pulling out onto the interstate. Kerrigan looks at me. "What do you think about everything Duke said back there?"

"I think I'm still processing," I answer, giving my brother a once-over. For the first time since this road trip began Duke's shoulders are lower, his demeanor more relaxed.

Kerrigan looks with me, then turns her appraising eyes

on our dad in the passenger seat. He is silent, sitting rigidly.

I look around and realize my mom is not sitting where she was before. "Where is Mom?"

Kerrigan points toward the bedroom. "She said she needed to lie down."

"Maybe the champagne got to her."

"Or maybe it was her oldest child."

"There you go again, Kerr, saying something that makes a whole lot of sense."

"Your brother shocked her," Grandma says, coming from the bedroom. "Neither one of you talk as quietly as you think you do. You never have. When you'd stay the night with me when you were little, I'd turn out the lights at bedtime and listen to you two gab for hours."

Kerrigan and I share a smile. Those nights were the best, and they usually meant we got out of whatever boring event our parents were trying to make us attend. We would beg and plead and cajole and if that wasn't enough, we'd call in the big guns: Savage Grandma. It isn't until now that I realize Duke is not a part of those memories because he was dutifully showing up for our parents the way they expected him to. Taking one for the team. I never stopped to consider whether Duke wanted to be there.

Without thinking too much more about it, I'm up from my seat and moving toward the front of the RV.

"Dad?" When he looks at me I ask, "Do you mind if I take a turn as passenger?"

He unbuckles and gets up, and I step aside for him to pass. He's quieter than usual, not only in a lack of speaking, but there's a quality about him I can't identify.

"Congratulations." I buckle my seat belt and prop my bare feet on the dash.

Duke lifts his eyebrows, "For what?"

"Shocking Dad into silence." Snow is gathered on either side of the road, but the pavement is clear.

"He expects defiance from you. From me? Not so much."

"Has he said anything to you since"—I thumb behind myself—"back there?"

Duke shakes his head. "He might never. You know how he is. He may rewrite history to make it so he doesn't have to face everything I said."

"Well, apparently you got to Mom. She's lying down. I guess the truth exhausted her."

"Was it me, or the champagne?"

"Probably a combination."

Duke nods. "Did you see the expression on Grandma's face?"

"I don't have eyes in the back of my head."

"She was smiling while I was talking. Full out beaming." He glances at me briefly before turning his attention back to the road. "Isn't that weird?"

"Actually, no. Last night I told you that I think she wants us to deal with our shit. Not just get along."

"It makes more sense than anything else," he says. "Why would she want to spend what she knows is the final portion of her life with family who refuse to be functional?"

"I think she knew if she forced us together, not only in physical proximity to one another but ample amounts of time, everything would eventually come to a boil." I look back at my dad, where he sits in the chair next to Kerrigan with his chin propped on his hand as he stares out the window. "The jury is out on Dad."

"I'm sorry I told Mom and Dad about your state of intoxication when you got married."

"In the interest of honesty, Dom and I originally planned to get it annulled right away. Then Grandma summoned us to her house, and Dad did that blustery thing where he tries to force me to do something for reasons that aren't even good, and then I did that thing where I get stubborn for no good reason other than I don't like being told what to do, and well"—I shrug—"here we are."

"You're staying married?"

My gaze flickers backward again, this time to my husband. He has his laptop out, and he's typing away. I hope coming on this road trip with me hasn't set him back too much at work. "We are. We're going to date. We went on a date once, when he was in town visiting his cousin. It was actually really nice, and we had a good time." No need to mention the miscommunication that occurred that evening. That can be an anecdote for later, sometime down the road. "For what it's worth, I'm sorry, too. I had no idea you felt that way about me moving to Phoenix. This whole time I thought you wanted to be where you are. Working for the family business."

"I do like working for the family business, but siblings who have parents like ours need to stick together, if only for the purpose of having another soul in the world who understands. I don't begrudge you leaving, but it sucked being left. If that makes sense."

Tears sting the backs of my eyes. "It does. I didn't think about you when I was leaving, and I'm sorry for that. All I could see was getting the hell out. Dad was so controlling. And his way of trying to control me was to make me feel bad about myself."

Duke nods knowingly. "One of many tactics he deploys. He tailors them to each one of his children. For me, it's been something along the lines of *you weren't good enough, but you could be.* The carrot he dangled in front of me was the possibility of greatness, which in turn led to his approval."

How did I never see that growing up? To me, Duke was the golden child. That made him easy to love. It was shortsighted of me, and very one-note. I missed the detail, the nuance, the subtext.

"What do you think Kerrigan's damage is?"

Duke chuckles. "I think she's good at hiding it, but offhand, I'd say she's a helicopter mom to a dog, enjoys shrooms more than she should, and pretends she's not as smart as she is."

It's hard to believe we started this trip in a dry, cacti-filled desert, full of hidden resentments and festering wounds. Look at us now, talking through our issues and driving through a world that looks like it has been dusted in powdered sugar.

I touch Duke's shoulder, lightly prodding him. "They sure did a number on us, didn't they?"

CHAPTER 51
Dominic

THE RED-BRICK HOTEL MONTE VISTA IN DOWNTOWN Flagstaff has every Hamptons arms crossed, their eyebrows tugging in either disbelief or discomfort. Even Cecily, who read about the hotel and knew this day was coming, looks perturbed.

"I am *not* staying in a haunted hotel," Kerrigan says.

Savage Grandma smiles at their expressions. "Yes, you are, you scaredy-cats." She looks at me. "Have you ever seen so many babies among a group of adults?"

"Never," I respond cheerfully.

Cecily narrows her eyes. I take her hand. Because I want to. Because I can.

"I'll keep you safe," I whisper into her hair as Ophelia leads the way into the famed haunted hotel.

She glares up at me. "If you do anything to scare me further, it's going to be you who needs to be kept safe from me."

I squeeze her waist. "Noted."

Browns and maroons decorate the hotel lobby, and

ornate gold filigree embellishes the ceiling molding. A gleaming cherry check-in desk takes up a large portion of the room. What looks to be a fireplace is actually a set of stairs leading down, metal lettering reading *Cocktail Lounge* on what should be a mantle. Framed black-and-white versions of the hotel throughout history line one wall.

To the young receptionist, Duke asks, "Can you please provide some background on why the hotel is believed to be haunted?" He sounds serious and unafraid, but I know the guy was standing in front of the building fewer than five minutes ago trembling in his Magnanni's.

She launches into a well-worn explanation of supernatural sightings. The Meat Man with the strange habit of hanging meat from his chandelier, the disturbing sounds of a baby crying in the basement, the Phantom Bellboy, and the infamous women of the night. Unsentimental, she says, "They were murdered and tossed from the third-story window."

Cecily leans her head against my arm, and I tip my head closer to hear her whisper, "Soiled doves and women of the night. This has turned into quite the road trip."

I snicker. It's the only appropriate word to describe the sound.

The receptionist looks at me. "You don't believe in ghost stories, do you?"

"Uh, no." I shake my head as I rock back on my feet. "I don't."

She nods her head decisively. "Perfect. We'll have you in room 306." Her tone is pleasant, but there is an undercurrent close to pleased mocking. Like she thinks she's setting me up.

"Why room 306?" Kerrigan asks, her hands wringing.

"Doesn't matter," I answer. "We'll be fine."

"Marilyn and I might take the motor home tonight," Glenn announces.

"I could sleep on the floor," Duke offers. "Is there a sleeping bag?" He shakes his head like he's clearing it. "Doesn't matter. I'll take the floor."

"I can definitely make that kitchenette table into a bed," Kerrigan adds, eyes lighting.

Given everything I have learned about this family, I did not see *shared fear of ghosts* as something that would unite them.

"You're sleeping here," Savage Grandma announces. "End of story."

The receptionist hands out keys. She dangles ours over my open palm and smirks. "Have a nice night."

"Way to go, Errand Boy," Cecily hisses when we step onto the elevator. She punches my upper arm for maximum display of vexation. "I looked it up. Room 306 is the room where the women of the night were murdered."

"She probably gets commission if she incites a level of fear that's still a little fun in the guests, like the perfect small shot of adrenaline. People are more likely to look for the supernatural and claim they see it if they're told to look out for it."

"Good luck," Duke says dryly, stepping off the elevator when it opens on the second floor. Kerrigan gets off too, saying to me, "You better hope you look nothing like the man who murdered those prostitutes." The ancient elevator doors shut with a clang.

Cecily deepens her voice. "I don't believe in ghost stories. Put me in the most haunted room in the hotel."

I press my lips to that inch of space below her ear, the spot I know she loves to feel my tongue glide over. "Is that how I sound, wife?"

She whimpers. "No, husband. You have a higher pitch."

I chuckle against her skin. The elevator doors open on the third floor.

We locate room 306, and slide our key into the lock. Cecily pushes open the door slowly, and it creaks.

"Did you hear that sound?" Her eyes are wide.

"This place is a hundred years old and you opened the door slowly. Of course it creaked."

She nods, mollified. "That makes sense." Her voice is small, and her lips are slightly jutted out.

I step in first to show her it's ok. It's a corner room with two windows letting in ample light. There is a dresser with a mirror above it on the wall, and a small seating area with a couch and rocking chair. Everything is old and worn, adding to the creepiness factor. Cecily edges in behind me.

"If that rocking chair moves on its own, I'll be stuffing my feet in my running shoes and hoofing it back to the valley."

"Better stretch now," I tease. "It could happen at any moment."

Cecily sends me a dark look. "That is not funny, Dominic."

"Please know that for the rest of our lives, I'm going to tease you mercilessly about this."

Yeah, I heard what I said. *The rest of our lives*. Bold of me, but not untrue.

Cecily drops her bag from her shoulder, and I drop both our duffels. She slides her arms around my neck. "The rest of our lives, huh?"

"Does that scare you?"

Her eyes roam my face, like she's drinking me in. "No. Maybe it should."

"There's no room for *should*. Not with us."

She rises on her toes, and I capture her mouth. Her hands find my hair, fingers fisting and pulling. She presses into me, gently biting my lower lip. The kiss is carnal, full of sex. If the fear of staying in this hotel has given her this adrenaline spike, made her this eager, I'm here for it.

Cecily stands back, sliding her joggers down her legs and kicking them off. She pulls off her T-shirt, and I could die right now, a happy man. A yellow lace bra, a matching scrap of underwear.

"Do those have a function?" I ask, my eyes glued to that perfect little spot on her body. "They're so flimsy they look like I could breathe on them and they would disintegrate."

Her lips curl up in a slow smile. "Why don't you find out for yourself?"

"Already planning on it, Menace. Daily vitamin, remember?" I poke her stomach with a single finger, urging her backwards until she's against the wall. "One day, I will stop an elevator and drop to my knees again. For now, this will have to do."

My knees hit the carpet. I lean in, press an open mouth to the lace. Cecily squirms. One hot breath against the fabric, then another. "Guess they're sturdier than they look."

"Mm-hmm," Cecily says, and I slide them down her legs.

All coherence ceases after that.

My tongue flattens against her. Using my mouth, I show my wife how much I care about her. How much I fucking adore this part of her, this beautiful spot only for me. A roll, and a nip. Two handfuls of her ass while my mouth loves on her. Her muscles tremble, and I hold her up while she falls apart around me.

"Dom," she whispers, when I turn my head and kiss the inside of her thigh. "You unravel me. Do you understand that? I'm just so...so...*undone* with you."

I look up. Cecily's looking down. "I feel the same way, Cecily."

Rising, I lift her up, and she locks her legs around me. Reaching between us, I yank down my shorts and position myself where my mouth was a moment ago. Cecily sinks down with a groan. "Right there," I growl, lifting her ass and slamming her back down. "Mine."

"Such a caveman," she gasps. "I love it."

Kneeling on the bed, I lie her back gently and come over her. Nose to nose, forehead to forehead, as I drive inside her. Heavy in the cradle of her legs, my strokes are slow and languid. She moans, an *mmm* that slides from closed lips. I press my lips to hers, wanting that sound to reverberate in my throat, ready to swallow it whole when she comes. My eyes close, my senses filled with her scent and her sound and the feel of her.

Cecily's hands are on my back, nails lightly scratching, and then they're on my throat, pressing in.

Hmm. Interesting. I don't hate it. The pressure increases, making it a little harder to breathe.

Cecily groans into my mouth and lets go of my neck. I sit up, grabbing one of her legs and throwing it over my shoulder. Gripping her hip, I increase my pace. Cecily's face tips up, luscious dark hair spilling around her head. Her hand dips between her legs, and I watch her fingers work, memorizing, so I can do it for her next time. I want to be everything for this woman. My wife.

Cecily's body spasms, her mouth in a silent *o*, eyes locked on mine. There's nothing more beautiful than watching my wife get pleasure from me. The look and sound and feel of her fracturing prompts my own, and I shut my eyes tight and do everything I can not to make noise. Cecily makes me want to become unhinged, roaring my release like I'm on a fucking savanna. I've never been so undone, just like she said. It's her. Only for her.

I fall down on the bed beside her, and she lays her head on my chest. "It was hard to be quiet, and this place is old. I'm sure the walls are paper thin."

I chuckle, running my fingers down her spine. "I'm sure whoever was in the room below us knows precisely what we were up to. The bed was moving."

There's a smile in her voice when she asks, "What if it's Duke or Kerrigan?"

"We're newlyweds. Aren't we supposed to be insatiable?"

"Perfect word. I like the leg over the shoulder move." She props her chin on my chest so she can look at me. Her cheeks are flushed, her hair a mess. My wife, freshly fucked.

"I'm not sure how I feel about the choking," I admit.

Her eyebrows cinch together, perplexed. "What choking?"

We walk into the cocktail bar at the Hotel Monte Vista on time. *We're Going To Have Fun, DAMMIT* informed us we'd be pre-gaming here before catching a party bike.

What I would like to know is if I can ride that party bike straight out of Flagstaff. I didn't need a dead prostitute's hands around my neck to make me believe in ghosts. An apparition sitting in that rocking chair would've sufficed.

Kerrigan catches sight of us first. She waves us over to the large high-top where she sits with Ophelia and Rainbow.

"I need a drink," I murmur to Cecily.

"Same," she says, in that breathless voice she's been using since ardently promising me she did not touch my neck even once during sex. At first I thought she was pulling a prank, but the more I considered it, the more I saw how impossible it would be for her to touch me like that from that angle. It would've been her thumbs at the front of my throat, and her fingers around the back of my neck. What I felt was the opposite.

We claim the two seats across from Ophelia and Kerrigan, and there must be some kind of look on our faces because Kerrigan immediately says, "What is wrong with you two?" She stirs the red cocktail straw in her drink, peering at us. "Another sexual mishap?" Kerrigan looks at me. "Did you come in her eye?"

"That is unbelievably disturbing," I say, at the same time Cecily mutters, "Seek help."

Kerrigan winks. "Call it what you want, but it distracted you from whatever is bothering you."

Cecily peeks at me, biting her lower lip. "We might have had an encounter of the paranormal kind."

Kerrigan sucks in a sharp breath. "I cannot stay here tonight."

There's no way we can reveal even a fraction of what happened in room 306. The Hampton family will end up pretzeled in the RV all night.

"You can, and you will," Ophelia says sternly.

"What happened?" Kerrigan demands.

Details of a sexual nature are not something I share, especially with my wife's family, so I say, "I thought I felt something touch me while I was changing."

Under the table, Cecily taps my thigh.

Kerrigan scrutinizes my clothes, giving me a *come on* look. "You're wearing the same clothes you've been wearing all day."

"I was creeped out. I put my clothes back on without getting new ones."

Her eyebrows raise as she sniffs out bullshit. "You felt something touch you? Where?"

"My backside."

"You're telling me the dead prostitute copped a feel?"

"Maybe she was trying to make him into a paying customer." Grandma sips her martini. "The first one is free, but the next one will cost you."

Kerrigan grins, cavalier because she believes we're bullshitting. If she knew the truth, she'd probably sleep in the shower of the RV. "In what currency do ghostly women of the night accept payment?"

"Are you about to tell a terrible joke?" I ask her, craning my neck for a cocktail server. Maybe alcohol will soothe the knot in my stomach.

"Nah." Kerrigan waves her hand. "I ran out of steam."

Cecily's parents and Duke arrive, and we finally get a

round of drinks. Kerrigan tells everyone a ghost groped me, while Cecily and I make quick work of our blueberry mojitos. They are nowhere near as good as the first time we had them, but maybe it was the company that makes them better in my memory.

"At least the ghost was friendly," Duke jokes.

It's like we've switched places. Lacking a plausible explanation for the tightening around my throat, I now officially believe in occurrences of the supernatural kind. The Hamptons, excluding Cecily, believe I've brought brevity to their fear, and somehow it has reduced it.

I glance around the table at every face except for Ophelia and Cecily. *I hope every one of you receives a visit from a dead woman of the night while you're sleeping.*

Petty, but I don't care.

We catch the party bike in the street out front of the hotel. There are twelve seats, ten with pedals and a bench-style seat on the back meant for someone to ride but not pedal. Ophelia takes the seat, and the rest of us assume our positions around the bike. Much like the Road Kraken on the first day of our road trip, an employee of the party bike company tells us how to operate it, and then he leaves with a parting instruction to park the bike where it sits now and he will be there to pick it up when we're finished.

"When was the last time you rode a bike?" Cecily asks, daintily setting her feet on the pedals.

"Years," I answer, toeing a pedal and watching it spin.

"Same," she responds, pressing her palm on the wooden bar top running the length of the pedaler. "There are ice chests here," she says, pointing at the space in the center.

"I had them stock it for us," Ophelia says. "Figured I

needed to get all of you liquored up before you sleep in a haunted hotel."

Cecily glances over her shoulder at me. I'm still rattled about what happened earlier, but the sight of Cecily leaning over and opening one of the ice chests makes for a great distraction. She's wearing a sweater similar to the one from our first date.

Cecily plunks hard seltzers in the drink cutouts in front of us. "Why are you looking at me like that?" She pops the top on her drink.

"I like what you're wearing. It reminds me of what you wore to Obstinate Daughter the first time we met."

Amusement trickles into her pretty brown eyes. "I can't believe you remember what I wore."

I reach for a strand of her hair, letting it slip through my fingers. "I remember everything about that evening."

A waving hand barges into our moment. "Hi, hello?" Kerrigan, of course. "Did I hear you say Cecily wore a sweater like this on your first date?" She pinches the fabric on Cecily's shoulder.

Cecily bats Kerrigan away, but Kerrigan isn't deterred. Her face lights up in triumph. "You wore a cardigan. You wore a *cardigan*."

"Is it just me or is 'cardigan' starting to sound like a weird word?" Duke asks.

Kerrigan sits back, shaking her head at Cecily. "Cardigan," she repeats, stabbing the air between them. "I told you."

"What's the story here?" I ask. The bike begins to move, but I'm not pedaling.

"It's a long story," Cecily says.

Kerrigan leans on the counter to look at me. "I was right. The end."

"It would be great if you three would contribute to the operating of this bike." Duke's grimacing, speaking between clenched teeth.

Ophelia smacks the countertop. "Baby is a bitch to move. It's all hands on deck."

CHAPTER 52

Cecily

I'M NOT DRUNK, BUT I AM MOST CERTAINLY NOT SOBER. WE'VE hopped from bar to bar. Dom and I line danced at the first place, and then he played pool at the second place, pairing up with Duke against my dad and Rainbow, who shocked us all by being a shark. The third and final destination had trivia night. We split up into two teams. Dom, Kerrigan, Rainbow, and my mom. That left me with Duke, my dad, and Grandma. We were neck and neck until the end, when the topic was classic literature.

Dmitri, Ivan, and Alexei are the three familial title characters in what 1879 novel?

Dom's hand shot into the air without a moment's hesitation.

The Brothers Karamazov.

I shot daggers at him, but he grinned broadly and strutted around the table to where I sat. My lips fought a grin at the sight, intent on being displeased. Dom, with lips that tasted like vodka and lime, reached for me, arms wrapping around my waist. "To the victor go the spoils," he murmured, his voice a rumble gliding over me. I tipped my face up, letting him kiss me in front of my family in a way that was partially indecent. Finally, Duke tapped Dom on the shoulder and said, "Dude, that's my sister."

The brotherly objection made me smile. I can't remember a time in my life when Duke took exception with anything having to do with me that wasn't born of my own behavior.

Dom had raised his hands in the air, either in a show of innocence or surrender, and when Duke's attention was stolen by something my grandma said, Dom reached around and pinched my butt.

We're in front of the Hotel Monte Vista now, checking the bike to make sure none of us have left our belongings behind. The group files in ahead of me and Dom, but Grandma hangs back and places her hand on my forearm.

"Little girl, I'd like to have a word with you."

"Ooh, sounds like I'm in trouble," I tease.

Her fingers move, lightly scratching my arm. "That remains to be seen."

I press a kiss to Dom's cheek. "I'll see you up there. Try not to get choked again."

Rainbow chooses a seat in the guest area near the check-in desk, settling in with one of the local magazines fanned over the side table.

Grandma leads me to the opposite side of the room, where a burgundy leather couch is unoccupied. She sits, arranging her caftan around her legs. My gaze strays to her ankles. I've been holding out hope the swelling was from travel or altitude as we climbed from valley to mountains. No such luck. The lining of her shoes digs into her swollen feet, giving way to puffy ankles.

"Grandma." I take her hands in mine as urgency washes over me. "Are you ok?"

Silly question. Of course she's not ok, and I know that. What I mean to ask is *are you ok in this exact moment, and will you not be ok in the next?*

"Well, I'm dying," she answers, sassy as ever. "But one could argue that we all are."

She pauses, waiting for me to have my customary reaction. A smirk, a laugh, something unserious. I can't find it in me. I knew what this road trip signaled, but I didn't have to face it with such clarity because we were on the starting line. Now we're halfway through. How much closer are we to the end of my grandma's life?

Maybe it's my expression, or my eyes that fill with pain like a boat taking on water, but Grandma's face falls. She loves our nickname for her, deriving a great deal of pleasure out of being sassy and savage, but she's more attuned to other's emotions than she appears.

"I asked you to hang back because I wanted to ask you how you felt about everything Duke said to you when we were stuck."

"Oh." I wasn't expecting that. "I felt bad. He's always been this soldier for Dad. I never questioned it, because it seemed like he wanted to be in that position. The good son. I didn't know he felt differently. And I really didn't know he felt that way toward me." Even now, picturing the frustration in the stern set of Duke's eyebrows, a pang of guilt hits me.

Grandma's nodding serenely as she listens, but there's something in her eyes I interpret as knowing.

"Has Duke talked to you about this before?"

"He has not. But you can learn a lot when you observe

carefully. Because I'm the grandma, I had a different viewpoint than you and your siblings."

"Why didn't you say anything?"

"It wasn't my place. And I wasn't sure if you were ready to hear it."

"You think I'm ready now?"

"Time is not on my side. Whether you have the internal fortitude for it no longer matters." She studies me. "But from what I've seen on this trip, I'd say you do. Dom is good for you."

"You don't care that I was drunk when I married him?"

"I'm not sure why anybody thought you weren't." She rolls her eyes. "It's Vegas."

"We didn't mean to. Get married, I mean. We were quite drunk. It was like...like a sitcom script." I laugh softly to myself, almost unable to believe how differently I feel toward Dom today. "We planned to get it annulled right away, but then you called the family meeting, and he got high with you."

She punctuates my sentence with a boisterous bark of a laugh.

"We definitely couldn't go get the annulment after that. And Dad was demanding I get one, and—"

"We all know how you feel about being told what to do."

"Correct."

"That boy came on our family road trip and put up with us. That's one hell of a task." She eyes me slyly. "You know what that means, don't you?"

"What?"

"He loves you."

"I'm not sure about that," I say, the argument automatic.

It's muscle memory. Safer to argue, to doubt. But it only takes a quick tally of all Dom's actions to know better.

The way he looks at me, all focus and attention on me like I'm the only other person present in a room of people.

How he listens, even if I'm saying something unimportant.

He's always there. Steady. Unshakable. Mine.

Just like that, my automatic denial feels like a lie I've been telling myself for too long. My chest tightens with something akin to hope, because maybe he does love me. Maybe he has for a while.

I look at my grandma. "He said he was coming on this trip because you asked it of him, and since you're, uh"—the word sits there on my tongue, heavy and repugnant—"um."

"Dying," Grandma supplies, unemotional.

"Right. Yes. That. He wanted to give you what you asked for."

"That can be true. And that makes me love him for you even more than I already do. But, Cecily, please believe me when I say men do not look at women the way Dom looks at you unless they're in love."

"How does he look at me?"

"Like he wants to exist in your orbit."

Dom's face comes to me easily. His smile in the morning when he opens his eyes and sees me beside him. The kisses he presses to the corner of my jaw, his voice husky. The way he shows up, time and time again, wanting nothing more than to be there for me. He's not asking me to be any different from the person I already am.

"I love him, Grandma."

She pats my leg. "I know you do. It couldn't be more obvious. You two have so much chemistry that sometimes it feels indecent to look at you."

I know exactly what she's talking about. Sometimes it feels indecent to stand beside him in public, like my private thoughts are suddenly visible on my forehead, and everyone can see how addicted to him I've become.

"You know," Grandma says thoughtfully, but I'm not fooled. Whatever she's about to say, she has been thinking about for a while. "If you were shocked to hear Duke feels the way he does, what's the likelihood your parents don't know how much they hurt you when you were growing up?"

The conversational about-face makes me shrink back. "How could they not know? I left Olive Township. I rarely go back."

Grandma shrugs. "I think people create stories around situations in order to protect their feelings. Their egos. Who knows what else? I bet your parents don't want to confront the poor parenting choices they've made. Although it seems Duke has already gotten the ball rolling on that conversation."

"Of all people."

"Seriously. I had my money on you."

"Is that why you asked us on this road trip? Were you trying to make us mend fences before you—"

I can't say it. I won't.

Grandma touches my shoulder, squeezing me gently. "You need to say it, honey."

"No." Unshed tears fill my whisper.

"Yes, sweet girl." She brushes hair back from my face,

tucking it behind my ear with such care. "You must face it. My death, and your parents. You have to be strong."

"I can't." I've never felt this powerless. This useless.

She curls a finger under my chin, urging me to look her in her eyes. Wrinkles burrow into her skin. Exhaustion plucks at her eyes, at her downturned mouth. "You were strong enough to leave your home when you needed to. You are strong enough to face all the reasons you left. It doesn't need to be tonight, or tomorrow. You'll know when the time is right. All you need to do is trust that you are capable of it."

I'm nodding, and trying like hell not to cry. Every moment I spend with her is precious, and I won't waste a moment crying. There will be time for that later.

She wraps me in a hug, into her body that used to have enough breadth to envelop me but now feels fragile. She smells of cinnamon gum and Red Door, and my heart fractures prematurely.

"I love you, honey," she says against my head.

"I love you too, Grandma."

She keeps me there, cocooned, until Rainbow interrupts. "Pardon me, Ophelia, but it's time for your medicine." She holds out her phone, where an alarm blinks.

"Yes, yes," Grandma says, letting me go.

I don't want her to release me. I want to be nine and in her kitchen with my sister, begging her to leave raw onions out of the tuna fish salad and listening to her lecture me on how it won't kill me to eat an onion.

I walk with Rainbow and my grandma to reception, and when I take a step for the elevators, they go in the opposite direction.

"Aren't you going upstairs?" I point above my head.

Rainbow's shoulders shake with suppressed mirth, and I narrow my eyes. Did I miss the joke?

"Fuck no," Grandma says. "We're sleeping in the motor home. Haven't you heard? This place is haunted."

I want to laugh, but I'm afraid it will devolve into tears. "Oh, Grandma. You really are savage."

She blows me a kiss, and I watch the two of them disappear through the front door. For the first time on this trip, I am grateful Grandma has Rainbow.

When I step off the elevator on floor three, Dom is there, peeking his head from the open door of room 306.

He reaches for me, pulling me inside and closing the door with his foot. "That was the third time I looked out there for you. I told myself the third time would be the charm." He looks into my eyes, and his happy expression disappears. "Are you ok?"

"She's dying." The admittance feels like defeat. The longer I put off saying the words out loud, the longer I could refuse their truth.

"Yes." Dom's voice is gentle, nearing apologetic. "I wish I could take this pain away from you. I wish I could feel it the way you do, so you don't have to."

Pressing my face to his chest, I tell him, "My grandma said that you want to exist in my orbit."

My head moves with the ripple of his chest as he chuckles. "She's right. That's why I gave my boss an ultimatum earlier. So I can exist in your orbit."

I step back, my sadness overshadowed by my surprise. "What?"

"I asked her if I can start a new arm of the agency in Phoenix. If not, I quit and I'm going to open up my own shop."

"Dom, are you serious?" It's the last thing I expected. Something I hadn't dared consider. But now that I know it's a possibility, I want it. Badly. Dom and I in the same city? Nothing sounds better. My hand presses to my chest, an attempt to contain my heart. It's galloping from my chest, overwhelmed with the notion Dom would do something so big for me.

"Cecily, this road trip is a fever dream. It's close quarters and high emotion and complex family dynamics. When it comes to you and me, I want to give us the best chance. Long distance, especially after an experience like this, doesn't accomplish that. I am desperately in love with you and I'd like to give all that I have to making this work."

YES. Yes one thousand times. I push him backward until he sinks onto the bed.

I scramble onto his lap, pressing myself against him as if I could soak into his skin. Diffuse him into my bloodstream. Have I ever been like this? Never. I want to put my mouth on him, and my hands. I want to sit under his gaze and listen to the details of his day. I want to drink blueberry mojitos with him on a Saturday afternoon, then go back to my place and make love, the slow kind where he rocks between my legs and our noses brush.

"Dom—"

He's shaking his head, quieting me. "Don't say it back. Not yet." His lips skim mine. Back and forth. Torturous. "Don't say it now when you're dealing with everything else this road trip requires of you. Save it for some other time, when everything that has your attention now has subsided. I'll still be here, Chestnut. I'll be beside you. Tell me then."

My lips lower to his throat. I swipe my tongue over his Adam's apple, his scruff coarse like sandpaper. "How will you know if I don't tell you?"

His hands roam. One sneaks into my hair, the other tightens on my hip. "Your actions, baby."

"Mmm." The sound vibrates my throat as I press down on the part of him that has grown under me. Suddenly I'm hungry for him. Ravenous. He is in soft shorts, no zipper, and I pull him out. My skirt has already ridden up around my hips, and when I lift up to my knees, Dom pulls my panties to the side. Gripping his shoulders, I take him. Slow. Drawing it out. Dom loses his patience and grips my hips, hurrying me down.

"I need you right there," he grounds out, moving my hips back and forth, pressing me against him. "Forever. I want you there forever. You hear me?"

He lifts me, then lowers me, over and over. I breathe out the only response I can form. "Forever. Yes."

I hold on to him, my hands in his unruly hair, scraping his shoulders, his upper back, everywhere I can touch.

Together we move, becoming frenzied and desperate. Mouth to mouth, nose to nose, forehead to forehead. Everything Dom has said makes the experience more profound.

The pleasure crests, and I rise up to meet it. Dom feels it, says, "Me too, baby." And then he holds me close while I shatter, and I hold him closer while he splinters.

He kisses my jaw, soft and sweet, and I run my hands through his hair as we both settle back into ourselves.

We get ready for bed, and when we crawl under the covers, Dom holds me tenderly. He doesn't say I love you again, but he doesn't have to. His actions speak for him.

CHAPTER 53

Cecily

I wake at 6:47 to the thrum of panic in my veins.

Beside me, Dom sleeps soundly, the white sheet twisted around his torso.

I can't shake the dread that pushes at my limbs, making them feel heavier than they are. After two minutes attempting to convince myself this is a trick of my mind, I slip quietly from bed. A T-shirt hangs from my duffel bag, wrinkled, and I pull it on. The closest bottom is the skirt I wore last night, so I drag that on, too. After I slide my feet into my sandals, I slip from the room.

The lobby is quiet. A young man sits behind the desk looking at his phone. He sets it down when he sees me.

I'm not sure where to go, or what I'm doing here. There was a force propelling me, and I responded. It is as simple as that, and just as confusing.

Behind me, the elevator dings. I turn to look, expecting Dom, but it's not him.

"Dad?"

My father, disheveled, silvery hair rumpled, wearing a

V-neck white T-shirt and shorts. His expression mirrors the bewilderment I feel. "Is everything ok, Cecily?" He comes closer, placing a hand on my shoulder.

I cannot recall the last time my father touched me, or looked at me with concern the way he is right now. "Y-yeah," I stammer. "Why are you down here?"

He shakes his head, his hand returning to his side. "I'm not sure. I don't know what woke me, but I felt—"

"Panicked," I whisper.

"Yes."

"And you came down here."

He nods. "I had an overwhelming urge, but"—he glances around the deserted lobby—"I don't know why."

"I did, too."

The realization arrives simultaneously. "Grandma," I say, at the same time he says, "Mom."

Dad spins around to the elevator, but I reach out, stopping him. "She slept in the motor home last night."

"Why did she do that?" he asks, following me out the front door.

We're jogging around the building, heading for the guest parking lot in the back.

"She didn't want to sleep in a haunted hotel."

He makes a sound that could be a laugh in the right context, but in this moment, it's more like sharp worry.

The motor home is at the back of the parking lot, where it takes up multiple spaces. I arrive first, prepared to pound on the door and endure my grandma's teasing later. But just as I raise a hand, the door flies open.

Rainbow stands there, eyes wide, face stricken. Her phone is in her hand.

"Ophelia," she says, looking from me to my dad. "She's unresponsive."

I don't know how it happens, but suddenly I'm in my dad's arms. He's stroking my hair and I'm crying, and his chest moves with an odd breathing pattern. He's sobbing.

Rainbow speaks with emergency services while we stand there, the rays of early morning sun gripping our skin. Snow huddles in the corners of the parking lot, stubbornly hanging on.

An ambulance screams into the parking lot within minutes, and people jump out, rushing into the RV.

I want to go in with them, yell at Grandma to wake up. She'd open her eyes and look at everyone, demanding to know what all the fuss is about.

But, no. I'm here, facing an eventuality I pretended did not exist.

And my dad is holding me while I cry.

CHAPTER 54

Dominic

OPHELIA'S HEART STOPPED WORKING AT 6:47 A.M. ON A Thursday.

I was the first to join Cecily and Glenn in the parking lot, after waking up and finding Cecily gone. I was followed closely by the rest of the Hampton family. Shock reverberated through them all, rendering them unable to make plans for what to do next. Even Duke, with his leadership skills, was at a loss.

I stepped in, arranging transport for Ophelia to a funeral home in Phoenix. I called the RV company, informing them we would be returning the RV early. Glenn drove us home, and I paged through the second half of **We're Going To Have Fun, DAMMIT**, calling the remaining destinations and canceling our bookings.

Cecily sat beside me, tucked up against my side while I dialed with one hand. I was unwilling to release her, even for a second. She was hollow, bereft, and I wanted her to feel the warmth of my palm.

We returned to the same parking lot we departed from just under two weeks ago. The same man waited for us, murmuring his condolences as Glenn handed him all three keys to the Road Kraken.

Now here we are, standing in a circle, our bags at our feet, unsure what to say next.

Cecily speaks first. "Well, um. I guess we'll call a car." She glances at me, and I nod. She digs in her purse for her phone.

Glenn asks, "Has anybody eaten today?"

Collectively, the group shakes their heads.

"There's a lunch spot over there." He inclines his head at the shops across the parking lot. "I don't know if it's any good, but it probably doesn't matter. Everyone needs to eat. Besides, uh…" He sniffs, hands going into his pockets. "I'm not sick of you yet, so, yeah."

It's Glenn's way of saying he'd like more time with his family.

"Sure," everyone murmurs.

Rainbow breaks off, walking toward the coffee shop where we all caffeinated before hitting the road.

"Rainbow," Kerrigan calls. "Where are you going?"

Rainbow's eyes are teary as she says, "My job is done."

"Sorry, no," Kerrigan replies. Her nose is red, her eyes puffy. "I have questions about moonstones. And vortexes. And sound bowl techniques."

Rainbow allows the faintest of smiles onto her face. "I suppose I could share my knowledge."

Lunch is odd, but everybody makes an effort. Cecily tells the story of the guy she went on a date with who tried to steal the salt shaker, and there are chuckles around the table. For a brief moment, there is a lighter feeling, but it is smacked down by the heaviness of the day. That is how grief works. It's a process.

Nobody tries to be happy, or anything they aren't. They are simply trying to do it together.

After lunch, we part ways. Everyone will see each other soon, and Glenn and Marilyn will stay in town to be a part of planning Ophelia's funeral.

Cecily asks me to come back to her place. When I offer to have Klein pick me up, she tells me she'd like to stay in my orbit.

This is precisely why I do not need to hear her tell me she loves me. Her actions make it clear.

When Cecily takes a shower that afternoon, I hear her crying. Stepping in behind her, I take her in my arms. Hold her while the warm water pours over us. Afterward, I towel dry her body and her hair, and she drapes across my chest in bed and falls asleep. While she softly snores, I look at the final text Ophelia sent me, just after she parted ways with Cecily last night. I didn't see it until I woke up this morning, when I checked my phone hoping to see Cecily's absence explained by her in a text.

> Ophelia: I'm happy she found you. Don't duck it up.

> Ophelia: Dammit. I said FUCK. Don't duck it up.

> Ophelia: DAMMIT.

I laugh silently at the words, hearing them in her voice. Salty heat burns my eyes, and they fill with tears. I've been staying strong for Cecily, for her family, but I'm hurting, too. I only knew Ophelia a short time, but to know her is to love her.

I try to control the shuddering of my chest, but it wakes Cecily anyway. She takes one look at me, sleepy-eyed, and knows.

Her tears spill forth. She cries and cries, hiccuping sobs that send me searching for tissues. I can't find a box, so I make my own with a wad of toilet paper, the end streaming like the tail of a kite.

Cecily noisily blows her nose, and I tell her, "My parents never bought tissues. They said it was a waste of money."

She smiles in the most wistful way. She's radiant in the late afternoon sun. "They were probably right."

Climbing back into her bed, I pull her onto me. She props herself on an elbow and brushes her hand over my chest. "I'm grateful you knew her."

"I am too."

Later, when the dehydration headaches we got from crying have subsided, I run out for groceries.

"How much did you hate driving my Jeep?" Cecily holds out her palm for her car keys when I return.

"It wasn't as bad as I remember." Lie. I hate that vehicle.

She smirks. "Sure."

"What exactly is your reason for"—I reach into the grocery bag—"this?"

Cecily's eyes grow wide. "I can explain."

I brandish the weird little doll. "It was under your passenger seat. An orange fell from the bag and rolled under. Imagine my surprise reaching for an orange but coming away with whatever this is." Despite the terrible hair, I see the similarities.

"First of all, no harm came to you as a result of that doll." Cecily snatches it from my hand.

I walk into her kitchen and unpack the groceries. "He needs to be thrown out."

"He has a name," she defends, reaching for the bottle of white wine I picked up.

"Yeah, I know. Dominic."

"His name is Malibu Dom."

I freeze. Turn around with the box of dried pasta. "Malibu Dom? As in, Barbie?"

Cecily lifts her chin. "Maybe."

"Are you saying I look like Malibu Ken?"

"I'm saying you look like Malibu Dom."

I shake my head at her. "Do you think your grandmother would've approved of me calling you Savage Cecily?"

Cecily nods. "Absolutely, yes." She twists the top off the wine and takes a long pull. "She would encourage me to drink my feelings, too."

I smack the counter. "Sit up here and drink your feelings while I make you dinner."

Cecily obliges, leaning sideways to awkwardly remove a small tumbler and pour some wine for me. She watches me look through all the cabinets and drawers, finding what I need to make chicken fettuccine alfredo.

I'm filling a pot with water when she asks, "Has your boss responded to your email yet? I'm sorry I forgot to ask."

"Don't apologize." I brush a hand over her thigh on my way past. "Today has been a hard day."

Cecily takes a sip, saying, "To put it mildly."

"Do you want to hear some good news?"

Cecily's eyes light up. "You know the answer to that."

"My boss said she prefers not to have me as competition."

Cecily sits up straighter. She leans forward, hands gripping the edge of the counter. "And that means?"

"She'd like me to open a Phoenix branch of the Whitaker Literary Agency." A thrill I haven't allowed myself to feel sweeps through me. Holding onto differing emotions simultaneously has not been without difficulty.

A smile breaks onto Cecily's face. The first genuine one I've seen from her all day. "Are you telling me my husband is going to live in the same city as me?"

I go to her, placing my hands on either side of her legs. "Exactly what I'm saying. We're going to have a favorite sushi place. Find the best donuts. Double date with Klein and Paisley."

Cecily holds my face in her hands, lightly scratching my scruff. "You'll appreciate the smell of rain again."

"That's the plan."

I finish cooking dinner, and Cecily carries the wine out to her patio. We eat dinner in the small space, balancing plates of pasta on our laps. The sunset is brilliant, the pink turning into ruby at the top and orange at the bottom.

Cecily twirls noodles on her fork. "It's hard to feel sad and happy at the same time. The happiness is a reminder that life goes on, but the sadness takes me back to yesterday, when she was alive."

"It'll probably be like that for a while."

"You sure you're ready to put up with all my grief?"

I tip my chin at her. "The past couple weeks should speak for me."

"True."

"I have one request, though."

Her eyebrows lift, waiting.

"Please get rid of Malibu Dom."

CHAPTER 55

Cecily

THE BEST THING ABOUT MORNINGS IS THAT FOR THAT BRIEF second when I first open my eyes, my grandma is still alive.

The worst thing about mornings is that the following second, I have to tell myself Grandma is gone.

It has been three days. Three mornings of forgetting and remembering, and I don't know if it will be like this forever, but I hope not. The bright spot in all of this is Dom.

Dom in my bed when I wake up.

Dom in my kitchen, pouring me coffee, preparing it the way I like it, with just the right amount of cream.

Dom washing the dishes from dinner.

He holds me close, and he calls me Menace because he knows it makes me smile.

"Do you want to meet for lunch today?" he asks. He's standing shirtless in my bathroom, brushing his teeth as I coax my hair into a ponytail.

I'm returning to work today. A week earlier than

planned, and Paisley told me to take all the time I need. But what I need is to bury myself in work, in clients, in content creation and marketing plans. My brain needs the exercise, my heart needs the distraction.

"I was supposed to go to lunch with Paisley and Paloma to our favorite place, but I can cancel." I finish tying the elastic around my hair.

Dom spits into the sink and rinses his mouth, shaking his head the whole time. "Don't cancel. I'll see if Klein is free. We need to discuss his book. That'll make it a work lunch, and I can use the company card."

Stepping behind him, I splay my fingers on his stomach and glide them up over his chest. I can't get enough of him. How can I be heartbroken and falling in love at the same time?

Because you're already in love. The thought comes to me, clear as day and in my grandmother's voice.

I press a kiss between Dom's shoulder blades. "I can't wait to hear about the potential sites for the new office." Dom has three appointments today to see office spaces, all within fifteen minutes of the heart of Scottsdale. "Dinner?"

Dom turns around, leaning back against the counter. "My parents were hoping to get dinner tonight." He pauses, gazing at me in a way that's hard to name. Reluctant? Bashful? *Apprehensive.* "With both of us. I told them everything. Mostly, anyway. They're looking forward to meeting you."

I step in closer, running my hand up and down his arm. "I can't wait to meet your parents, Dom."

Relief loosens the set of his eyebrows. "They're going to love you."

"And I will love the people responsible for creating

you." I rise on tiptoe, brushing a mint-flavored kiss over Dom's lips. He deepens the kiss, leaving me wishing I'd taken Paisley up on her offer to take more time off.

Dom drives me to work in the Jeep he pretends not to mind but I know he still hates. One of *many* items on his moving checklist is buying himself a vehicle. It'll be his first time owning a car, and I can tell he's excited at the prospect, immersing himself in safety ratings and such.

Dom pulls up to the curb in front of P Squared Marketing. Paisley and Paloma are already there, unlocking the front door. Paisley carries two coffees, one of which I know is for me because Paloma's already holding one. They offer a wave and hustle inside.

"See you for dinner." I lean over to kiss Dom goodbye.

"And I'm having you for dessert," he growls, the rumble running the length of my spine.

Away from the parameters set by a meticulously planned road trip, Dom and I have been insatiable. The stolen moments in the RV, against the boulder, and the elevator were great, but this is even better. Last night it started when I placed my feet in his lap while he was reading a book. Two days ago, it was me bending over in the kitchen searching for the right container to store leftovers.

Dom waits for me to step through the front door of the office before pulling away from the curb.

Paisley and Paloma might've gone inside, but they didn't go far. Waiting just inside the door for me, I'm hardly inside the building before they pounce.

"Wife'd." Paloma jams a bright pink fingernail my direction.

"It's nice to see you, too." I look at Paisley. "What is she talking about?"

Paisley shrugs and hands me the second coffee she carries. "How should I know? I only keep her around because she has a nice rack."

Paloma sticks out her chest and bounces. The performance ends and she holds up two fingers. "Two things. First, we are sorry for your loss. You thought you would have more time with your grandma, and you didn't, and that sucks." She pauses, letting me speak if I want to. When I don't say anything, she continues. "Second, you have domesticity written on your forehead." Using the tip of one nail, she draws a line across my forehead.

I bat her away. "No, I do not. Am I allowed to go to my office now?"

Paisley beams. "Dom told Klein you're not getting an annulment."

"That's correct." I want to stand on the roof and shout it through a megaphone. I want to wear a stupid hat that says *Mrs.* I want to do all the things I always thought were ridiculous, but I simply don't know how to hold space for all of that effervescent happiness and my grief at the same time.

Paisley grabs my hand. "When you're ready, we can't wait to celebrate you. I'm thinking a night on the town. We'll dance until we're sweaty."

I raise my eyebrows at her. "You do realize that's how I ended up married?"

She laughs. "Good point."

For the next few hours, I immerse myself in catching up. It isn't until Paisley sticks her head in my office that I realize it's well past lunchtime.

"I'm starving," she says, rubbing her stomach.

Being late for lunch has its perks. The restaurant that is usually packed midday is only half full. We snag a seat on the covered patio. Water flows through the canal between us and the buildings we've just walked from. The sunshine is warm, but not yet hot.

Pressing my toes into a pocket of sunlight beside our table, I say, "It's hard to believe I was stuck in a snowstorm less than a week ago."

Paisley and Paloma stare at me. "What?"

"The RV we rode around in got stuck on the side of the road. It was crazy. This cowboy showed up to help pull us out." I'll have to ask Kerrigan if she's heard from him.

Paloma throws up her hands. "Why is it never me who gets rescued by a cowboy? It's always someone else."

Paisley side-eyes her. "How many other people do you know who have been rescued by cowboys?"

Paloma pointedly ignores her. "Tell us more stories, Cecily."

Paisley and I share a silent laugh before I launch into everything I remember about the trip.

We're dunking focaccia in pesto when my dad calls. Startled by the name flashing on the screen, I stare at it for a full three seconds before saying, "I should answer this."

"Dad, hi." I get up from the table, walking around the corner of the patio until I'm on the sidewalk. I don't need privacy for the conversation, but I have the urge to pace.

"Cecily. How are you?"

Why does he sound that way? Softer. Like he cares.

"Unbelievably sad," I answer honestly. "How about you?"

"Like I can't see or talk to the person I used to be able to see or talk to anytime of day."

The answer is so honest, so raw, and it takes me aback. Have I ever heard my dad talk like this? No.

"I was wondering if you would like to help me plan Grandma's memorial? Kerrigan and Duke were close to her, but you and Grandma had a unique relationship." He falters. "She was there for you when your mother and I were..."

My breath hangs in my throat as I wait for him to finish his sentence. I can't imagine how he's going to end it.

He sighs, then finally says, "When we were assholes."

That one word does not capture the depth and breadth of what it felt like to grow up in his household, but it's a start. A small turn on the pressure valve.

We have a lot to work through, and who knows how long it will take, but it all starts with a single step. *The ball is in your court*, I hear my grandma say.

I tell my dad I will help him, and we make plans to meet at my grandma's house tomorrow when I'm done with work. I hang up and return to the table. Our lunches have arrived, along with three flutes of champagne.

"What's with the bubbly?" I ask, taking my seat.

"No particular reason," Paisley answers. "Just wanted to celebrate the fact that you exist. I missed you."

Tears spring to my eyes, and I am mortified.

Paloma smacks Paisley's arm. "You made her cry."

"Happy tears," I clarify, picking up my glass. "My dad asked me to help plan my grandma's memorial. That probably doesn't seem like a big deal to you, but it is. He's..." I search for the words, but I cannot find them. "He's..."

Paisley smiles kindly. She picks up her own glass. "I get

it. My dad is something indescribable, too." She extends her glass to the middle of the table. "To daddy issues."

I clink. "To daddy issues."

Paloma hangs back with her drink in hand. "I can't cheers to that. I don't have daddy issues."

Paisley and I dissolve into laughter. "You bitch," Paisley says before taking a big sip.

It feels so good to laugh with these women.

"You ready?" Dom asks, sliding my Jeep into Park.

"We're not walking to the gallows," I gently remind him, slipping my hand into his as we walk to the restaurant.

Dom chose a place that has outdoor seating and yard games, to give us something to do aside from making conversation.

A man and woman wait outside the restaurant door for us, and based on the way their eyes light up when they see us, I'm guessing it's Dom's parents.

"Domino!" the man yells, starting for us.

"Well, that is unbelievably cute," I murmur.

"Forget you heard it," Dom whispers.

"Never," I whisper back, letting go of Dom's hand to introduce myself.

Dom has his dad's infectious smile, and his mom's straight nose. They are both warm, eschewing my offered hand for hugs.

Later, when we're playing shuffleboard, Dom's mom

thanks me for bringing her boy home. "I'd feared he'd meet someone and stay in New York City forever." Then she chucks my chin and I most definitely fall in love with her.

We go to a nearby place for gelato, and Dom's dad, with a mouthful of pistachio, asks, "Did Dom tell you I had a brush with the law?"

I clear my throat, trying to swallow down my lemon and white chocolate flavor. "Um, yeah. He did. How'd that work out for you?"

He shrugs. "About as well as it could have, I suppose."

"Does that mean it's over?" Dom asks, voice strained.

"Yeah," Ron nods, cinnamon hair bouncing on his forehead. "That slippery asshole got caught in another town doing the same thing. My name is clear again." He winks at me.

I bite back a smile. Dom's dad is a bit like a naughty child who knows he's a rascal but means well.

Before we leave there are hugs all around, and a promise to see one another soon.

"Thank you," Dom says, brushing a kiss over my knuckles as he drives my Jeep away.

My hand settles on his thigh. "After you spent all that time with my family, I'd say I have at least thirty more interactions with your parents before we're even."

Dom's shaking his head. "That's not how I operate. There's no tallying with me. We'll do what we can to make one another's lives better without keeping score."

At the next red light, I lean over and kiss him. "That sounds like everything I never knew to ask for."

CHAPTER 56

Cecily

THE FOLLOWING DAY, I MEET MY DAD AT MY GRANDMA'S house. I was nervous about being in her home without her, but that feeling fizzled the moment I stepped inside. My grandma's personality shines through in this huge home with the eclectic decor. The teal carpeted living room I once thought of as weird now sends a pang through my chest. *Everyone forgets beige,* Grandma had said. *Nobody forgets teal.*

My dad is out back on a chaise lounge beside the pool, his laptop balanced on his lap. He looks up as I approach, squinting into the sun behind me.

"Put me to work," I say, instead of hello. My dad is the other reason I'm nervous today. I don't know what to expect from him. For years, I knew exactly what I was going to get when I interacted with my father. It wasn't pleasant, but it was *stable.* Whoever he is now, or whomever he is trying to become, disrupts established norms. We cannot get to the other side of whatever this all is without growing pains, but *damn.*

He closes his laptop. "I admire your eagerness. But first, I think we should talk."

A different set of doors leading from the pool into the house opens. Out steps my mother. She smiles at me, and though it's a little forced, it's a positive response to seeing me when nobody is around to benefit from it. Grandma isn't present, no appeasing is necessary. Her smile is, well, *meant for me.*

My mom walks out, and my dad turns his legs so my mom can sit with him. A part of me wishes I could run away, but I sink down on the seat beside him, dropping my purse to my feet. "What about?"

My parents share a knowing glance.

Dad starts. "Your brother has brought some things to our attention that were...not great. Ways your mother and I behaved when we were raising the three of you. Duke and I had a long talk yesterday, and he made it very clear that these were his experiences, and he's not speaking for you or Kerrigan. But considering both of you moved away, and only one of you comes back to visit, I'm guessing you might share Duke's feelings."

"I don't know exactly what he said to you." I have a pretty good idea though, if it was anything like our talk that day in the motor home after we were saved from the snow. I take a deep breath, steadying myself. It was easier to hide out two hours away from my parents than it is to confront them.

"When I was fifteen, you told me I made it difficult to love me. I have never forgotten that. It plays over and over in my head, even now. It was cruel. It may have also been slightly true." Dad opens his mouth, and I don't know what he's going to say, but I halt him with a lifted palm.

"Duke was your eager first-born boy. A little prince, ready to serve his kingdom. Kerrigan was the baby, easygoing and flexible and open. I was none of those things. I was headstrong and opinionated. So it probably *was* more difficult to love me. For a long time I thought greater difficulty meant it wasn't worth the hassle. That *I* wasn't worth the hassle. And that is just not true."

At some point while I was speaking, my mom raised her hand to her lips. Now she presses down so hard her lips have lost color. "Mom, you sort of floated away at some point. You stopped being there, even when you were standing in the same room."

She nods, and when she moves her fingers from her mouth, her lips bloom with color again. "I am sorry, Cecily. Please know that it wasn't you. It wasn't any of you. It was me. The older you grew, the less I knew how to parent you. It seemed like you didn't want me anymore. I know that sounds childish, but at the time it felt like a deep rejection from all three of my children. I felt useless. I turned to other activities, friends, whatever else I could do to fill my time. Nobody appeared to care when I did that, or notice." She and my dad share a second look, this one full of empathy, and I realize this is not the first time my dad has heard my mom say this. He is also guilty of not caring, and not noticing.

"I'm sorry you felt that way, Mom. That sounds very lonely."

"It was, but sweetheart, it wasn't your fault."
Sweetheart.

A memory vaults upward into my mind, as if I've plucked it. My mother calling me *sweet baby Cece.*

Dad runs a hand through his thinning silvery hair.

"There's nothing I can say to change what I said back then. I vividly remember the day I said it, the way your eyes lit up with fury. At the time you didn't seem sad, but clearly, it devastated you. I don't know if I've ever been filled with such regret. Not until now, anyway, listening to your brother, and you, tell me how I've hurt you both." His hands steeple under his chin. "It's no excuse, of course, but when you were young I was building the Hampton brand, and it became all I could see. All I could think about. There comes a point when a person gets so mired in the day-to-day they stop seeing what's beyond the business. An obsession, in a way. And I became obsessed with making something of myself, on my own." He shakes his head. "That was something your grandma and I had to work out during the road trip. Separate from all the work that needed to be done in my own family."

I hadn't known there was anything to be worked out between my dad and my grandma. The RV was huge, but how did all those hard feelings fit in there?

"I've already told your brother, and now I'll tell you." Dad takes Mom's hand. "I am retiring from Hampton & Co. From here on out, your brother is the CEO. Mom and I are going to spend some time traveling after Grandma's memorial." His thumb brushes her knuckles. "We have a marriage to repair."

"Wow," I say, soaking in the announcement. "That's...great? Is Duke ok with taking over?"

"Yes." My dad chuckles. "I think he's ready for me to leave. He has plans for the company, and it's time to let him execute."

"I was hoping," my mother says, "that you might let us throw a reception for you and Dom when we return from our travels. Not for any reason other than to celebrate you two."

"Does this mean you'll stop telling me to get an annulment?"

"Yes," Mom hurries to say.

Dad gives me a look. "You have to admit it looked suspicious."

"Dom would live with me in a cardboard box." He kind of already is. My apartment is tiny.

"We're happy for you, Cecily. Really. Seeing you like this, in love like you are"—Mom glances at Dad, who nods —"well, it makes us happy to see you happy. I guess that's all I need to say."

Mom invites me to stay for dinner, and when I tell her I have plans to meet Dom (technically true. The plans consist of making cacio e pepe pasta and rolling around in the sheets for the remainder of the evening), she says she has a little surprise. The doorbell rings, and there's Dom, holding flowers for my mom and a bottle of wine.

My mother graciously accepts the flowers and wine. Dom greets me with a kiss in the foyer once we're alone, and says, "It feels like we're dating and I'm having dinner at your parents' house for the first time." He brushes a kiss over the side of my throat. "Never mind the fact I've shared at least twenty meals with them already."

I glance back toward the kitchen, where my mother has turned on Italian dinner music. "It does feel like that." I run my palms over his chest. "You know, I never brought a boy home to meet my parents. You're the first."

"Technically, you didn't bring a *boy* home."

I scoff. "Sorry. A *man*."

He pinches my top between two fingers and tugs me closer. "You brought your *husband* home."

Satisfaction ripples through me. I love that word. *Husband*.

In the kitchen, my mother has turned out a spread, but there's no unifying theme to it, at least not that I can tell. Pork ribs dripping in barbecue sauce, ahi tuna sushi rolls, green chili enchiladas, pink and white Circus cookies, and Bugles.

Dad surveys the spread and says, "Not that I don't love a smorgasbord, but what's the theme here?"

Dean Martin sings Mambo Italiano, and it makes the scene even more disjointed. And then it hits me.

"These were my favorites. I mean, they still are." I snatch a pink animal-shaped cookie from a platter. "I haven't had these in years." I look at my mom. "Did you shop for this?"

She nods, and say it isn't so *is she looking bashful*?

"I wasn't sure if you still liked any of this, but I wanted to do something nice for you. I got everything I could remember you liking, and hoped at least one item would work. Even if it was only Bugles." She grabs a few from the bowl and fits them over her fingers. "You used to eat them like this."

"She still does," Dom says, hand slipping around my waist. Does he know the state of shock I'm in? Is he literally providing me with what I need to stay upright?

"This looks amazing, Mom. Thank you. I haven't eaten since lunch, and I have big plans to do a lot of damage right now."

Emotion sweeps over my mom's face, but she flutters

her hands and says, "Ok, ok, everybody grab a plate. And wine!" She finds Dom's wine and uncorks it.

We eat outdoors, at the same table where I stood across from my father and refused to get an annulment. My parents ask Dom about his upbringing, his parents, and his job. It very much feels like they are getting to know each other for the first time. It kind of feels like I am, too. Who will my parents be from here on out?

Later that night, when we're in bed and I'm recounting the day for Dom, he says, "Savage Grandma was a mastermind."

"That's exactly what she was. She knew what she was doing every step of the way."

Dom lightly strokes my arm. "Except for me. I don't think she saw me coming."

I draw circles on his chest. "She liked you right away."

He presses his nose to my hair, nuzzling. "She liked me for you."

"She liked you for you. But also for me."

Dom flips us over so he's looking down at me. Lips poised at the hollow of my throat, he says, "I'll have to go back to New York next week, after the memorial. Dee wants to meet with me in-person, and then I have to start the process of moving back here."

I pretend to think. "It's been awhile since I've been to New York. Maybe I should go back, make sure it hasn't changed."

Dom's lips sweep over my chest, his hair not swaying as much with the movement as it did last week. The first item on his agenda before going to look at new office space in Scottsdale was to get a haircut.

He lifts his eyes, finding my gaze. "Are you fishing for an invite, Menace?"

I beat back a grin. "There's nothing stopping me from hopping on a plane right now if I wanted. But yeah, I'm hoping a certain someone might invite me to tag along."

Dom's head dips lower, burrowing his face in the valley of my breasts. Muffled now, he says, "You're my wife. You don't need an invite. You're a given."

My nails rake over his back, scratching just the way he likes. "Keep talking like that and you're guaranteed to get laid."

"A man can dream," he says, moving down my body.

CHAPTER 57

Dominic

THE FOLLOWING THURSDAY, OPHELIA IS LAID TO REST. CECILY helped her father implement Ophelia's plans for her memorial, and to nobody's surprise, it's heavily attended. Cecily addresses the attendees, her voice clear as a bell until she recounts the time she and Ophelia were at a bookstore when Cecily was thirteen. "I had an unfortunate haircut, and a boy made fun of me. Grandma threw a book at him. She literally threw a hardback at his head." Cecily sniffles, but a smile emerges through her tears. "And then, when he was looking at her with astonishment, she told him"—Cecily laughs—"to go clean the cheese off his weasel." She laughs harder now, and other people join in. "I asked her what that meant, and she said, "I don't flipping know, but my dad used to say it and it's disgusting. Always made me feel gross inside, and I'd like to make that little shit feel gross inside, too." She put her arm around me and told me nobody messed with me on her watch." Cue the tears. From Cecily, and everyone else.

Afterward, Cecily is inundated with people she doesn't

know telling her the funny things Ophelia said to them over the years.

Duke's friends from Olive Township attend, and they hug Cecily and tell me stories about her as a kid. Mallory, the wife of one of Duke's friends, tells me she is also Cecily's client, and that Cecily is responsible for getting her true crime podcast picked up by a network. I'm not surprised. My wife is creative and witty.

The Hampton family stays until the last person leaves. In the morning, Cecily's parents will return with Duke to Olive Township, and Glenn will begin the process of officially retiring from Hampton & Co. Around the same time, Cecily and I will head to the airport to catch our flight to New York.

Glenn calls Cecily that evening while we're packing for our trip.

"Hi, Dad," she says, and I know she's getting used to sounding casual when he calls. Baby steps.

"Oh." She drops onto the bed, right on the pile of clothes she's laid out. "Are you sure?"

Getting her attention with a hand on her arm, I silently ask if everything is alright.

She nods, but her eyes are wide. Shocked.

"Yeah," she says, breathless. "Yes. We'll meet with him when we get back."

Cecily hangs up. "My grandma left her house to me."

I sit down on my clothes, too. "How do you feel about that?"

Cecily faces me, tucking a knee up onto the bed. "I...I don't know. I wasn't expecting anything. I hadn't thought about it, honestly. If I had thought about it, I would've assumed it was all going to my dad, or sitting in a trust or,

I don't know, the local cat shelter." Cecily presses her fingers to her eyes. "It might sound weird, but it was easy to forget my grandma was wealthy. She never acted like it. Whatever it means to act like it."

That makes sense. When I was a kid, I pictured wealth as diamond bezel watches, private jets, and tigers on leashes. Now I understand those are displays of wealth, and true wealth is something different.

"Cecily, I want you to know that I would live with you in a shoebox. Or you can move into the house your grandma left you, and I will get an apartment if that's what you think is best for us while we date."

Cecily's face crumples in horror. "Why in the world would you get an apartment?"

I like the strength of her objection. I like it *very* much. "Believe it or not, I've never been in this situation before. I just want you to know that all paths are welcome, as long as they end at the same point."

Cecily fingers a button on my shirt. "And what point is that?"

"You and I, married."

She smirks and taps the button. "We already are." Using her palm, she pushes me to lie flat on the bed. Her face appears above me, backlit by the overhead light. "In fact, I think we should skip all the dating nonsense and be married."

"Is that right?"

She nods, her finger trailing over my chest. "I love you, Dom." The words are soft, a reverent claim. "But you knew that."

"I *hoped*." And now that I know, I could soar. Cecily

doesn't love easily, making these words from her exponentially sweeter.

Cecily cradles my face, tipping it up to hers. "I love you, Dominic." This time the words have strength, as if she has already become used to them. "What started as the worst mistake of my life turned out to be the best choice I've ever made."

My thumb runs over her lower lip, tugging gently. "You are by far my favorite bad choice."

She grins and wiggles her eyebrows.

I find her left hand and cover it with my own. "I've noticed your ring finger is bare."

"Very bare," she agrees, pouting playfully. "Like yours."

"Let's remedy that."

"Ok."

"Right now."

Her eyebrows tug in the center. "I think the stores are closed by now."

Moving quickly, I wrap my arms around her and roll her over. She gasps in surprise as I hold my weight on a forearm, reaching into the bag I'd been packing.

"Dom, what are you—" Cecily cuts off when she sees what's in my hand. "That's a ring box."

"It is," I confirm, situating myself so I'm lying alongside her. "And I've had it for a while."

Cecily's brown-eyed gaze slices to mine. "A while?"

"Since Sierra Grande."

"You bought a ring for me in Sierra Grande?"

I shake my head, using my thumb to open the ring box seam. "That is when your grandma gave me her ring."

Cecily sucks in a shocked breath. Instantly her eyes

grow shiny. "She must have really believed in us, Dom. In you."

"I told her she might want to hang on to it. That our story was complicated. She told me to knock off my crybaby antics and put her ring on your finger when we were ready."

Cecily breathes a shaky laugh. "That sounds exactly like her."

I push up a little, so I can use both hands. "She said a few curse words, too, but I left those out." I pluck the brilliant pear-shaped diamond ring from where it nestles in the box. The gold band is delicate, intricately woven in a design that gives it an antique feel. "If it's not your style, we'll get something else." I don't want her to feel pressured to wear something that doesn't suit her.

Cecily's head shakes vehemently. "My whole life I've admired my grandma's ring, and she knew it. She'd remove it to put lotion on her hands and I'd slip it on my finger and pretend it was mine."

With two fingers, I hold the ring in the air between us. "Can I put this on your finger, Cecily? Make you mine?"

A tear slips from the corner of her eye. "I already am. But, yes. Of course."

She offers her left hand, and I slide the ring on, feeling something heady and powerful. Humbling, too. This incredible woman has agreed to be my partner for the rest of our lives. To let me be hers.

I take her hand, the feel of the cool, hard metal new against my palm. I brush a kiss along her knuckles.

"Let's get yours when we're in New York," she says, a trace of urgency in her tone. "I want to put a ring on your finger."

I like all facets of Cecily, but this side of her is special. Possessive and eager. "Let's do it."

Cecily turns her face to me, letting me know she wants to be kissed. I love it. And I give her what she wants.

When we come up for air, cheeks pink and breathless, she says, "My mom wants to throw us a party, and this time it's for the right reasons."

I trace the curve of her cheek. "I'll have to invite my parents. But first, I'll need to give all the Hamptons a crash course on how to handle my dad and his ideas."

"At least we know that from here on out family gatherings cannot possibly be boring."

I kiss her again, something slow and easy. We have time.

"I love you, Cecily." It's a truth that exists without fanfare. Basic, and fundamental.

"I love you too, Dominic."

Epilogue

Dominic

I feel bad for Klein. But not *that* bad.

He and Paisley returned from their honeymoon in Switzerland last week. Dinner out to hear about their trip was only a front. I have waited a long time to watch people point at him and laugh at his T-shirt.

The patrons of this crowded restaurant did not disappoint. Our reservation was for nine on a Friday night, when I assumed the crowd would be sufficiently half in the bag. I requested a table at the far end of the restaurant so Klein would be viewable to everybody, including the rowdiest spot in the place: the bar.

"Ooh shit," some guy says, clapping Klein on the shoulders from behind. "I don't know if I would call you hotter than a hoochie's coochie, but you are handsome." He cackles and moves on.

I side-eye Klein's shirt, lips pursed to keep from laughing. There's a retro feel to the design, with a faded circle and the bold text saying Hotter Than A Hoochie's Coochie.

Klein glares at me. "I hate you."

I shrug. "Mild payback. I walked through Vegas in my shirt."

"I'm surprised they let you in here wearing that." Klein's older sister, Eden, pipes up from over the top of her menu. One of the many benefits to living in the valley again is spending time with Eden and her preteen son, Oliver. Tomorrow I'm meeting Klein at Oliver's soccer game.

"The bouncer found his shirt funny," Paisley adds, hand pressed to her mouth and shoulders shaking.

Cecily swipes a finger through the salted rim of her margarita. "I can't believe a restaurant needs a bouncer. This place is a slightly toned down version of a club." She opens her mouth and flattens her tongue, swiping the salt across it. A knot forms in my stomach. It doesn't matter how many times I've had my wife, I want her endlessly.

A woman in a bustier with a towering rose headband dances past our table, breathing fire. She breaks character when she reads Klein's shirt, a laugh bursting forth and sending the flame shooting sideways.

Paisley laughs so hard she snorts. "You made the fire dancer lose focus."

"It's a talent," Klein deadpans.

"Ok, ok," Eden says after we order platters of tacos. "Before my brother and my new sister-in-law"—she sends an elated grin at Paisley—"tell us about their honeymoon, I want to hear about how you two got together." Eden levels me and Cecily with a look that is downright parental. "I don't know where I was when you told this story at their wedding, but I missed it. Don't leave anything out. I am but a lonely single mother spending my days picking up dirty socks and subtly suggesting to an eleven-year-old boy that he bathe and wear deodorant."

"Who, Klein?" I point at my cousin.

"Fuck you very much," he announces, fielding yet another exuberant and probably drunken guffaw from a man passing by.

I press a kiss to my wife's hair. "Do you want to go first, Chestnut?"

"Sure," she says, squeezing my thigh. "We made plans to meet for a drink, and then I walked into Obstinate Daughter..."

We've told this story enough that I know exactly where Cecily will pause, or throw a look my way.

I love my wife. Love listening to her tell our story, the way she smirks and smiles and rolls her eyes, but it all has an undercurrent of happiness.

"She loathed me," I interject, when Cecily talks about the gummy I ate with Savage Grandma.

"I did," she confirms. "But only because my feelings were hurt."

Eden oohs and ahhs when Cecily tells her how we fell in love in the midst of familial chaos, how it stripped away the pretext that usually accompanies the beginning of a relationship.

When dinner is over, we head home to that huge house on the mountain I used to look at as a kid. For now we've made one of the guest rooms into our bedroom. We are slowly incorporating our personalities into the home. Cecily ripped up the teal carpeting the day after we moved in, revealing a beautiful wood floor beneath. "Grandma will definitely haunt me for that," Cecily had said, smacking the dust from her hands.

Growing up I did not have a pool, but I can stay with absolute certainty, the best part of having your own pool is swimming in it naked.

"This is our third night this week skinny-dipping," Cecily says as she glides past, naked outline visible under the water. The back patio lights are out, and I set the pool light to low. Below us, the lights of the city twinkle. Above us, the city lights mute the stars, and in the distance airplanes blink red upon takeoff and landing at Sky Harbor International.

Living up here with Cecily has a dreamlike quality to it. Being with her at all has the same feeling. She is a dream come true.

The Phoenix branch of the Whitaker Literary Agency is officially up and running. Dee visited for the opening, but Sally stayed home. There were internal rumblings that Sally herself was the author of the western horror, writing under a pseudonym. I didn't have to care, or be involved in the drama. Working across the country is a blessing, for many reasons.

Cecily slices through the water and appears in front of me. "Your parents are coming over Sunday afternoon," she says, slicking her hair back from her face. She keeps her body below the waterline, only her shoulders and head showing. "I still can't believe you lied to them about my last name."

"The worst part was that I forgot I did that." I'd claimed I'd misspoke, but I think my mom knew better.

"You know I like your dad. He's a character."

My eyes fall to Cecily's chest, where an inch of cleavage

bobs above the water. "I told my Dad he's not allowed to post pictures on his social media like he did last time."

Cecily grins. "It was a creative caption."

My groan amplifies my grimace. Deepening my voice, I quote, "*My son changed his name to Richie Rich.*"

Cecily laughs. "But he spelled it Rich E. Rich."

The mortification lingers. "He agreed no more photos. No more posts."

Cecily rises on tiptoe, her nipples poking out from the water. The only word to describe the look on her face is *flirtatious.*

"Are you teasing me, Mrs. Bellinger?"

Cecily sighs. Blows on her fingernails. Flicks her wet hair off her shoulder. "I'm just living."

I strike before she can finish her sentence, hauling her flush against me. She giggles and gasps and pretends to struggle.

Lifting her over my shoulder, I deliver a smack to her backside, the water giving it a sharper sound. "So crude," Cecily teases. "I bet you have scars on your knuckles from all that dragging."

Dripping water, I carry her from the pool and through the house to the guest bedroom. It's the same wrought-iron bed, but new bedding. A rug, and a painting of a scene from an old western town. I framed the photo I took of Cecily on the trail ride, and when she tried to hide it away in the dresser drawer, I intercepted her. I told her as many times as she gets rid of that photo, I will print it out and reframe it. That's my lady on the day we had our first real kiss, and the picture stays. She acquiesced.

The bedroom window is open wide, the heat of the summer night pouring in. I lower Cecily onto our bed, and she scrambles to all fours. I'm frozen in place, admiring her. Every day she's more beautiful to me. Every day she does something that makes me love her more. Yesterday she slipped her leg between my knees when I hugged her, and I thought it was the cutest thing.

The way she's looking at me now is not at all sweet. Glancing over her shoulder, wet hair tumbling sideways. "Are you not up to the task, Errand Boy?"

Taunting me. We might have moved past her loathing me, but she still loves to get a rise out of me.

Climbing onto the bed and coming up behind her, I lean down, nipping at her shoulder. "Hold on, Menace."

She laughs, that throaty sound I love so much. My left hand runs along her spine, the simple wedding band I wear gliding over her skin. She's told me before that she likes the feel of it.

I hope so.

I'll be wearing it until the end of time.

The End

Ready for more romantic comedies set in this universe?
Please visit Amazon to
preorder the third book in the
Serendipity & Shenanigans series (Eden's story).
If you missed Klein and Paisley's story in
Here For The Cake, visit Amazon or click here.

<u>**The Time Series**</u>

Our Finest Hour

Magic Minutes

The Lifetime of A Second

Acknowledgments

Readers - my biggest and most heartfelt thanks goes to you. Without your readership and support of my work, I wouldn't get to do what I love. I should also say thank you specifically for letting Here For The Cake into your hearts the way you did. What was intended as a standalone turned into more, and Hard Feelings was born as a result. Thank you a thousand times!

Thank you to everyone who made this book shine - Rosie Fables for your cover art, Sarah Hanson for your cover design, Nicole McCurdy for your developmental edit, and Darlene and Athena for proofreading. It takes a team!

My beta readers: Meagan, Mindie, Amanda, Danie, Erica, Paramita, Lillian, Mary, Natalie, and Crystal. Thank you for being willing to give me honest feedback! I am forever grateful to you.

Jennifer Millikin is a bestselling author of contemporary romance and women's fiction. She is the two-time recipient of the Readers' Favorite Gold Star Award, and readers have called her work "emotionally riveting" and "unputdownable". She lives in the Arizona desert with her husband, children, and her dogs Liberty and Magnus. With twenty novels published so far, she plans to continue her passion for storytelling.